Stoner

By
Darnell Clevenger

**Cover Design by
Pam Fraley Cutrone**

Text Copyright © 2019
Darnell Clevenger
All Rights Reserved
ISBN 978-0-578-50268-7

1

The tension in the atmosphere slammed into Stoner the instant he stepped through the door. A heavy silence floated thick and yellow in the cloud of tobacco smoke. The customers formed two separate groups. Alone behind the bar an emaciated bartender pretended interest in polishing his whiskey glasses. A quick glance from Stoner's cold, grey eyes uncovered the pretext. The thin man kept glancing furtively at the group of men to Stoner's right. These men, a half dozen strong, sat at a table close to the end of the bar, coins and folding money scattered in front of each man, cigarettes sending spirals of smoke ceiling-ward from fingers and lips. A bottle stood in the middle of the table. One man, a big man, beefy and heavy shouldered, was shuffling a deck of cards. As he shuffled he stared at the other occupied table. At the table he was watching sat a young man about his own age, in his mid-twenties. His hat hung on the chair beside him. His clothes and blonde hair were rumpled and dirty and his face sprouted a week's growth of sandy beard. He sat hunched over his drink, both hands cupping the glass as if it might fly away if he let loose. He faced the table of six but he seemed to stare through them as if they didn't exist. His eyes were glazed and his face slack from booze.

Beside the young man, facing Stoner, stood a young woman of eighteen to twenty. She was tall, willowy, with breasts barely contained by a soft, green blouse and full lips that sent a flash of excitement through Stoner's loins. Her black hair danced around proud shoulders and her green eyes snapped as she talked in a voice so low that Stoner only became aware of it through the movement of her lips. Her face showed traces of red as if from embarrassment or anger.

Or both. In any case she didn't belong in a saloon, Stoner realized.

Reading her lips, Stoner made out a few isolated words, nothing more: home, worried, mother. Realizing suddenly that he was staring at the girl, ashamed by his rudeness, he shook off the hypnotic spell she had cast on him and started toward the bar. He hadn't completed the first step, however, when the beefy-shouldered man at the poker table spoke roughly.

"Hey, Linda, I'm talking to you. You want company, come over here. I sure as hell won't ignore a woman wearing a blouse like that."

Stoner froze, anger surging into his eyes, turning them the icy grey of a winter sea. He glanced at the girl for her reaction. She continued talking as if she had heard nothing. Her companion continued staring into space. Stoner shrugged and once more headed for the bar.

"Hey, saddle bum, watch where you're goin'," the beefy man yelled at him before he had taken three more steps. "I was talkin' to my lady love and you cut right in between us. That ain't polite. Tell the lady you're sorry."

At the first words, Stoner swung to face the poker table. His left foot moved forward an inch or two in front of his right one, his arms dropped lazily to his sides, a cold smile pursed his lips, and his eyes sparkled deceptively. For several moments the big man stared at Stoner, a sneer on his lips, unaware that he teetered on the brink of death. Then the moment passed. Stoner shrugged, turned, and walked to the bar where he ordered a beer. Snickers and catcalls followed him but he shook off the anger and ignored them.

"Hey, saddle bum, I told you to apologize. The lady's waitin'."

Deliberately Stoner kept his back to the heckler. The bartender nervously moved out of the line of fire.

The center of the big man's attention was Linda Peters, who had ridden to town to find her brother, Rob. Not for the first time since entering the saloon did she tell herself that she shouldn't have come to Chasco without some of the Rocking H hands. But Rob had left the ranch six days before and hadn't returned. Several times word had reached the ranch that he was drinking steadily, although peacefully. Linda and her mom had sent two of their hands to Chasco to herd Rob back to the ranch; they returned empty-handed to report failure.

"Rob said he wasn't gonna come with us nohow," with an embarrassed grin Cactus Newel complained to Mrs. Peters. "Hell's bells, ma'am, beggin' your pardon, the kid threw his hogleg on us again. And like the other times, he was so drunk he couldn't see nor hold the damn thing steady. It was wavin' all over the place. Me'n Tack, we was scared he'd shoot us and not even know it. So we got out of there like coyotes runnin' from scattered buckshot."

"If he was as drunk as you say, why didn't you take his pistol away and pack him home across his saddle?" Linda had interrupted angrily.

"Well, Miss Linda," Cactus had grinned disarmingly, "There's times when a man with a few drinks under his belt can be mighty dangerous. And me, I ain't one of your storybook heroes. Sides, your maw said no rough stuff. We wasn't to break no bones nor shoot him up none. Not even no bruises, she said." He turned back to her mother before continuing, "Now wasn't that what you said, ma'am?"

Mrs. Peters simply shook her head with dismay and disgust steeped in humor and dismissed the two cowhands. Later she told Linda that Cactus and Tack had probably made the right choice. Rob was dangerous when he was drinking. In the past few months he had twice shot at Rocking H hands trying to stop his drinking and rustle him back to the ranch. Luckily he missed both times. And even more luckily, both times he had shot at Cactus or Tack.

"They're both easygoing men" she continued. "If it was Tall Will, or maybe even Pate, I reckon they might've shot back. Tall Will's got a bad temper. And Pate, well, I've got him pegged as a man who'd shoot first and ask questions later. I think he might just shoot automatic like, before he could stop himself."

"Mom, we've got to stop Rob's drinking somehow. We need him to manage the cattle and hands," Linda commented angrily, then added with amused chagrin: "I can handle everything but those damn cowhands. I tell them to do something and they do whatever they want to and then give me those damn silly, innocent grins and say with a stupid drawl, 'But Miss Linda, ma'am, I sure thought that was what you told me to do.' I get so mad I have to laugh or I might shoot one of them myself."

The conversation had taken place the previous day. This day, when Rob had not appeared in the night or during the early morning hours, Linda's anger had increased until mid-afternoon, when she saddled and set off alone for Chasco. How, she didn't know, but she planned to take her brother back to the Rocking H and his responsibilities.

Barstow's attempt to badger the stranger into apologizing to her for nothing made her anger flare hot and uncontrollable. She was frightened but pride kept the fear from showing. Only the anger crept into her actions and speech: anger at herself, anger at Rob, and most of all anger at Barstow and his Bar B hands for their crude behavior.

"Leave him alone, Nate," her voice, even in anger, came out modulated and commanding. "Your fight's with the Rocking H."

"Ha, ha, ha," Barstow roared. "Fight? A drunk, some broken down cowhands, and a girl who's all woman but thinks she's a man? Against an outfit like the Bar B? We've got more'n a dozen hands year round and twice that many durin' roundup. You know that, sweetheart." Again he roared with laughter. "Hell, callin' that a fight's like callin' it a fight when a elephant steps on a ant. That'd be like callin' it a fight if I was to throw that drunk brother of yours out of here. Which I been thinkin' pretty serious about doin'. Now, if you was to be nice to me I might leave him alone. I might even help you sober him up."

Barstow's comrades laughed and openly ribbed him about his offer.

"C'mon, Nate, she's too good for the likes of us poor cow chasers. She's been back east to get edification on how to run a ranch."

"She wouldn't spit on you, Nate. You're too ugly and dumb like the rest of us poor Bar B cowpokes."

"Save your offer for them that don't put on airs, Nate. She wants a man she can whip every day and twice on Sundays."

"Hey, Romeo, get too close and she'll put a knife in you. Story is she carries one in that blouse of hers."

"Yeah, maybe I better check and see about that knife before we get too cozy," Barstow grinned and took a long pull at the bottle. "I bet you'd like that, wouldn't you, little lady?"

Suddenly he slammed the bottle down on the table and, with a bound, leaped to his feet and strode purposely toward the table where the girl had turned her back and was again pleading earnestly with her drunken brother.

The girl whirled to meet the onslaught. Her brother half rose with an angry cry, but his feet became tangled in the legs of his chair. Before he could straighten to his full height he tumbled to the floor, taking chair and table with him. As the girl swung to meet him, Barstow grabbed a handful of her blouse and began half dragging, half carrying her toward the table where his companions sat laughing and cheering. He had not taken two steps with the girl in tow, however, when a pistol barrel smashed against the flesh and bone of his forearm, paralyzing his hand and freeing the girl's blouse. Almost simultaneously a blow from Stoner's fist sent him reeling into the table where his comrades sat. Money, whiskey, table, chairs, and men crashed into a pile against the wall.

With a roar of anger Barstow struggled to his feet, followed closely by the others. The angry muttering froze one sound at a time as each man found himself staring into the deadly barrel of a Colt .45 and, above it, a pair of wintry grey eyes.

"I don't much like bullies," Stoner let a deadly smile touch his lips and eyes, "especially ones that push women around. I figure they're the same ones that beat up kids and drunks when no one's looking. And torment horses and other animals just for the hell of it. There's no vermin lower, I don't reckon. The best thing to do with critters like that is squash them before they spread the sickness to others. That's what I should do to you, squash you before you manhandle some other lady, or do something worse." Flecks of gold suddenly began to dance and glitter in Stoner's eyes. "But I reckon I'll let you off with an apology. Like you were going to do me," his eyes and pistol focused unwaveringly on Barstow's belt buckle. "Now, apologize to the lady."

"You've picked a bronc you can't ride, stranger," the beefy-shouldered man blustered. "There's only one of you and six of us. I was you, I'd hightail it out of here now."

The roar of the shot in the low-ceilinged room sounded deafening. One of the punchers behind and to Barstow's right screamed in pain. The pistol he had surreptitiously drawn clattered to the floor as he stared dazedly at the bloody, ragged hole in his bicep. No one else made a move. After he had felled Barstow, Stoner had moved a few steps to his right so as to be out of line with the girl and her brother in case shooting began. From there he spoke into the silence of the room.

"You," his pistol pointed straight at the Bar B foreman's belly, "the one they call Barstow. The lady's waiting. Apologize."

"And if I don't?"

Barstow spoke with no sign of fear. But Stoner saw the flicker of doubt in the beefy man's narrowed eyes.

"Then I'll put a bullet through the arm you grabbed her with, a bullet you won't soon forget."

"You ain't got the nerve to shoot an unarmed man," Barstow's voice continued strong and unafraid but Stoner noted a nervous tic developing at the edge of the foreman's right eye.

"I don't reckon you're unarmed," Stoner chuckled, the sound like the distant rumble of a glacier. "You've got a .38 tucked in the back of your belt and four rannies around you with sidearms. But I don't reckon I invited you to any duel either. What you've got coming is punishment for insulting and manhandling a lady. You can apologize or you can take a bullet through your right arm. If I shoot, you won't use the arm for a long time, maybe never." Stoner grinned. This time the winter cold was completely gone from his eyes, replaced by the imp of deviltry. "You've got ten seconds."

The hands around Barstow stared at Stoner in fascination. No one made a sound or a move toward a pistol. The wounded puncher had slumped into a chair. He sat with his head down, supported by his good arm, his wounded arm hanging limply as blood dripped down over his fingers and onto the sawdust-covered floor. The girl had picked herself up from where she had fallen when Stoner's pistol paralyzed Barstow's arm. She was trying to help her brother to his feet, unsuccessfully.

"Okay, okay," Barstow spoke slowly, murder glaring from his black eyes. "I ain't gonna let no back-shooter cut me down when I ain't got no weapon." A note of sarcastic bravado crept into his voice. "Besides, I reckon I was out of line, Miss Peters, ma'am. I let the whiskey get the best of me," he bowed almost graciously. "But you," he turned to Stoner, "I was you I wouldn't be around here tomorrow come sunup. Any Bar B rider sees you, he shoots." He glared, his eyes angry with frustrated violence, then spoke to his companions without taking his eyes from Stoner. "Let's go. We'll take Manny to the doc and head for the Bar B."

"Well, ma'am," Stoner drawled to the object of Barstow's abuse, his pistol still lined on the Bar B foreman's midriff, "what do you think? You satisfied with such heartfelt apology?"

"Yes, please," the young lady insisted quickly. She had succeeded in getting her brother into a chair, but he threatened to fall out of it at any moment in spite of her restraining hand. "No more trouble, please. Mr. Barstow's just drunk. He's not usually that way. He didn't used to be, anyway."

Stoner shrugged, lowered his .45, and stepped further from the door.

After a last meaningful glare at Stoner and a puzzled look at the girl, Barstow led his crew from the room. Stoner followed them out. He returned only after the five Bar B punchers had deposited their wounded comrade at a house on the edge of town, collected their horses from in front of the saloon, and ridden out of town. The girl was still trying to get her brother onto his feet. The bartender was explaining apologetically that, since there was no business, he wanted to close for the night and go home to his family.

"Sir," the girl turned to Stoner, her manner proud but ashamed, her voice filled with disgust. "My brother's too drunk to stand. Could you help me put him on his horse? It's out back, with mine. If we could tie him on I could get him home."

Stoner doffed his flat-crowned Stetson. "Begging your pardon, ma'am, but how far's home?"

"About three hours north on a walking horse. But I don't think...."

"That's a far piece," Stoner interrupted. "If something happened out there...you know, the horses spooked or something like that, you might not have a brother come morning, what with him tied on his horse and in the condition he's in. And it coming on night and all...." He hesitated lamely.

"I've got to get home. And take him with me," the girl's voice became desperate. "Mom'll worry as long as he's in town."

"I don't reckon your brother can ride under his own steam tonight, not in his condition," Stoner tried to reason with the girl. "And unless your mama's dying, you won't help her by bringing a drunk brother home. Why not find a place in town? Tomorrow he'll be sober and the ride'll be more pleasant for both of you."

"Thank you. You've been kind. Without you..., well, I don't know what Nate Barstow would have done. I've never seen him like that before. He was...he was an animal. But that doesn't change anything. I've got to take Rob home tonight. If we stay until tomorrow, he'll just start in all over again. That's the way he is." Embarrassment at discussing family skeletons with a stranger mingled with desperation made her voice breathless and hurried. "He's okay when he's on the ranch, but in town...."

Stoner interrupted gently. "If you trust me, I'll ride out with you. The two of us should be able to keep your brother on his horse without tying him. You can put me up at the ranch tonight and feed me in the morning. After that I'll be on my way. Okay?"

The girl studied him for some time before she answered. As he returned her look, Stoner thought he had never seen eyes so deep and penetrating.

"Okay," she agreed finally. "Thank you. But we'll pay you for your time."

Stoner shrugged. "We can talk about that tomorrow."

Soon they had her brother mounted on his horse. Stoner walked alongside and held the young man on while the girl led the two horses. Within moments they reached the front of the saloon and Stoner's horse. Stoner and the girl mounted and they set out three abreast, with the former holding the young man in the saddle. After nearly an hour the boy sobered up enough to ride without help if they kept the pace to a walk. The going had become rougher, the trail narrower, so the girl forged into the lead. Stoner dropped to the rear. They plodded along in silence, each rider caught up in his own thoughts. Stoner dozed in the saddle, half awake, half asleep. Linda Peters wandered in and out of his sleep like a warm vision of all he had lost in his wandering life. Most of the women he had ever known very well were those working in the saloons and cribs of towns he had passed through, or the foul-mouthed woman of some outlaw acquaintance. The others, the toil-worn wives and daughters of farmers and isolated ranchers, he had mostly stayed clear of. None had ever attracted him much and he had long before learned that keeping away from them was the best way to avoid trouble with their menfolk. But Linda Peters was different. When he closed his eyes he could easily call forth the sparkling anger in her eyes when Barstow addressed her or the gentle smile on her lips when she looked at her brother. From time to time he found his mind creating intimacies with the soft curves of her lithe body. Each time he shook himself with irritation. He wanted nothing tying him to the valley. He planned to leave in the morning.

2

When they reached the Rocking H, Mrs. Peters was sitting outside on the long veranda, anxiously awaiting the arrival of her children. Dim lights in the bunkhouse witnessed that the hands also hadn't bedded down for the night. Linda called one of the punchers to take care of the three horses and to put Stoner's gear in the bunkhouse. After briefly explaining what had happened to her mother, she disappeared with her brother while Mrs. Peters herded the stranger into the kitchen, where she fed him steak, fried potatoes, and eggs, and good-naturedly grumbled when he refused a second helping.

"A man as big as you are shouldn't have a problem putting away two steaks."

"I reckon he could if they were ordinary, but not when the whole steer's in one steak," Stoner returned her smile. He liked what he saw in the energetic woman. She was in her early to mid-forties, he figured, probably the latter, but he didn't think she looked it even though her hair was completely grey and wrinkles crowded the corners of her eyes and mouth. She had spread out in the rear and middle, no doubt, but the reflection of lost beauty was still there in her sparkling eyes and smiling lips and the way she held herself as she moved efficiently but gracefully around the kitchen.

Mrs. Peters, for her part, also liked what she saw in the young man seated at her table, in spite of the fact that she pegged him immediately as a man who had killed and would kill again. He was a dangerous man, she had no doubts, but one to whom hard work was no stranger. He was broad and angular, several inches over six feet with at least two hundred pounds on a deceptively lean frame.   His hands were calloused, the skin laced with scars from old cuts and rope burns. The muscles of his arms and shoulders rippled as he crossed the room to take a chair at the table. His black hair curled over his neck like the mane of a wild stallion she had once seen on the range. A deep scar on his left cheek showed pale against sun-browned skin as dark as that of an Indian. Another jagged scar down the side of his neck disappeared under his shirt collar. His beaked nose appeared to have been broken and healed on its own, leaving it slightly twisted below the crown. His eyes were a sun-faded blue-grey, cold and penetrating until he smiled, when the blue filled with tiny specks of dancing light. She was certain he was a man of deep emotions, but one who prided himself on controlling those same emotions, just as she was certain he was a gunfighter. What he was showed in the way he walked with his eyes always on the move and his right hand hovering near his holster, the way he chose a chair hidden from the window, with its back to the wall and facing the door, the sometimes haunted look in his eyes when he thought no one was looking. She was no expert on gunfighters. But she had seen a few of them in her life: Bat Masterson in New Mexico and Wild Bill one time while passing through Dodge City. And now and then she came in contact with one passing through the valley on the way to somewhere, or nowhere. It was easy to recognize the breed in the man sitting at her table, no matter that he appeared so young. She guessed him to be in his mid-twenties. No older than her Rob. But there was a world of difference between the two young men. And she wasn't sure it was all in Rob's favor. Maybe none of it was. Deep inside herself she shrugged sadly. Rob had been her major disappointment, hers and her husband's before the latter had died. He was arrogant when sober, arrogant and cruel when drinking. When he was drunk he became cold and distant, retreating further and further into himself until even Linda couldn't reach him; yet when he was sober Linda was the only person he seemed to love and respect, the only one he treated decently now that his father was gone.

"Stoner," she commented as she cut a wedge of dried apple pie and set it before the young man. "Is that what people call you, or is that your family name? If you're going to sit at my table I reckon I should call you by something else besides your last name."

"Just Stoner, ma'am. That's what they call me."

She filled his coffee cup, poured herself a cup, and sat down across the table from him.

"Well, now, Stoner," she smiled, "I know I shouldn't be nosey. But, well, stuck out here on the ranch like I am, I don't see many strangers. Fact is, we don't get many guests any more, not since the Bar B started riding roughshod over every stranger that passes through the valley...um...almost two years ago now. So I get kind of starved for conversation and sometimes pry too much when I do have someone to talk to. You'll forgive me that, won't you? If I ask questions I shouldn't?"

"Ma'am, after that steak and this pie, I don't reckon there's anything I wouldn't forgive you," a deep chuckle escaped Stoner's throat.

"Remember, you asked for it," Mrs. Peters echoed his chuckle. "I'm dying with curiosity, so here goes: You sound like an educated person. An education suggests family. Yet you only have one name. How is that?"

"I didn't say I only had one name, ma'am. I said people call me Stoner, just Stoner." He smiled at the twinkling pair of brown eyes locked on his face. "My Christian name's Jacob. Friends used to call me Jake. But I like Stoner or Jacob better."

"Maybe I'll call you Jacob, then. I like that. My husband's name was Jacob."

"Was, ma'am?"

"Yes. He died in an accident almost a year ago today. It was at roundup. He was herding a bunch of cattle along the rim of a canyon on the northeastern corner of the ranch. A bull turned on his horse. The horse panicked." Mrs. Peters paused to wipe her eyes with the corner of her apron. "All three went over the side of the canyon. It was a three-hundred-foot drop."

"I'm sorry, ma'am. He must have been some man if a woman like you loved him."

"Why, thank you, Jacob. I reckon you had a decent upbringing to come up with compliments like that."

"Yes, ma'am, I did. My folks were nice people."

"From your accent I'd say you come from back east somewhere," Mrs. Peters' voice had turned soft at the glimpse she caught into Stoner's soul. When he mentioned his parents a deep hurt seemed to quiver fleetingly in his eyes. "Will you tell me about them?" she added.

Stoner shrugged uneasily. For years his early life had lain deeply buried. Not for a long time had he told anyone that he had a family in his past. He thought he had put it all away, stored below the hurt level of memory if not completely dead and buried. Now this pleasant, kindly woman had brought the hurt again welling up from the mire of his inner being. Somehow he found it impossible to deny her request; she reminded him of the woman he had once called mother and had long before left cold and dead under the earth of the Indiana countryside.

"Not much to tell, ma'am," he forced the embarrassment from his voice and decided to level with the woman, although he didn't know why. "I was born and raised outside a mud-spot called Sunset, Indiana. We were dirt farmers. There were eight of us kids to feed, ten bellies in all, so we did a lot of hunting and fishing to make it through to the harvesting every year. Me, I stood in the top middle of the pack. We scrimped and saved and went hungry a lot, but Maw saw to it that we went to school till the teacher said we weren't progressing any more. Maw, she had eight years of schooling and was proud of it. Me, I guess I take after her; I like to read a lot and I was still in school the winter she died, had been for nine years. I was fifteen." Stoner paused and meditated for a moment. "It was a dry spring and summer and then a bad winter following, one of the coldest in his memory, Paw said.

Along about February the food gave out. There wasn't any game to talk about that year either. The neighbors couldn't help much; they were struggling too. Paw and us boys hunted further and further. One day Paw went out by himself and didn't come home. Two days later the sheriff showed up to tell us Paw had been killed stealing meat from a farmer about ten miles away. We never did get his body back or find out who killed him. Maw took to bed and died several weeks later. Lung congestion, the doctor said. Grief, I think. After she died the sheriff came for us, to put the younger ones in an orphan home and serve papers on the rest to get off the farm. Paw had mortgaged the farm sometime and the bank was foreclosing, they said. They didn't figure the two older kids could make the farm pay. Me and Sammy--he was a year younger--the sheriff was going to put us on other farms where they didn't have kids. Sammy didn't mind. He went. I did mind. I ran away. I've been on the move ever since, almost ten years now."

"Never went back?" Mrs. Peters had heard similar stories more than once in the seven years since she and her Jacob had packed children and belongings and moved west from Pennsylvania, from young men working the ranches of the valley as well as from those riding the grub line. But, somehow, Stoner's story touched her as none of the others had. Why, she didn't know, unless it was because he resembled her Jacob when he talked and smiled. He even looked like her dead husband in some ways--the same height and carriage, the same color eyes, similar facial features. Her Jacob had had light hair, been heavier, more sedentary, softer, used to hard work but also to enjoying family life and the fruits of his toil. The constantly moving eyes of the hunter so evident in the young man at her table had been absent from her husband's eyes; his had sometimes been filled with fatigue, sometimes with hurt or failure, but mostly with simple well-being.

"Nope," Stoner answered thoughtfully. "I've thought about it more'n once. A couple of times I made plans to go.

One time I even bought a train ticket to Chicago. But I turned it in the next day." He shrugged. "I guess there ain't much draws me back there anymore. Maw and Sammy were the only ones I was close to. Maw's gone. So's Sammy. He died in a flood on the Mississinewa near where it hooks up with the Wabash. Must've been a couple of years after Maw and Paw died." At Mrs. Peter's inquisitive glance, he explained, "I met a gambler down in El Paso, not more'n four or five month after Sammy died. He was from a town close by Sunset. He told me. He didn't know what'd happened to the rest of the kids, though."

"I understand," Mrs. Peters reached across the table and touched his arm. A tear gleamed in her eye and her voice shook slightly as she spoke. "My Jacob's parents died before we came west. Mine died shortly after we came out here, within a few months of each other. I didn't go back either time, but I've always wished I had after Mother passed away. I could have spent some time with Dad before he was gone. But I've never really wanted to return for any other reason." She smiled through the sadness of the moment. "I never liked Jacob's brother. Oddly, I've never missed my two sisters either, even though I liked them well enough before I left. I can understand why Linda fell in love with them while she was back east to school. They were always a lot of fun, gave the greatest parties and were always surrounded by interesting people. But..., I don't know why," she laughed, "but I guess I've always been more attracted to the sufferers of the world. Jacob used to tell me I'd take in any stray creature that came my way as long as it was hurt in some way. Oh," she suddenly realized how what she had said might sound to the young man. "I didn't mean you...." She stopped. Her eyes twinkled. "If I had any self-respect and decency, I'd be ashamed of myself for suggesting you're a stray."

She burst out laughing and Stoner joined her. The more he sat and talked to the friendly, pleasant woman before him, the more he found himself under her spell. Just as she had found something of her husband in him, so in her he had encountered much that he remembered about his mother--the ability to laugh at herself, the way she rambled a little when she talked, the tenderness, the caring for those who suffered, the love that continuously bubbled up from just beneath the surface.

"I reckon I am a stray, ma'am," he grinned at her, his blue eyes reflecting his youth for the first time in years. "That's what I've been saying. For over ten years now I ain't stayed in one place more'n a year, mostly a few months. Except for Socorro, over in New Mexico. I worked on a ranch there for almost two years. I thought I'd found a permanent home. That's where I was working before I came this way."

"Why'd you leave?" Mrs. Peters asked inquisitively. "I know it's rude of me to ask," she laughed," but like I said, I'm a nosey biddy."

For the first time during the evening, she noted, Stoner didn't meet her eyes right away. He stared at his coffee cup as if trying to put off the answer as long as possible. Then his eyes met hers. She saw the anger deep inside him.

"I reckon I left for the reason I seem to leave most places, ma'am. One of the other hands found out who I am and reckoned he was faster'n me."

When Stoner seemed reluctant to continue, Mrs. Peters prodded him curiously. "Was he?"

Stoner smiled sadly, "Well, ma'am, I'm here, ain't I?" He added in a more serious tone, "The owner, he didn't want a killer around, he said, so I sloped."

Mrs. Peters decided to stop prying. She noticed that Stoner's face had hardened as he told of his reason for leaving the ranch in Socorro. Beneath the surface, however, she thought she caught the brief reflection of a soul in torment.

"So," the young man's voice had turned to stone, "I decided to go back to using my own name again. I reckon if people don't want me around it's best to know from the beginning."

"I think you're probably right, Jacob. Are you looking for a job or just riding through?"

For a long moment their eyes locked. On the ride out from town Linda had mentioned that they had had trouble with the Bar B before and conflict seemed to be developing again. He figured Mrs. Peters was offering him a job. For him, he decided, the question was if he liked this woman well enough to stay on and help fight the Bar B, because that was what she wanted in him, his gun, whether she realized it or not.

"Regular wages or gun wages?" he finally asked.

He liked her better when he saw the blush spread outward from her eyes.

"Yes, I guess you're right," she admitted honestly, meeting his eyes without flinching. "We need fighters right now. But even more, we need someone that can boss the crew. We lost our foreman two months back, scared off by the Bar B. No one else on the crew could handle the job, I didn't think. But Rob wanted it bad so I let him have it, against my better judgement. Now I've got a worse problem. I need someone that can keep Rob in line. He's turning mean. He's drinking more and more and when he's sober he pushes the men too hard, a lot of times without reason or direction. I'm afraid I'm going to lose him and the crew. If I lose the crew, well, I reckon it'll just be a matter of time before the Bar B takes over the ranch. Not many cowhands in the valley would come to work for us now, knowing they'd have to fight the Bar B. If I lose Rob...," she gave an embarrassed shrug, "he's my son; I don't know what I'd do if I lost him." She sat silently for a while, swirling her coffee cup in the rings on the table. "I might lose Linda along with Rob; they've been really close since she returned from back east."

"What's your beef with the Bar B?" Stoner asked quietly.

"It's the biggest spread in the area and it borders on ours. The Bartlemans own it, old Joseph Bartleman and his two sons, Matthew and Samuel," Mrs. Peters paused and grinned mischievously. "Joe, Matt, and Sam, the peas in a pod you always hear about. Matt and Sam are twins. About the only way you can tell them apart is that Matt's right-handed and Sam's left-handed. The only way you can tell the sons apart from their paw is that he's older. They ride alike, walk alike, talk alike, think alike, act alike...why," she giggled like a girl, "I bet they even do their duty alike." She blushed, "Sorry, I got carried away. But every time I think about them I have to laugh, they're so much like each other."

"They don't sound dangerous," Stoner commented, to move the conversation back to the point.

"No," as Mrs. Peters met his eyes she turned serious, "they don't seem dangerous when I think of how much alike they are. But don't let that fool you. They're dangerous alright. They're all three good with guns. But Sam now, he's a whiz-bang. With Colt or rifle, no one around here can touch him. Or Matt or old Joe either...because they're some shakes themselves. Worse yet, anyone goes against one of them goes against all three. No matter who's in the wrong."

"Ma'am," Stoner interrupted gently, "you haven't told me what your trouble with them is."

"Jacob, never become impatient when an old woman rambles," Mrs. Peters smiled. "Besides, I want you to know what you'll be letting yourself in for if you take the job. It won't be easy. You might get yourself killed. You'll have to face those three and Nate Barstow too. He's the one you crossed in town to help Linda." At Stoner's look of embarrassment she reached across the table and patted his hand. "No need to be modest; it was a grand thing to do. And dangerous. Nate's the foreman of the Bar B, if you don't know. He's the only one in the valley the Bartleman boys don't bully around. He killed a poor nester with his bare hands a couple years ago, they say. No one saw the fight, but the man's back was broken. And he was some bigger than Nate, my Jacob said. Jacob also said Nate's faster with a pistol than Matt and Joe Bartleman, but not Sam. He said he saw them drawing and shooting at targets once; Nate beat Matt and Joe every time."

"Sounds like you're trying to talk me out of taking the job," Stoner chuckled.

"Maybe," Mrs. Peters answered seriously. "I like you. I wouldn't want you hurt on my account. But I have to have someone now, not tomorrow or the next day, and you seem like a man that can take care of himself. You showed that in Chasco." At Stoner's shrug, she continued with bitterness evident in her voice. "What the Bar B wants now is some of our best grass and water. What they want eventually is the whole Rocking H."

Mrs. Peters paused to catch her breath before going on, "The Bar B's the biggest ranch in the valley, like I said, probably three or four times our size." She hesitated. "Actually, though, there are two valleys, the small one running east to west and the main valley which runs northwest to southeast, more or less. We claim the small valley and some of the mountain country around it as well as the pass and some of the hilly area running between our little valley and the main valley. The boundaries of the Bar B run the entire length of our southern boundaries and part way up the eastern line. They want the whole Rocking H. Make no mistake about that. They want it and they plan to have it. But first they want a section of our land we call Loma Linda," she laughed, "although it's really a series of small hills and canyons. It has year-round water and some of the best grass anywhere; of course all of our water is permanent because it comes from the permanent spring at the Loma." Mrs. Peters paused again to catch her breath. "The Bartlemans have made moves on the area for two years now. The grass spills over our boundary onto the Bar B, but they don't have water on their side. That whole area of theirs is dry. To get to Bar B water, their cattle have to travel long distances over some pretty rough ground, or use the spring I'm talking about. It comes out of the ground right near the boundary line between the Rocking H and Bar B and then forms Rushing Creek as it flows this way; Rushing Creek is the little stream that runs through the middle of our valley and fills the pond over there behind the house," she motioned with her thumb. "You came in too late to see it; it was too dark. We let the Bartlemans use the spring until a little over two years ago when they started increasing their herds in that section of their ranch. That was okay as long as only a few Bar B cows strayed beyond. But one day the Bartlemans moved a large herd of their cattle to Rocking H land around the spring and this side of it. Jacob drove the cattle back to the Bar B and asked Joe Bartleman to cut the herd and keep his cattle on his own land. By the next year the Bar B had tripled its herd in the area; they were running some of the cattle on our land. Jacob drove the Bar B cattle back to Bar B land again and fenced the boundary line. Why the Bartlemans accepted the wire without a fight, Jacob couldn't figure out. But they did and drove most of the cattle to other areas of their ranch. Then Jacob died, not more than a month after the fence was completed. There've been a number of incidents since, like shootings from ambush just to scare somebody or a cow killed now and then. Earlier this summer they cut the wire at the Loma so their cattle could get to the spring. We patched it up. The men tell me they've recently doubled their herd in the area again."

"Who saw your husband's accident, ma'am?" Stoner's curiosity had become aroused by the coincidence of Jacob Peters' death so soon after his run-in with the owners of the Bar B.

Mrs. Peters smiled sadly. "Oh, it was an accident. When Carl--he was one of the hands at the time--when Carl brought the news that night my first thought was that Jacob had been killed by the Bartlemans or Nate Barstow. Carl didn't know anything except that Jacob had gone over the cliff and that he was dead. He'd ridden on ahead of the wagon bringing Jacob's body in." She paused and wiped her eyes with her sleeve. "When the wagon came in, I knew right away Rob had been involved. He was guilty, angry, hurt, ashamed-- all of those and more. Something inside him had died. I could see it in his eyes when he told me how the accident had happened. He and his dad had been working as a team chousing cattle out of the brush and gullies near the edge of the cliff. Rob decided he'd had enough so he tied his horse under a mesquite tree and sat down in the shade, not more than a few yards from the cliff, without telling his father. He'd no more than settled in when a bull came running out of a pile of boulders and underbrush nearby and charged him and his horse. Behind the animal came Jacob, herding a few cows along the edge of the drop off. The bull was in the bunch he was driving. Rob pulled his Colt and fired in the air to frighten the bull away from him and his horse. When he fired, the animal turned on Jacob. Rob doesn't think Jacob even saw the bull turn until it smashed into the side of his horse and all three went over the cliff; Jacob was too busy trying to stay on his horse. You see, Rob's shot also frightened Jacob's horse, set it to bucking right there on the edge of the bluff." Again she wiped the dampness from her cheeks. "It's not hard to understand Rob's guilt. He loved his father even though the two had lots of problems getting along. He was 24, yet he still followed Jacob around like a puppy, like he had as soon as he was old enough to walk. Jacob couldn't ride anywhere without Rob tagging along, on the ranch, to town, anywhere. He was flattered by their relationship. He loved Rob. But it made him unhappy too. He worried about Rob's cruelty and he wanted his son to grow up and earn responsibility as well as independence. Rob...well, he wanted more responsibility alright. He wanted to become Jacob's foreman. Jacob didn't think he was ready, though, and Rob thought he was. They argued about it a lot the last few months before Jacob's death. I just wish...."

"I don't reckon Rob'd be any too pleased if you made me foreman," Stoner commented dryly.

"I don't reckon," Mrs. Peters agreed sadly.

"Can you make it stick?"

She shrugged, "I'm the sole proprietor, as our lawyer says. Jacob left everything to me."

It was Stoner's turn to shrug, "I mean, do you have the sand to make it stick? If Rob's like you say, he might get nasty. He might go after me. He might go after both of us. Or he might decide to leave for good. Could you stand up to him?"

Mrs. Peters returned his penetrating gaze, "Yes, I believe so. He's my son. I love him and I'm not sure what it would do to me if I lost him. But I'd almost rather see him gone or dead than what he's becoming."

"I wouldn't kill him if I took the job," Stoner promised solemnly, sorry for the proud, strong woman before him. "If it came to that, I'd leave the valley first."

"Thank you, Jacob," Mrs. Peters spoke with tears in her eyes. "But I wouldn't want you to sacrifice your own life for Rob's. As much shame and hurt as it gives me to say so, I'm not sure his life's worth yours. Not the way he is now."

3

A half hour later, having spent the time asking about the characteristics and potential reactions of the hands and of Linda, and having decided that he would be a fool to get involved in the Rocking H's problems, Stoner told Mrs. Peters he'd give her an answer the next morning. He felt guilty about not telling her right out about his decision to ride on his way as he had originally planned, but he couldn't bring himself to destroy the glimmer of hope that had gladdened her face as they talked. Unable to meet her eyes he said goodnight and headed for the bunkhouse, cursing himself for a coward as he walked through the crisp night air.

All five hands were present when he entered the dimly lit room. The door and windows were open to the cool night breeze. Even so, clouds of dense smoke hovered over the table where the five punchers were playing cards with a dog-eared deck and piles of matches. Conversation came to a halt as he entered the room. All eyes turned curiously in his direction.

"That the nursemaid you was talkin' about, Cactus?" a young puncher asked of a grizzled old man beside him, standing up and stretching to his full height as he spoke. "He don't look like much, leastways not enough to buffalo the Bar B. A mite skinny and underfed, I figure. You reckon Miss Linda made that story up to fun us poor cowpokes?"

The old man referred to made a toothless grimace meant for a grin. "Nope. Miss Linda don't make jokes. I don't expect I seen her make a joke once since she come back from the east. That's what they teach them back there, I reckon, to take theirselves and life serious."

Stoner surveyed the grinning punchers from right of the doorway. Mrs. Peters had told him a little about each one of them and warned him that they were an unruly bunch. The old man would be Cactus Newel. He had been with the ranch when the Peters family bought it. He was a loyal, hard-working hand who seldom left the ranch even to go to town. But once every year, in the late winter months, he disappeared for three or four weeks, only to reappear again and resume his duties as if nothing had happened. No one knew for sure where he went, but most of the other hands suspected a woman somewhere. Old Cactus always returned in a good mood, contented, with a few extra pounds added to his girth. And broke--his year's savings gone.

The heavy-shouldered puncher who had made the comment to Cactus was Tall Will Johnson, a giant of a youth with a perpetual, reckless grin on his face and a Colt tied low on his thigh. He was the joker of the outfit, always ready for anything: hard work, a joke, a drink, a good time, a fight. He was a natural-born leader, Mrs. Peters had commented, but he was still too young, hot-tempered, and full of the devil for the foreman's job. His loyalty was also a problem. Like her son, Rob, he had doted on her Jacob. He had been a grub line rider passing through the valley when Jacob had pulled him out of a developing shooting scrape with the Bartlemans, in Chasco. Then and there he had accepted a riding job with the Rocking H and had remained. He would have ridden to hell and back for her Jacob. But when the older man died, he had turned reticent toward her and Rob, not always, but occasionally. She was sure he stayed on only because of Linda, who alternately flirted with and ignored him. She didn't figure he would remain at the ranch much longer unless Linda became serious about him.

The other three hands ranged from their early to late thirties. The youngest of the three was little more than thirty, Stoner felt sure, in spite of his being almost completely bald. He was known simply as Pate, no other name, and had signed on shortly before Jacob Peters' death. He too had developed a crush on Linda. "Those two are going to fight one of these days," Mrs. Peters predicted with a half-humorous, half-disgusted shake of her head, referring to Pate and Tall Will. "And my daughter will be the cause of poor Pate's death if she doesn't quit flirting with both of them." As he surveyed the group, Stoner wasn't sure that Mrs. Peters was right about the outcome of a fight between Tall Will and Pate. Will had the advantage in height and arm length, and in bulk. But not in determination and knowhow, Stoner decided as he caught the bald puncher's eyes on his own. Sitting indolently with his chair tilted back against the wall, Pate looked like he would stand three or four inches below Will's six four and probably weigh in at twenty to thirty pounds lighter. But there was no give in his eyes. Stoner had once seen such eyes on a mastiff down in Tucson as the animal fought two of its own kind, killing them methodically one at a time in spite of the lifeblood pouring from its own body. Any fight between Will and Pate would be to the death, he had no doubt, with whatever weapons Pate could get his hands on.

The final two were called Tack Guthrie and Sonora Vasquez. Like Cactus, Sonora had ridden for the previous owners of the Rocking H. Tack was a more recent hire, having appeared in the valley a year or so after the Peterses took over the ranch. Both were approaching forty and were men who had spent most of their lives in the saddle: leathery-faced, bow-legged, slender-shanked men without an ounce of fat on their bodies. They would fight for the brand, Stoner concluded his survey of the two.

"Can't say's I know what Miss Peters told you," he grinned at Tall Will. "But buffaloing the Bar B doesn't sound like anything I've done."

Tall Will returned Stoner's grin, "You ain't callin' Miss Linda a liar, are you?"

"Not me," Stoner's smile froze on his lips and his eyes turned an icy grey. "I'm just a peaceable cowpoke that's sleepier'n a bear before hibernation. So I reckon if you gentlemen'll excuse me I'll turn in." So saying he headed for the bunk where his gear had been piled.

"I don't reckon we'll excuse you just yet," Tall Will's words were a mocking imitation of Stoner's. "We wanta find out if you're the wildcat Miss Linda thinks."

"No we don't," Cactus interrupted. "You do, Will. The rest of us told you we wasn't gonna help hooraw nobody. He stood up for Miss Linda and Rob; that's enough for the rest of us."

Tall Will laughed. "Well, stranger, Stoner or whatever you call yourself, you heard the man. It's just you and me. I say it was a setup to plant you on the Rocking H. Nobody could make Nate Barstow and his bunch of toughs eat crow that easy."

Stoner shook his head disgustedly and again turned toward the bunk where his gear was.

"I ain't through with you, by God," Tall Will lunged forward several steps. "I reckon you're a damned spy for the Bar B and I'm gonna send you back, over the saddle or just bruised up. Your choice."

Stoner stopped and turned to face the angry young cowhand. "Well," he drawled, winter's ice cracking in his voice, "maybe you've got good reason to suspect me. Or maybe there's some other reason you're all lathered up to pick a fight with me. I don't know. But you asked for it and you've got it. But not with fists. That's a Colt in your holster there. Anytime you're ready, go for it." As he spoke the final words of challenge, he slipped into a crouch. His right hand hovered claw-like inches from his own Colt.

Instantly Tall Will's hand streaked for his sidearm. Just as suddenly he stopped, his Colt still in its holster not more than an inch above where it had rested before he reached for it. A look of fear, consternation and bewilderment slowly spread over his face. Stoner's Colt had appeared as if by sleight of hand, cocked and aimed chest-level almost before Tall Will had touched his own.

"You want to continue this set-to?" Stoner asked, his eyes cold, probing.

"Jesus," Tack breathed. "I ain't seen anything that fast since I seen Doc Holliday in action back in Jacksborough."

None of the others uttered a word. Tall Will's face turned ashen, but he didn't flinch from the bullet he expected at any moment. Stoner also remained frozen in his crouch for what seemed minutes to the others in the room, his eyes unblinkingly locked on the eyes of his antagonist.

"You reckon this little fracas is over?" he finally asked, a mirthless smile touching his lips.

"Yeah," Tall Will started to speak but only a husky whisper came from his mouth. He cleared his throat. "Yeah, it's over."

"For now or for good?" Stoner remained crouched as if frozen in stone. Nothing about him moved, not so much as an unconscious tremor of muscle or flesh, or the blink of an eye, except for the slow spread of the icy smile from eyes to lips. Before Tall Will had time to answer, he continued, "I'm gonna sack out and I wouldn't like to wake up dead."

"I'm no back-shooter," Tall Will's voice echoed a mixture of anger and chagrin at both the defeat and the suggestion, as well as deep relief at being alive. "You beat me fair and square. You coulda shot me but you didn't. The way I figure it, I owe you for that. And for what I said about you and the Bar B bunch. The way you throwed that hogleg...well, anybody that says you didn't buffalo Nate Barstow and his cronies is a liar. And that includes me."

"Fair enough." Stoner holstered his pistol and extended his right hand. "No hard feelings?"

Tall Will took the proffered hand and pumped it with nervous enthusiasm. His green eyes once again glimmered with youthful humor and self-confidence.

"But I'd sure like for another chance to get even. Say a friendly fistfight some time."

His antagonist looked the younger man over and returned the grin when their eyes met, "No thanks." His voice was somber in spite of the grin. "I don't fight for fun. And I don't fight friends. I never did see anything friendly about a fight of any kind. Never got any satisfaction out of punching or kicking another man senseless, maybe crippling him for life. Or taking the chance of being crippled. I don't pull a gun or take a punch at a man unless I'm ready to kill to win." He shrugged in mock self-deprecation. "Sorry, but that's the way I am. A man without much of a sense of humor."

Cactus chuckled and commented in a low voice, "Now me, I can understand that." Tack and Sonora both grunted assent. Pate shook his head as if in amazement. Tall Will alternately frowned and smiled halfheartedly as if not quite sure but what he was being poked fun at.

"No offense meant," Stoner raised his hands palm forward in continued peace offering. "And that's not to say I don't like to watch a good fight. I reckon I'm about as bloodthirsty as the next fellow when it comes to someone else being pounded around. So with that sermon," he concluded with a chuckle, "me for about ten hours sleep. Hell, it must be almost morning already."

"There sure as hell won't be no ten hours sleep if'n you want breakfast. We'd all better hit the sack," Cactus added, cackling loudly. "That damn Chew Lin'll bang his pan before sunup."

At the newcomer's puzzled look, Tall Will explained, "Chew Lin's the Chinaman cook. He sleeps in the cookhouse, that long building north of us and the main house. When chow's ready, he takes one of his biggest pans and this here big wood spoon he don't use for nothing else and he bangs away on that there pan so you can hear him all the way to Chasco. If you don't show up quick-like he raises old Ned."

At Tall Will's explanation, the other hands laughingly agreed.

"Then I better get what sleep I can," Stoner commented as he piled his blanket roll, saddlebags, and cartridge belt on the floor; put his pistol under the pillow; pulled off his boots, socks and outer clothes; and with a sigh of relief rolled into bed.

The next thing he knew a horrible din reverberated up and down the murky hallways of his unconsciousness. He pounced from bed, his pistol in his hand and cocked.

Five faces above five fully clothed bodies grinned innocently at him from five different bunks. He grinned back sheepishly before turning to dress. Chew Lin's hideous clanging continued.

"You reckon he's awake now?" Tack Guthrie asked the room in general.

"I reckon, or he mighta shot one of us poor cowpokes in the leg, or somewhere more private. As weak as he looks in the mornin' I don't reckon he could lift that big hogleg any higher," Tall Will laughed good-humoredly. "You'd reckon there'd be a law against a man that careless totin' a pistola like he does. Thank God Almighty Chew Lin woke him up before he did shoot one of us poor critters. Miss Linda'd have his head for sure, the way she hates weapons and fightin' and such like."

"What I think," Sonora chimed in, "is that he's a caballero from a rich hacienda somewhere. He likes to sleep all the day and court the ladies all the night."

"You sayin' he's a lady's man?" Pate rolled his eyes and threw his hands up in mock consternation. "With a mug like that? You sure must be a damn poor judge of what pleases the ladies, Sonora."

"That's why he courts them at night," Tall Will laughed. "Now me, I...."

"Whoops," Cactus interrupted with a roar. "Don't let Tall Will get started on how dangerous he is to the womenfolk. He'll run on for an hour or two, or the whole damn day maybe. He runs off at the mouth every time he talks about hisself and the ladies. Let's go eat," he added after a slight pause. "Chew Lin ain't bangin' that pan no more; he's gonna raise a ruckus the whole time we're eatin'."

After devouring the morning meal of flapjacks and eggs, the latter from Mrs. Peters' brood of hens, the crew stood around outside the long, squat building used for a chow hall, occasionally making a comment, awaiting working instructions for the day. Stoner mosied on back to the bunkhouse to collect his things. He planned to saddle the black and then talk to Mrs. Peters before heading to town to stock up with food for the trail. He didn't look forward to telling the Rocking H owner about his decision. She was a good woman, a person to ride the river with. He had liked her the moment he laid eyes on her. He felt something comfortable in her, the secure comfort of home and family. It was odd, he thought, but in some way he felt like a deserter. She had treated him like one of her own. She had made him an honest offer. But he couldn't take it. And he couldn't give her an honest answer for not doing so. He couldn't tell her that he was simply too tired of fighting. And worse, he couldn't tell her that he was too attracted to her daughter, that if he stayed he might make a fool of himself over the girl, or do something for which he'd have to fight one of her crew, maybe more than one of them. The very thought of the girl's youthful curves sent soft, warm fingers of pleasure wandering through his belly and groin. But she, well, Stoner had noted the scorn hidden deep in her eyes as she looked him over in the saloon, from his drawn pistol to his faded, torn Levi's and shirt. She wouldn't have anything personal to do with a gunfighter, much less a ragged grub line rider who usurped her brother's authority. If he stayed he wouldn't be able to help himself. He'd try for the girl even though he'd already seen the not-quite-hidden evidence of her scorn. He couldn't stay and not try. She was more than enough reason for him to go, before he caused Mrs. Peters problems he didn't want to. But Rob Peters...there was the main reason he should keep moving. He didn't figure Rob would stand peacefully by and watch another man take over the authority that should by rights of birth belong to him. Rob wouldn't accept another man as head of the ranch. On the other hand, if he, Stoner, became foreman he wouldn't have a shirker and troublemaker on the ranch. He'd have to make Rob knuckle under or get out. That would mean a fight, with fists or guns. Not that he was afraid of young Peters. Rather he was afraid of himself and what he might do. If he crippled or killed the young man, Linda Peters would never forgive him. Neither would Mrs. Peters, in spite of what she thought. And finally there was the coming fight with the Bar B. Without the other two problems, the Peters children, he might stay and fight for Mrs. Peters in spite of the odds and his feelings. All three problems, he grimaced to himself, he didn't want to face.

He soon had his gear ready; he headed for the corrals to find his horse and saddle, planning to ride back past the bunkhouse to pick up the gear. A deep sense of loneliness overcame him as he saddled the dust-shaded black. Mrs. Peters had made him feel comfortable, as if he had finally come home after years of wandering. He had liked the crew, even Tall Will. He missed the camaraderie of ranch work that he had left in New Mexico and the meaning that it had given his life. The thought of continuing his wandering existence twisted his gut. He tried to shake off the melancholy. But forcing his mind to concentrate solely on the world around him only increased his sense of loss. The Rocking H exuded a fertile permanence and peace that he had never felt before, even on the ranch in New Mexico, which at one time he had planned to make his home. The rambling buildings of Rocking H headquarters sat at the bottom of the pass which led from the larger valley that he, Linda and Rob had followed from Chasco into a smaller, lower valley. The buildings blended comfortably with their surroundings. Made of logs and natural wooden shakes and sitting in a stand of pines and aspens and old, twisted oaks, the buildings and corrals meandered unobtrusively across the narrow break in the hills. The break led from the larger valley into a little valley that spread westward like a thumb of its larger neighbor. The ranch buildings stood guard over the small, fertile valley, sentinels hidden among the trees that lined the approach. The valley itself spread out before them, not more than a few hundred yards wide and three miles long. A small, shallow stream meandered along the center of the valley, its silvery water occasionally visible through the trees and deep grass that lined its banks. It flowed lazily into a miniature lake behind the ranch buildings, a lake whose placid surface was surrounded by green rushes knee-high to a rider on a tall horse. The central floor of the valley gleamed a dark green which faded to lighter greens and browns and yellows outward toward the lower slopes of the hills surrounding it. Higher up, the slopes became the dark greenish black of pine forests. Above the eastern slopes of the valley the morning sky glowed in the deep, cloudless blue of infinity. The sun had risen a blazing ball well over the horizon but hadn't yet burned heaven and earth to dry reflections of itself.

To the east, hidden from Stoner's sight by the small range of hills through which the pass meandered, but not from his memory since he had ridden through it the previous day, the larger valley spread yellow and brown in every direction, to eventually merge with mountain peaks that dwarfed those enclosing the smaller valley. "Must be twenty miles or more to the eastern side," Stoner reflected as he gazed at the far peaks.

"A man'd never tire of the view," he mused aloud, noticing the way the black pranced nervously and stared toward the east, its ears pointed, its nostrils slightly flared. When the animal snorted he commented softly, rubbing its ears, "That's okay, Blacky; I see them."

Along the trail that wound down through the pass appeared three riders trotting their mounts toward the Rocking H ranch buildings. Stoner silently watched the riders approach to within less than a hundred yards. All three rode big horses, two bays and a roan, horses that moved with an easy rocking gait suggesting both speed and stamina. The three riders were all of a size, big like their mounts, wide-shouldered, deep-chested men with sidearms at their hips and rifles in saddle boots. Stoner grinned to himself as he noticed the similarity of dress too, from the flat-crowned black Stetsons and red shirts to the Levi's and black boots. The only apparent difference between the two younger men was that one wore his pistol on the left side, for a left-handed draw.

"I reckon those three are the Bartlemans," Stoner drawled in the dusty black's ear as the three riders drew abreast of him and passed by, pulling their mounts to a walk for the final approach to the house, their piercing eyes studying him momentarily. "I'd lay a few thousand to one they'd be a mite tough to buck. All three look like scrappers if you don't take them by surprise, and if they're as good with those hoglegs as Mrs. Peters says."

Without another word he turned, climbed over the fence, and cut straight past the bunkhouse to the house. He reached the front porch just as the Peters family appeared, called by Tall Will who was standing to the left of the family, on the edge of the porch, watching the approaching riders. To Stoner, Linda exuded an overwhelming aura of domestic tranquility and permanence. And physical attraction. He found it close to impossible to tear his eyes from her. The sleeves of her dress were rolled above the elbows. Several small patches of flour spotted the light green of her apron and clung to her bare arms, round, golden, soft, as if those spots had been missed in a hurried attempt to ready herself for company. Her arms and face still radiated the red heat of the fire. A few strands had escaped the dark green ribbon that held her hair spread along her back almost to her waist, keeping it from falling forward over her shoulders. Those loose strands fell in wavy disarray over her forehead and ears. Her face reflected a faint irritation at the disruption, and curiosity, nothing more. As she stepped to the edge of the porch and shaded her eyes to better see the approaching riders, Sam caught a whiff of something warm and appetizing--bread, pie, cookies, cake, something fresh from the oven. Mrs. Peters looked like she had been in the kitchen also. As with Linda, her face was flushed with heat and her apron spotted and crumpled. She'd been wiping her hands on a towel as she came through the door. She continued to carry the towel in her left hand. Rob showed the effects of his drinking bout. His eyes were bloodshot, his skin pale, his lips dry, his hands unsteady as he nervously mopped at his hair or tried to straighten the shirt he must have hurriedly thrown on when Tall Will announced that riders were approaching. But he had come armed; a pistol hung from the holster at his side.

Stoner moved to the far right of the others, near the edge of the porch. He, Rob and Tall Will were the only ones with weapons. If trouble started, he figured, he and Will would have the Bartlemans in a crossfire and at the same time would draw the fire of the three men away from the Peters family. But if Rob drew without shifting his position, he would draw fire toward his mother and sister. Stoner grimaced to himself. He wondered if Rob had enough sense to move from where he presently stood.

He had barely taken his position when the three riders pulled up in front of the porch. The elder Bartleman doffed his sombrero but the cold emptiness of his eyes belied the gesture and the words that followed.

"Mrs. Peters," he nodded his head slightly, "you look bright and chipper this morning. It appears like you and Miss Linda've been doing some cooking. Reminds a man of what he's been missing since his wife died."

"Good morning, Mr. Bartleman." A noncommittal smile touched the corner of Mrs. Peters' eyes. "If you were Irish I'd say you had a little of the blarney in you this morning. But, anyway, I appreciate the compliment. A woman doesn't receive many stuck out here away from town like I am."

"That could change. I'll buy you out any time you say the word. You should know that. Lord knows, I offered to buy your husband out more'n once."

"I know you did," Mrs. Peters searched the elder Bartleman's face, anger clouding the depths of her eyes. "But as far as Jacob was concerned, you never made a serious offer. Your last offer averaged out less than a dollar a head for the cattle and less than ten cents an acre for the land. You couldn't have expected him to sell for that, so he never thought you really meant to buy us out. Besides," she continued after a heavy pause, "Jacob wasn't interested in selling and neither am I."

"Well, now, after your husband's death I decided to wait, figurin' you'd see you can't run a ranch like the Rockin' H. But the waitin's over," Bartleman's voice dripped scorn, changing to an arrogant pitch as he talked. "A woman alone with a son that's a drunkard and a girl that's spent too much time back east learnin' how to talk and look good--hell, she don't even know enough to stay out of saloons." Sam guffawed at his father's words. "What's she gonna do when it's brandin' and cuttin' time?" Again Sam guffawed, ogling Linda while the older man stared disgustedly at Mrs. Peters. "And that son of yours. Hell, he's drunk half the time, I hear. How's the two of them gonna keep a ranch runnin'? And you too. You ain't never run no ranch. Hell's bells, Jacob Peters done all the real work around here. He run the ranch and you know it. You ain't got no experience with proper grazin' and doctorin' sick cows and knowin' when to sell. Those two pups ain't neither. A year. Two maybe, and you'll be dead broke. Your cattle gone to rustlers and the weather and...well, hell, I didn't ride all the way over here to talk about your problems or to make another offer for your spread. I reckon I'll get it soon enough as it is." The elder Bartleman let his eyes roam freely over the two Peters women and Rob, scorn curling his lips. Then for a few moments he silently studied Tall Will.

When he spoke his words were for the tall puncher alone, "I recall we had a little run-in in town once. I told you to get out of the valley but old Jacob said he was hirin' you. Well, Jacob Peters's dead and you ain't left yet. We'll talk about that sometime, but right now I got somethin' to say to the boss lady."

Joe Bartleman's eyes, arrogant and devoid of feeling, swung back to Mrs. Peters, his movement dismissing Tall Will as if the latter no longer existed. The tall puncher's face turned white around the gills at the threat, but he held his peace and his eyes never wavered from the frigid glare of the older man, his hand never moved from near his pistol. When the elder Bartleman turned away from him, Will's eyes returned to those of Matt, who sat his horse facing the Rocking

H hand. Will'll do, Stoner thought to himself as he studied Sam Bartleman, who had pulled up a few feet away and was sitting slouched in the saddle rolling a smoke and staring at Stoner, a sneer resembling his old man's curling his lips.

"What I've got to say, Mrs. Peters, is this," Bartleman began.

Stoner let a smile tweak the corners of his mouth. Bartleman had never once let on that he had noticed Stoner, as if the latter were a statue or a part of the natural scenery. Yet Stoner knew that the edge of the man's eyes had studied him more than once, thoughtfully, carefully.

"We moved Bar B cattle onto the grass at Loma Linda. Figured there was enough water and grass there for both of us. I hope you won't cause no trouble. The water's there. So's the grass. Plenty of it. We figure we got as much right to both as Rocking H has."

Mrs. Peters studied her neighbor's face before she responded. No smile breached her lips or touched her eyes. Her hands remained calmly at her sides. But Stoner noted a slight tightening of her shoulders, as if what she had heard disturbed her temper, but not enough to make her lose control.

"Jacob saw fit to let you use the water from the spring. You took advantage of him, overstocking your side of the grass and then driving your cattle over onto our side." She paused, continuing to study the elder Bartleman. "You're right, of course. There's plenty of water for both the Rocking H and the Bar B. There's enough grass on both sides, too, if we both use our heads and don't overstock the graze." Again she paused thoughtfully. "I'll have the whole fence in that area taken down so your cattle can easily get to the water and grass."

"That won't be necessary," Bartleman bowed mockingly. "We took a piece of the fence along our side of the spring down some time ago, as I reckon you know because your men put it back up; yesterday we took down a longer section of the fence. We'll be moving more cattle in soon."

"You what!" Rob interrupted with an angry shout, stepping in front of his mother. "You had no right to tear that fence down. It's well inside our land. We have a clear title to all of the area on our side of the fence, including the spring."

"So, what you gonna do about it?" Sam Bartleman spoke for the first time.

"Drive your cattle back where they belong and put the fence up again," Rob shouted, beside himself with anger.

"You'll play hell," Sam laughed tauntingly, his words a deliberate insult. "A drunk, two women, and a bunch of broken-down grub-line riders? Course, one of the women could make this whole problem a lot easier on all of us if she was a mind to."

He grinned and leered at Linda. His father guffawed. Swearing hoarsely, Rob grabbed for his pistol.

Stoner had watched the drama unfold. Flashing through his mind at Joe Bartleman's first words to Mrs. Peters had come the warning that the Rocking H owners were maybe being set up by the Bartlemans, that if the latter could kill Rob and Tall Will, and maybe himself, and if Mrs. Peters died from an accidental bullet, the battle would be over before it had begun, the Bartlemans clear victors. He had begun to move even before Rob grabbed for his sidearm. His Colt slipped into his hand, he slammed one bullet into the ground between the front feet of Sam's mount as he dived into Rob, smashing the latter into Mrs. Peters. A split second later, as his shoulder connected with the solid wood of the house and he rebounded with a tigerish leap to the front of the porch, another bullet from his Colt caught Joe Bartleman in the right shoulder, tearing the latter's arm from the gun he was trying to draw. With a piercing shriek, Joe's mount reared sharply at the sound of the shots and the biting sting of gunpowder on its muzzle.

Sam's horse had already begun to swap ends at the crack of the first shot and the slap of the bullet into the ground near where its muzzle drooped tiredly. Sam was unprepared for the sudden move of the animal. His whole attention had been concentrated on killing Rob and the new man who had had the run-in with the Bar B punchers over the Peters girl. Matt, he was confident, would take care of the puncher called Tall Will. Joe would be shooting too, ostensibly in Rob's direction but actually at Mrs. Peters and her daughter. The plan had been his and Joe's, as was most of the planning at the Bar B. It had been a simple plan. The three would ride up to the house, call the Peterses out for a talk, start a fight, and kill anyone who had come out to face them. Later they would claim that the Rocking H had started the gun battle and stray bullets had killed the women. That all three Peterses were there and that they were backed by only two punchers had been luck. That Joe had wound up facing the two women, thus becoming responsible for their death, was also luck.

Even before he reached for his gun Sam knew that something had gone wrong. The new puncher was already moving, his hand filled with a Colt .45. Sam had no time to prepare himself. At the same moment when the sight of the movement and the pistol hit his retina, the shot blasted near his horse's face. With a bleat of fear the animal leaped straight up and began swapping ends before it hit the ground again. At the first leap Sam lost the right stirrup. The pistol he had been drawing slipped from his fingers. At the second leap he felt himself falling and grabbed for leather. At that moment Joe's horse came down across his. A front hoof caught him a glancing blow behind the right elbow, in the ribs. He lost consciousness as he was smashed from the saddle. He was unaware that two ribs had been broken. He was unaware that, if Stoner hadn't leaped from the porch and, with superhuman effort, dragged Joe's horse off of his, he would probably have been trampled to death in the dust, a few feet from the people he had come to kill, or squashed as hundreds of pounds of horseflesh fell on top of him.

Agilely, as his shoulder smashed into the wall and his second bullet plowed into Joe, Stoner gave a leap that put him beside Tall Will, between Matt Bartleman and the Peterses, who had all wound up in a heap against the wall behind Tall

Will's position. He relaxed as he saw that Will had Matt covered, the latter with his pistol still in its holster.

A split second later he dived for Joe's horse, yanking it and Sam's mount from over the prostrate body of the twin. In the process he dumped Joe onto the ground near Sam. Joe landed on his wounded shoulder and, without a sound, lost consciousness.

Once he had the horses calmed and hitched to the rail at the side of the house, Stoner returned to the porch area. The rest of the hands had appeared with weapons drawn and ready, but too late to see action.

"We was outside the bunkhouse jawin'," Cactus was ruefully explaining the crew's absence to Mrs. Peters. "We heard the Bartlemans ride up, but we sure didn't expect no shootin', not with you women folks present. We didn't figure it was none of our business what you all was talkin' about so we stayed put. That was a real mistake."

"Maybe it was best you stayed put. It all turned out okay for us, thanks to Jacob," Mrs. Peters commented as she directed the hands to carry Sam and Joe into the house, where she and Linda began working on the two wounded men.

Stoner silently watched the men and women disappear into the cool interior of the building. Remaining outside were four of them. Rob and Will stood on the porch with their sidearms trained on Matt Bartleman, who still sat his horse at the edge of the porch, his pistol in its holster, his hands resting motionlessly on his saddle horn, his eyes moving nervously from Rob to Tall Will and back to Rob. Stoner walked over to the young Bartleman and drew the man's pistol from its holster, then the rifle from its scabbard. He studied the rider but found no evidence of a hideout gun.

Stepping back, he ordered, pointing with his head to the edge of the porch, "Get down and sit." He turned to Rob and Will, "You can put those pistolas away. I don't reckon the man's very dangerous now, not with him having no weapons and there being three of us with Colts."

For a moment he thought Rob was going to refuse the order. Their eyes locked. After a while Rob's eyes dropped and he reluctantly holstered his pistol.

"Might's well," he accepted. "The catamount's teeth have been pulled."

"Not because of anything you done, Peters," Matt spoke for the first time, his eyes locked on Will. "You," he spoke to the tall Rocking H puncher, "me and you'll have it out some other time, when there ain't no others to get in the way."

A good-natured grin spread over Tall Will's face, but it never reached his eyes, which remained cold and emotionless. "Any time you say, but I reckon your paw's got first chance. Or so he says."

"Enough," Stoner's voice cracked like a whip. "I told you to get off your horse," each word cracked loudly in the silence that had followed his first command.

The Bar B twin ignored the command. Looking at Stoner with an insolent grin on his lips, he wrapped one leg around the pommel of his saddle and reached into his shirt pocket for his tobacco. Without warning, as swiftly as a striking sidewinder, Stoner took one step, grabbed the young man by the arm and shirt and, with a twisting movement of muscular arms and shoulders, swinging his feet rhythmically to the motion of his upper torso, heaved his victim into the dust.

Matt lit with a heavy thump, on his back, his arms and legs akimbo. He lay where he fell, unmoving, frantically gasping for the breath that the fall had smashed from his lungs. Stoner stood above him and watched, no expression in his eyes.

For five long minutes Matt struggled to force air into his tortured lungs. For several more he gloried in the feel and taste of the oxygen as it returned strength to his body. Above him, a couple of feet from his outstretched arms, stood the man who had pulled him from his horse. He surged from the ground, his mind registering a blind need to smash and destroy.

He didn't quite reach his feet. The toe of Stoner's boot connected with his chin, stunning him momentarily. A split second later the same toe smashed into his temple. The world blacked out.

4

Over a half hour later Matt woke up with a splitting headache. For some moments he thought he was still being beaten by the man who had thrown him from his horse. He began to fight back but quickly realized that there was nothing to fight, that the pain in his head was not coming from being hit but from being bounced around in the back of a wagon.

He forced his eyes open and began to take note of his surroundings. He was lying on his back with his head at the tail of the bouncing vehicle. On one side of him lay Sam, apparently unconscious, groaning with each bounce. On the other side lay Joe, his eyes open and staring angrily into the empty void above, his lips clamped against any expression of his pain. Backward on the wagon seat so as to face the three Bartlemans, his rifle carelessly pointed at Joe's middle, sat the Rocking H puncher called Pate. Driving was the man they called Cactus, the one, as the local wags claimed, that had been on the Rocking H when Columbus discovered the New World.

After several attempts to form words with a tongue that stuck to the roof of his mouth, through lips that were as parched as last year's corn, Matt finally emitted a hoarse whisper, "Where we goin'?"

Pate stared at him for a long time without answering. Finally, however, offering a smile that resembled a death mask, he answered laconically, "Chasco."

"Our horses? I never figured the Rocking H for horse thieves."

Again Pate stared at him for a long while before answering. When he did answer his voice was as expressionless as his eyes, "I reckon I'll pretend you didn't say that. You was a well man and had you a gun in that holster,

I'd shoot you right where you are, like I would a mad coyote. I ain't got no truck for men that try to shoot women down. Was me, I'd a hung the three of you back there at the Rocking H. But Mrs. Peters wanted you taken to town to the doc and I follow orders. She's too damn nice for her own good, I reckon."

"I...," Matt started but stopped, not knowing what to say.

"Your horses're tied on behind if you'll look. Now shut the hell up. I gotta haul you to town but I ain't gotta listen to your crap. You make one more peep and I may shoot you in the leg, just for the hell of it. I don't like ridin' in one of these contraptions and I don't like nursemaidin' killers. That don't put me in no mood for small talk."

Matt decided to shut up, as advised. He didn't figure Pate would shoot him. But there was no need antagonizing the man. There was always that possibility no matter how slight that he might shoot. More to the point, however, he might decide to dump the three wounded Bartlemans out in the middle of nowhere. And, from the looks of things, Sam might not make it if he had to ride a horse for any distance. And riding in the saddle wouldn't do Joe any good either, although Matt wasn't sure the movement of a horse could be any harder on a wounded man than the bouncing of the wagon.

Between half closed eyes he studied Pate.

What he saw he didn't like, nor did he like what had just taken place at the ranch. He didn't like it for two reasons. One, Joe and Sam had convinced him that the Rocking H would be a pushover and that the hands and the Peters family would fold at the first sign of real trouble. They'd been wrong, his father and brother had. He hadn't seen any weakness in Mrs. Peters, or in Rob, unless it was the latter's lack of self-control, which could be a greater danger to himself and those around him than to the enemy. But the important thing was that he wasn't one to cut and run in the face of trouble, young Peters wasn't. It was a mistake to think so, Matt believed, and Joe and Sam didn't make mistakes very often, not ones that could be mortal. But this time they had; they had underestimated Rob and his mother. Worse, they had underestimated the Rocking H punchers. This man guarding him, this man they called Pate, didn't look to be a man to back down for anyone, Matt thought, as he studied the man's face and eyes and the way he held his rifle, loose, relaxed, no longer pointed at anyone in particular but never wavering from the direction of the three Bartlemans. Neither was the one they called Tall Will slow to action, as Matt himself had learned to his shame, although he hadn't been set for the gunplay and so was caught flat-footed when the Rocking H puncher made his play. But the worst mistake of all had been underestimating the new rider and in ignoring the possibility that he might be on hand at the Rocking H, the rider who had taken on Nate Barstow and the Bar B men with him. All three of them, Sam, Joe and himself, had figured the incident in the Chasco saloon for a freak accident, just as Nate and the others had described it: drunken punchers with their instincts impaired and their minds on Linda Peters, a grub line rider sober and not considered a threat. The newcomer had drawn when no one was expecting it and thus had gotten the drop on Nate and the boys. They had accepted that line of reasoning and so weren't prepared for the tornado they had encountered.

The other reason he didn't like what had just taken place at the Rocking H had to do with Joe and Sam and what the man Pate had just said about women killers. Neither his father nor his brother respected women much. Their attitude was plenty clear to Matt in spite of how they acted around respectable women. The way they talked when only the three of them were present, the way they had treated his mother when she still lived, the cruel manner in which they treated the whores in Chasco--Matt had realized long ago that they thought of women as having been created to serve a man's pleasure and other needs, nothing more.

But he'd never thought they would actually kill a woman, not until Pate's words sent his mind wandering back over the confrontation at the Rocking H and on to the earlier ride from the Bar B. Joe and Sam had made several comments that now made him wonder if they had made plans of which he wasn't aware. They had talked about how easy it would be for them to get the whole Rocking H if Mrs. Peters accidentally died. They didn't figure Rob and Linda could keep it running.

"Hell," Joe had said in disgust, "the boy'd put ever cent they made down his gullet and the girl'd put the rest on that ripe little body of hers."

"It ain't so little in some places," Sam laughed with a leer.

"Keep your mind on your business and off the scenery," Joe returned the leer. "If everything goes right today, won't be long before the Rocking H'll be ours. Then you can maybe figure out what to do with that little bit of goose down, if she don't drop dead before then." He leered at his son.

"You really think they won't do anything about our cows on the Loma?" Matt asked.

Joe and Sam exchanged a knowing grin. At the time Matt had thought nothing of it.

"Won't make no difference what they do," Sam claimed. "We're on the land now and old Jacob Peters's dead. They ain't got the men or the leadership to do anything about it. And after today...."

He finished his sentence with a shrug and a quick glance at Joe.

"What about after today?" Matt asked suspiciously. "What we gonna do next?"

"He means once we lay down the law to Mrs. Peters, won't be nothin' she can do about it. About our cattle on the Loma, or about the other herd we're gonna put there next week."

"Won't be enough grass for our cows and theirs if we drive another herd there," Matt commented.

"Yeah," Joe and Sam answered in unison, making no further comment.

Matt had known that his father and brother had the fence cut to the spring on the Loma, again; he had also known that they had some Bar B cattle driven onto Rocking H land. But he hadn't known that they planned to drive more cattle onto the Peters ranch. They hadn't told him of their plans, he realized, because they knew what his reaction would be. Before Jacob Peters had died, when they'd invaded Rocking H grass with their cattle and Jacob had driven the cattle back to Bar B land, Joe and Sam had been ready to take the warpath. Only Matt's angry insistence had kept them from going after Jacob or taking their men and driving the Rocking H cattle and men both from the Loma Linda range.

Now, lying in the rear of the wagon, looking down the barrel of Pate's rifle, he worried about the future. Losing the battle at the Rocking H would make Joe and Sam as mean as wounded grizzlies.

"Will Paw and Sam be satisfied with just killin' Rob Peters and those two hands that faced us down?" Matt asked himself.

He knew the answer even before he formulated the question. No. The answer was no. They wanted the Rocking H. They had wanted it for a long time and they would probably have had it already if not for him standing in their way.

All of which led to his next question: How far would they go to get the ranch? Another empty question, he thought. Both Sam and Joe had killed more than once for little if any reason. To think they would hesitate to kill for a ranch as rich as the Rocking H was naive, especially now that hate would be mixed with their greed. But the women? Matt shook his head at this last of his hopeful doubts, or, more reasonably stated, he told himself, doubtful hope.

And himself, he wondered how far he would go. They were his only kin, Joe and Sam, the only ones he knew of anyway. He had always followed their lead. As he was growing through childhood into adolescence Joe had been the supreme power. Neither son had dared challenge his orders. They did as he said or faced immediate retribution--belt, board or fists, whichever was most handy at the time. Later, as the two sons grew through the teen years, Sam grew more and more rebellious. As the years passed Joe found it more and more difficult to discipline his fractious son. So he began to listen to Sam's suggestions. Later he began to accept the boy's decisions. Some time, precisely when, Matt didn't know, but as he and Sam grew into young manhood Sam became a full partner in the authority of the ranch and he, Matt, became a shadow of his brother and father, a member of the family who followed orders as did any other hand on the ranch, but who could sometimes keep his father and brother in check if he stood firm and unbending.

5

As Pate and Cactus rolled away with their load of Bartlemans, Stoner made a decision. He climbed back onto the porch of the ranch house and knocked at the door. To the shouted call to come in he entered and followed the sound of conversation into the kitchen. As he entered the room the talking stopped. Mrs. Peters smiled and greeted him. Her children simply waited, silently, for him to state his reason for being there.

After a brief glance at Linda and Rob, Stoner ignored them and addressed himself to Mrs. Peters, stoically accepting their apparent dislike of him although irritated by what he considered the injustice of their attitude, especially Linda's.

"I reckon I came to accept your offer of a job," he returned the friendly smile in the eyes watching him. "That is, if you still want me."

"We don't need no foreman," Rob interrupted. "I'll be ramroddin' the Rockin' H."

Stoner's eyes flicked briefly over young Peters, dismissed him, and then returned to those of Mrs. Peters. He noted the hurt deep in the brown eyes that locked on his.

"I told Linda and Rob about the offer," Mrs. Peters commented softly. "They don't like it but it still stands."

"You can't do this, Mother," Linda spoke for the first time, continuing to ignore Stoner as if he weren't there. "It's not fair to Rob. Besides, we don't know anything about this man. He's just a drifting gunfighter. He'll probably desert us if the Bartlemans make him a better offer."

"He saved you a mauling in Chasco, maybe worse," a soft note of scorn touched Mrs. Peters' words. "You ought to be thankful."

"I am, Mother, but that doesn't mean we have to make him foreman. Rob and I can run the ranch. We don't need help from a stranger. We can pay Mr. Stoner for his services or, if you insist, we can give him a riding job although we don't need any more hands right now."

"He saved your brother from the Bartlemans today. Maybe he saved all of us. Tall Will thinks they were set to kill us all."

"Rob and I don't think so, Mother," Linda was becoming agitated with anger and embarrassment, Stoner noticed. "Rob shouldn't have lost his temper, but he'd have had the drop on the Bartlemans if Mr. Stoner hadn't interfered. Mr. Stoner did all the shooting and almost got Rob shot."

"That's not the way I see it," no edge sounded in Mrs. Peters' words, but in the tone of voice rang a quality which allowed for no further argument. "As of this moment Jacob is foreman. If Rob wants to work he'll take orders from Jacob. So will you, Linda." She turned to Stoner. "I apologize for this little show of family dissension."

Stoner stood awkwardly kneading his sombrero, embarrassed by the exchange of words, embarrassed and worried. After his one comment, Rob had remained uncharacteristically silent. Yet violence lurked in the glazed stare of his eyes, in the set of his mouth, and in the rigid stance of his body.

"In any case," Mrs. Peters continued after a momentary pause, glancing first at Rob and then at Linda before returning her gaze to Stoner, "the job is yours."

At her words Rob turned and stomped from the room. Linda started to say something, apparently thought better of it, and followed her brother.

"Thank you," Stoner smiled naturally for the first time since entering the room. "But I reckon your children aren't any too happy."

"I hope they get over it. If not...," Mrs. Peters shrugged helplessly before regaining control of her emotions. "What should we do about the Loma Linda range?"

"Take it back now," Stoner didn't hesitate. "Take it back while the Bartlemans are stove up, if we can take it without a long, drawn-out battle," he sounded a note of caution. "Depends on what they did to the wire and posts and how much their cows have mingled with yours, and if they left anyone on guard. And how many," he suddenly grinned at her. "I'm a lot of help when it comes to answering questions, ain't I?"

In spite of the circumstances, Mrs. Peters couldn't help but return his smile. When he smiled his flashing teeth and shining eyes were contagious. They made him look like a boy again, a happy, mischievous boy setting out to pull a prank on someone.

Immediately they became serious again. They talked for some time about the ranch--the graze, the water, the cattle, Mrs. Peters' hopes for the future.

"I reckon I'll have to ride out and look the Loma range over," Stoner spoke thoughtfully. "I can make a decision then about what to do and when."

"Take some of the men with you," Mrs. Peters advised.

"I reckon, in case the way's clear to take it back now," Stoner agreed, then mused aloud. "I don't know when Pate and Cactus'll get back. They might stick around Chasco all day and half the night. Who knows? I don't reckon I better wait on them if I want to check the Loma before the Bartlemans realize what we plan on doing; I need to learn the lay of the land before I make any decisions and I need to do that soon. So I'll take Tall Will and Sonora and leave Tack here in case Nate Barstow and the Bar B come calling, although Tack and Rob won't be much defense if the Bar B comes in force."

"I don't figure the Bar B'll show up here," Mrs. Peters said. "The hands probably won't know anything happened to the Bartlemans until late in the day, too late for them to try anything before tomorrow. And I don't figure Joe'll let Nate and the men come over here anyway; he'll want you for himself, you and Tall Will."

"I hate to leave you unprotected, you and Linda and Rob."

"I can shoot; so can Linda," Mrs. Peters smiled at his worry. "But if there's going to be a fight today or tomorrow, it won't be here; it'll be out there at the spring. You take the boys with you. We'll be okay until Pate and Cactus return." She hesitated for a moment, her eyes swinging toward the back of the house, where Linda and Rob had disappeared, before adding, "Take Rob with you. Please. It might mend the fences between you a little."

Stoner nodded reluctant agreement but wondered how he could fulfill her request without alienating Rob further. His mind was still preoccupied with her request when he stepped into the bunkhouse. If not, he might not have fallen into the trap set for him.

Linda and Rob stalked off after their mother made known her decision to appoint Stoner foreman of the Rocking H, slamming out the rear door in their anger. Once outside, they talked in low voices for several minutes and then walked swiftly to the bunkhouse. Tall Will, Tack Guthrie, and Sonora Vasquez were sitting outside. Rob gave orders to Tack and Sonora.

"You two saddle Stoner's horse and a horse for each of us five. Stoner'll be leaving shortly so take his gear and put it on his horse. The rest of us'll be riding out to check on the spring at Loma Linda. We're gonna drive those damn Bar B cows back on their own land, and any Bar B gunhands we find. We'll meet you at the corral shortly. Wait there."

"Stoner's horse's already saddled," Tack commented. "I reckon he was ready to head out before the fracas started."

"So, saddle the rest of them and put his gear on his saddle," Rob made no attempt to hide his irritation. "Just get it done."

When Tack and Sonora had headed for the corral, Linda took Tall Will's arm and led him into the bunkhouse. Rob followed them inside.

Once inside, Linda dropped the puncher's arm and turned to face him. Rob moved up beside her.

She almost laughed aloud at the comical expression of bewilderment on Tall Will's face as she led him inside and then stepped away so she could face him without straining her neck, but she caught herself in time. He was likeable and humorous, Will was. He was fun to be around at a social or a dance, or even on something as simple as a ride or a picnic. But he wore his feelings on his sleeve where she was concerned. Too often in her short time back from the East she had unwittingly caused black eyes and bloody noses, and an occasional broken bone, mostly the result of Tall Will's fists driven by what he perceived as insults to her character but occasionally driven by his anger at her for embarrassing him.

During thoughtful moments she was torn by the tall puncher's reaction to her. On the one hand she was young enough to glory in her power over him. On the other hand she had matured enough to condemn both the feeling her power gave her and his reaction to it.

In the present situation the shame lay heavy on her mind. She had never consciously instigated a fight between two men. She had despised those women who did. Yet here she was, at Rob's suggestion, ready to set Will against someone who had done her no harm but had rather befriended her and her brother in Chasco, a man she felt strangely attracted to at the same time that she felt only contempt for what he was. As she whirled to face the tall puncher, an image flashed before her eyes, the image of another face. It was a hard face chiseled in granite and framed by soft black hair. The blue eyes were grey with controlled anger at one moment and gentle, admiring blue at the next, but always with a deep sadness hidden just under the surface. She thought of being dragged ignominiously, frighteningly across the saloon floor toward a group of drunken brutes. The terror and the shame returned, leaving her as weak as she had been during the ordeal itself. Then an iron hand appeared from nowhere and smashed the arm that was dragging her. She was free, safe. But she felt herself falling until another hand, companion to the one that had freed her, gently steadied her while she caught her balance.

She shook her head, trying to free herself from the memory of Stoner's hand on her arm, steadying her, and of his eyes watching her, admiring her, as she stood on the porch waiting for the Bartlemans. Again she shook her head, angry that she couldn't free her mind of the image of a drifting gunfighter.

"Tell him, Sis," Rob interrupted her memories, "or I will."

"Tell me what?" Tall Will asked suspiciously.

"I don't know, Rob...," she began, shame and fear making her hesitate.

"Aw, that damn gunfighter," Rob answered Will. "Sis's afraid of him and now Ma's gone and made him foreman. He...."

"Afraid?" Will interrupted, addressing his question to Linda. "What'd he do?"

Linda found it impossible to meet his eyes. They were too angry, too honest and angry.

"Nothing. He...."

"Nothin'?" Rob exploded, talking to the puncher. "Like hell nothin'! Me and Linda didn't want him to come out here but he came anyhow, like maybe he figures he's got something comin' from Linda, the way he keeps watchin' her. Now he's talked Ma into makin' him foreman. Jesus, you know how she's a sucker for any lazy tramp that comes her way. I guess they had a long heart-to-heart talk last night," his voice overflowed with sarcasm. "His calculatin' heart to Ma's bleedin' one. He weaseled the foreman job out of her and that leaves you and me out in the cold, Will. I was gonna make you foreman when I took over runnin' the ranch."

The tall puncher had not taken his eyes from Linda's face.

What she saw in those eyes frightened Linda. She had agreed to Rob's plan for getting rid of Stoner only because she didn't want a gunfighter around. Stoner had saved her in

Chasco, but he had almost gotten Rob killed on the porch, and he had almost killed Joe and Sam Bartleman. It was only luck, she thought, that he hadn't killed one of the two men, or both. She was convinced that war with the Bartlemans was inevitable if he remained at the Rocking H. When their wounds healed the Bartlemans would come looking for him. They would come prepared for war if the Rocking H protected him. In order to avoid a war, he had to go. And she had to control Rob and find a compromise with the Bartlemans on the Loma Linda problem. She didn't agree with her mother that they wanted the entire Rocking H and wouldn't stop until they had it.

She pulled her mind back to Rob and Tall Will. Rob was outlining his plan for getting rid of the gunfighter. The violent light still glowed in the tall puncher's eyes; it scared Linda; so did Rob's plan; somebody could get hurt and she wanted to avoid that.

"When he comes in," Rob was saying, "me and you'll face him. Right here," he stepped to within five feet of the door. "Not too close so he gets scared and goes for his gun, but close enough so we can get to him quick. One step; that'll do it," he took a step toward the door. "One step'll put us in arm's reach. Linda, she'll be right here," he took his sister's arm and led her to a position beside the door. "She'll grab his right arm as he comes in so he can't draw his pistol. And we'll do the rest," he ended triumphantly.

"Do what?" Tall Will asked dubiously.

"Take his gun away and march him down to the corral. We'll put him on his horse and send him off the Rocking H. He's a gunfighter. If he ain't got no weapons he ain't gonna put up a fight. He'll go peaceable."

"We could face him and order him off without the sneaky part," Will's voice still echoed his uncertainty. "I reckon he'd go peaceable."

"Maybe, but I don't think so," Rob's temper began to rise. "He wheedled the foreman's job out of Ma and he's got his eye on Linda. I don't think he'll go. If he don't...," he paused with an expressive shrug, eyeing first Will and then Linda, "if he goes for a gun, Linda might get hurt. Killed even. Or he might kill one of us. Me, I don't think the foreman's job is worth killing or getting killed about."

"I don't either," Linda agreed hesitantly. "Maybe you're right, Rob."

"I reckon," Tall Will reluctantly accepted her decision. "But I sure don't like it. I could take his gun away and work him over a little." The angry light returned to his eyes as he expressed what he would really like to do. He hadn't quite gotten over being so easily bested the previous night. What really made him furious, however, was that Stoner had followed Linda against her wishes and was maybe imposing himself on her.

"No," Linda raised her voice, reacting to Will's last comment, "I don't want him hurt any more than necessary. We'll take his guns and pay him for his services. I have the money on me." She showed Will a small roll of bills.

"You sendin' him away without no weapons?"

"He can pick them up tomorrow, at the town marshal's office," Linda answered. "We'll send somebody in with them."

"What about the Bartlemans? And Nate Barstow and the Bar B punchers? Stoner'll need his weapons if he meets up with any of them, after what he's done."

"They won't shoot an unarmed man," Linda answered with confidence. "If he doesn't have his weapons he'll be safer; he won't be able to start a fight like he did today with the Bartlemans."

Tall Will was beginning to have second thoughts. He too had been at the house when the Bartlemans arrived, he told himself. From what he'd seen, Stoner hadn't started anything but had rather defused a potentially deadly situation, quickly and efficiently. Moreover, from what he had seen and heard of the Bartlemans since he'd been in the valley, he couldn't agree with Linda's optimism. They were killers, quick to anger, quick to shoot. However, he didn't know how to refuse Linda. If she wanted Stoner gone, he'd see that the gunfighter left.

At that moment Rob spoke from the window through which he had been watching the house, "He's comin'."

He moved over beside Will, who stood facing the door. Linda took her position. As she waited she found it impossible to meet Tall Will's eyes.

Stoner barged through the door carelessly. He was preoccupied with the problem at Loma Linda and with finding a way to appease the younger members of the Peters family. Even when he found himself facing Rob and Will, with Linda close by on his right, possible treachery didn't enter his mind. It might have if he'd taken a closer look at the two men before him, at the strained look around their eyes or the set of their lips, but he didn't. His thoughts focused on Linda. He wondered what she was doing in the bunkhouse. He wondered why she and Rob were talking to Tall Will. He wondered why her very nearness sent alternating heat waves and chills running up and down his spine and into his loins.

Then it was too late. Linda took a step as if to move over beside her brother. As she passed Stoner she stopped and grabbed his pistol with both hands. With the instinctive reaction of a wild animal scenting danger Stoner swept her hands from his weapon and lurched to the left; his palm slapped into the walnut handle, his fingers closed around the metal, his arm contracted to speed upward.

It never began its motion. Tall Will's fist connected with his chin, a glancing blow thrown off by the sudden move. He slammed into the wall, the violent contact tearing his hand from his Colt. He might have recovered to put up a defense, but as he rebounded, trying to shake free of his dazed condition, Rob's pistol connected with his head. Once. Twice. A third time.

The last thing he felt was this hat sliding from his head. The last thing he heard was Linda's scream, "Don't! You'll kill him."

When he came to, his head lay in Mrs. Peters' lap. She was washing his face with a wet cloth and talking to him.

"I'm sorry, Jacob. I didn't think...."

"Jesus, Ma," Rob's complaining voice reached Stoner as if from a great distance. "Quit slobbering over him, will you? He's a no-good drifting gunfighter, that's all. If somebody paid him enough, he'd shoot you or me or anybody."

"I don't be...," Mrs. Peters started to answer.

"You can't send him off like this, Rob." Stoner recognized Linda's voice as it interrupted uneasily. "He might be hurt bad; you hit him awful hard."

Two of the punchers seconded Linda's comment--Tall Will and Tack Guthrie. Stoner recognized their voices. But Rob had taken command. In a loud, angry voice he overrode their concern.

"It don't make a damn bit of difference if he don't make it to Chasco or anywhere else. He ain't nothin' but a killer. The world'd be better off without him if he did die somewhere."

"You can't mean that, Rob," Linda's voice rose with distress.

"You goddamn right I mean it," Rob's voice rode roughshod over his sister's. "He made his play for the ranch. I stopped him. I sure as hell ain't gonna let him make another play. That'd be smart, now wouldn't it? He'd maybe decide to shoot me next time. I know his kind."

Linda continued arguing with her brother, seconded by Mrs. Peters. The punchers remained silent.

Stoner heard the voices as if from somewhere in a fog. He tried to move but couldn't. He tried to concentrate on what was being said but found his mind wandering in and out of the fog. The pain in his head became more intense, throbbing, but at the same time some voice inside him told him he'd be okay. Wishful thinking or something subconscious telling him that he didn't have a concussion, that he had been worse hurt and recovered, quickly--he didn't know which and couldn't concentrate long enough to make a rational decision. Several times he tried to touch the source of the ache, to determine how bad it was, but he couldn't move his hands. He didn't realize they had been roped to his sides. Soon he felt rough hands handling him. His arms were freed. Instinctively he started to move his hands to his head. But somebody grabbed his arms. He felt himself lifted and then thrown into the saddle. His mind cleared. He realized what was happening to him. He struggled but he was too weak to make much of an effort at defending himself. His legs were tied together under his horse's belly; he was bent forward and his arms tied under the animal's neck.

"That should hold him," Rob's voice rose in a shout of triumph. "Now turn the damn animal loose. Head it back toward town and turn it loose. When he comes to, he can get those ropes off his wrists."

"What if he doesn't come to?" Tall Will asked doubtfully.

"Hell, look at his eyes," Rob gave an angry snort that sounded like the irritated grunt of a javelina. "He's already coming out of it. We were too damn easy on him."

"You would have killed him, Rob," Linda accused her brother.

"No more'n he deserved," Rob shrugged. "Sonora, lead his horse down the trail a ways and turn it loose, but make sure it heads toward Chasco. Next time I see him I'll kill him," Rob's voice rose arrogantly. He had forgotten that Linda and Tall Will had helped him overpower Stoner. In his mind Stoner had become the vanquished, himself the conqueror.

"I'll do it, Sonora," Linda interrupted, taking the black's reins from the cowhand. "You go ahead, Rob. I'm not riding out to the Loma with you."

Rob didn't answer at first. When he did, his words and tone of voice were curt, authoritative, "Don't let that killer come back here, Linda. You do, I'll kill him. And don't you go to Chasco. I don't want someone to have to drag you out of a saloon again. Stay where you belong."

With a brusque "Let's go!" to the hands, Rob spurred his horse around the south side of the lake.

6

As he rode at the head of the column, Rob gazed contentedly around him. Overhead the sun smiled among white, fluffy clouds lining the immense blue from horizon to horizon. The slopes of the mountains surrounding the valley were dotted with stands of pine and aspen and the darker moving shadows of the clouds. The valley unfolded before them, green and fertile with scattered bits of color where cattle browsed in the sun. The crystal stream flowed cold and peaceful over its rocky bed, spreading life around it.

"The valley's mine now," Rob told himself, exulting in the words until the shadow of his dead father rose from the mire of his subconscious and cast gloom over his thoughts. Suddenly he needed a drink. Automatically he reached for his saddlebags, but he immediately pulled his hand back to the pommel. He didn't have a bottle. Besides, he had quit drinking again. He swore under his breath. He cursed himself for not having brought a bottle and he cursed himself for wanting a drink in the first place.

Somehow...somehow he had to come to terms with his part in his father's death. Worse yet, he had to come to terms with how he had felt as his father's horse lost its footing and stumbled over the side of the cliff. He had found himself smiling into the last glimpse he had of his father's eyes.

He could live with the lie he had told his mother, that the death had been an accident, but he was finding it more and more difficult to live with the truth. It was true that he and his father had been working together chousing cattle from the underbrush near the cliff, that they had become separated and he had dismounted in the shade of a thick mesquite, and that a few minutes later Jacob had ridden up. But from then on the episode did not develop as he had told her.

"Come on, Rob," Jacob had spoken with irritation, doffing his sombrero and wiping the sweat from his forehead with a bandanna. "You've been dogging it all day. I'm tired too, but the boys're coming in from the other direction and I'd hate to have them clear this whole quarter mile stretch by themselves."

"Why not? That's what we pay them for," Rob let his own irritation show in answer to his father's.

"Yes," Jacob answered slowly, without raising his voice. "But that's just it. We pay them a wage. There ain't no reason for them to work any harder than they have to, except loyalty and pride in a job well done, I reckon."

"And wantin' to keep their jobs," Rob sneered.

"But us," Jacob continued, ignoring Rob's words, "our wages come from profit, and profit is tied to hard work as much as it is to being smart and bossing other people around. Now, come on, let's get back to work and do our share along this stretch of underbrush."

Rob struggled to keep his temper. In one form or another he and Jacob had had the same discussion a half dozen times that day. Each time he had given in, mounted, and followed his father back into the brush. This time he remained where he was.

"I'm takin' a break," he spoke sullenly. "I'll come help in a little while."

Jacob stared at him for several moments. Rob could see the words forming in the older man's mind and he steeled himself against whatever argument might come. But finally, with a shrug of his shoulders, Jacob rode off. Oddly, the silent withdrawal made Rob madder than a lecture would have. As he sat there doing nothing his anger grew until, when he begrudgingly ended his break and mounted to follow his father, he was seething with murderous rage.

He had no sooner settled his boots in the stirrups than he looked up and saw Jacob sitting his horse near the edge of the cliff, facing an angry bull. Between Rob and Jacob a small bunch of cattle were milling nervously, watching the face-off.

Jacob began reining his horse away from the edge of the cliff, careful not to make a sudden move. Rob knew he should stay where he was, quietly, until Jacob was safely away from the drop-off, but suddenly he found himself shouting and riding toward the bunch of cattle between him and Jacob. The next thing he knew, he had drawn and fired his pistol in the air. The cattle stampeded toward the bull and Jacob. Jacob's mount panicked and reared, trying to unseat its rider. Before Jacob could regain control, the bull plowed into him and his horse, several of the cattle on his heels. As the animals collided, Jacob's eyes locked on those of his son, hurt, accusing, questioning. Rob smiled unconsciously as his father disappeared in the midst of the screaming melee of frightened animals. A few moments later came the terrible thudding impact. Rob gave a ghastly chuckle and turned away.

Rob shuddered as the memory again washed over him. He glanced at the men riding with him, to see if they had noticed. But they seemed wrapped up in their own thoughts.

Later they made a sharp turn to follow the creek into the canyon that led to the spring at Loma Linda. In a few moments Tall Will urged his mount up beside Rob's.

"We could be ridin' into a trap," he spoke above the dull thud of the horses' hooves on the sod.

Rob pulled up and studied the terrain. They had just entered the mouth of the canyon. The walls started a couple hundred feet on each side of them and rose to five hundred feet above the creek bed in places. There were some good ambush spots, Rob knew, but he didn't think the Bar B riders would be expecting an attack. They wouldn't know about the clash with the Bartlemans, and they wouldn't think anyone at the Rocking H knew about the takeover of the spring. Besides, to put a man up on each wall of the canyon to scout for an ambush would slow them down too much.

"Slow's better'n bein' put to bed with a pick and shovel," Tack spoke softly after Rob had rejected putting scouts out.

"Scared?" Rob asked with a sneer on his lips.

"Leery as a whore in church," Tack ignored the sneer but his eyes bored into Rob's until the younger man turned and gazed up the canyon. "What do you say, Sonora?"

Sonora shrugged nervously without answering.

"One of us could ride out front un poco," he finally spoke up. "He might see any bushwhackers before the rest get in range."

"Not in some of those rock piles we'll be ridin' by," Tack disagreed. "They're too thick and high on the slopes. If there's any bushwhackers out there, a scout'll be dead or we will because we'll put too much trust in him bein' out front. If they let him go by without shootin' we'll ride right into them."

"If they do start shootin', there ain't much protection any place in the bottom of the canyon," Will added.

"Yeah, well, 'if' don't get the cows branded," Rob interrupted sarcastically. "I'm ridin'. You ladies can come along or you can go back to the ranch."

He spurred his horse on up the canyon, not glancing back to see if the hands were following. In his mind, though, uncertainty struggled with irritation at their hesitancy. He promised himself that any of the three who didn't follow him would find themselves without a job as soon as they returned to the ranch. But a few moments later the three riders pulled in behind him.

As for a possible ambush, he scoffed at the idea. He didn't believe the Bartlemans wanted the Loma spring badly enough to start a shooting war over it. They wanted it all right. And they would make a play for it, figuring that, with Jacob gone, the Rocking H would be a pushover. But when they realized he was willing to fight for the water they'd back off quickly enough, just as they would have backed off at the ranch house if Stoner hadn't interfered.

"Damned gunfighter!" Rob swore. Then he smiled to himself at the mental picture of Stoner beaten and tied to his horse. Immediately he dismissed his thoughts and began planning for a potential face-off with a couple of Bar B hands at the spring.

The further they rode up the canyon without encountering evidence of Bar B riders or cattle, the more Rob became convinced that the Bartleman forces were not expecting opposition. He ignored the continued advice from his companions to send out scouts when they were approaching good ambush sites. Just before the attack Tall Will reined up beside him.

"The three of us been talkin'," he said. As he spoke he pointed at masses of boulders lining each side of the trail a couple hundred yards ahead and high up on the canyon wall. "We should stop here and send someone ahead to take a look-see in those boulders. We ain't far from the spring now and I reckon this is about the best place in the whole canyon for a bushwhackin', lots of cover for them, next to none for us."

Rob pulled his horse to a halt and reined it around to face his three hands. "Like I said before," he commented sarcastically, "anyone don't like what I'm doin' can ride back." He stared at each rider before adding, "But if you do ride off, keep ridin'. Nobody works for me if he don't follow orders."

"Yeah, well," Will spoke up again, his voice a carefully controlled drawl, "ain't nobody gonna ride away from no fight, I don't reckon. But I'd sure feel safer if someone looked over them boulders before we all go ridin' on up the canyon."

"Someone besides you, you mean?" Rob's voice dripped scorn.

"That's not what I meant," Will could not hide his angry reaction to Rob's words. He had never liked young Peters. He had remained at the Rocking H for several reasons, not the least of which was that he liked Jacob Peters and his wife. Linda, though, was the main reason. He lived with the hope that something might develop between him and her. On the other hand, Rob was an excellent reason to ride on to another job. The man had a sharp tongue and little respect for the abilities of others.

"If you want someone to scout those rocks, I volunteer," Will continued when he could again control his voice. "But someone better do it. It's stupid as all hell not to. When we ride under them we'll be out in the open."

"My feelin's exactly," Tack seconded Tall Will's words.

Rob stared at the two, then at Sonora. Sonora said nothing but Rob could see that he agreed with his fellow cowpunchers. Suddenly the anger welled up in Rob's chest, the same blind fury that had killed his father.

"I'm boss of the Rocking H now," he gritted, fighting against the anger. "There's no way any Bar B riders at the spring know we're on our way up here. And if they do, they ain't goin to ambush us. The Bartlemans don't want a shootin' war no more'n we do. Now come on," he shouted over his shoulder as he yanked his mount's head around and dug his spurs into its flanks.

The three punchers shrugged in futility and spurred their horses in pursuit. They had no sooner caught up, below the rock formation on the right, when the first shot came. Rob went down first, cursing and flopping. Then Sonora grunted and dropped from the saddle like a stone. Will grabbed his rifle and Sonora and struggled into a rocky depression. A moment later Tack and Rob followed him.

Will wrapped himself around a small boulder and then looked around. What he saw caused his stomach to churn in fear. He and his companions couldn't fight back without exposing themselves. The firing was coming from both slopes, pinning them down completely. They were dead unless help came, he figured, because the riflemen on the slopes weren't asking them to surrender; they were shooting at any movement. They had already winged Tack and nicked Rob again.

7

Immediately after Rob and the hands headed for Loma Linda, Mrs. Peters stepped over beside the black and began untying Stoner's wrists, ignoring Linda's expression of doubt about freeing Stoner before he was off the Rocking H.

"Are you all right, Jacob?" she asked anxiously.

"Yes," he forced a smile to his lips, but couldn't control the icy grey flecks in his eyes or the throbbing in his head. "I don't think anything's broken. I've got a pretty hard head."

"I'm worried," Mrs. Peters ignored his attempt at humor. "I'm worried about you, I'm worried about you and Rob, and I'm worried about Rob taking those poor cowboys out there to maybe face the Bar B."

Stoner leaned over to help her untie his ankles before he answered, ignoring the waves of throbbing pain caused by putting his head down. His first instinct was to ride after the departing riders and beat Rob within an inch of his life. His second, whether he completed the first or not, was to ride out of the valley and away from the brewing fight. Then he looked into Mrs. Peters' face. Their eyes met. He read the hurt, the worry, the anger, the fear, all the conflicting emotions that she was trying to control with a forced smile and trembling lips. Again his feelings for the woman melted his own anger.

"I promised you I wouldn't kill Rob," he put his hand on her arm and squeezed softly.

"But will you help him?" she pleaded. "After what he did, I won't blame you for saying no, but I'd be forever in your debt if you did."

"Mother," Linda interrupted, ignoring Stoner, "Rob doesn't want the help of a gunfighter who's too quick to shoot. Why won't you let him show you what he can do?"

"Nobody said he shouldn't," Mrs. Peters shook her head sadly as if caught in a recurring argument. "But he's no fighter, and that's what we need if we expect to save the ranch from the Bartlemans."

"Rob won't stand for it, Mother," Linda spoke stubbornly. "Nor will I."

"I don't see that there's much you can do about it," Mrs. Peters shrugged disconsolately. "If Rob won't abide by my decision, he'll have to leave the ranch."

"What about me?"

"You'll have to make up your mind too. I own the Rocking H. It's my ranch. I'm willing to listen to you and Rob, but my decisions are final. No more going against them, as you and Rob did just today," she paused. "I made Jacob foreman. He'll continue as foreman if he wants to. If he won't, I won't blame him, not after the way you and Rob treated him. But I'll find someone else who will, and he might not be as easy on Rob as Jacob has promised to be."

"What if Rob takes back the Loma Linda graze?"

"I might have to change some of my thoughts about him. But he has more to prove than that he can go off half-cocked and shoot up a bunch of Bar B punchers or run Bar B cattle back onto their own range. I want him to accept his responsibilities consistently, to the men, to the cattle and horses, to me. Your father thought of us as God's caretakers over this little bit of earth. I agree. We owe it to Him to keep the land in as good shape as we received it in and to at least treat the animals we use decently until they meet their fate, just as we hope God will treat us decently in this life until we meet ours. We also owe it to ourselves to do as well as we can in whatever we do. That's what your father believed and that's what I believed with him. And I still believe it."

Stoner felt the anger drain from him as he listened to the woman's words. He felt the same warmth and humility wash over him as he had the night before while he sat at the kitchen table and listened to her talk. He felt the ache of loneliness for someone to care for him as she had cared for her husband

and as she cared for her children and for the ranch. He felt the need to become a better person, someone she would admire.

"I know, Mother," tears glistened in Linda's eyes as she spoke. "We've talked about this before, too many times. You know I agree with you in most things, but Rob does as good a job as he can. I think he turns to drink because he can't face his limitations. It's a terrible cycle. He sees his own cruelty, he realizes how little he knows or how little he can do, he realizes how incompetent he can be sometimes, and cruel, so he begins to drink, but that only makes the problem worse. He...."

"I know," Mrs. Peters whole body sagged dejectedly. "I know how you feel, although I'm not sure I agree about his reasons for what he does. I've loved him and cared for him and fretted over him for a quarter of a century. And I've hurt for him every time he was hurting. That's the worst, to see him hurting and not be able to do anything but echo his hurt. He may be your brother, Linda honey, but don't forget he's my son. He was made of my flesh, torn from it. He'll always be part of my flesh and blood. I'll always cry when he cries and laugh when he laughs. I'll always hurt when he hurts. That I can't help. But I can try to keep him from destroying what your father built for both of you until he's capable of protecting it or until I'm dead. And I can try to help him become a decent human being. If I don't try my best to do those things, then I'm not being faithful to your father's memory. Or to my love for the two of you"

As Mrs. Peters finished speaking, Stoner decided to dismount in spite of the dizziness and the dull ache. He slowly stepped to the ground and stood with his head down for a few moments, until the world quit its slow gyration.

"Are you all right, Jacob?" Mrs. Peters asked with concern.

"Yeah, I reckon so," he tried to smile reassuringly, but his attempt brought only a grimace to his lips.

He tried to focus his eyes on Mrs. Peters but found himself looking at Linda instead. She refused to meet his gaze but he had noticed the look of concern on her face as she watched him dismount.

"If you've got my guns" he addressed his words to Mrs. Peters, "I'll ride out and see what's going on at Loma Linda."

"Where'd Rob put Jacob's pistol and rifle?" Mrs. Peters asked Linda.

"Mother," Linda answered sharply, "I don't think you should interfere with Rob this time."

"I won't interfere if he's doing okay," Stoner broke in. "I'll be added insurance in case the Rocking H needs help. If he does okay in this little set-to," he shrugged and glanced at Mrs. Peters, "I reckon I can back off and hang around Chasco for a while to see how things go. If he does okay and the Bar B leaves you alone, I'll ride on. If not, well, whatever happens, I'll be around if you need me."

"What is it you want?" Linda interrupted suspiciously. "Why are you trying to help us?"

"Not you," Stoner looked at her from cold eyes. "I helped you once and didn't get much for it except a sore head. It's your mother I'm trying to help. She's a real lady. It'd make any man proud to help her."

Linda blushed with anger and shame. She conceded to herself that the gunfighter had a right to be angry with her. Given all his help, she hadn't treated him very well. But she couldn't bring herself to befriend a man who lived by his gun and who, she was convinced, was trying to replace Rob as acting head of the Rocking H. Nor could she forgive a man for whom, from the first time she saw him step through the door of the Watering Hole Saloon in Chasco, she had felt such an uncontrollable physical attraction.

Although she remained skeptical of his motivation, she decided to give up the guns and to go with him. Rob and the hands might need all the help they could get.

While Stoner followed Mrs. Peters to the house to have the cuts on his head taken care of, Linda hurried to the bunkhouse for his weapons and on to the house for her own rifle. Soon, despite Stoner's protests that she should remain at the house, the two were riding eastward. They hadn't ridden far when Stoner pulled up.

"Riding down the middle of the valley like this, can we be seen from the Loma area?" he asked Linda when she had pulled her horse up beside his.

"Not from the Loma, but from that rounded peak this side of it," came her terse reply. "The one that sticks out by itself up there," she pointed to a long rounded hill that swung out from the peaks around it as if marking a curve in the valley floor. "A lookout up there can't see us yet. The land's too low on this end of the valley. But we're climbing. In a few more minutes we'll be high enough so anyone up there can spot us."

"Any way we can get to the spring without being seen by a lookout up there?"

Linda didn't answer for a while, trying to study out the reason for his question.

"If the Bar B has a lookout up there, we don't want to ride into a trap."

"Do you think Rob and the boys rode into a trap?" For the first time Linda felt worried for her brother, but doubts of this man beside her and anger at his rugged confidence still nagged at her emotions. She tried to force a sneer into her voice but failed, and also failed to hide the worry, "Or are you afraid Rob and the boys will ambush you?"

"I don't think either one," Stoner studied her with an amused half-smile on his lips. "I don't think either and I consider both as possibilities. A man's a fool to ride blind into any situation, potentially dangerous or not. And this one at the spring has all the makings of a gunfight if the Bartlemans left riders there." He paused, wondering why the sparks seemed to fly every time he spoke to the girl beside him. "We could walk into a fight already going on. We could walk into a standoff. Your brother could be a prisoner of the Bar B, or he could be in control. Hell, I don't know. But no matter who's in charge or what's going on, it'll be dangerous for me. I've got a headache to prove it." He forced a grin. "So I damn well know I'm not announcing my arrival if I can help it. That'll give me a little edge, maybe enough to keep from getting killed. Or enough to keep from killing someone else, your brother included."

Linda bristled at his words, "You kill Rob and I'll kill you."

Looking at her, Stoner had no doubts that she meant what she said. Whether she could carry through with actually killing a human being was something else, something he didn't care to find out. He shook his head in admiration and disgust. She was a beautiful woman, all woman. Her riding skirt framed long, shapely legs that looked strong enough to grip a horse's flanks for hours on end. A green cotton blouse molded wide shoulders and full breasts that surged against the buttons and out the open neck, soft, round, white, tempting. Her suntanned arms were long, firm, her neck inviting. Her lips were full, her chin strong, her cheekbones high, her eyes sad, expressive of some longing beyond masculine understanding.

Stoner felt himself becoming lost in the labyrinth of her being, in the powerful physical presence of her body and in the even more powerful sense of untamed passion and spirit that flowed from somewhere deep inside her. Why, he asked himself angrily, why had he stayed to face the torment of being near her with the ever-present knowledge that he would never touch her?

"Is there a back way in and which way is it?" he finally repeated his question, ignoring her threat, his voice thick with irritation.

She pointed, "Up there an old game trail cuts through the foothills. It comes out high above the Loma, but we can leave it just short of where it ends and take a canyon that swings around and drops down above the spring. Not many people know about it. Besides, the canyon is so rocky and its mouth so overgrown with trees and shrubs that we can ride right out onto the slope above the spring before anybody knows we're there, even if they do expect us."

Stoner didn't ask about potential ambush sites along the trail or in the canyon. He could do that as they rode. With a gesture toward where Linda had pointed, he grunted, "Lead out; I'll follow."

"You're trusting," Linda commented sarcastically as she reined her horse uphill.

For a moment Stoner sat bewildered by her words, not quite sure what they meant. Then he chuckled and spoke loud enough for her to hear, "I'm afraid of getting lost, not of getting shot in the back."

Her answering laughter, spontaneous, floated back to him as he spurred the black up the hillside.

Shortly before they reached the opening into the canyon they heard the sporadic shooting. Linda reined in her mount and looked back at Stoner. He pulled up and sat listening for several minutes before answering the questioning fear in her eyes.

"Sounds like maybe a dozen rifles." After a long silence he continued, "No, there aren't that many, I don't think. More like eight, ten." They were on a wide section of the trail. He had pulled his mount up beside hers. As he spoke he put his hand on her arm to help soothe her fears but, when she jerked her arm away as if stung, he felt a wave of angry embarrassment wash over him. When he gained control of his emotions, he continued, "As long as a fight's going on, some of them are still alive. But we'd better get down there." He motioned for her to lead the way.

Soon they entered the canyon. When they rode out onto the slope above the spring, Stoner found himself in a tangle of juniper, aspen, and brush as high as his horse's shoulder. Below him a long rolling slope angled downward to a depression made up mostly of a small body of water not much bigger than a large pond. The spring, he decided. On the far side of the pond, the water overflowed down a gentle embankment to form a small creek. The creek flowed through a series of winding, sloping meadows to disappear in the distance. All around the spring and the meandering creek were slopes of open meadow land, some steep, some moderate. The upper parts of the slopes were covered with pines and aspen.

Linda dismounted, tied her horse to a sapling, took her rifle from the boot, and began making her way downhill through the brush.   Stoner followed suit. When they reached the edge of the trees and brush they stopped. Stoner studied the gun battle taking place two hundred yards away on one of the slopes below the timber line. Four men were trapped in a hollow with little cover except for a few small boulders. Surrounding them he counted five riflemen, all shooting from good cover.   Far beyond the hollow four horses were scattered, grazing peacefully, too far off for the men in the hollow to reach them.

"Looks like the Rocking H down there in that little bowl," he commented to the girl beside him. "They're stuck there, I reckon, unless we take a hand in the game. There's five men with rifles on the slopes. Got them pinned down good. One of those Rocking H boys gets careless, he's gonna be dead mighty quick. Not enough cover for a snake down there."

"If I go down there, maybe they'll quit shooting," Linda looked at Stoner questioningly.

"Maybe," Stoner answered laconically. "Maybe not. I don't reckon it's worth a gamble, not when I can get on the slopes above the bushwhackers and maybe get the drop on them."

For the first time in the less than twenty-four hours since he first saw her in the saloon, Stoner realized, Linda appeared uncertain, hesitant.

"I think you should stay here, away from the fighting," he said. "You'll be safer. You go out there," he motioned in the direction of the fighting, "they might shoot you before they see who you are. Or they might capture you. They capture you, they've got a hostage to use against the Rocking H boys down there. Besides," he added, hoping to stave off the anger he saw flash over her face at his words, "I'll need somebody to guard my back. You've got a clear field of fire from here. I'm going to move in on those two on the north first. You see one of them or one of those yahoos on the south try to flank me, shoot him, pin him down, or something. If you can't stop him, fire three quick shots, wait a few seconds, then fire three more quick ones to warn me someone's coming. If I have to get out of there quick-like or if I get pinned down or caught out in the open or something, cover me. Think you can do that?"

As soon as he spoke the last five words, Stoner realized his mistake. He cringed, waiting for the tongue lashing.

"Don't be so damned condescending," Linda's anger exploded immediately. "I know you're a professional gunfighter, but I've been shooting a rifle almost as long as I've been walking. I can hit what I shoot at," she glared at him as if her greatest pleasure of the moment would be to shoot him rather than the Bar B punchers below.

Stoner sensed the beginnings of a grin touch his eyes and lips. He quickly suppressed it. "I reckon shooting humans is a little different from shooting targets and game," he stared out at the gun battle in order to hide the gleam in his eyes.

"I reckon," she angrily mimicked his drawl. "But I've done it before. Apaches raided the ranch twice the summer I was eleven. We all had to fight. Mother and I loaded the weapons, but we had to shoot too; there were only seven of us and lots of them," she visibly shuddered.

"Hit anything?" Stoner asked, curious, sympathetic, but forcing all emotion from his voice.

"Yes," her words came out in a hoarse whisper. She paused until Stoner had almost decided she was not going to continue. Then the whisper rose again, "The bunkhouse was burning. We were in the house. An Indian was trying to get through the window in the back. His face was painted all black and horrible. He was screeching like a wild animal." Again the long silence. Stoner waited patiently, not completely certain of what was to follow. "I shot him...right in the face...his eye...his...sometimes I still have nightmares about his face. It...."

"I know," Stoner interrupted, his voice an echo of hers. "I know. I used to think they'd go away some day, but they don't."

For some time they stood quietly looking at each other, understanding and sympathy closing the space between them.

Finally Linda spoke, "I'll stay here and cover you if you really think that's best, but don't ask me to stay just to protect me. It's my brother out there and I won't be treated like a helpless female," she laughed shrilly, nervously, but good naturedly, "even though I may be one in this situation."

"It's best," Stoner chuckled with her although not completely certain he was right. He didn't know whether the two of them had been spotted or not; he didn't know which way the Bar B would run if they did run; he didn't know if they knew about the canyon above the spring; he didn't know whether Linda would have to fire and give away her position, and what might happen if she did; he didn't know whether a Bar B puncher had gone for reinforcements and, if one had, when that help might arrive and from where. But he couldn't change what had to be done, he knew. He hadn't had any control over whether or not Linda rode with him. He didn't have any control over what he had to do now. He had to do what he would have done if she weren't along: play the cards as they were dealt in the game he had chosen to sit in on, the struggle between the Rocking H and the Bar B. He had to neutralize as many of the Bar B rifles on the slopes below him as he could.

He opened his saddlebags and took out the old pair of moccasins he'd bought from an Indian woman in Socorro. With them on and his pockets filled with ammunition for his Winchester, he trotted along the slope, keeping well back inside the tree line as it meandered along the slopes. Much later, just as he had decided that he had overshot his objective, a rifle spoke downslope from where he stood. He eased himself to the edge of the trees and brush. Below him and to his right he could make out two men not more than forty yards from where he stood. "Careless," he muttered to himself. They lay behind the trunk of a fallen tree. They were well hidden from the punchers in the depression below them, but they were clear targets to Stoner. The tree, a fallen juniper, was little more than a long trunk, old, rotten, its limbs having long since dropped off. The two gunmen had no place to escape Stoner's fire. On the other side of the log they would become clear targets for the Rocking H hands two hundred yards beyond them.

Sighting quickly but carefully, Stoner put a shot between the two. A faint smile touched his lips at their startled yell.

"Leave your weapons and work your way up here," he shouted when the two turned fearfully and looked his way.

"What if we don't," came a shouted response.

"I shoot to kill."

"I don't reckon you'd kill us in cold blood," one of the two shouted arrogantly.

For answer, Stoner put a bullet into the tree trunk a few inches from the shouter's head. "The next one goes in a leg," he yelled. If I can hit it, he thought.

He didn't have long to wait. One, taller, older than the other, spoke first, loudly. Stoner couldn't make out the words but he figured the tone sounded reconciliatory, so he waited patiently.

"I don't know about you, Lew, but I ain't gonna lay out here in the wide open and git shot at. I don't know that feller up there. He might not shoot. But again, he might. If he does shoot, he might hit where he aims. Hell," the bushwhacker rolled onto his back and scrubbed at his two-day growth of beard, "he might get his jollies out of cripplin' a man."

"Goddamn it, Tate," his companion swore. He was a short, skinny youth. "I don't like this. Nate said to hold the spring. He ain't gonna like this neither. You know Nate."

"Yeah, I know Nate Barstow," Tate answered tonelessly. "He's liable to take out after us with those iron fists of his. That's all he knows, pound on somebody." He paused. "But he don't pound on me, you notice. He knows better. I'd take a pig sticker to him sometime he ain't lookin'."

"Yeah, I heard that before," Lew answered derisively.

"I'm goin'," came Tate's only answer. He began working his way up the slope, careful to use the lay of the land as cover from the punchers in the depression below.

In a few moments he heard his partner scraping along behind him. The going was rough. The rocks under the grass tore at his flesh and clothes. The slope was steeper than he remembered, but he had crawled downhill the first time, not uphill. He soon ran out of air and began panting hoarsely, gasping in shallow breaths that hurt his lungs. He began swearing angrily, cursing himself and life with each gasp. He spit and sure enough the blood was there. He had first noticed it, Gawd, how long ago? A year? Two? Yeah, maybe more. He continued swearing and crawling, and coughing and gasping, cursing the fates and struggling up a slope that wouldn't cause more than a little heavy breathing for a normal man. He knew he should see a doctor, but he couldn't bring himself to admit what he might have.

When he finally crawled into the tree line, he flopped onto his back and lay there gasping and hacking, eyes closed, mind also closed for the moment. Lew soon joined him.

"Where is he, old man?" the young puncher asked. "Ain't nobody here but you and me, you on your back coughing your guts out and me standin' here ready and willin' to fight this bushwhacker when he shows up. If he shows up."

Tate forced himself to his knees and looked around. He saw nothing.

"I don't know," he said, again dropping tiredly onto his back. "Let me get my breath and we'll look around."

"No need to look around, Tate," the voice he heard echoed from his distant past. "I'm over here."

Tate forced himself to sit up. His energy was beginning to return. The wracking coughs were becoming fewer and fewer.

"I recall that voice," he said raspingly, "but I can't put face nor name to it."

"Tell your partner to drop that pistol he's got under his shirt and we'll talk," Stoner kept his rifle on the younger Bar B puncher as he spoke. He stood twenty yards away, hidden behind the trunk of a large pine.

"Jesus, Lew," Tate groused. "You may be a kid but you should know better'n to try a hideout on a man that's got you covered."

"Hell," Lew answered, his irritation making his voice sharp, "how was I to know he ain't old and blind like you. Anyhow, you was the one told me to use every trick you can."

Wracked by another coughing fit, Tate didn't answer. Lew could make out the barrel of the rifle pointed at him, but not the form behind it. He pulled the pistol from his belt and angrily tossed it downhill in the direction of the rifle, hoping he could find both later.

"Now the knife you stuck in your boot," the voice cut the silence.

"Goddamn it," Lew exploded, but he carefully extracted the knife and tossed it toward where the pistol had landed.

Stoner stepped into view. Lew watched him bitterly but made no comment. Tate didn't glance up.

"You gonna be okay, Tate?" Stoner asked with concern in his voice.

The old Bar B puncher looked up.

"I'll be damned," he shouted, bringing on another attack of coughing. When he had the spasms under control again, he continued in a quieter voice, but one loaded with pleasant memories. "What's it been now, five years, six? Boy," he turned to Lew, "this here's Jacob Stoner. I reckon you've heard of him. You ain't, you've got your head in the sand. Gunfighter, outlaw, marshal, general hell raiser, I reckon there ain't much he ain't done if it's dangerous, even to savin' this worthless old hide of mine from the Apaches." He stopped and grinned at Stoner. "We had some real good times around El Paso and down in Old Mexico before you rode out. Never could figure why you left. That border pistolero you shot just before you took out didn't have no friends. The law, rangers and all, was glad to see him put away. So was about everybody. Weren't no need to run."

"I'd about had it with that life," Stoner smiled at his old comrade. "I was getting damned tired of drinking, fighting, taking anything not tied down, and generally raising hell like a bunch of kids."

"Hell, ain't nothin' wrong with havin' a good time." Tate coughed and spit blood into the dirt, then added sheepishly, "But I reckon I've had one too many over the years."

"Anybody can get consumption," Stoner looked at the emaciated form of his old friend and wondered how long he had to live. "It doesn't come from drinking and raising hell, I don't figure."

"I reckon," Tate answered tiredly. "But I sure doubt if they help it much."

"What the hell do you two know?" Lew sneered. "You think you're a sawbones or somethin'?"

Stoner ignored the youth, but the words jerked him back to the reality of his situation and that of the punchers down below in the hollow.

"The shape you're in, I'd as soon not have to tie you up while I go after your friends across the way," he spoke to Tate and waved his hand in the direction of the sporadic shooting on the far slope.

"I wouldn't blame you if you did," Tate glanced up from where he was sitting in the dirt. "We was ordered to kill any Rockin' H hands that showed up." He paused. "I been thinkin' for some time about headin' north, up to Colorado, up in the high mountains somewhere west of Denver. High mountains're good for consumption, I hear. Now that you've dealt yourself in this here game, I reckon I'll quit thinkin' and start doin'." He hesitated, glancing swiftly at Lew. "Our horses're right up there," he waved his hand, "just over the top of the slope. Turn me loose and you won't see me around here no more. Although I'd sure as hell like to be around when you meet Sam Bartleman. That'll be some fight."

"Shit," Lew broke in, "he won't get past Nate."

Tate looked at the youth and shook his head in disgust, then grinned at Stoner, "What you gonna do with kids like that? I've seen both you and Nate Barstow in action. He's seen Nate use a handgun but he ain't never seen you. Now here he is predictin' what Nate'll do to you when you meet."

After a few moments of silence, he asked insistently, "What about it? You gonna turn me loose?"

"You up to going back down the slope for your weapons?"

"Yeah, if I take my time. Why?"

"You go get your guns. Bring the kid's too if it's not too much trouble. Meantime me and Lew'll go get your horses. We'll bring them here. You can leave as soon as we get back"

Without a word Tate started downhill. Motioning Lew to walk in front, Stoner headed up the slope. Twenty minutes later they returned to find Tate sitting quietly against the trunk of an aspen.

"What about Lew?" the latter asked as Stoner and the youth came to a stop a few feet away. "You gonna turn him loose?"

"No way," Stoner shook his head. "I wouldn't trust him any further than I can see him in a heavy ground fog on a dark night in a forest.   I can't figure you being partners with somebody like him, Tate."

"Aw, you got him all wrong," Tate spoke with a mixture of embarrassment and anger. "He's just a kid. Give him a few years and he'll be okay."

"Screw you, old man," Lew burst out angrily. "I don't need no broken down old fart makin' excuses for me. I'll do my own talkin'."

"So talk," Stoner reacted angrily, irritated by the way the boy spoke to Tate, a man he, Stoner, had had a great deal of respect for in the past.

"Screw you too, and the horse you rode in on," Lew sneered at Stoner. "I get a chance, I'll put a bullet in your guts. You're dead meat anyway when Nate finds out what you've done here."

"Sorry," Stoner addressed his words to Tate, "but you can see the problem. You're free to go. He stays." For long seconds he stared at Tate. "But get out of the valley and stay out till this fight with the Bar B's over. I see you before that...," he shrugged.

"Yeah, I know," Tate interrupted. "Don't say it. I'd rather we stayed friends, but if you threaten me...," it was his turn to shrug and hesitate.

Stoner switched his pistol to his left hand and stuck out his right. Tate stood up and gladly took the proffered symbol of friendship. Lew chose that moment to attack Stoner, but it was a futile attack, quickly put down. Tate kicked out with his booted foot and caught the charging boy in the knee. At the same time Stoner dodged and his right fist, swinging in a backward roundhouse, caught the boy on the ear. The latter plowed into the dirt face first. He struggled to his feet, cursing violently, ready to charge again, but stopped. Stoner stood a few feet away, his Colt in his right hand, waiting.

"You won't shoot," Lew gritted. He stood poised on the balls of his feet, his fists clenched and his eyes slitted murderously.

"Maybe," Stoner stared at him emotionlessly. "Maybe not." He trained the barrel of the Colt on Lew's chest and waited.

For a long time the youth returned Stoner's stare belligerently, before finally turning toward Tate. "You'll get yours someday, old man. Whose side you on anyway?"

"I figure I saved you a broken skull at the least, possibly a bullet in the gut. You're not very bright attacking a man like Stoner when he's armed and you ain't."

Lew swore angrily, holding his ear with one hand. "You goddamn traitor. You had his right hand," he mumbled. "All you had to do was hang on. He couldn't get his hogleg in play quick enough, I figure."

"You don't know Stoner," Tate shook his head in disgust. "I'd hung onto that hand or tried to stop him from shootin' you, we'd both been dead, me first. He can shoot almost as good with his left hand as he can with the other. And he sure as hell was ready to shoot me when I kicked you. I seen it in his eyes." He glanced speculatively, questioningly at Stoner.

"Yeah," Stoner met Tate's eyes with a glimmer of self-mockery in his own. He made a show of easing the hammer back down on the Colt. "That's how close you came. I was squeezing the trigger when you let go of my hand. Lucky for both of you that you let go quick enough." He glared coldly at Lew. "Because I sure as hell wouldn't have let this young bastard live if he made me kill you."

Lew stared at the pistol and then at Stoner, respect mingled on his face with the anger. After the single attempt he submitted docilely, but he refused to meet Tate's eyes or answer his farewell when the latter took his leave and rode leisurely away from the looming fight, planning to ride over the mountains and then swing northeast toward Denver.

When his old friend had disappeared through the trees, Stoner tried to shake off the feeling of gloom that had begun spreading through him as soon as Tate turned his horse uphill. He failed. The dull sense of loss remained. It made no difference that Tate had invited him to ride along. It made no difference that Tate had said he would stick around Durango a year or so, waiting for Stoner to join him. It made no difference that Tate had not been part of his life for five years or more, or that they had actually ridden together for less than two years. The man represented the essential nature of Stoner's life--always on the go, getting to know people and places only to move on to new people and places, always with an emptiness in his gut, the sharp emptiness of recent loss, the dull emptiness of old losses, the cold emptiness of knowing he would move on sooner or later, the lonely emptiness of living on other people's land, among other people's friends, never on his own land, among his own people.

Leading Lew's horse, Lew himself walking angrily in front of him, he skirted the slopes toward the mouth of the canyon where he had left Linda. She was alert and heard him coming.

"I've got a captive for you," Stoner spoke as he and Lew entered the small opening in the heavy brush. "I'll leave him here while I see what I can do about those other bushwhackers." He motioned Lew to sit down with his back to a large pine at the edge of the glade.

"You're not going to tie him up?" Linda asked in a startled voice. "I can watch him. He's so young," a note of scorn entered her voice. "He surely can't be very dangerous."

"He didn't get that bloody ear by being peaceful," Stoner continued tying Lew to the tree, stretching the rope around the tree and tying it to each wrist. "If it hadn't been for his partner, one of us'd be dead."

"What happened to his partner?" Linda asked, still skeptical, but now also fearful that someone had been killed. She couldn't believe that this boy, a ragamuffin of a boy with mistrustful, faded blue eyes, could pose a threat to an experienced gunman like Stoner.

"He was an old friend," came Stoner's curt answer as he finished tying his prisoner and stood back to check his handiwork. The boy could move his hands and arms to a fairly comfortable position, but he couldn't reach his pockets and he couldn't reach the knots with his fingers or teeth. "He's got consumption. He decided Colorado'd be good for his health. So I turned him loose."

Stoner felt the irritation mount as Linda looked at him with clear disbelief written all over her. Why, he wondered, did she seem to think he lied every time he opened his mouth? He could have killed Nate Barstow in the saloon. He could have killed the puncher who drew on him in the saloon. He could have killed the Bartlemans at the Rocking H. He could have killed Tate. He could have killed Lew. But he hadn't. Yet she persisted in thinking the worst of him, in spite of what he had already done for her and her family.

His aggravation gritting in each word, he asked her to keep an eye on Lew while she guarded against a possible flanking movement from the three remaining Bar B punchers.

"What are you going to do with him?" LInda asked, eyeing Lew with what Stoner thought was a combination of disgust and pity.

Stoner shrugged, "Turn him loose, I reckon, once I don't have to worry about my back."

He threw the words over his shoulder as he set off along the slope toward a point he had chosen for the beginning of his campaign against the other three bushwhackers, a ledge above where their shots seemed to be coming from. The shooting had almost died out completely. Only occasionally did a shot echo over the slopes. Once he thought he heard a yelp from the hollow below, immediately after the sound of a shot, as if someone had been hit, but he couldn't be sure and the sound, whatever it was, didn't repeat itself. He worked his way upward through brush and over and around boulders until he had the tops of the slopes between him and the Bar B riflemen, then he trotted rapidly toward the peak that stood its lone vigil above the battle below. When he reached his first destination, he moved quickly downslope until near the tree line, then crawled the rest of the way through a ravine that skirted the rear of the ledge above the Bar B riflemen before turning and dropping steeply downward.

8

Lew waited for a long time after Stoner had trotted out of hearing before he spoke up. With an effort he forced the contempt from his voice. He'd not been one of the Bar B riders with Nate Barstow in the Chasco saloon the previous day. But he later absorbed the story as embellished by his bunkmates and he'd concluded that Linda Peters was no better than the women he ran into in saloons.

"That gunfighter your man?" he asked Linda, watching her closely for her reaction.

Linda felt the anger rise in her chest, anger and something else, something warm and vital that, at the reference to Stoner as her man, flowed upward from her belly and soothed the anger. She looked closely at the young Bar B puncher. What she saw cooled her first reaction, but left her with another mixed reaction to the young puncher and his question. Ground-in dirt, added to the effects of the sun, turned his face and hands a blackish brown. His hair had been bleached white by the sun's rays, but it appeared grey because of the dirt and bits of twigs and leaves and other things hiding in it; it hadn't felt a comb for months or been washed in the same length of time, she figured. His eyes expressed scorn and mistrust, and something else she couldn't quite make out, something lurking just under the surface. His narrow lips seemed set in a perpetual sneer and his ears were much too large for his head, sticking out like those of a jackrabbit. He body was skinny, with the wiry scrawniness of active adolescence. He probably hadn't changed his clothes for weeks, even to sleep, or taken a bath. She wrinkled her nose at the odor he emitted. She grimaced to herself at her sudden desire to drag him to the closest water and scrub him clean. She almost laughed aloud at the

86

conflicting emotions she felt, the desire to mother the young Bar B rider and at the same time the disgust and the fear that came from something she couldn't pinpoint.

"You gonna answer or not?" the young puncher interrupted her thoughts. "You too stuck up to talk to someone like me?"

The words forced her emotional reactions into her subconscious self. Curiously she asked, "No, he's not. I really don't even like him much. But what's that to you? Why should I talk to you anyway? Why should I talk to someone who was trying to kill my brother?"

His eyes glittered momentarily at her questions. He didn't try to hide the scorn he felt. He ignored her questions. "That's what they say. Ever since you come back with all that travel and schooling, you're too uppity to talk to the common folk less'n you want something, like maybe to order them to do something or get a favor. You think you're better'n the rest of us, they say."

Linda started to react angrily, a sarcastic comment appearing of its own accord on the tip of her tongue. But she caught herself. "I don't think I'm a snob," the clipped tones of her voice expressed her irritation. "Besides, who I do and don't talk to is no one's business but my own."

The boy didn't answer her, but his eyes never left her face, nor the smirk his lips. Annoyed, she turned to the battle taking place down the canyon. Nothing had changed in the moments taken up by Stoner's return and departure and by her brief talk with the young Bar B puncher. An occasional puff of smoke followed instantaneously by a muffled shot attested to the continued standoff. Once Stoner's head and shoulders appeared briefly at the top of a slope, then disappeared as he made his way toward the ambushers. She felt as if she were watching some silly comedy. She felt like a spectator in a seat so far removed from the stage that the actors seemed more like ants or miniature dolls than real, live human beings. She found it difficult to believe that someone might soon die, yet she knew that Rob lay hidden down there, caught in a real trap with real bullets seeking his lifeblood, as did others well known to her. She knew the scene had tragic potential.   Yet, for a few brief moments she had trouble accepting the reality of the situation. She glanced at Lew, hoping to pull herself from the momentary lethargy, the sense of unreality into which she had slipped.

The boy watched her silently, the smirk no longer on his lips, his eyes empty. Finally he again spoke, "That's your brother down there, you say? The one called Rob?"

"Yes," she answered with a smile, hoping conversation might pull her from her emotional inertia. "Do you know Rob?"

"Yeah, we've talked some," Lew lied with a poker face. "We had a few beers at the bar the other day before he got pie-eyed. That's when I left. I don't much like bein' around drunks."

He smirked to himself, careful not to let it show. Nate had said that the girl didn't like for her brother to drink. He watched her closely for her reaction to his words, wondering if he could get her to free him.

"You're kind of young to be drinking and hanging around saloons," Linda looked at him dubiously.

"I ain't so young," Lew didn't have to force irritation into his voice. He had always looked younger than his actual years and the fact galled him. He wanted respect, respect and fear. What he generally got was laughter and a pat on the back, until he flashed his knife and took a slice out of somebody. Then the people nearby took notice. He'd never killed anybody yet; the thought made him squirm. But he had cut more than one man for making light of him.

His eyes drifted to a spot near the girl, where his weapons lay, tossed into the dirt by Stoner. The hilt of the knife was visible above the scabbard attached to the pistol belt. Quickly he shifted his eyes to the sky, hoping Linda hadn't noticed. Again he wondered how far he could play her.

"Fifteen, sixteen maybe?" Linda asked, the kindly humor in the words sparkling in her eyes.

"You dumb bitch!" Lew swore to himself, refusing to meet her eyes until he had control of his emotions. "I ain't real sure because my parents died when I was just a baby," he spoke in a whisper as if ashamed of what he was saying, almost chuckling out loud at how easy the lie came, "but if the woman that run the orphan home was right, it's eighteen or nineteen, more'n likely nineteen."

"You don't look it." Disbelief hung thickly around each word.

"I can't help how I look, ma'am," Lew kept his eyes on the ground to hide the irritation. "I can't help it if people're always pickin' on me because of my looks, neither. Rob never did, though."

"How long have you known Rob?" Linda asked, interested in spite of her doubts. Her knowledge of her brother didn't entail an image of him consorting with someone as dirty as Lew, especially some hired hand working for the Bar B.

"Not long. About a year, I guess. I reckon we've downed a beer or two together four, maybe five times. I don't know him good. The Bar B and Rockin' H ain't exactly friendly. But I ain't got nothin' against you or your brother, or your hands." Caught up in his fabrication, he couldn't help adding a little boast about his manhood, "I don't drink much but I drink when I want and I drink with anybody I want. The Bartlemans nor nobody ain't gonna tell me what to do when I ain't workin'."

Linda raised her hand to her forehead, pushing at an imaginary strand of hair in order to hide the smile his childish brag evoked. She didn't like this boy, she clearly realized. She didn't like the way his eyes looked at her. She didn't like the perpetual smirk on his lips or the dirt ground into his skin. Nor did she trust him. Something warped lay embedded deep in his muddy eyes. He was lying about Rob, she had no doubts; Rob would never associate with someone as filthy as this young Bar B rider. Still and all, she mused to herself, she pitied the boy. He was too young to be tied up like a criminal.

"You know we wasn't plannin' on killin' them Rockin' H punchers."

Lew was preparing the ground for his next move. He wanted loose and he had decided that she was his only hope. He couldn't work his wrists free of the loops that bound them, nor could he work his fingers around to the knots holding the loops in place.

"That's not what it looks like," she answered brusquely, staring at him questioningly.

"We wasn't," he continued stubbornly. "We was supposed to keep them pinned down till dark, then let them sneak off. Them was Nate's orders, and Mr. Bartleman's too. Nobody was supposed to get hurt."

Linda stared thoughtfully at the youth. She didn't trust him. She still sensed something inimical lurking below the surface of his murky eyes and in the sneer on his lips, but she began to wonder if what she sensed might not exist more in her reaction to the dirt than to the boy. His words reminded her of her own first response to the morning's action on the porch. She had felt that Stoner started the shooting. Later, talking to Rob, she had become certain of it, which made her question the necessity of the gunplay in the saloon. But on the ride out from the ranch house, talking to the gunfighter, she had begun to question her own interpretation of events. He was pleasant. He seemed reasonable and capable, not a man to go off half-cocked. Still and all, she wondered if his physical appeal was clouding her judgment. The previous day, at the first sight of him in the saloon, and that very morning as he approached the porch with the alert freshness of morning on his face and in his stride, she had felt the impact of a powerful force that left her knees weak and her lungs short of breath; yet there was something more in the attraction too, something that gave her a sense of safety and comfort, and, when he looked at her, of being all female and desirable.

"Well, we wasn't," Lew persisted stubbornly, watching her closely for signs of sympathy or interest. "You can believe me or not. I reckon it don't make no never minds now, not after what that gunfighter done to Tate."

"Who's Tate?" Linda asked curiously. She didn't notice the glint of triumph and cunning in Lew's eyes.

"My partner," he stared down at the ground and hesitated for a long while, as if something sad and unbelievable were preying on his mind, before continuing in a low voice. "The old man that was with me over there on the slope, the man your gunfighter said was his friend too and that he let go."

"He's not my gunfighter," her voice cracked with irritation.

"Sorry," he searched her eyes and face. "But he killed my partner so I reckon I don't feel none too friendly to him or the people supportin' him."

"He killed your partner?" Linda felt only shock. The words came so unexpectedly that she forgot the questionable character of the boy facing her. "He said your partner was sick, so he let him go."

"Yeah, he was sick alright. He was dyin'. Had consumption. The gunfighter told the truth there. He was old too, over eighty." Lew paused, frantically searching his mind for more lies. "He was leavin' at the end of the month, on payday. He planned to ride up Colorado way, up into the high country. Said it'd be good for his sickness, maybe let him live longer. The gunfighter told the truth about that too."

"Stoner," Linda commented, stunned and unable to think of anything else to say. "His name's Stoner."

"Yeah, that's what he told me after he shot Tate." He again searched Linda's face carefully and felt a thrill of success flash through his chest.

"Said it like it meant something. Like he wanted everybody to know who killed Tate and I was supposed to spread the news. I reckon he's like all them gunfighters; he wants people to know about his killin's so they'll be scared of him."

"He said your partner was a friend of his," Linda attempted to shake free of the shock the boy's words had given her, but she found it impossible; her words came out in a hoarse whisper.

"They was friends once, I reckon," Lew couldn't quite keep an undercurrent of gloating from his voice, but he didn't think the girl noticed. "Leastways, that's the way it seemed at first, after the gunfighter got the drop on us. They was talkin' over old times, tellin' war stories and all, and Tate was tellin' about his consumption. He'd just said he was headin' for Colorado shortly when that damned gunfighter of yours up and shot him. Without warnin' nor nothin'. He just cocked his sixgun and shot him in the gut. He wasn't no farther away than I am from you." Lew stared down at the ground, hiding his eyes, trying to keep his face as long and mournful as he could. He waited until he felt his words had sunk in before adding, "You ever seen a man gut shot, ma'am? It ain't nice. Old Tate, he was rollin' around on the ground and groanin' and coughin' and spittin' up blood. He must've been sufferin' somethin' fierce. Me, I started over to help him but that Stoner waved me back with his pistol. Told me he'd shoot me too if I didn't sit down and shut up. So, well, I ain't crazy. There wasn't nothing I could do for poor old Tate anyhow; he was dyin', slow and hurtin', but dyin'. I sat down pronto. And you know what that bloodthirsty gunfighter of yours did?"

He looked up. Linda couldn't look at him. She didn't see the gleam of triumph that lighted his eyes and twisted his lips into a wolfish grin.

"What?" she asked, her voice barely audible.

"He shot Tate in the face," Lew forced his words out in a husky whisper. "He walked over and stood right over him. His pistol wasn't more'n two feet from Tate's face when he shot him between the eyes. There wasn't no call for it. Tate was dyin' anyway. But...well, what the hell, when I cussed him for a murderer and a coward, that damn Stoner said he was puttin' him out of his misery, like he would any sufferin' animal.

I reckon I'll have nightmares the rest of my life about that killin'."

Linda couldn't answer. She sat in shocked silence, trying to reconcile her own mixed feelings about Stoner with the image the young Bar B rider had given her over the past minutes.

Lew watched her closely but held his peace. His cunning mind told him she needed to absorb what he had told her. In the process, he hoped, she would begin to mistrust, even fear, the gunfighter. He waited until the color began to return to her face and her eyes once more began to move and focus on things nearby.

"Why he didn't kill me when he killed old Tate, I don't know, ma'am," he mused aloud. "I figured there for a moment, right after he shot Tate in the gut...I figured he was gonna gut shoot me too. It was in his eyes, the killin' desire was. But it passed and he didn't shoot me. Why?" He shrugged, "I don't know. But I sure am scared of what he might do when he gets back from down below."

"I won't let him hurt you," Linda spoke angrily. Her emotion was directed as much at herself as at anybody. She couldn't quite accept the Bar B puncher's picture of Stoner. A gunfighter he was. She didn't doubt that. He was lightning fast. He seemed to fear nothing and no one. In the saloon he had attacked a half dozen men and held them at bay. On the porch he had attacked three men who were all known as fast with pistols. Here on the Loma he had immediately taken it upon himself to free Rob and the Rocking H hands. He didn't hesitate to enter battle or to use his pistols. But in the saloon and on the porch he hadn't killed anyone. Maybe that was because there were credible witnesses. Maybe he had wanted to kill. At first she had thought so. Then his peaceful reaction to what she and Rob had done to him in the bunkhouse and the ride out from the ranch house had begun to change her mind. Now, she reminded herself, she only had the young Bar B hand's word about Stoner killing Tate, and that word conflicted directly with Stoner's brief description of what had happened. She stared at the boy before her. She didn't really trust him, she thought, but what if he was right?

"What if I turned you loose?" she asked suddenly, trying to make a decision. If Stoner had not killed Tate, she reasoned, it didn't really matter if she let Lew go, not if he left for the Bar B. On the other hand, if Stoner had killed Tate he might kill the boy when he returned. She shuddered. She wouldn't want the boy's death on her conscience, no matter what she thought of him.

"What do you mean?" Lew asked, hiding his elation.

"Would you take your horse and head for the Bar B right away?"

"Ma'am," he forced himself to meet her eyes straight on, "you wouldn't even see my dust, I'd ride so fast."

"Let me think it over for a while," she answered hesitantly, uncertainty paralyzing her.

"What's to think over?" Lew asked insistently, his voice made shrill by a sudden fear that she might back out of her promise.

"I don't know," she shook her head angrily. "But I need to think." She rose and paced around the clearing, nervous, her mind trying to work its way through the paralysis that had suddenly blocked it.

"What's to think about?" Lew pleaded. "Just let me loose! I'll run like the Devil's after me." When she continued pacing as if she hadn't heard him, he burst out angrily, "If that gunfighter of yours comes back before I get away and kills me, you'll be as guilty as him!"

Linda stopped walking and looked at the prisoner. He was just a boy, she told herself. If Stoner had killed his partner, he was probably scared to death that the same thing might happen to him.

"Okay," she finally spoke aloud, staring at Lew but not really seeing him because her mind was beset by images of Stoner as he freed her and then faced the Bar B hands in the saloon, of his face when he looked at her as he approached the porch that morning, of his eyes smiling as he talked to her on their ride to the Loma Linda. "Okay, I'll turn you loose, but I can't believe Stoner killed your partner in cold blood."

Lew kept his head down, mumbling false words of gratitude, as Linda cut his bonds with his own knife. Even when his hands were free, he remained motionless except for the chafing motion of his hands as each tried to rub life back into the other. From the corner of his eyes, however, he watched Linda carefully, like a mountain cat waiting for its prey to approach near enough for it to spring. Her rifle lay ten yards away, to the right along the slope, where she had left it when she left her post to free him. It lay out of reach of both of them. She had not drawn the pistol at her belt, but she had put her hand on the butt and stepped back out of his reach. As he watched, she tossed his knife toward where his pistol and saddle gun lay near her rifle. He rolled over onto his hands and knees, pretending he was trying to stand up but really rolling closer to the girl and at the same time working the kinks out of his back and legs. Unconsciously he groaned at the sharp needles of sleep-pain that flashed through his legs.

"Are you hurt?" Linda asked sympathetically as she stepped closer to put her hand on his shoulder.

He exploded. The touch became the fuse. He lunged from the ground with a roar, tackling her around the hips. His momentum, badly judged, sent them both tumbling downhill, rolling end over end until he came to rest against a small pine and she flopped into a clump of low-lying catclaw. His head hit the tree trunk, stunning him. For a moment he lay against the solid bark, unable to move, his eyes wild as he watched her trying unsuccessfully to extricate herself from the clinging branches. He grinned viciously at the sounds of ripping cloth and torn flesh. The next moment he scrambled over the ground separating them. Mercilessly he grabbed her by the hair and dragged her toward the tree where he had been tied, laughing gleefully at the increased sounds of tearing cloth and cries of pain caused by ripping flesh. Somehow she got hold of his right ankle as he began a step, tripping him. Unconsciously he let go his hold on her hair to save himself from a hard fall. She scrambled to her feet as he hit the ground; her hand darted toward the pistol still in her belt. But he was too quick. As the pistol came free and started to align with his torso, he tackled her again, both arms swinging. One hand connected with her wrist; the pistol went flying. The other hand connected with the side of her face; she reeled downhill, lost her footing, and again landed in the catclaw.

Swearing like a madman, Lew chased her into the brambles. Again he grabbed her by the hair and dragged her free, ignoring her squeals of pain. Once he had her free, wildly pummeling her head and shoulders with his fist all the time he was dragging her...as soon as he had her free, laughing savagely, he pulled her to her feet and threw her back into the thorns, then dragged her out. Once, twice, three times he repeated the torture, laughing insanely all the while, ignoring her pleas as if he didn't hear them.

Finally he stopped. She lay where he had thrown her. She was a mass of dirt, leaves and twigs from hair to shoes. And scratches. Cuts and scratches oozing splotches of blood covered her bare skin. Her riding skirt, thicker than her blouse, had come through the battle with only a few rips. But her blouse draped from her body in shreds. Above her skirt only one breast was completely covered. Her back, too, was almost completely exposed.

She tried to cover her exposed breast, but she had nothing with which to do so. She tried to stand but her legs refused to support her.

Lew watched her struggles as he worked to catch his breath and calm his anger, grinning triumphantly, cruelly, all the while. Slowly the cruelty gave way to lewd, savage passion. His faded blue eyes, fixed on her naked breast, clouded over, became hypnotized. He grabbed her by the hair and began pulling her toward the tree to which he had been tied. His mind no longer focused on vengeance or murder; it had been overcome by a stronger emotion, a sensual desire that permeated every pore of his body, made it impossible for him to draw an easy breath, and flashed fiery throbs of pleasure through his loins.

He got her to the tree. But the cut pieces of rope were not long enough to tie her as he had been tied. Driven blindly by his passion, he trussed her up like a calf. Sadistically, glorying in her pain and helplessness, he yanked her ankles up behind her back and tied them to her wrists, ignoring her pleas for mercy. The job completed, he sat back on his heels and stared at her, his eyes glazed over and a drop of spittle on his lips. He began to fondle her exposed breast. Then he heard her frantic words.

"The fight's over. They're not shooting anymore. They'll come for me now. If you do anything to me, they'll kill you."

He continued fondling her breast as her words seeped into his consciousness. Suddenly he felt uncertain as to what to do next. What if the gunfighter did show up? The possibility of Stoner catching him unprepared doused him with cold water.

He stood up and hurried to the spot where Linda had been keeping watch, the only spot in the clearing with an open view of the gun battle. Cold thorns of fear twisted into his gut as he glanced down the gully and bare slopes below. The gunfighter was returning. As he watched, Stoner spurred up the slopes and into the trees, still angling toward the clearing.

"Damn," Lew exclaimed, but immediately the fear disappeared and the desire to kill the gunfighter pushed all else from his mind.

Swiftly he gathered his weapons and dashed back to where he'd left Linda. Quickly he untied her and prodded her toward their horses.

"We're going uphill and set up a ambush," he chortled. "I'll tie you up again when we get to a good place. After I kill that damned gunfighter you and me'll have us some fun. I reckon you'll like that," his laughter turned ugly as he completed his words. "Hell," he added, staring at her, "maybe you can show me a good time till he gets back."

9

Soon after leaving Linda with the captive, Stoner sprawled on his belly on a ledge overlooking the ambush. He couldn't see the Rocking H punchers clearly, but he could see their position and every move on their part appeared to bring an arm or leg or some other body part into view for a brief moment before it was quickly jerked from sight. The Bar B riflemen were firing only when part of a body showed. The Rocking H hands were no longer answering the fire from above them. Only three of the men seemed to be moving around from time to time, which made Stoner wonder if the fourth man had been badly wounded. One of the punchers-- Sonora, he thought--had something red wrapped around his head; another--he couldn't tell which one for sure but thought it was Tack--had his shirt sleeve torn off and wrapped around his upper arm.

Stoner turned his attention to the three Bar B riflemen. The area of the slope he was on had been formed by an avalanche in the distant past. It dropped into the hollow in a series of four sharp descents, broken up by four rocky ledges, and then the gentle slope at the bottom which flowed outward to form the hollow in which the Rocking H had forted up. Each ledge extended three to four feet deep and ten to fifteen long. At each end they merged with the less abrupt slopes that flowed together into the hollow. He lay on the top ledge; the Bar B bushwhackers lay on the next ledge down, about forty yards below his position, a ledge that sloped out and upward from a few yards of roughly level mountainside. The ledge was almost completely exposed to his position. By hugging the wall of the slope the three men could find some cover from his rifle, but they would be even more exposed than the Rocking H punchers in the hollow were to their rifles.

Of the three Bar B riflemen, Stoner had a clear shot at two. They lay on their bellies in plain sight. The other rifleman lay alongside a boulder, under its overhang, nothing but a boot heel showing to Stoner. But he too had made the mistake of ignoring a possible attack from above. He couldn't shoot uphill without exiting his hole and worming his way back in feet first.

Stoner hesitated for no longer than a split second, then called out, "Okay, you Bar B punchers! Toss your rifles down the slope, one at a time, you on the right first."

The two exposed bushwhackers turned onto their sides and looked up, seeing nothing but a rifle barrel and a shock of hair behind it. They tossed their rifles down the slope. The man under the overhang made no move to comply with the command.

The Rocking H punchers below were taking quick furtive glances uphill.

"Okay, I'll deal with your pard in a moment," Stoner drawled coldly. "Now throw those sidearms after the rifles, again one at a time, the man on the right first."

When the two were unarmed, Stoner spoke to them in a voice loud enough, he hoped, to carry on down into the hollow. He wanted the Rocking H punchers to know what was going on so they wouldn't shoot an unarmed man, or shoot him. "You two are out of it now. Stay that way. You try to buy back in the hand and you're dead." He paused for effect. "You under the boulder, that ledge you're on looks a lot like the one I'm on. Mostly solid rock with about a half inch of gravel covering it. If I shoot from here, I can send bullets ricocheting under that overhang; from this distance I can put them about anywhere I want them. Those bullets're gonna ricochet all over the place and take a lot of dirt and gravel with them. After a few, you're gonna be cut to pieces. A few more and I reckon you'll be dead or maybe wish you were." Stoner paused, then added, "I figure you other two should talk him out of there. You've got two minutes."

He lay quietly, watching. They talked low so he couldn't hear what was being said, but from the insistent, angry tones that reached him he figured a full-scale argument was going on. He waited patiently, preferring a peaceful rather than a violent resolution to the final stage of the fight. The two minutes passed and became five, he figured, and the holdout showed no signs of relenting. Finally, without warning, Stoner aimed a few inches to the right of where the overhang connected with the ledge and fired. The echo of the shot along the slopes drowned the accompanying echoes of the bullet as it ricocheted off the ledge, into the boulder, back into the ledge, higher up, and then off the top of the boulder and out someplace onto the slopes that met in the hollow below. The sound didn't hide the frightened yelp from the rifleman under the overhang.

When silence again reigned along the slopes, Stoner spoke in a loud voice, "The next one goes under the overhang. You've got five seconds to get the hell out from under there, friend."

"Okay, okay," he heard the muffled shout, "I'm coming out. Don't shoot."

The rifleman began backing out of his ambuscade, his boots and then legs showing first, ultimately his head. When he was clear he stood up. Stoner recognized him as one of the Bar B punchers in the Chasco saloon, a short, squat man with unkempt dark hair and beard and a nose flattened over much of his lower face. At Stoner's orders, the rifleman threw his weapons down the slope, careful not to show himself to the Rocking H rifles below.

Stoner knew he couldn't make his way down to the ledge holding the Bar B punchers without losing sight of the men themselves. He didn't figure to take a chance on being ambushed with a hideout gun or a rock. So he shouted to the Rocking H punchers below, asking a couple of them to come up the slope, get the tossed weapons, and cover the prisoners while he descended. Three of them, all except Rob, had stood up and were staring uncertainly upward. They must have understood some but not all of his words because Tall Will left the group and began climbing.

Stoner waited patiently. When the tall puncher had climbed into easy voice range, he again explained what he wanted. With a huge grin, Will began collecting the weapons and heaving them downhill. All three pistols landed in the hollow, yards from the Rocking H punchers, who began laughing and shouting what seemed to Stoner, from the few words he caught, instructions on pitching form and bets on whether the weapons would reach the bottom. One rifle made it by air into the hollow, where its stock shattered against a rock. The other two landed on the hillside and bounded downward, one reaching the hollow in a single piece, the other in two pieces, its barrel and stock having been separated by the boulder it hit at the end of its originating flight.

Stoner shook his head and grinned. In spite of Will's part in the assault at the bunkhouse, he liked the tall, rowdy puncher.

After he had tossed all the weapons to the bottom of the slope, Will climbed on up to the ledge where the three Bar B punchers stood under Stoner's rifle. He kept the three bushwhackers covered while Stoner made his way down to join him.

"What happened?" the gunfighter asked curiously when he reached the ledge. "How'd you come to get trapped down there in that hollow?"

"Ah, hell!" Will burst out in disgust. "Me and Sonora and Tack, we damn well figured the Bar B might be waitin' for us. What Rob was thinkin'," he shrugged his shoulders expressively, "who knows? We told him. Back when we was just climbin' out of the valley, we told him we'd best send out scouts or leave the trail and ride the top of these slopes through the trees till we reached the hills above the spring. That way, we figured, if we run into an ambush, we'd maybe have a chance to fight back. They wouldn't catch us out in the open. And maybe, just maybe, we could turn the tables and catch them campin' out on the flats by the spring or bushwhacked out on one of these slopes." He waved his free arm. "But Rob, hell," his eyes and a shrug expressed his chagrin, "he don't figure anybody but him's got any brains." He paused and his eyes locked on Stoner's, "Hadn't a been for you, maybe none of us'd got out of that hollow alive. These bastards was sure wantin' to send us down the dark trail," his eyes turned to ice as they shifted from one prisoner to the next. "A good thing for us you didn't leave the Rockin' H like Rob told you to." He again looked directly at Stoner and there was no doubt of his gratitude. "You won't have no problem with Rob for a while, I'd lay odds. He caught one in the leg and another in the hip. They ain't serious to life and limb, I don't reckon, if blood poison don't set in, but he'll more'n likely not be ridin' for a few days and he'll have a limp for longer'n that. Sonora and Tack got hit too, but they're just scratches."

As Tall Will talked on about the fight, Stoner studied the prisoners. Of the three, the short, stocky hombre who had used the rock overhang for cover appeared the most immediately dangerous. There was a smoldering violence in the rigid set of his shoulders, in the way he stood slightly forward on the balls of his feet, and in the anger lurking under the surface of his eyes. Little stood out about the other two except a dull, animal-like glaze in their expressions and the fact that their eyes never stopped moving, darting from place to place, person to person as if searching for danger or escape, never quite meeting the gaze of another person. Everything else about them was nondescript, their clothing, their height, their weight, the two-day stubble on their faces, the brown hair not quite unkempt, not quite neat. Stoner wondered if a mutual bloodline had formed them in similar molds or if time had, a time shared as saddle pards maybe.

"I don't reckon you three want to tell us what this's all about?" he asked, letting his gaze rest heavily on each one in turn.

After a few moments of silence one of the look-alikes spoke in a low mumble, shrugging his shoulders several times as he spoke, "Hell, it ain't no secret. We brung a small bunch of cows up from the home ranch. We was supposed to get here the day before yesterday, but we didn't get to the spring till yesterday morning. We was supposed to scatter the cows over Rockin' H range and make sure nobody interfered. When we seen your punchers comin', we ambushed them. We figured to keep them pinned down till the herd scattered."

Stoner grinned mockingly, "You didn't have orders to kill anybody from the Rockin' H that showed up here?"

"Naw," the two look-alikes answered in unison.

"Yeah, like hell," Will burst out. "Them bullets sure had killin' on the mind, if you didn't."

"You callin' me a liar?" one of the Bar B punchers growled indignantly.

"You calling Tate a liar?" Stoner interrupted.

At Stoner's question, fear flickered momentarily on the puncher's face. He didn't answer. Stoner told Will about Tate and Lew.

"These rannies might've sent for more guns," Will put in. "When they ambushed us, I think there was one of them on the ledge you was on. I ain't sure. Neither is Sonora or Tack. But we think there was. And he ain't there now."

Will's news gave Stoner a start. Tate hadn't mentioned a messenger.

"Did you send a man back to Bar B headquarters?" he asked the three prisoners.

The short, stocky puncher glared at him. The other two avoided his eyes. No one answered.

Suddenly worried, Stoner asked the prisoners where they had left their horses. When they continued their stubborn silence he spoke coldly, "You can walk or ride, but you sure as hell won't ride our horses."

"They're over there," the Bar B rider who had talked previously pointed up the slope, "on the other side of the hill, in a stand of juniper that's got a burned out spot on one corner of the stand, like it was hit by lightning."

Stoner remembered the stand. He had seen it as he approached the fight. It was easily visible from the top of the slope they were on, so he told Will how to find it and sent him after the horses.

"You sure you don't need help gettin' these yahoos down into the hollow?" Will asked dubiously.

"No," Stoner answered with a pointed glance at the prisoners and a quick grin that only Will could see. "It'd give me great pleasure if one of them made a break for it. I need the target practice."

As soon as Will began climbing up the slope, Stoner started the prisoners downhill. Sonora and Tack were standing in the open below, eyes on the prisoners, rifles ready, so Stoner backed off and trailed behind the three, far enough to give those below a clear shot if anyone made a break for it, close enough that his own rifle could quickly cover any false movement. He and his prisoners were soon standing near the hollow in which Rob still lay. He left the Bar B punchers under the guns of Tack and Sonora and walked over to Rob.

"Want me to look at those wounds?" he asked.

Rob lay on his back, his face pale and drawn with pain. The right leg of his Levi's had been slit on the inside to the crotch and on the outside almost to the waist. A long strip from somebody's red shirt was wrapped around his thigh just above the knee. Another strip from the same shirt covered his lower hip.

He had felt the same elation as the others when the firing ceased on the north slope.

"They're leavin'," Tall Will had been the first to spot the withdrawal. "They're movin' back and I don't see nobody replacin' them."

Relief and hope had buoyed their spirits for a while, until they realized that the riflemen on the south slope had made no move to withdraw.

"I reckon those two on the north slope rode to the Bar B for help," Tack had expressed his suspicions, not realizing what had really happened. "It don't change nothin' here though. Those three up there can keep us pinned down till dark without any help."

"They already sent for help, I bet," Sonora spoke up. "I bet there was a man on that second ledge, like we thought, and they sent him to the Bar B soon as they bushwhacked us."

"Then where'd those two on the north slope go?" Rob asked, irritated that he had lost control of the men as well as the situation. Shortly after the ambush they had quit talking to him. Mostly they talked to each other as if he weren't there.

Nobody said anything else. Only the sporadic rifle fire from above and the ricochet of a bullet or its dull impact in the dirt near them broke the gloomy silence. Only sporadically did one of them return the fire. It was too dangerous. And futile-- the three bushwhackers were too well protected by the rocky ledge on which they lay.

Rob and the Rocking H hands had given up the fight. They were waiting for nightfall, hoping no Bar B reinforcements would arrive before then. After dark, if they hadn't been surrounded, they would try to make it to the horses and flee back down the canyon. Failing that, they would head into the hills and make their way back to Rocking H headquarters, hoping to lose any pursuit in the barrancas and along the pine-covered slopes between them and ranch headquarters.

At last, when their morale had sunk to its lowest ebb, they heard Stoner's challenge from above.

"Jesus, it's Stoner," Will exclaimed, jubilation in his voice.

Will's shout sent relief and fear flashing together through Rob's guts, relief that he was safe from the Bar B riflemen, fear for what Stoner might do to him. He asked himself how Stoner had gotten free and why he had followed the Rocking H riders. Had Rob's mother freed him and sent him to help out in case of a fight with the Bar B? Or had he somehow broken free and come seeking vengeance? Rob told himself that his mother must have freed the gunfighter. Otherwise the man wouldn't have gotten the drop on the Bar B. He would have joined them.

Rob's reasoning eased his fear a little, but doubts still gnawed at his gut. Surreptitiously he pulled his pistol, which had remained in its holster throughout the ordeal of the ambush. He held it across his chest and fought to overcome the icy chill that was spreading through him, steeling himself to face Stoner.

"A mess, huh?" Rob grimaced in an attempted smile as Stoner strode up. The gunfighter's words didn't alleviate the fear that his appearance caused.

"I don't know," Stoner answered, thinking Rob was referring to the wounds. "Who put the bandages on?"

"Sonora, while Will was heading up the hill to join you." Rob rambled on in a shaky voice, unable to control his thoughts. "He's always got salve and pills and things with him. Used to be a medicine man or something down in Mexico. Curandero, he calls it, whatever that is. He put something on my wounds and bandaged them. Said the bullets only hit flesh and went on through."

Rob stopped talking. He had not yet looked directly at Stoner, except for quick, fleeting glances that expressed a mixture of shame and relief as he realized that Stoner's attitude was not threatening.

"I didn't mean my wounds were a mess, though they are," he continued, trying to return Stoner's steady gaze but failing miserably. "I meant what happened here was. I rode right into their ambush. Will and Tack and Sonora, all of them tried to get me to turn off the trail and send out scouts. I was too goddamn stubborn. Dad always said I was too bullheaded for my own good.   Well," his whole body sagged with his shame while his fists clenched and unclenched spasmodically, angrily, "I sure proved him right. I...."

"You made a choice," Stoner interrupted. "Life's full of choices. Every time a man gets up and puts on his boots he's made a choice, maybe two or three of them. "Every time he stops at a saloon or tops a mean bronc he's made a choice. He didn't have to stop at the saloon; he could've stopped someplace else or just ridden on. He didn't have to ride the bronc; he could've let somebody else do it or he could've ridden some other, easier horse or, hell, he could've taken up walking." Stoner took off his sombrero and ran his fingers through his hair. He had set out to ease Rob's sense of guilt but found himself stumbling for ideas and then for the words to express them. He continued hesitantly, "Some of the choices we make are important. Some aren't. It doesn't take much brain-power to know that. But the thing is, a man doesn't run from making choices just because he makes a few bad ones. If he's worth his salt he'll learn from the bad choices. And he'll learn not to worry about what's already done. It sure can't be helped."

"That doesn't change the fact that I almost got four of us killed here, not to mention what I did at the house," Rob interspersed, bitterly reproaching himself more for his failure in both cases than for the decisions and actions themselves and offering a half-hearted apology at the same time. "I went off half-cocked in both cases. That's what Dad always said was one of my problems. I don't think before I leap. If you hadn't...."

"Yeah, well, none of that can be changed, so it's time to forget it and begin deciding what to do next," Stoner shrugged, watching the other man carefully. He wondered if the bitter self-accusations were honest and long-lasting or simply a momentary chest-beating unconsciously meant as quick atonement. He hoped the former, for the sake of Mrs. Peters and Linda.

"I almost got us killed and you saved us," Rob continued his self-abasement as if he hadn't heard Stoner's comment, caught up in his attempt to placate Stoner and his bitter sense of his own failure. "You saved us after all I did to you." A note of amazement had entered his voice. "I'm not sure I would've done that. Paw would've. Me, I...."

"Maybe," Stoner interrupted, becoming a little embarrassed by the continued direction of the conversation. "Maybe not. Maybe you never let yourself go. Maybe you weren't meant to be like him even. The fact is, you're not you paw. That's pretty damned obvious. Maybe you tried to imitate him so much you never had time to become whatever it is you're supposed to be. Or maybe you are like him. Maybe that's your problem. You're like him in some ways, but not in the ways you want to be. Jesus," Stoner threw up his hands in despair. "I must sound like a cow looks chewing its cud, lots of posing, not much happening."

Rob laughed nervously. Stoner grinned. Their eyes met and held until Rob looked away.

"Your mom asked me to take over running the Rockin' H," Stoner made the words a question.

A mad desire to kill Stoner swept over Rob like a flash flood. His fist tightened spasmodically on his pistol. His eyes took in the form before him. Stoner stood with his balance resting lightly on the balls of both feet, his rifle in his left hand, his right hand hanging loosely near the Colt in his holster. Rob's stomach lurched and his fist relaxed. Stoner was watching him with a half-smile in his eyes. "He knows what I'm thinking," Rob thought and the desire to kill deserted him, leaving him weak and frightened.

"I'll step aside," he lowered his eyes..

"No," Stoner mused aloud. He had noticed the killing rage flash into Rob's eyes and then fade. He promised himself never to turn his back when Rob had anything to be mad about. "I don't reckon that's what she'd want, not now. She was afraid of your drinking, and of the meanness. And mostly she was afraid you couldn't handle the Bar B, afraid you'd get killed trying to stop them." When Rob started to interrupt, he held up his hand for silence. "It doesn't make any difference whether you can or can't, or whether you drink too much or don't, or whether you get mean as a wounded coyote when you do drink or when you're crossed. I don't know you well enough to say one way or the other. The important thing is, your maw worries about you. So I promised her I'd take the job of riding herd on the ranch." He paused and studied Rob. Again Rob looked up and began to say something. Again Stoner held his hand up, palm forward, for silence. "But I don't want the job," he continued. "Your ma's just about the nicest woman I've ever run into. I took the job because she wanted me to. Hell, I just couldn't say no. I started to, but then the Bartlemans rode up and I knew I couldn't ride off and desert her. I just couldn't do it."

"Jesus, man," Rob exclaimed, his eyes still averted. "You don't have to explain your reasons to me. After what you've done today, the job's yours. I'll take orders."

"No," Stoner refused the offer, wondering how long Rob's acquiescence would last. "You've had lots of experience here on the Rockin' H. You know the land. You know the cattle business. It's your ranch. Your ma'd be proud if you did take over running it. You manage it, you and your sister. Your maw would like that. Me, I'll stick around. I know a little about cattle too. I'll be here if you want advice. I reckon the other punchers would be happy to tell you all about running a ranch, too," he chuckled. "But there's one condition," he locked his eyes on Rob's face.

"Name it," for the first time since Stoner's arrival Rob spoke with confidence but still couldn't meet the gunfighter's cold, probing eyes.

Stoner could see his own relief reflected on Rob's face. "I'll be war chief or head gunhand or whatever. When it comes to fighting the Bar B, I make the final decisions."

"You've got a deal," Rob tried to stand up but fell back with a groan and ended by offering his hand from his reclining position. His anger had disappeared to be replaced by relief and a renewed sense of his own importance. He realized how much he had feared and hated the gunfighter, and still did, he admitted to himself, but not as irrationally as before.

Stoner gripped the proffered hand.

Tall Will soon came down off the slope leading the Bar B horses. Immediately he and Tack mounted two of the horses and set off to round up the Rocking H mounts. As they were reining their mounts away, Stoner spoke up from beside Rob, where he was still standing.

"Keep these Bar B rannies here till I get back, will you? We may have some use for them. I left Miss Peters up on a slope above the spring." He waved his hands in the general direction, before continuing, "I'm going to bring her and our other prisoner back." With those words, ignoring the startled looks of the Rocking H punchers at the mention of Linda, he straddled the third Bar B mount and headed up the narrow valley formed by the merging slopes.

The sky overhead seemed limitless, a faded blue dome receding forever. Not a cloud marred the surface horizon to horizon. The sun beamed its innocent ferocity without interference. The stream, little wider or deeper than when it flowed into the pond behind Rocking H headquarters, meandered its way slowly through the narrow strip of land at the feet of the grassy, treeless slopes. Nothing protected the water from the rays of the sun. Rocks and gravel lined its banks.

As Stoner rode he studied the terrain around him. A couple dozen cattle grazed on the slope below the canyon mouth he was headed for. Not far beyond that another small herd stood with their heads down, some grazing, some seeming to doze in the sun.

Sweat rolled down Stoner's torso. His shirt was soaked and grimy from his exertions, his Levi's little better. The sweatband of his sombrero was too wet to hold the flow out of his hair. He took the sombrero off and, as he rode, used his bandanna to mop the water from forehead and neck. Subconsciously he studied the heavily wooded area where Linda was supposed to be waiting. Nothing moved up there. Except for the cows, nothing was moving between the bushwhack site and where the narrow valley swung around the foot of a small, rounded hill and disappeared.

"That's strange," Stoner mused aloud. "Linda could see the fight easy enough. She knows it's over. Why isn't she showing herself?"

He reined his mount to the right and kneed it uphill. Once among the trees he dropped to the ground. Leaving the animal tied loosely to the low limb of a tree, carrying his Winchester, he glided rapidly toward where he'd left Linda and the young Bar B rider. Minutes before he closed in on his objective he became even more certain that something had gone wrong. No noise reached his ears, no whisper of voices or movement, except for the occasional whinny of a horse--his black, he was sure.

His first glimpse of the opening confirmed his fears. His black stood alone. Lew no longer sat at the base of the tree to which he had been tied. There was no sign of Linda. He made a quick circle of the clearing, noting the tracks made by his and Linda's horses entering the clearing and by two horses heading back up the canyon. Nothing caught his attention--no sound, no movement, no odor. So he glided into the open and circled again, carefully studying the ground ahead of him. Nobody had been in the clearing but Lew and Linda, and himself earlier, nothing that he could find evidence of anyway. The ropes binding Lew had been cut, by Linda, he figured, although there was no way to tell for sure since the area around the tree had been pretty well covered by all three sets of tracks. There had been a fight after Lew had been freed. His boots and Linda's, Stoner concluded, had torn up the grass and weeds near the tree. The impression of a struggling body being dragged marked two distinct lines down the slope. A few drops of blood were scattered here and there near the draggings. A torn piece of green material lay at the edge of the battleground; he quickly recognized it as part of a sleeve from Linda's blouse. But near where the horses had been tied footprints showed that Linda had mounted without help, so she had been alive when she left the clearing.

Stoner stood up from examining the footprints and stepped toward the black. As he did so, a movement flickered in the corner of his eye and then froze, somewhere in the distant shadows. Stoner dived to the right and rolled toward the safety of the tree that had held Lew just as a shot reverberated through the woods and a bullet ripped the air where he had stood a split second before.

From behind the tree Stoner studied the heavily wooded canyon above him. He could see nothing but trees and underbrush and occasional glimpses of blue sky. Except for a jay scolding something far back along the slopes toward where the Rocking H had been pinned down, he could hear nothing. He decided to take the chance that the bushwhacker had lost sight of him because of intervening vegetation and terrain; quickly he snaked around the tree and into the underbrush. Carefully he began working his way up the canyon. He had covered little over what he considered half the distance to where he had noted the movement when Lew shouted.

"Hey you, Stoner! I've got your woman. Show yourself or I'll cut her. She won't look so pretty with her face all sliced up."

Fear tore at Stoner's vitals, its icy fog spreading into his chest, but he ignored the command. He prayed the boy wouldn't carry through with his threat, but if he did.... Stoner shrugged angrily. If Lew did then he, Stoner, would carry a terrible guilt to his grave. He continued working his way up the canyon, having a target now in the sound of the voice.

"Show yourself, goddamn it," Lew shouted again, his voice high pitched with a note of hysteria. "You heard what I said. If you don't show yourself, you can't blame me for what happens."

"The hell I can't," Stoner swore to himself. He had reached a rocky outcrop ranging from two to three feet high and made of a single flat-topped slab surrounded on all sides by several yards of broken granite and underbrush. He crawled around the left side of the slab and eased his body in among a jumble of brush and rocks and small boulders until he could look between two of the largest boulders and see Lew's position, while remaining unseen himself.

The boy had chosen well. He too lay hidden in a confused pile of brush and boulders and small trees about thirty yards from Stoner's position.

"This's your last chance," Lew shouted again, nerves turning his voice into a squeal toward the last word. "By God, I ain't gonna wait no longer."

Stoner watched carefully for any sign of movement. He had a clear shot, he figured, if Lew showed any part of himself. The barrel of his Winchester rested on a rock wedged between the two boulders behind which he lay. His left arm, also relaxed against the rock, held it in place. The butt snuggled against his shoulder; his finger curled loosely around the trigger. With a barely perceptible roll of his torso he could cover the entire thicket that hid Lew and his prisoner.

"Yeah, well," he shouted, "that woman doesn't mean anything to me. She sure as hell ain't worth my life. Not to me anyhow." He waited for a moment, hoping Lew would show himself, but the boy didn't. "Tell you what, though, you hurt her in any way and I'll kill you slow and terrible; you'll be begging me to kill you before I'm through. I don't hold with hurting women and kids."

"Ah, crap," Lew shouted back, ridicule edging in with the nervousness. "I don't think you got the guts to do no such thing."

Stoner didn't answer. He was concentrating on the left edge of Lew's shelter. He thought he'd seen a flicker of movement there and was becoming more and more convinced that the sound of Lew's voice came from that area. After interminable minutes of silence, his patience was rewarded. A patch of yellow appeared at the base of a small juniper. Lew, he remembered, was wearing a dirty yellow bandana around his neck. Linda had nothing yellow on. He let his eyes relax; then looked again, shifting his gaze around the immediate vicinity of the yellow splotch. Nothing, he couldn't make out any human shape. He had just about decided that his sight was failing him, that the yellow spot was a flower or a leaf or something, when Lew spoke again. As he spoke the yellow moved, became more visible, more pronounced, and what Stoner took to be Lew's dirty hair appeared in the shadows above the yellow.

"Time's up. You...."

Stoner had aimed a few inches above the yellow patch. He squeezed the trigger as Lew spoke. Lew's words were drowned in the sharp burst of the shot. The yellow patch suddenly rose several feet straight up, then Lew flapped into view, blood streaming from what had been the area between his lips and nose, his feet churning the ground behind him as they frantically tried to get him upright, his arms, having dropped the rifle as he clambered to his knees and tried to stand, flailing the air. The unconscious, macabre pantomime of a gorging vulture frightened from its prey and unsuccessfully trying to become air-born lasted but a few seconds. Lew tilted lower and lower as his legs continued their instinctive churning until his chin collided with the ground, then his body hit and lay still, his legs for a while continuing to beat out their last attempt at living motion. He had been dead even as he tried to stand. The bullet had smashed his upper teeth, passed through his mouth, and exited at the back, snipping the spinal cord on its way.

Stoner carefully made his way to the body. He didn't figure any more of the Bar B was around but he wasn't taking any chances. He reached what was left of the young cowboy without glimpse or sound of movement in the canyon around him. For a moment he stood looking down at the corpse. A sense of empty futility spread through him like icy, numbing mist. The kid had had a warped idea of what being a man was all about. He hadn't known the difference between valor and foolhardiness. He hadn't seemed to know the meaning of kindness or friendship. In the few moments that Stoner had known him, the kid had seemed cold and cruel, without the slightest inkling of brotherhood or love or mercy. He wouldn't have lasted long anyway, Stoner reckoned. He was too careless of the intelligence of others, too cocksure of his own superior skill and wisdom.

"But he was just a boy, damn it," Stoner thought sadly as he looked at the sightless eyes and mutilated face.

He started to pull the boy's jacket off in order to cover the face and eyes, especially the eyes, when thrashing in the bushes nearby sent him diving for cover. A moment later he reappeared sheepishly and walked quickly to the underbrush behind Lew's position.

Linda lay awkwardly on her side in a large clump of tomatillo. Her ankles had been cruelly forced up behind her and tied to her wrists. Her skirt lay in crumpled, soiled folds, barely covering her slender hips. Dirt smudges and scratches seemed to dot every square inch of exposed skin. Deeper scratches marred her shapely thighs and calves. An especially nasty cut zigzagged down one shin. Her blouse had been ripped open, baring one full white breast and pink nipple. Her hair, disheveled, covered with dirt, broken twigs, and bits of leaves, hid most of her face. A sleeve torn from her blouse had been jammed into her mouth and tied in place with a length of dirty rope.

Stoner felt hot passion surge through his loins and into his chest. His breath came in short bursts. He felt the sweat burst through the pores of his neck and forehead and torso. He stopped, shaken to the core of his being by the violence of his lust, frozen in place, unable to see anything but the warm flesh of the girl lying helplessly in the bushes before him. Until he caught a glimpse of her eyes. Hurt, anguish, supplication, violence, a killing hate, a deep, quivering fear--all lurked in the large dark spheres almost hidden behind the dirty, knotted strands of hair. Suddenly, shame cooled his passion as if it had been submerged in an icy mountain creek. He could move again.

As he approached, Linda's struggles became more violent, her unintelligible growls angrier. Swiftly, as gently as he could, Stoner stooped and freed her mouth before taking his knife to the rope binding hands and ankles.

At first she couldn't speak. Her efforts resulted in the same mumbled monosyllables as before the gag had been removed. She struggled to stand but only succeeded in falling and then scooting laboriously along the ground as she tried again and again. The ropes had cut off the circulation in her arms and legs, which now moved like the limbs of a baby who hadn't yet learned how to use them. Speaking soothingly, Stoner carried her to an area of soft pine needles and grass, then knelt beside her and began to massage her forearms and wrists, moving slowly toward her hands.

"Please," she whispered hoarsely, having succumbed to his ministrations after a brief, weak attempt to free herself from his hands, "please cover me." As she spoke she wondered at the multitude of conflicting emotions raging inside her--scorn for this man who lived by violence struggled with a physical attraction that turned her weak and passive. An angry desire to strike out at something, to take vengeance for her pain and degradation, fought with a desperate need of the moment for tenderness and affection. She was acutely aware that Stoner could not keep his eyes from her naked breast, yet she did not feel the contempt she often felt when men ogled her body openly or covertly, nor did she feel the irritation that she thought she should feel under the circumstances, only a slight embarrassment. Why, she wondered. "Please," she repeated, "cover me."

"I don't...," Stoner started to say he had nothing to use, but he stopped, mentally cursing himself for a fool. He'd been so worried about the girl, so worried that she might have been physically hurt, badly, or that she might at any minute go off the deep end emotionally, and at the same time so intimidated by her semi-naked presence that his mind had quit. He could think of nothing to do but to get her on her feet and functioning independently as quickly as possible. In answer to her request, however, he stripped off his shirt and awkwardly helped her put it on, backwards so it covered her better; he didn't figure she wanted the dead boy's jacket draped over her.

"You hurt anywhere?" he asked awkwardly. "Any broken bones or...?"

"No," Linda answered seriously, before forcing a smile and looking into his eyes with mingled embarrassment and gratitude. "No broken bones I'm sure. But I hurt all over."

Stoner noticed the smile and felt relief spread through his gut and chest. His breathing eased. His body relaxed.

"If you won't go away," he returned her smile, "I'll go back downhill and get my other shirt. It's in the saddlebags. That way I won't feel so naked."

Linda blushed at his words, reminded of her own bared breast and general disarray when he had found her. Abashed, avoiding a direct glance into his eyes, she searched his face, wondering if his words were meant to be suggestive.

"Sorry," Stoner also turned red under his sun-darkened skin as he realized what he had said. Under his breath he cursed his verbal clumsiness.

"I'll be back," he commented gruffly and turned to go downhill to the black.

"Wait!" Linda's command sounded peremptory to her own ears; she softened her voice as she continued even though both the realization and the subsequent change irked her. She was becoming too interested in a wandering gunfighter, too worried about his feelings, she thought. "My mare is up there," she pointed uphill. "That Bar B rider...," she shuddered at the cruelty of her former captor and yet sorrowed for the death of someone so young. "That boy led our horses up there. He wasn't gone but a few minutes; he couldn't have gone more than fifty yards." Tensely she watched Stoner as he hesitated. "I have an old slicker in the saddlebags. It's all torn and ripped, but...," she hesitated and forced a nervous laugh. "I don't know why I'm cold. But I'd feel better if I had it," she blushed and refused to meet his probing eyes.

Stoner wondered if she was going to have a case of nerves now that the rough stuff was over.

"You gonna be okay?" he asked.

"My God!" she exclaimed, ignoring his question, her face turning pale, deep concern making her gasp the words. "How is Rob? And the boys with him?" Her eyes searched his face.

"I must be self-centered like Mother says. I was so worried about myself, I forgot all about them." A plea for his understanding, maybe for his forgiveness as well, seemed to hang just under the surface of the words.

For some moments neither broke the silence. Her eyes continued searching his face as if there, somehow, she would find not only the answer to her question but also absolution for her selfishness. His thoughts stumbled clumsily between the plea and the question; his mind, destroyed by the powerful image of her lips and eyes begging for forgiveness, added to the sensual image of her body in disarray, could not bring his tongue and thoughts together in a coherent statement.

Finally, with an effort that left him as weak as a starving lion kitten, he forced his thoughts into rational order, "I don't reckon it's selfish to worry about what a skunk like Lew's gonna do when he's got you tied up like he did. He was a coldblooded killer, I figure, not a speck of human feeling in his bones. You're lucky you're alive. He's the type that'd rape a woman or torture a man and then slit their throats, laughing all the time. And head for the nearest saloon when he was done." Stoner paused, feeling his strength returning. "Your brother and the hands? They're okay. A scratch here and there. Nothing serious. Rob got the worst of it, I reckon. He'll walk a little slow for a while, but he's not in any danger if blood poisoning doesn't set in."

He described Rob's wounds and Sonora's ministrations, followed by an outline of the conversation the two of them had had. When he had finished she looked at him thoughtfully but made no comment. Again promising to return shortly, he set off uphill, jogging. He found the horses with no trouble. No prints showed in the soft mat of pine needles, but it was easy to follow the trail of freshly broken twigs and trampled shrubs. As he approached the area where the two animals had been tethered to the branches of a fallen aspen, one of them whinnied. Shortly afterwards he led them into the small clearing where he had left Linda.

The girl was sitting up, leaning against the trunk of the pine near where he had left her. She had the sleeves of his shirt rolled up and two or three top buttons holding it in place. Her own blouse she had torn into several large pieces and with them was trying to clean and bandage her worst cuts. She smiled in relief at his return.

"I guess I'm still scared," she commented guiltily, not meeting his eyes, a little self-conscious because of his naked torso. Seeing a man nude to the waist was no novelty. She had also seen more muscular men with their shirts off, men with broader shoulders, men more handsome. But something about Stoner's smooth, cat-like movements, something about the way his muscles rippled with each rhythmic motion, caused her breathing to increase raggedly and her legs to become weak and rubbery. "I almost hid when I first heard you coming back. My first thought was that you were somebody from the Bar B."

"I reckon a person would be a little skittish after what you went through," he smiled and squatted on his heels beside her, the canteen from her saddle horn in his hands. "Here, let me do that," he set the canteen on the ground and, beside it, put a half full bottle of whiskey he had taken from Lew's saddlebags. Gently he took the rags from her hands. "If it hurts just sock me one. Or better yet, yell like the Devil's coming. That way you won't have to doctor my bruises."

"Your bruises?" she asked, baffled.

He grinned, "The ones you might give me if you don't shout out the pain. Wiping the dirt and stuff out of the cuts'll hurt bad enough, I reckon, but the whiskey will burn like sin."

His breathing made difficult by her nearness, struggling against a hot trembling deep inside his chest, he inspected her arms and face, trying to ignore how softly warm her skin was to his touch and how her riding skirt draped sensually over her thighs well above her knees. The scratches were everywhere but mostly minor. The blood on one cheek and arm, he figured, must have come from her legs, spread by her hands since both of those also had dried blood on them. He wet a piece of her blouse with alcohol and cleansed the scratched areas as well as possible before beginning on her legs. Once he glanced up. Her gaze was fixed on him, hypnotized. A tender glow flowed from her eyes to his when they met. Startled, he quickly glanced back to his work, but not before he noted a mist of surprise spreading outward through the tenderness. Swiftly he cleaned the shallower cuts and scratches, leaving two on her thigh and the deep one on her shin until last.

"You better hold on now," he commented when he was ready for the last three cuts. "These last ones are deep and the whiskey'll burn like blue blazes."

"What should I hold on to?"

He glanced up at her question, only to find her eyes again fixed on his face, but this time with a teasing smile matching the softer one on her lips.

"Well," he felt his breath again rampaging around his chest and fought unsuccessfully to control it. "Well," he repeated, forcing a grin, momentarily gaining control over his voice if not his breathing, "you might grab hold of my arm and dig in. The pain might bring me back from this wild dreamland I seem to be in."

"And what kind of a world is that?" her nervous laughter rose liltingly into the silence around them. "Or maybe I shouldn't ask," she hastened to add, blushing. "Maybe it's not something a girl should know."

He suddenly chuckled, her teasing helping return a semblance of self-control to his inner being. For the second time he could see a natural, likeable, spontaneous female under the veneer of sophisticated defensiveness. His mind flashed the image with the first one, the picture of her on the porch of the ranch house, sleeves rolled up, flour spotted here and there over body and dress, still warm and flushed from the heat of the oven. "I reckon most women have a good idea about what kind of emotions they cause in a man. I've always figured they know a lot more about that than a man does, know more about him than he does himself sometimes."

"I think," Linda began, turned modest and serious by a sudden fear of herself more than of the gunfighter, "I think we had better talk about other things and you had better get on with your task. Rob'll wonder what happened to us. And I'd like to see him, see if his wounds are no worse than you say."

Stoner stared at her, letting the moments flow around him as he probed deeper into the eyes meeting his. He wondered if she felt the same desire he did, if their nearness to each other was playing the same havoc with her emotions that it was with his, or if her eyes only expressed a warm, open thanks for his freeing her from Lew and doctoring her cuts.

Without a word he began cleaning the last three cuts. He too thought they should hurry. Not for the reason she did. He wasn't worried about Rob. He worried about the Bar B making an appearance. If a messenger had been sent he could have already met Bar B riders nearby and be on his way back with them. He finished cleaning the girl's cuts, his respect for her rising as neither his awkward attempts to wipe the dirt from the wounds nor the whiskey brought a complaint from her. As he worked she explained how Lew had gotten the upper hand, pausing only to grit her teeth as he poured alcohol into her scratches or when he touched an especially deep cut. He listened without comment. He figured she blamed herself enough for the fight and for Lew's death. Nothing he could say would help her sense of guilt. What he wanted to say would only antagonize her. No one liked to be called stupid. So he remained silent.

He finished cleaning and bandaging the deep cut on her shin. Next he tied Lew across his saddle, helped Linda mount and put on her slicker, and headed downhill to get his black and his shirt, leading Lew's horse, followed closely by Linda. In short order they were riding down the open canyon.

10

Halfway to the rocks where the men had been forted up, they met Tall Will and Tack Guthrie.

"We was worried you all had got lost," Tack commented straight-faced but with a twinkle in his eye. "Now that I see you, I reckon they wasn't no need to worry. You been chasin' bears and wrestlin' them for the hell of it."

Linda turned red; her eyes flashed fire. Then she caught herself with an effort."

"I caught the bear easy enough. He was pretty slow," she coolly imitated Tack's drawl. "I tackled him and was wrestlin' him somethin' fierce. I about had him pinned when Stoner came along and shot him. Spoiled my fun." She laughed at the startled look on Tack's face and the huge grin on Will's.

"We was worried," Will laughed. "So we rode up to help."

"I left the kid with Miss Peters," Stoner broke in to save Linda the embarrassment of explaining how Lew had gotten loose and what had happened later. "Like I told you. I reckon I didn't do a good job of tying him. He got loose and sneaked up on Miss Peters while she was keeping watch on the battle down here. He tied her up and was laying in ambush for me." He shrugged and let his eyes meet Linda's. Her smile expressed her relief and gratitude. "Well, he got the drop on me and took my gun. But Miss Peters, she'd got loose somehow; she tackled him. Damned spunky, him with that pistol." He shrugged and grinned. "What could I do? I didn't have my sidearm so I jumped in the pile before he could get off a shot. It was touch and go there for a minute. Miss Peters got thrown into a big patch of catclaw and knocked around in there some by the two of us. The boy got free and dived for his pistol. He'd dropped mine right beside me. I beat him to the shot. That's it."

He looked at the two punchers. Both glanced at his shirt on Linda's small frame; she had taken the slicker off on the hot ride down the canyon and it lay across the saddle in front of her. Neither made a comment. They fell in behind and silently rode back to join Rob and Sonora and their prisoners. Rob looked better. His color had returned and he was sitting up helping Sonora guard the prisoners, who were sitting in a row against a shelf of rock. Linda made straight for Rob but he waved her worried questions away, irritated by her show of emotion.

"I'm okay," he growled suspiciously, "but you look like you've been wrestling a cougar."

In a low, hurried voice Linda explained what had happened, taking the blame for Lew getting away, but not mentioning that her captor planned to rape her. When she had finished, Stoner discussed the situation with her, Rob and Will. He suggested that he, Will and Tack remain on the Loma with the prisoners.

"They can damn well help drive the Bar B cows back where they belong and fix the fence," he grinned coldly at the prisoners.   "Tack's arm wound is no problem, but Sonora's head wound needs rest and attention, so he can escort you and Linda to headquarters," he directed his final comments to Rob. "I'd appreciate it if you'd take Lew's body with you. Send Cactus to town with it, have him turn it over to the sheriff and tell him what happened. Send Pate out to the Loma with tools to repair fence, in case we need them."

"I don't figure the Bar B cows've had time to scatter much," Will broke in, addressing Stoner. "The graze is good around the spring. That'll keep them put for a while. The problem'll be separatin' Bar B from Rockin' H cows if there's been much mixin'. But we ain't got a lot of stock in there right now, so I reckon we can have the Bar B herd back on home range soon, maybe today. I don't reckon the Bartlemans sent more'n a hundred head or so. That's the way they done it before. They'll figure on drivin' in about that much more if we don't do anything about the cattle already on Rockin' H land. And more later."

Rob nodded his head in agreement, "What about the fence? I'm pissed off enough to fence the spring off again."

"I don't figure that'd be a good idea," Stoner spoke thoughtfully. "Your dad," he looked closely at Rob. "Your dad let the Bar B use the spring before they began pushing their cows onto Rockin' H grass. I think you should start there again. Fence their cows off from your range but leave an opening from Bar B range to the spring. Serve notice that you're good neighbors. You'll let their stock water at the spring even if it is on your range. They're welcome to the water. But not to Rockin' H grass." He looked closely at Rob and then Will. "It'd be worth a try, I figure. Might avert a war in the near future." He grinned starkly. "I doubt if it will in the long run. But if nothing else, it'll maybe buy us a few weeks to get ready."

After some heated discussion, Rob and Will reluctantly agreed.

"I hate to give them coyotes anything," Will complained angrily. "They cut our fences, drive their cows on our range, ambush us, shoot us up, and we turn around and let them keep some of what they took. Don't seem right we should reward their thievin' and murderin' ways."

"Yeah, I feel the same way, Will," Stoner shrugged. "But I don't reckon they've got off free. They've got a couple wounded Bartlemans stove up for a while, one dead puncher, and another puncher that rode north. And they'll soon have their cattle back on the Bar B." He gazed thoughtfully at Will, then Rob. "It might be a mistake. But if it is, it's not a big one. The big mistake was in not killing the Bartlemans this morning. Cut off the head and a wolf isn't very dangerous any more. I should have killed them. The fight would be over," he shrugged again. "But as things turned out it would have been murder, and I'm not one to kill a man in cold blood." He paused and gazed off into the distance. "We've won this hand, I reckon. Let's give a little and hope the other side backs off."

There seemed little more to say. At that moment not one of the three thought the Bartlemans would actually back away from their desire to take over the Loma Linda area, or from their desire to ultimately take over the entire Rocking H. But, after hearing Stoner out and talking his suggestion over for a few minutes, Rob and Will both agreed that his might be the best way. Linda said nothing.

They discussed what they needed to do to get ready for a fight with the Bar B. A few minutes later Rob, Linda and Sonora headed for the ranch house, leading Lew's horse with the corpse draped belly down over the saddle. The other three rode up the canyon with their prisoners in tow. As they approached the spring they estimated a hundred head of Bar B cattle scattered over the canyon and its slopes. Grouped in the neighborhood of the spring they found another hundred head. Almost twenty yards of fence along the line between the two ranches had been pulled down and rolled into a pile at the foot of a rocky cliff.

"Ha, ha," Tack laughed after they had inspected the area. "These Bar B hands was too lazy to pull down much of the fence."

"Yeah," added Will with a boyish grin, "and too lazy or dumb to scatter the whole herd down the canyon. Won't take long to get those cow critters back home and fix this mess here by the spring."

Stoner studied the area. The spring bubbled up from the depths near the head of the canyon. The water hole it formed spread out over an acre of land. The stream they had followed up the canyon flowed deep and narrow from the lower end of the pond, but soon became wide and shallow as it drifted down toward the valley floor. Beyond the spring the canyon slowly folded outward, broad and shallow, gentle slopes alternating with steep drop-offs, the slopes covered with small stands of pine and aspen.

"You two take these punchers, ride back, and haze all the Bar B critters this way, one of you on each side of the creek," Stoner motioned to Will and Tack. "Split the prisoners any way you want, but keep a close eye on them. We don't want them escaping. They might spread the word about where we are and what we're doing. Me, I'll try to be around when you get this far."

"Where you goin', boss?" Tack looked concerned as his eyes roamed over the Bar B land beyond the fence.

"I reckon I'll haze those animals back through the fence," he jerked his thumb toward a large herd of Bar B cattle grazing on the slope above where the creek left the pond. The rest had grazed down the canyon and broken up into small bunches of a half dozen or more. "Won't take much. Then I'll ride over yonder, beyond the fence, and look around, look for traces of horses riding this way from Bar B land. You two keep a sharp lookout. So far we're still all of us alive. Let's try to keep it that way."

"You watch yourself," Tack commented as he reined his horse back along the canyon. "If they're comin', the other Bar B riders could be here any time."

Stoner watched his two companions ride away with the prisoners until Will forded the creek and they continued riding separately, one group along each side of the water. When he could no longer see any of the riders, he skirted the spring and began moving the herd of cattle along the slope toward the hole in the fence. Once he had them on Bar B land he drove them along the fence until he found a small bowl with decent graze, enough, he figured, to last the herd until after nightfall. Satisfied that the cattle probably wouldn't stray back toward the spring and down the canyon until evening, at least, he kneed the black further into Bar B land, angling back toward the canyon mouth above the spring. Winchester at the ready, he eased up the slope and into the trees and brush that lined either side of the canyon as it opened onto the top of the mountain down which it meandered its course. There he dismounted and led his horse. His eyes moving ceaselessly, his ears keenly attuned to the sounds of the natural world around him, remaining in the shadow of the trees, he ghosted over the top of the mountain and down the other side until he could see the trail that both Tack and Will had mentioned as the probable one any riders coming from the Bar B would take. From where he stood deep in the shadows of the tree line, his eyes could follow much of the trail as it zigzagged for close to a half mile down the slopes of the mountain and then made a sweeping curve and disappeared into the timber. He settled in for a wait. Less than a quarter of an hour later four horsemen rode out of the trees at a slow trot and entered the curve.

"Luck," he spoke softly to the black. "I'm a lucky damned son of a gun sometimes."

He studied the trail between him and the horsemen. Often it disappeared for a few yards as it dipped into a ravine, skirted a stand of timber, or worked its way through rocky terrain. A little more than a hundred yards from his position it squeezed through a jumble of cabin-sized boulders as it climbed onto an open, treeless flat of cactus and sage. To his left a ravine plunged down the slope to within forty yards of the boulders before making a sharp right turn. Quickly Stoner ground-hitched the black and ducked into the ravine. Minutes later he reached the point where the ravine swung right. A quick glance over the edge showed that his judgment had been correct. The jumble of boulders hid him from the approaching horsemen. Swiftly he climbed out of the ravine and trotted along the slope until he reached his destination, making sure he remained hidden from the lower reaches of the trail. A quick examination of the area put him behind a boulder on the upper edge of the jumble; he was hidden from the approaching riders but, through a narrow opening between two boulders, he could watch them approach. Once they passed through the boulders and entered the open land beyond, with one short step he could place himself behind the protection of another boulder but at the same time above the riders, above and behind them. He would have a clear field of fire from a distance of twenty or thirty feet. If everything worked out as he planned, no more men would die that day. No one would die, but the approaching riders would help repair the cut fence. Stoner grinned to himself. The potential of the situation tickled him. He was still young enough to appreciate a good joke, even when dangerous.

He checked his rifle to make sure he had already jacked a cartridge into the firing chamber. Satisfied, he settled in to wait, watching the horsemen wind toward him.

They continued their approach at an unhurried trot. Stoner recognized a couple of them; they had been with the Bar B foreman the previous day, in the saloon. He had not seen either of the other two. Barstow was not riding with them.

Within minutes the two leaders entered the jumble of boulders through which the trail wound its course. Less than a minute later all four riders passed Stoner's position and trotted into the open meadow beyond.

"Far enough!" Stoner roared, his voice loud and deadly in the still air. "The first one makes a move without my sayso is a dead man."

His first words brought the riders to a startled halt, horses prancing nervously, hands dropping to grasp at sixguns. At his second sentence, the hands froze in place, then carefully, slowly rose to shoulder height.

"What's this? A holdup?" one of the riders in the lead blustered.

"I guess you could say that," Stoner chuckled coldly. "I want your weapons, one at a time. Shuck your saddle gun, first, then the pistol. Start with you front right there, the yahoo with the big mouth and the copper conchas on his sombrero. Drop your guns right beside the trail."

Stoner ordered each Bar B Rider in turn to drop his weapons. Next he had them ride forward ten yards, spread out and, still facing away from him, dismount one at a time, each man backing up five paces after dismounting, dropping onto his stomach, and finally spreading his arms straight out from his body. None of the riders seemed in a mood to argue.

The horses, freed of their burden, ambled forward in search of grass, reins dragging. Stoner grunted disgustedly; the Bar B animals hadn't been trained to ground hitch.

"Serve them right if they have to walk back to the Bar B," he grunted as he walked from his ambush, his eyes never straying from his captives except for an occasional quick glance back along the trail and up along the edge of the timber. He didn't figure any riders were following them, but he didn't plan on taking any more chances than he had to.

He leaned his rifle against a large rock near where the enemy hardware lay and drew his Colt before approaching the riders. He mistrusted a rifle at close quarters.

One at a time he frisked his captives. He came up with two pocketknives and a derringer. These he tossed beside the other weapons.

"Okay," he ordered next. "On your feet. We've got a little walk ahead of us.

It didn't take long to cover the half mile back to the spring, although his captives were limping and complaining of sore toes by the time they arrived.

"We might as well sit down and wait," Stoner grinned at his prisoners when they reached the spring. "I hear the cows coming but it'll be a while before the hands get them here, I reckon. Meantime, you boys can get a drink if this short little walk in the country has made you all hot and dusty and thirsty. One at a time," he spoke brusquely as all of his prisoners started for the water at the same time. "I don't reckon on torturing you boys by keeping you from water, but I want to return you to your boss alive, alive and healthy. That might not happen if I don't keep a close watch out; you boys seem a mite quick around water. Somebody might fall in and drown. Or stub a toe trying to escape."

After the Bar B riders had all had a chance at the water, Stoner ordered them to sit down on a rocky ledge up one of the slopes, along where the fence still ran uncut. Pistol on his knees, he squatted nearby, where he could keep an eye on all four. As he waited for the cattle to appear, he studied the four men. As he had noticed before, two had been with Barstow in the saloon; they were young, tall, bronze-faced, cold-eyed. One was whipcord thin, the other big enough to wrestle a grizzly. They hadn't seen more than twenty or twenty-one summers. They resembled many cowboys Stoner had known, young daredevils ready for anything from a lark to a fight. Yet the similarity ended at the surface. "The big one," Stoner warned himself as he looked them over, "doesn't fight for fun. I doubt he does anything for fun. For enough money though, I reckon he'd do anything from fighting or killing to running off a man's stock or crippling his son. Or scaring his women. Or beating them or worse if the boss says to. I don't reckon I'd turn my back on him."

He moved his eyes to the other two prisoners, one in his forties, one well over fifty, he estimated. They too were gunhands, not simple cowhands. Both wore tied-down holsters. Both wore gun belts that had seen years of use. But there the similarity ended. The younger and shorter of the two had hands without a callous in sight. He had spent more time inside saloons and bunkhouses than out in the weather. He refused to meet Stoner's eyes directly but rather gazed off into the distance while watching his captor from the corner of his vision. "Back-shooter," Stoner mumbled under his breath. "Bushwhacker. More dangerous in a prolonged fight than his compadre, but I'll bet a peso to a centavo he doesn't move without careful planning and the odds on his side." Stoner recognized the fourth man from years back, but he couldn't remember exactly where or when. He was an old man by the standards of his trade, probably in his late fifties, an inch or two short of six feet, completely baldheaded except for a ring of short-cropped grey hair around the back of his head, from ear to ear. He hadn't shaved for a day or two but his clothes appeared clean under a thin layer of dust and sweat, evidence of the ride from Bar B headquarters. His brown eyes met Stoner's with a glint of humor shining from their depths. Stoner answered the glint of recognition with an almost imperceptible nod.

"What you plannin' on doin' with us?" the thinner of the younger two asked, the youth with the long blond hair and straggly white fuzz on his face.

"Hell, Wib, he ain't gonna do nothin'," his companion laughed sarcastically. "He's just gonna keep us here a while. You know, he's gonna try and scare us shitless with that mean old stare of his. Then he's gonna send us back to the Bar B. He ain't got the backbone to face off with Nate Barstow and the Bartlemans. He knows they'd eat him alive."

"Shut up, Cal," the taller of the two older gunmen ordered without raising his voice. "You gotta learn to keep your mouth shut when it can't do nothin' but get you in more trouble."

"You ain't my daddy, old man," Cal sneered.

"Hell," the older man returned the sneer, chuckling mirthlessly. "You wouldn't know if I was. You nor your ma."

"Dodge," the youth bounded to his feet and stepped toward the other. "You watch your mouth or one of these days I'm gonna stop it up permanent-like. You hear?" Fists clenched, body hunched for attack, he stood over his opponent.

"Sit down!" Stoner's voice didn't rise above a normal, conversational tone, but a note of iron finality rang in the words. He didn't move, but the barrel of his pistol shifted slightly.

"Go to hell," Cal growled, turning on his captor. "Put that pistol down and then tell me to sit down, if you got the guts."

Stoner stared up into the empty blue eyes ten feet away. As he watched, a dull glimmer of cruelty appeared somewhere in the depths and spread outward like ripples in a muddy puddle. The young rider's lips curled into a sneer. His chin jutted out. His hulking frame hunched forward slightly, threatening, ready to attack.

Stoner didn't want to kill the young Bar B hand, but he knew he had to do something or lose control. The boy had lost all fear. He was convinced that Stoner wouldn't shoot and so was determined to push what he saw as his advantage against an adversary unwilling to kill.

Stoner decided to try a bluff. "The barrel of this Colt is pointed at your belly," he spoke coldly, clearly. "I don't reckon I can miss at this distance. But if you want to try me just keep standing for another ten seconds."

"Bull crap," Cal exploded. "You wouldn't shoot nobody in cold blood. If you was gonna shoot us, you'd of done it back there at the rocks, when you had us out in the open, dead to rights."

Stoner remained silent, but the gunhand called Dodge laughed, an icy laugh without a note of emotion or mirth. Then he spoke up, still chuckling, "That's Stoner, Jacob Stoner. I don't reckon I'd dare him to shoot me. He might just do it, shoot me and bury me naked in some canyon around here, then plant a cholla on my grave. Like he did to Pete Cameron down El Paso way. Pete thought he was some punkins, with a pistola or knife or fists or anythin' else." Dodge winked and grinned at Stoner, showing more gaps than teeth. "We was camped out in a canyon south of town, a bunch of us that had pulled a job for a rancher. No need to mention names," he again grinned at Stoner. "There wasn't much to do. We'd been hidin' out over two weeks, waitin' for orders for another job. Pete, he was bored and getting' louder and meaner every day. One day..., well, he wasn't very bright, Pete wasn't. He'd been ridin' Stoner somethin' fierce for a long time, even before we lit out for the canyon. One day he started in like usual, callin' Stoner here names, bumpin' him and throwin' things in his direction and yellin' catch after they was already in the air, anything from rocks to sticks and dried horse turds, tellin' Stoner what he was goin' to do to him some day. The thing is, the day it happened he'd come outside the cabin without his sidearm. He didn't have his rifle either. And there he was, like a damned crazy coyote, tormentin' Stoner up one side and down the other. I reckon he figured he was safe with or without his weapons."

Dodge stopped talking. After several minutes, Cal's voice, irritated and sarcastic, interrupted the silence, "So, old man, tell us what happened. What did your hero here do? Scare Pete to death with words?"

The older Bar B rider looked up at the young rider and shook his head in disgust before speaking, "Pete went too far, I reckon. He picked up a clod of dirt and threw it at Stoner. When it was already in the air he yelled for Stoner to catch it. Stoner, well, he drew his Colt and shot that clod dead center. Splattered it all over the place, all over Pete and everything else nearby." Dodge shook his head in admiration. "Pete wasn't more'n ten feet from Stoner when he threw the damned thing. He yelled about the time it left his hand, and he sure as hell didn't lob it; he sent it scootin'. Well," he paused for effect, eyeing his audience, "I never seen Stoner draw, but the clod was still closer to Pete than him when that there bullet sent it flying back where it come from, in pieces. Pete, he started cussin' like a mad man. He called Stoner and his kin ever rotten thing he could think of, I reckon, him not bein' a educated man. All the while he was cussin' and rantin', Stoner just stood there where he'd been standin' before. When Pete appeared finished he said, 'I think you'd best sit down and shut up, Pete. I got a pistol. You ain't.' Pete now," the old gunfighter's eyes twinkled, "he commenced cussin' again. But he didn't get more'n a half dozen words out of his mouth when Stoner shot him right between the eyes, up and shot him like you'd shoot a snake. Never said a word. No warnin' this time, no time for Pete to even know what was happenin'. He just aimed his pistol careless like and bang. Pete flopped over and died. Later Stoner stripped the body and dragged it out away from camp. The next day we found the grave with a little cholla planted on it. The rest of the time we was camped there in that canyon, every evenin', Stoner watered that cactus. When we rode off for good, it was healthy as a doggie bein' fed by the boss's daughter with a baby bottle."

"I reckon you're windy as hell, old man," Cal scoffed. "Besides, he's more'n likely grown soft like you."

With the effortless grace of a cat, Stoner rose to his feet. "I was wondering where we'd met," he spoke to the old gunfighter without looking at him, without cracking a smile, his eyes fixed on the young Bar B hand named Cal. "Now I remember it all. That's been a long time back. I was a little shaver back then, not even dry behind the ears yet, kind of like this young mule here. If my memory hasn't gone to pot like the rest of me, we had some great times in those days. But, hell, Dodge, since then I've got religion. I've become as peaceable as an old range bull that's too old to smell the heifers in heat and too stove up to do anything about it anyway if he did accidentally wander close enough to get a whiff."

As he talked, Stoner moved slowly toward Cal. The latter watched him approach, suspicious but arrogantly unafraid. Stoner felt a twinge of shame for what he planned to do, for what he figured he had to do if he didn't want to lose control of his prisoners, especially the two young ones.

Three feet from the boy, he faked a swing of the Colt to the head, moving to the left with the same motion. Cal's shoulder dropped with Stoner's fake, then rose slightly; his mouth split in a wide grin; he lunged forward, his right fist swinging in a roundhouse loop for Stoner's jaw. Stoner's move to the left had put him beyond the range of the swing that might have broken his jaw if it had landed. Even as he felt the breeze from the near miss, he lunged forward and brought the barrel of his pistol around in an arc that skimmed over Cal's reaching arm and thudded dully against his nose. Without waiting for the flow of blood that instantly followed the crack of broken cartilage, he rammed the barrel into his foe directly under the point where the lower ribs met, hard. Cal folded to his knees, gasping frantically, painfully for breath, the blood choking him with each gasp.

As soon as his Colt connected with Cal's gut, Stoner stepped back and away from the other prisoners, putting Cal between him and them. Dodge had made no move. He sat with his back against the rocky ledge, relaxed, a slight, sardonic smile twisting his lips and crinkling the corners of his eyes. His partner had leaned forward, his shoulders hunched, his legs tight, ready to spring to his feet. When Stoner stepped back and swung his Colt to bear on the three, the gunhand relaxed, the wolfish killing light left his eyes, his face again turned vacant, a slight shrug twitched his shoulders, as if to say, "Some other time." Wib had bounded to his feet and darted forward as the barrel of Stoner's weapon smashed against Cal's nose. When the Colt's barrel swung to his chest and froze in place, he was still moving, not more than five feet from his target. Suddenly the bony, ice-cold fingers of death clutched at his vitals and flashed over his face, turning it ghostly white. He stopped, frozen as motionless as the pistol in Stoner's hands. His eyes had risen from the weapon to the eyes of the man behind it. There, reflected in the merciless lashing of sleet in a winter storm, he saw his own death. Sweat broke out in every hidden corner of his body, running down his face, his chest and back, his legs. His stomach churned. He fought to breathe, just as did his saddle partner who had fallen onto his side and lay there thrashing and gasping like a fish pulled from a stream and thrown up on the bank to die. Carefully, deliberately he turned his palms outward and raised his hands above his head, moving backward step by step in the same slow, deliberate fashion.

"I'm out of it," his voice rose from a broken whisper to a husky plea.

Stoner shook himself like an old dog just come in out of the rain, forcing the killing fury from his system before it had time to spread into the control mechanism. "Okay," his voice flowed even and strong but with violence barely hidden under the surface, controlled for the moment with great effort, but ready to burst forth at the least danger.

"Help your pard then," Stoner shrugged, backing up until he could once again sit down on the rock he had occupied before the hassle with Cal. "But keep him quiet. Next time he causes me a problem, I might shoot. And if I do, I'll damn sure shoot to kill. I'm tired of fiddle-farting around with a goddamn kid that came here to kill Rockin' H hands; he can take the medicine I hand out free, or he can buy a lead pill. It's his choice from now on."

Stoner glanced at the two older gunmen as he spoke, his face a cold mask. Down deep, however, he grimaced to himself. He didn't want to kill the young would-be tough, not him or anyone else. Killing Lew had brought the haunting sickness back into his gut. It would be weeks, maybe months, before the boy's empty eyes and deathly white face quit haunting his sleep or, at odd moments of solitude, floating cold and clammy upward into his chest, filling his lungs with the rotten smell of death and his mind with memories of the grave.

He watched as the Bar B rider called Wib worked over his partner, waiting until his breathing had returned to normal, then staunching the blood by tearing strips from Cal's bandanna and stuffing them up the bleeding nostrils. The two talked in low tones, from time to time glancing threateningly in Stoner's direction. The latter grinned to himself but otherwise ignored them. He had his mind focused on the cattle that had just appeared at the edge of his vision, down the canyon. He watched as the two Bar B riders closely guarded by Will hazed a herd of sixty to seventy animals toward the spring and the Bar B range beyond. A few moments later Tack appeared with his prisoner and a smaller bunch of cattle.

At the first appearance of cattle and prisoners, Cal sat up, swearing bitterly. He started to stand but, with an angry glance at Stoner, sat back down.

"I mighta knowed," Dodge chuckled mirthlessly. "Jacob Stoner don't do nothin' half way. I reckon the four of us're gonna help fix some fence."

Nobody else said a word. Stoner watched the cattle and riders moving slowly up the canyon. Tall Will and Tack brought up the rear, herding their prisoners along while the latter hazed the cattle. The two Rocking H hands seemed to be enjoying themselves. Tack rode alertly two to three horse lengths behind the Bar B rider, rifle in his right hand, reins in the left. Will rode slack-shouldered, left leg cocked around the pommel, rifle barrel resting on his knee, reins draped over the barrel. He kept inching his mount up on the heels of the Bar B horses as if daring the two riders to fight or make a run for it. Stoner shook his head, irritated and tickled at the same time.

"He's an ornery cuss, Will is," he chuckled to himself, a chuckle as empty of mirth as was Dodge's, "hell-bent on fighting the Bar B or anybody else that ruffles his feathers. I reckon one of these days he'll kill someone or get killed himself. Either way it'll slow him down some," he spoke the final words aloud, laughing as he did.

Startled at his words, the four Bar B prisoners stared at him inquisitively. He ignored them. He had caught a sound from further down the canyon, the sound of a distant shout. A few moments later Pate rounded the first bend and rode into sight, leading two packhorses. Stoner glanced up at the empty, faded blue of the sky. The sun burned fiery hot in the west, well above the peaks. The air along the earth was as clear as the sky itself. They had at least five hours until sunset, he figured, when their mountainous world would be plunged into almost instantaneous darkness. With the help they had, they should have time to finish repairing the fence before nightfall. He planned to leave the deep, steep-sided gully he had picked out unfenced so the Bar B cattle could reach the spring; they would have to drag and pile some logs and brush and boulders at the gully's mouth until they could bring more barbed wire up from the ranch house, to keep the cattle from scattering onto Rocking H land, but that shouldn't take long. The fence posts still stood solidly in place. The barbed wire, three strands of it, had been snipped in several places and loosened from the poles but otherwise left intact. They should have plenty of time before dark, he figured, if the Bar B riders would work. He grinned at the four men staring curiously at him. He grinned because it was his job to see that they did work, swiftly and efficiently, and because he was already enjoying the job even though it hadn't yet begun.

He waited until the cattle had been driven onto Bar B land and scattered beyond the mouth of the canyon, until Pate had ridden up with his packhorses, and until Tack and Will had returned with their prisoners. Then he immediately sent Tack to bring in the Bar B mounts and weapons as well as his black.

"Take one of the prisoners with you. When you get back," he continued softly, indicating the food supplies on one of the two packhorses, "the two of you build a fire over there in that open, flat area." With his finger he indicated a place two dozen yards from where the spring gushed out of the ground, "And get supper cooking. Make it a big fire. We don't want any of these Bar B yahoos getting lost in the dark later. The rest of us are going to build fence."

"The rest of who?" Cal asked belligerently.

"Like hell!" exploded Dobbs, the short, squat man with the unkempt hair and beard and the flattened nose, the rifleman who had been the last of the bushwhackers to surrender.

"I reckon you two'd best wait and see what Stoner's offer is before you say no," Dodge spoke from the ledge he had been sitting on. He alone among Stoner's four prisoners had remained sitting when the others rode up.

"You can wait till hell and back, old man," Cal sneered. "Me, I ain't fixin' no fence. It don't belong to the Bar B and I didn't ride all the way out here to take orders from some loud mouth from the Rockin' H."

"You sure are doin' a lot of yelpin' for a coyote with a squashed nose," Dodge shook his head disgustedly.

Swearing violently, Cal dove for the old man. But Stoner had anticipated the move. With Dodge's first words of reconciliation, he edged closer to the two antagonists until he was almost standing between them, within arm's reach of the younger man. As Cal moved, Stoner swung his pistol barrel up and down in a short, vicious arc. It connected with the shoulder, at the base of the neck. Cal folded, moaning with pain, momentarily paralyzed. Bar B and Rocking H hands froze in place.

Stoner swung to face the remaining prisoners. "You men rode out here to cut Rocking H fence, drive Bar B cattle on Rocking H land, and shoot any Rocking H punchers that interfered." His voice, low but knife-sharp, cut the silence, drowning the low moans coming from the writhing Cal. "Five of you bushwhacked three Rocking H hands and one of the owners. One of you attacked Linda Peters; his name was Lew; he's dead and his old saddle partner headed north. The other four of you came out here to help finish off the ambushed Rocking H hands. Me, I'm tired of listening to your bellyaching. I should put a noose around your necks and be done with it. I'll sure as hell regret it that I didn't, I reckon. But I figure any man should get a second chance. So we're not going to string you up. But you are going to pay the piper one way or the other. Those who won't help repair the fence, I'll tie them up till we're finished." He paused and glared at his audience. "I don't reckon you'll like the way I tie you up, especially if we don't finish the fence today. You'll stay tied up till we finish it, till tomorrow or the next day if we don't finish till then. You might lose the use of an arm or leg in the process." He again glared angrily along the line of faces. "If you don't work, you don't eat. And you walk home, without boots, down through the valley, with me right behind you on horseback, making sure you step on lots of rocks. Those who work and work well, they get fed and get their horses to ride home. If everybody works with a will we should finish in two or three hours. You can ride out tonight. If we don't finish tonight, the men that put their shoulders into the job can ride out tonight anyway. The goof-offs stay over to help again tomorrow. They'll be hogtied for the night, of course. Without blankets." He paused for effect. "And it gets colder than hell up here at night, as you damn well know."

When no one answered or met his eyes, he began giving orders. He sent Dodge with Tack, figuring him for the least dangerous of the Bar B gunhands under the present circumstances. Tack would need help bringing in the five horses and the guns left out by the boulders where Stoner had disarmed the Bar B riders. And Dodge, Stoner had decided, would be the least likely to try for an escape or for the guns. He seemed to be enjoying the situation, as well as a renewed acquaintance with Stoner himself. The three bushwhackers and the gunhand who had been riding with Dodge, he sent with Will and Pate to drag whatever they could find to fill in the sides of the gully as it opened onto the spring. He considered Dodge's pard and Dobbs the most dangerous of the prisoners, but he figured Will and Pate could handle them. As for the younger two, he sent Wib to help mend the fence and he kept Cal with him, to unpack the food supplies and tools, set up camp, and round up plenty of firewood in case they had to stay the night.

Tack and Dodge took off on foot, leaving Tack's mount for Slicker, Dodge's partner. They planned to find Stoner's black horse first and then use it to round up the Bar B cayuses, figuring the latter had strayed some and might be hard to approach on foot. Tall Will and Pate soon had their prisoners mounted and riding. Pate had spoken quietly to Stoner as his tall companion was getting the four Bar B gunhands mounted.

"Anyway you look at it," Pate began the conversation with a glint of laughter in his eyes, his voice easily carrying to Will and his charges, "that old man and the splay-shouldered one are spooky. They look like they might start a fandango or a shivaree or some such wild time given half a chance. It make any difference to you if I shoot the legs out from under one or both...if they try somethin' dumb? I won't shoot them for nothin', I guess," he shook his head in mock sorrow. "That way, with some lead weighin' them down, they won't dance so good and show us poor Rockin' H mavericks up for the clodhoppers we sometimes appear to be."

Stoner laughed and entered into the humor of the words. "I don't reckon I'd lose sleep over a little innocent shooting, Pate," he too spoke loud enough for the Bar B hands to hear. "But use your old bullets. The new ones cost too much to waste on the likes of those rannies. And don't shoot any joints. You know, knees and ankles and such. We don't want any crippled punchers on our hands. Who'd do the work?"

As Pate and Tall Will rode off with their unwilling hands, Stoner turned the full force of his gaze to the remaining prisoner. Cal still sat on the ground, rubbing his neck and glaring at the Rocking H foreman.

"That about shooting a man in the legs, you don't mean that, do you?"

The tone of the voice, speculative and uncertain, made Stoner study the young rider more carefully.

He shrugged and eyed the young Bar B hand reflectively. "Put yourself in my place," he finally spoke, his voice cold and unbending. "We didn't start this shindig. There're four of us, four reps from the Rockin' H. We're on Rockin' H range. We didn't attack anybody. There're seven of you Bar B gunnies. You attacked us, without provocation, as they say in the courts. You tried a land grab, and you weren't worrying none if you had to kill a few Rockin' H hands to get the land. This morning your boss and his boys, the Bartlemans, started a shoot-out up at the Peters house, with Mrs. Peters and her daughter present and in the way of catching some lead." He paused and stared emotionlessly, noting that the news about the Bartlemans didn't appear to surprise the young rider. "Me, I reckon it's in my rights to string you up, take you in to the sheriff, shoot you right here, or anything else I might decide. But I've said I'll let you go and that's what I'll do, unless you screw up. The question is, are you going to help or not?" Stoner swung his full gaze to Cal, who sat staring up at him, frowning angrily. "So far I've taken it easy on you," he spoke softly. "The talking's over as of now. You either get up off your ass and help unload these supplies," he pointed toward the two packhorses, "or I tie you up. Right now. What do you say?"

"There ain't no sense in me bein' the only holdout," Cal grumbled. "The rest of these women I ride with have folded, so I reckon they ain't nothin' for me to do but go along for the time bein'."

The harsh tone of Cal's words reflected the smoldering anger and hate lurking in ambush under the surface, Stoner decided. He would have to stay on his guard around the young Bar B hand. In the meantime, however, he was happy to have the crisis over and the Bar B hands ready to pitch in, no matter how unwillingly. It flashed through his mind that he might have been better off sending them home, without their weapons. But he discarded the thought almost as quickly as it ambushed him. If he had sent them home, they might have circled back and caught him and his riders unaware, strung out repairing the fence or sleeping. They might have ridden home and back by morning, picking up more riders at the Bar B. Once armed, knowing that he and most of the Rocking H hands were absent, they might have attacked Rocking H headquarters. They might have ambushed him and his men on their way back to the ranch house. Too many ifs, he thought. Besides, he had already made his decision; he had no choice but to make it work.

Shrugging his shoulders fatalistically, he herded his prisoner to the packhorses. The two of them made short work of unpacking the supplies, the food and cooking utensils in the open space Stoner had designated for the camp fire and the fencing equipment by the first post from which the fence had been cut.

"We won't need the digger and shovel," Stoner remarked aloud after testing the empty posts.

"Those lazy bastards," Cal grumbled. "If I'd been here there wouldn't be no fence posts standing"

Stoner ignored the comment.

While he and Cal brought in firewood, Tall Will, Pate and their charges dragged two fallen pine trunks into place at the mouth of the gully Stoner had chosen for Bar B access to the pond. Soon afterward Tack and Dodge reappeared, three Bar B horses in tow, the saddles of all three decorated with firearms.

"They've all been unloaded, boss," Tack commented loudly. "I've got all the ammunition here." He patted his saddlebags. "There was lots of shells in them belts but, what the hell, me'n Dodge've had lots of practice so we emptied them right smart."

Stoner noted the glare that Cal turned on Dodge. He wondered how long the old man would last when he returned to the Bar B.

"These saddlebags're gonna stay at my right hand till after we eat," Tack concluded, grinning at Cal, whose frown of anger he too had caught. "And at my hand there's gonna be a meat knife. First strange hand I spot sneaking toward them bags is gonna separate itself from whatever's behind it."

"Well, pot pusher," one of the bushwhackers laughed drily, "it won't be my hand if you can boil water without burnin' it and fry meat without scorchin' it. My hands'll be busy stuffin' water and food down my gullet. I'm damn near dry enough to drink downstream of a herd of cows with the trots and hungry enough to eat what they're trotting."

His words brought roars of laughter from everybody except Cal, whose sour expression never changed. The tension between them eased by the laughter, everybody pitched in to get the work done so they could eat. Stoner left Cal to help Dodge and Tack with the meal. In short order the others had the sides of the gully lined five feet high and the fence up; soon afterward several of them were helping the three cooks burn steaks which Tack was slicing off a slab of beef Pate had carried on the pack horses. The sun's glow was just beginning to touch the western horizon when they completed cleaning up after the meal.

"It's gonna be cold up here before morning," Cal commented. "I've got a blanket. So's everybody else, I suppose. Us Bar B men, at least. But it's gonna be cold."

"Might be some rain toward morning," one of the bushwhackers nodded toward the north and a little west. "Those look like rain clouds way off there and they look to be comin' this way."

"Well," Stoner laughed at the obvious reason for the comments, "I figured we all might camp out for the night. Get a little fresh air. Tell stories around the fire. Look at the stars and moon about the girls that got away."

His sally brought a salvo of laughter.

"Man," one of the bushwhackers commented. "If I had a twenty-dollar gold piece for every time I've had to sleep without a roof over my poor old balding head, damned if I wouldn't ride for Mexico and live like a king the rest of my life."

"Hell, Baldy," Dodge spoke up for the first time since before the meal, "I always figured the only time you ever slept outside was when you passed out in the alley behind some saloon."

Again laughter made the rounds of the circle of men around the camp fire.

"You Bar B men want to ride for home this late?"

Several loud comments in the affirmative answered Stoner's question.

"You're free to go anytime." Stoner was relieved that they wanted to ride out. He didn't relish the thought of having to guard them all night, nor, like them, did he want to spend the night out in the open. Pate had brought no tent or blankets. He, Stoner, had his heavy Mexican serape on his saddle, but he had noticed that none of the other Rocking H punchers carried a blanket.

"What about our guns?" the short, broad-shouldered bushwhacker asked brusquely.

Stoner considered the question for several moments. Earlier, he had planned to keep their weapons and leave them in Chasco in a few days. After considering the question carefully, however, he decided that there was no reason to keep the weapons. The Bar B riders had no ammunition, so their weapons were of no value until they reached Bar B headquarters.

"Take them," he answered. "But we'll keep the bullets. We'll leave them in Chasco one of these days."

After some grumbling, the Bar B riders accepted his decision.

     "I reckon we'll ride out then, soon as we can tighten the cinches," the gunfighter called Slicker spoke from his squatting position by the fire, the most words he had spoken since being taken prisoner. From the grunts of assent around the fire, Stoner figured the man was speaking for his companions. "We can make a few miles before it gets too dark to ride, hole up somewhere if we have to until the moon comes out, and ride on in to a warm bunkhouse and soft bed. I reckon that'd suit you too."

     "Reckon you're right," Stoner agreed lazily. "Ride out any time you want."

     Within ten minutes the sound of moving horses faded into the encroaching twilight beyond the fence. Stoner turned to Dodge, who stood a few yards off, next to Tack.

     As the other Bar B hands were preparing to leave Dodge had approached Stoner.

     "Got anything against me stayin' around?"

     "Cal?"

     "Yeah, we been havin' trouble for some time. The kid's mean, meaner'n a cougar with a smashed tail. He likes to chew on things that don't chew back, just to hear them squeal. Me, I don't squeal, but I'm getting' too old and tired to chew back, so he just keeps chewin', figurin' someday I'll have to squeal or run. Well," he paused sadly, thinking of how life had mellowed him, "tomorrow's the day, I reckon. If I go back he won't stop till all the flesh is gone. He won't let me run, not after the way I crossed him and stood up for you." He paused and stared off into the distance. "What the hell," he shrugged and continued. "Now, well, Nate Barstow, he's kind of stood up for me in the past, kept Cal's tormentin' from forcin' me to draw on the boy. But Nate don't take kindly to what he calls treason. After today he's gonna be mad as all hell about us not doin' what we come to do. When he finds out we helped put that fence back up...Jesus!" the old man exploded with a mirthless chuckle. "He'll want a scapegoat and I reckon I'll be it. If I go back to the Bar B, with Cal and Nate both after me, I'm dead meat."

"Okay," Sam looked thoughtfully at the older man, "stick around. If you want, ride back to headquarters with us. I'll talk to Rob about hiring you. If he won't, you can stop over for a few days anyway."

As the last sound of the Bar B horsemen faded into the silence of evening, Stoner turned to the Rocking H hands, "Pack up. We're leaving."

"Already packed," Tack commented from his squatting position by the fire. "We figured you'd wanta ride out."

Within minutes they had the packs on the pack horses, their own mounts saddled, and the campfire smothered with rocks and dirt.

As they reined their horses down the canyon, Pate's voice rose softly over the creak of leather and the thud of hooves, "That storm ain't gonna hit for three or four hours. Until then it's gonna be a clear night, lots of stars. I don't reckon we'll need the moon to see by.

11

Linda and Rob spoke little on the ride from the Loma to Rocking H headquarters. Neither wanted to talk in front of Sonora.

At the house Sonora again cleaned and dressed Rob's wounds and then allowed Mrs. Peters to tend to his own head wound, while Cactus headed to town with Lew's body and Pate packed for the trip to the Loma. Later, after they had all eaten and Pate had ridden out, Sonora retired to the bunkhouse.

As soon as the hands were gone, Mrs. Peters asked Rob with concern, "You're sure we don't need to send for Doctor Zimmerman?"

"No, Mom, I'll be okay," Rob snapped. "I lost a lot of blood but I feel okay now that I've eaten and can rest. The bullets went right on through, so there's nothing to dig for and no bones or organs damaged. Sonora does as good a job as that old drunk Zimmerman does anyway."

Mrs. Peters acquiesced, although reluctantly. She agreed that Sonora was probably as capable as Doctor Zimmerman when it came to treating wounds of all kinds, but she would have preferred a second opinion.

"Was there something you didn't tell me about the fight while Sonora and Cactus were here?" she asked, looking closely at both Rob and Linda, especially Linda, whose condition had caused Mrs. Peters as much alarm as had Rob's.

Linda caught herself as a nervous sigh of distress escaped her lips. She realized that her nerves were frayed. A number of times on the ride home, and since arriving, she had felt her body begin to shake and had only gained control of herself with an extreme effort of will. She needed to sleep;

sleep would help repair the damage to her nervous system caused by the danger to Rob and by the struggles with the boy Lew. But first she wanted a bath. She desperately needed to wash the memory of the boy's hands and filthy suggestions from her body and mind.

Before leaving for town Cactus had filled the tub in the washroom in back of the house and started a fire under it. Another quarter hour and the water would be hot; she could scrub herself clean.

She and Rob began to speak at the same time.

"Go ahead, Sis," Rob laughed.

Startled at how nervous he too seemed, Linda looked at him closely. His perpetual air of boredom was gone. He almost seemed happy. His eyes glinted. His lips no longer pouted. The arrogant lift of his shoulders had dropped so that now they seemed to express the same calm pride she had admired and loved in her father. The tired droop of his body only added to the aura of self-confidence.

"You seem proud of yourself," she couldn't keep from commenting, pleased at the change in him and wishing it would last.

"You talk first," he insisted. "I'd like to know what you're doing with Stoner's shirt on. You didn't tell that part back at the Loma."

"I'd like to know that too," Mrs. Peters cut in. "I didn't want to ask until we were alone, but since Rob noticed too...," she let her voice trail off into silence.

Linda retold the story she had earlier told Rob and which he had summarized for their mother, this time adding the struggle with Lew but still leaving out the part about his hands caressing her naked skin.

When she had finished, Mrs. Peters spoke first, "Thank God for Jacob Stoner."

Rob remained silent, his eyes locked on those of his sister, wondering if she had changed her mind about the gunfighter and realizing that he couldn't blame her if she had. He himself had found that he could get along with Stoner but, even more importantly, he had decided that he could fool the man as easily as he could his mother. If he played his cards right, he thought, he could drive a wedge between his mother and the gunfighter. As for Linda, he had always been able to control her. Finally, after an interminable silence, he began to talk tiredly, choosing his words and tone carefully.

He emphasized that it was his failure to accept advice which had brought about the near disaster. As he talked he watched the two women, trying to measure the impact of his words on them. "I would have killed the man," he added. "Now," he shook his head in exaggerated disgust at himself and, looking closely at Linda, said the words that he thought his mother wanted to hear, some of which he couldn't reject as easily as he had earlier in the day even though he wasn't completely convinced of their truth, "looking back, I agree with Ma. He saved us here on the porch this morning. He saved you a mauling in Chasco. And he saved us on the Loma. I guess I've been a real horse's ass."

His mother walked up behind him and ran her fingers through his hair, a gesture she had not made since his father had died. Fighting the hot tears that flooded into his eyes in spite of the fact that he was playing a part, he took her hand and squeezed it. Then he told her about his agreement with Stoner.

"I'd like to work with him if it's okay with you," he ended his explanation, not meeting her eyes. "It may not work, I know that. I'll have to fight against booze and my temper, which won't be easy. I may lose, but it's something I want to do. I'm tired of myself as I am. When we were pinned down in the canyon," he spoke broodingly, truthfully, before adding a final lie, "for a while there I didn't think we were going to make it. A man thinks a lot in a situation like that, about himself and what he's done and not done. I didn't like myself much after an hour or so of going over my past. Then somebody took out the two bushwhackers on the north slope, although at the time we weren't sure what had happened to them. Later we heard Stoner on the slope above us. I made myself two promises then and there: If Stoner got us out of that trap I'd be grateful to him for the rest of my life. And I'd turn over a new leaf."

"Oh, Rob," his mother began to cry. "You don't know how happy that makes me." For some time she struggled with her emotions, finally giving up and laughing through the flowing tears. "As long as you remember you can't fire Stoner. He works for me."

"Agreed," Rob returned her laugh, adding, "This calls for a drink." At his mother's look of consternation, he grinned boyishly, "Of water."

This time Linda joined in the laughter. A moment later she left to take a bath, promising to save enough hot water for Rob. When she returned, her mother sat alone, waiting. Rob had gone to the bunkhouse on his way to take his bath. Linda sat down beside her mother.

"Have you told us everything that happened between you and that awful boy?"

Startled, feeling the heat of embarrassment rise into her face, Linda looked closely at her mother. She wondered why she had thought she could fool anybody, and why she had wanted to fool them unless it was because of the foolish pride she had struggled against ever since returning from the East. While still at Loma Linda she had realized that she hadn't fooled the cowboys; she had noticed their surreptitious glances after she had told her story to Rob, leaving out any mention of the struggle with Lew before Stoner's arrival. She had also caught Rob's look when she finished telling her story to her mother. He hadn't been fooled. And now her mother was showing her own suspicions.

"Oh, Mother," her voice barely broke a whisper. "I feel so...," she fought unsuccessfully against the angry tears forcing their way into her eyes, "I feel so dirty."

"The bath didn't clean your feelings, did it," Mrs. Peters took her daughter's hand and held it gently. She knew that something more had happened between Linda and her captor, something the girl had not mentioned. She prayed that her daughter had not been raped. She didn't know if Linda's youthful pride could cope with that.

"No," Linda agreed. She had hoped to keep secret that the boy Lew had torn her blouse and put his dirty hands on her. She still couldn't quite accept what might have happened if Stoner hadn't arrived on time or if he had lost the fight. She wondered if she could face the gunfighter again. The feel of his eyes caressing her bare breast sent conflicting shivers racing up and down her spine; yet she knew that he had looked in spite of himself. His embarrassment and sympathy had been evident. His piercing eyes had only lingered for a moment as he struggled to force them elsewhere.

"I feel so dirty," she added, shuddering.

"It wasn't your fault, whatever happened," Mrs. Peters was hesitant about forcing Linda to express her private feelings. Before her daughter had gone east, the two of them had been close, two women surrounded by men. They openly discussed their thoughts and preoccupations about everything from men to religion. They laughed together at how the cowboys postured and showed off in Linda's presence, like roosters in a hen house. They laughed together at Linda's awkward attempts to become an adult. Mrs. Peters had gloried in the straightforward honesty of their relationship. She loved her daughter and she knew that Linda loved her.

Then Linda had gone east to continue her education and had returned a sophisticated young lady. In the process she had grown self-possessed and distant from her mother, unable to share her innermost thoughts and feelings as she once had.

"I know, Mother," Linda spoke with her eyes downcast. "But that doesn't help much. He was such a liar. And the awful thing for me is that I felt sorry for him. I believed him. I didn't see how sneaky he really was, or how cruel, until it was too late. Almost too late," she added in a whisper. "If Stoner hadn't arrived when he did," again she shuddered uncontrollably.

"What really happened?"

In a low voice, Linda told her mother the story from the moment of turning Lew loose until Stoner gave her his shirt to cover herself with.

"I've never been so scared, and so embarrassed, and so...," as she ended her story her voice dwindled to silence.

"And so dirty," her mother smiled at her, sadly, with profound understanding.

"Yes," with an effort she returned the smile.

"I suppose a lot of women feel that way sometime in their life, those that have been physically molested, at least. So many of us seem to have a split personality about our bodies. If we give ourselves freely, in love, we think of it as something natural no matter how unsatisfactory. But if we're taken by force, well, we feel guilty as if we somehow share in the blame. We seem to feel that our forced participation, no matter how unwilling, has somehow debased us. It's not fair but that's the way it is."

Linda stared at her mother in shocked silence. For the first time since returning from the East she ached for the closeness the two of them had once had, two women in a world of men. She yearned for the mutual confidences and the occasional, unforgettable moments of shared laughter or tears. She wondered why a gulf of taboos had developed between them.

"Were you ever...?" she found it impossible to continue. Why, she asked herself, couldn't she be as open and honest with her mother as she had once been, and as her mother had always tried to be with her?

"Molested? Raped?" Mrs. Peters smiled regretfully at her daughter. She wondered if she and Jacob had been wrong in sending Linda east to finish her education. The girl had returned with too many of the sophisticated eastern mannerisms that she and Jacob had gladly left behind when they headed west. Worse, the East had somehow destroyed the bond that she and her daughter had once had. In some ways they had become strangers.

"Yes and no," she spoke thoughtfully, watching Linda carefully as she spoke. "I can't really say I was raped. What the law would say about it, I don't know. The church, I suspect, would blame me and the boy both. But the only important thing, for me, is what I thought about it and what I think about it now." She paused, worried that she might not be doing the right thing in sharing this episode of her life with her daughter. She had never told another soul about it, except her husband. "I was fourteen at the time. The boy was eighteen. He lived next door so I saw him a lot. He teased me and protected me from other boys. We laughed and played games. I thought we were a lot like brother and sister," Mrs. Peters laughed ruefully. "That was long before I realized how difficult it is for normal, healthy males and females to be friends, just plain old friends. And long before your father and I became sweethearts." She caught Linda's eyes with her own and held them. "The boy caught me in the barn one time when nobody else was at home. I fought him at first. But he was a lot bigger and stronger. He held me down until I quit struggling. Afterwards," she shrugged and smiled sadly, "I felt so terribly guilty. I thought I had been ruined forever. I was scared to death that I was pregnant, but luckily I wasn't. So life went on and I began to think of the episode as just one more experience in the shaping of my character. Maybe," she again smiled into her daughter's eyes, "maybe your father would have escaped my wiles if I'd been as innocent when we met as I was before that day in the barn. Who knows?"

"Your wiles?" Linda laughed softly, sadly. "I think I remember the story of how you trapped poor Dad. He was so smitten from the first time he saw you that he moped around after you until you took pity on him and proposed."

"I didn't tell you that," Mrs. Peters' laughter joined Linda's.

"Dad did. You know how he liked to tell fibs about you and him."

"Someday maybe I'll tell you the truth about our courting days."

Linda felt her curiosity rise. But she held her tongue. For the first time in years she felt the old affinity with her mother and she didn't want to do anything to destroy it.

"That boy," she returned to the story her mother had been telling, "did you...?"

"One mistake is enough," Mrs. Peters interrupted. "I wasn't physically attracted to him; I made sure he never caught me alone again. So, I guess he turned elsewhere. In any case, about a year later he left town. The rumor was that he barely escaped the two brothers and irate father of another girl."

"Men are all the same," Linda spoke disgustedly. "I get so tired of their stares and suggestive comments."

"How would you feel if they never looked at you?"

Startled at the question, Linda pondered for a while before answering. She knew what her mother was getting at. She knew her mother was probably right. But she still wished that men were less aggressive in expressing their desires. Most times she hated the ogling stares, the suggestive comments, and the not-very-subtle attempts to get her alone. Yet, ruefully, she had to admit that at times, from some men, she welcomed the same looks and comments and aggression that with other men and at other times she rejected.

"I know, Mother," she finally answered. "I wouldn't want to be a wallflower that men never wanted. But I just wish that more men were like Dad was."

Her mother looked at her, an amused smile on her lips, "I don't think you knew your father very well. When we first met he was a normal young man, hot-blooded and explosive but also gentle and compassionate when I got to know him. Those sharp eyes of his didn't miss much, including a beautiful woman's anatomy." She paused and studied her daughter, wondering if something more than her recent experiences in Chasco and on the Loma had embittered her a little. "I hope he enjoyed looking at a pretty woman to the day he died. There are many joys we have in this life. One of them is looking at beautiful things, at a sunset, a snowcapped mountain, the desert in bloom, children playing. Seeing them makes us feel more alive, I think. But there's an added something about looking at a beautiful specimen of the opposite sex. I suppose it's the tint of sexuality added to the beauty. I don't know what else it could be. But whatever it is, there's nothing else quite like it. It's different, just as enjoying the sky is different from enjoying a herd of cattle grazing on a mountain meadow."

"Mother," Linda exclaimed, bursting into delighted laughter. "I didn't know you were a poet."

"I didn't either," Mrs. Peters' laughter joined her daughter's. She was happy that she had made Linda laugh. She hoped the experience with the boy Lew would become just a minor incident in Linda's memory.

"I guess I never thought of Dad as a man," Linda confessed after the hilarity died away. "I mean," she interrupted herself, embarrassed, "he was my father and...."

"I know," Mrs. Peters interrupted. "I know. It's difficult to imagine your parents as real human beings like everyone else, with all the blundering and coarse passions that go with being human. You know they are, but, well, knowing and feeling are two different things." After Mrs. Peters' words, both women found themselves silent, at a momentary loss for something to talk about, slightly embarrassed. "What do you think of Jacob now?" Mrs. Peters broke the silence.

"Jacob?" Linda blurted, bewildered.

"Stoner, Jacob Stoner."

"Oh, the gunfighter. I'm sorry, Mother. I was still thinking of Dad."

"I know," Mrs. Peters smiled at her daughter. "I could see it in your eyes. But what do you think of him, of your gunfighter, now that you've had a chance to get to know him?"

Linda dropped her eyes from her mother's penetrating gaze. She didn't want anyone suspecting the powerful physical attraction she felt for Stoner, especially not her mother or Rob.

"He saved me from Nate Barstow yesterday," she spoke reluctantly. "He saved Rob and the men today, and me. I was so naive. I let that boy loose, not so much because I really believed what he told me, but because I was afraid of what Stoner might do to him. And I thought he was telling the truth about being scared and heading for the Bar B if he was untied." For her mother's benefit, she reiterated the story Lew had told her about his capture and also the story Stoner had told. "I still don't know who to believe."

"You would take the word of that brutal boy against Jacob's?"

Linda shrugged angrily, "I know I should be thankful to Stoner. I am. I'm thankful that he and Rob reached an agreement. I'm thankful he's going to help us against the Bartlemans." She paused and, seeing the irritation on her mother's face, tried to soften her words. "He can be thoughtful and gentle. I saw that side of him after he killed Lew, when he gave me his shirt to cover up with," she blushed. "But he's a killer, Mother. I saw that side of him too."

"There's a difference between a killer and a fighter who kills to protect himself or others, Linda," Mrs. Peters smothered her irritation at her daughter's intransigence. "Most of us human beings would kill to protect ourselves and our loved ones. Your father killed more than one man in the war and protecting this ranch. That didn't make him a killer. If we're forced to fight the Bar B, Rob may have to kill. I hope that doesn't make him a killer, not in the way you mean. And I don't think Jacob Stoner is a killer in that way, either. I don't think he kills because he enjoys it, or because of his temper, or because it's the easiest thing to do in a specific situation. If he was a killer, he'd have killed somebody in the Chasco saloon, or here on the porch. Oh, I know he's killed for money in the past. He told me so. But I think he's ashamed of it. I think it haunts him and that's one of the reasons he never stays in one place very long. His past catches up with him, so he runs from it. "

Suddenly Mrs. Peters realized how tenacious her angry defense of Stoner had become. Startled, she looked at her daughter. Both women smiled to show their understanding.

"He is interesting, Mother," Linda admitted. "But don't try to marry me off to the man. He's a gunfighter and when I marry I want a steady man like Dad was."

A little later Linda trudged off to bed. Mrs. Peters remained seated, waiting for Rob to return. When he did, she smiled happily to herself. He moved with a self-assurance she hadn't seen in him since his early adolescent years. They talked for a couple of hours about what needed to be done around the ranch. Then Rob also headed off to bed. Mrs. Peters sat on alone during what remained of the evening, thinking, remembering. When twilight turned to dusk, she lighted a lamp and began to read. What little remained of the evening light slowly turned into darkness. When the words became little more than a blur on the page, she doused the lamp and made her way to her own bedroom, feeling her way through the familiar house, her mind re-creating memories of her husband and their past together. Later she slept. She did not hear Stoner and the hands ride in.

12

The next morning, at Stoner's recommendation, Rob hired Dodge.

"I know you don't need another puncher," Stoner said. "But it can't hurt to have another gunhand around if this range war with the Bar B heats up. Until we know what the Bartlemans are going to do, we'll need somebody here at headquarters all the time, one more hand besides the cook. We don't want to leave your mother and sister unprotected, not after what happened yesterday. I don't think the Bartlemans'll try the same thing again," he shrugged, "but who knows?" He added, "You'll also need to keep a sharp eye out while you're working the ranch. It might be best to work all in a bunch and keep one man on guard all the time."

Rob agreed and a half hour later led his crew back toward the Loma, to fence the gully left open to Bar B cattle, to check and repair the fence for several miles both directions from the spring, and to drive any Bar B cattle missed the previous day back to their own range. He left Tall Will behind.

The tall cowboy and Stoner were leaning against the corral fence as the men rode out.

"I think I'll ride into town, try to get a feel for the Bartlemans and what they might do next," Stoner commented as he watched the horses and riders moving slowly down the middle of the valley.

"Yeah, I reckon the Bartlemans're still in Chasco," Tall Will too watched the slow-moving cavalcade. "Sam Bartleman won't be ridin' for some time, not with two busted ribs and a cracked collar bone. Old Joe, well, that shot of yours took a lot of flesh and some bone fragments with it. It didn't break nothin', but more'n likely the old man won't be usin' that shoulder for a while, maybe never like he did before you shot him."

"How do you know all that?" Stoner asked curiously.

"Sonora's surmise from the quick once-over he give them before Pate and Cactus carted them off. And Doc Zimmerman told Pate the same thing when the old drunk first looked his patients over."

"I might pay them a neighborly visit, ask them what their intentions are."

"Yeah," Will remarked drily, "and they might have some Bar B hands around standing guard or some such thing. The Bar B hands might not take kindly to neighbors calling without no invitation."

Stoner chuckled, "I reckon I could read them a passage from the good-neighbor book."

Tall Will shook his head and grinned, "What I meant was, you should take a friend like me with you. Some of the Bar B gunnies might be in town." He shuffled his feet in embarrassment, not meeting Stoner's eyes. "After yesterday, well, you saved my bacon out there on the Loma. If you go to town alone and get shot, I'm gonna have one hell of a time livin' with myself."

"Thanks, Will," Stoner felt a catch in his throat. It had been years since friendship had been offered to him with no strings attached. He held out his hand. "Friends?" the words came huskily from deep within him.

Will clasped the proffered hand in his own huge, calloused mitt. In spite of his efforts at self-control, his lips split in a broad grin and his eyes gleamed with happiness.

"I couldn't ask for a better pard," his voice too shook huskily.

"If you're through telling Stoner how great he is," Linda interrupted smilingly from nearby, addressing Will, "you can saddle Moccasin for me."

Neither man had seen her approach. Her words startled them. Stoner glanced rapidly around, cursing himself for a careless fool. He was standing in the open, an easy target from any number of ambush sights, yet his mind had been dwelling on other matters, completely ignoring the alert habits that years of danger had instilled in him. Uneasily he followed Linda and Will into the barn.

"I'm riding into town," he commented as Linda led her white-stockinged roan mare from its stall and held it while Will threw the saddle on and began tightening the cinches. "You can ride in with me. I don't want you riding around alone." He noticed Will try to hide a startled grin but the reason for it didn't strike his consciousness. "I figure the Bartlemans want you dead and I'm not sure about their foreman, but he may too. You...."

"You don't want what?" Linda didn't hear Stoner's last sentence. She had come to the barn prepared to deal in a friendly way with the gunfighter. He had saved her honor if not her life. Her mother liked the man. Rob now appeared to respect him. Both wanted to work with him. Stoner was a brave man, brave and, in a way, kind and considerate. She too had begun to admire him in spite of what he was. But his first words and the peremptory tone she heard conveying them fired her temper. Before she realized what she was doing the words escaped her.

Angered as much by her own words as by Stoner's, she turned to face him, hands on hips, eyes flaming.

Behind her, Tall Will's grin grew wider as he struggled to keep from bursting into a guffaw. More than once he had tried to convince Linda that riding alone was dangerous for her. Too many Bar B riders rode the mountains between their range and the Rocking H, too many grub-line cowboys and hunters roamed the mountains surrounding the valley. The latter occasionally camped in the valley at night, sometimes for several nights, beside the water or in one of the many canyons leading up into the hills. .

"Answer my question," Linda demanded haughtily, hands on hips and eyes blazing.

Stoner found his own temper flaring, in spite of the admiration he felt for the girl's independence.

"I don't think you should ride alone," he tried to smile but he felt the stiffness of his face and the anger in his eyes. "It's too dangerous."

"You want to ride with me, is that it?" Linda's voice oozed contempt.

"I didn't say that," Stoner gained control of his anger. He understood why Will was grinning. His command had been like that of a husband or father. He understood, but he couldn't smile at the humor nor could he apologize and start over, as he should. "What I said was, I'm riding to town. You're welcome to ride along."

Linda insisted on an honest answer, "Do you want me to ride with you?"

"I'd rather you ride with me than ride alone," Stoner stubbornly refused to answer her question directly.

"I'm not riding to town. I'm going for a ride."

"Where?"

"That's none of your business. You're my mother's hired gunfighter. You seem to have ingratiated yourself with her easily enough. Now you've also won Rob's favor. I can understand why. In the short time you've been here, you've saved us all. For that I'm grateful." She paused for a moment and added as if in reconciliation, "You're also very considerate. But as long as you stay here, you'd better remember one thing: I don't take orders very well, not from anyone, especially not from a hired hand."

"I don't think you should ride alone."

"I don't care what you think. I'm old enough to do what I want."

Linda stared at Stoner. She read the concern in his eyes and began to feel sorry for her reaction. She wondered if she was doing the right thing in ignoring his warning. A moment later, however, she shrugged off the momentary lapse. The man had no right to order her around.

Stoner returned the stare, mentally kicking himself for the clumsy way he had tried to stop the girl.

"What about taking Will along," he tried his hand at reconciliation. "I think that would make us all feel better, your mom, Will, me, Rob if he knew you were planning on riding alone."

Without a word, her anger beginning to return at Stoner's insistence, Linda pulled the reins of her roan from Will's hands, led the animal out into the open, and mounted.

To Stoner who, along with Will, had followed her through the door of the barn, she threw a few parting words over her shoulder as she kneed the roan around the corner of the corral and away from the buildings, "You work for my mother; give her your advice. My brother admires you, he says; give him advice if he wants it. But any advice you have for me, keep it to yourself. I don't want it."

Will and Stoner stood side by side, listening to the soft thuds of the animal dissipate at a trot down the valley.

"You have a way with the ladies," the tall puncher commented, chuckling.

"It comes natural," Stoner answered in disgust at himself. "They always do what I tell them, or else. That's plenty clear for anybody with eyes."

13

Later, by the time he was walking his mount into Chasco, his restless eyes studying the shadows and other potential ambush sites, Stoner had forced his confrontation with Linda from his mind. He had admitted to himself that she was correct. He had no right to interfere with her plans or actions. His agreements had been with Rob and Mrs. Peters, not Linda. Yet his admission didn't ease the worry he felt for her riding alone through the countryside.

He pulled the dusty black up to the railing before the Chasco Saloon, beside the three horses that already stood there dozing in the heat of the afternoon sun. He didn't recognize the brand on the animals, but didn't rule out that the riders worked for the Bar B. Inside the dim room of the saloon, he paused, letting his eyes become accustomed to the change in light and surveying the room as he did so.

At a card table sat three Bar B riders: Cal, Slicker, and Dobbs. They glanced up as Stoner entered but then returned to their game as if they didn't recognize him. He had the distinct feeling that they had known he was coming and were ready for him, that they were simply waiting for something, some sign, somebody, before they made their play.

He was right. And wrong.

The night before, the three and their comrades had arrived frustrated and irascible at Bar B headquarters. When they reported what had happened at the Loma Linda, Barstow's angry reaction did their tempers no good.

"One man took all of you?" he exclaimed, anger struggling with sarcasm in his tone. "Hell, I thought I sent men to do a man's job, not boys. The next time you can bet I will."

"You didn't do so well against that gunfighter yesterday," Slicker sneered.

The foreman glared at him without a word until he turned away.

"Give me five men and I'll go back out tomorrow and do the job right," Cal swore.

"You'll get your chance maybe. I just come back from seein' Joe in town. He's mad as a rattler a horse stepped on." He grinned without humor. "Wants the new Rockin' H gunhand taken care of. Pronto. You three," he nodded to Cal, Dobbs, and Slicker, "head for Chasco first thing in the morning. Hang around. If the gunfighter shows up, take him out. Make it look good, though. No back shooting, not in town," he growled. "Start a fight. The three of you should be able to take one man, if you don't let him sneak up on you again," he chuckled mirthlessly. "If you can't, hell, wait till he leaves town, follow him and shoot the bastard in the back."

Barstow stood silently watching the three gunhands, a faint sneer touching his lips. The three turned away. Deciding that the Rocking H gunfighter might not ride into town, the foreman turned to another gunhand standing nearby, one of the men who had ambushed Rob and his hands on their ride to the spring.

"Think you can keep an eye on the Rockin' H, Thorn, trail the gunfighter when he rides out and put a bullet in him?"

"Yeah," Thorn smirked. "You want, I'll put a bullet in him right there at Rockin' H headquarters."

"No," Barstow shook his head, "Joe doesn't want any more shooting around the Peters women, not for a while anyhow." He chuckled. "The sheriff and a few of Chasco's respectable citizens visited him and Sam after the doc was through with them." His chuckle turned to a humorless guffaw. "They said they'd heard the gunfight started with the Peters women present. That upset them, said they didn't want to hear of anything happenin' to those two women. Seems they wouldn't accept Joe's word that the Rockin' H gunfighter started the shootin'." He paused, still grinning, "So no shootin' near the Rockin' H or around the women. Anyplace else...," he put his finger to his temple and spit on the floor of the bunkhouse.

In Chasco, as his vision adjusted to the dim light in the room, Stoner swung his eyes away from the three Bar B gunhands seated around the table. At the far end of the bar, leaning against the back wall of the saloon, stood the same bartender who had been there two days previously. Near him, slumped, his elbows supporting him on the bar, the youngest Bartleman was talking to the bartender.

Stoner moved over to the bar and took up a position near the front of the building, where he could face Matt Bartleman as well as keep an eye on the three men at the table. The bartender turned to face him and he ordered a beer.

"Mind if I join you?" Matt asked as the bartender was pouring Stoner's drink.

Surprised, Stoner looked more closely at the man. What he saw, he liked. Matt was tall, about Stoner's height, a little heavier, with a clean, strong, agile look about him. He was freshly shaved and his hair had been trimmed recently. He had piercing grey eyes, high cheekbones and a square chin. There was something honest and open about the way he looked at a person.

"I'll buy," Stoner answered Matt's question. "I see your beer's gone."

"I usually don't drink this time of the day," Matt walked over to join Stoner. "But I guess two beers won't hurt me none."

The bartender drew the second beer, set the drinks in front of the two men, and withdrew to the far end of the bar.

"You weren't very sociable the last time we met," Stoner grinned, raising his beer in salute.

Shrugging, Matt forced an answering grin, "Nope. But neither were you. Leastways I wouldn't call it friendly to knock a man out of the saddle, not when all he's got to land on is the hard ground."

"I don't remember."

Matt raised his beer to return Stoner's salute and to accept what he took as a peace offering. "Me, I forgot too," he said.

The two changed the subject and talked about conditions in the valley, about ranching, grass, the weather, and the people.

Finally Matt broached what was eating at his insides. "You should talk the Peterses into selling out and moving someplace else," he spoke slowly, softly, as if the words hurt.

"Why?"

"You know why," Matt spoke with irritation. "You knew why when we rode in to the Rocking H yesterday, else you wouldn't have reacted so fast. No need for me to say it."

"You don't think your pa'll back off."

"No," Matt stared into his empty glass. "He wants the Rocking H. So does Sam. They won't neither one back off."

"You?" Sam asked curiously.

"I'm satisfied with what we got, but Sam and Pa have the say-so, not me," Matt answered, his tone apologizing for his lack of control over his brother and father. "I got them to back off when Jacob Peters closed the Loma Linda spring to us. I've been able to keep them in line since, mostly, although they don't always let me know what they're gonna do. But they planned the Rocking H set-to without letting me know what they were planning. I thought we were gonna offer to buy Mrs. Peters out, nothing more." He shook his head angrily and stopped talking, deciding he had said too much. For the past twenty-four hours his mind had been a battleground where his values and his loyalty struggled for dominance. Neither side had won yet; the battle raged on. But he was slowly reaching a compromise, one that made him sick inside, but one that had made it possible for him to talk to Stoner and warn the man. He would follow his father wherever the older man led, except for killing the Peters women. "But I can't stop them," he finally added. "They want the Rocking H and they'll get it one way or another."

"Will you stay out of the fight?" Stoner asked, hoping the answer would be yes but certain it would be no. His respect for Matt Bartleman had grown considerably in the past few minutes, as had his like for the man. He didn't want to fight him. But he didn't see any way to avoid it. He knew Matt would remain loyal to his father and brother. And he was certain Matt was right about the two; they wouldn't give up until they had the Rocking H.

"I can't do that," Matt answered with anguish. "All I can hope to do is slow them down and keep them from hurting Linda and Mrs. Peters. And I have doubts about being able to do that."

Neither man spoke for a long while. Matt toyed aimlessly with his beer glass. Stoner divided his attention between Matt, the bartender, and the three men at the table, who seemed completely absorbed in their game. When Matt again began speaking, he talked of his father's role in settling the valley and making it safe from renegade Apaches and outlaws.

"He thinks he's earned a right to as much of the land as he wants," Matt commented.

Soon afterwards, he left. Stoner ordered another small beer, planning to drink it and then find a place to eat. After eating, as he had told Matt, he would talk to Joe and Sam Bartleman, try to talk them out of going ahead with their attempts to take over the Rocking H. It wouldn't do any good, he figured, but it wouldn't hurt to try. If nothing else, it would give him another chance to size up the two men.

"Matt don't have much say-so about what the Bar B does. His paw and Sam run the whole shebang."

At the words Stoner turned to face the table where the Bar B riders were sitting. The three men had not moved, but they were no longer pretending to be absorbed in their game. Suddenly he realized why they were there and what they had been waiting for--the departure of Matt Bartleman. Briefly he considered that Matt had been in on the set-up, but immediately he rejected the thought. He didn't believe Matt was a man who would send others to do his killing for him.

"And they don't want you around," Cal continued talking, a killing light in his eyes and a sneer on his lips.

Stoner studied the three. A thick bandage covered Cal's nose, with a thin piece of cloth slanting down under both cheekbones and around the back of his neck to hold the bandage in place. Both eyes glared at Stoner from out of thick black semi-circles.

Stoner grinned. "How's your nose?" he asked Cal as he studied the young Bar B rider's companions. Dobbs met his probing eyes with a cold stare, his hand suggestively caressing the butt of his .45. This time, unlike yesterday, Slicker also met his glance. Their eyes locked for several seconds before the Bar B gunman smirked and shifted his gaze to some point on Stoner's chest.

Stoner noted that Cal was wearing two pistols slung low, his companions a single sidearm each.

"Go to hell," Cal angrily answered his question.

"I reckon I will someday," Stoner slowly stepped away from the bar, forcing a wider grin as he returned Cal's angry glare. "But I reckon you'll beat me there."

"No," Cal laughed suddenly, the noise harsh, menacing in the quiet of the saloon, "I reckon I'll be drinkin' beer and lovin' the girls long after the cactus covers your grave. Fact is, you'd better say your prayers now, before it's too late."

As Cal spoke, he and his companions stood up. Dobbs began inching to the right, Slicker to the left. Cal remained where he stood, behind his chair, the anchor in the deadly game of crossfire the three were planning.

"Yesterday you had all the aces," Cal continued, his lips split in an attempted grin which made him look like a cornered coyote snarling at its tormentor. "Today we've got three of them to your one. I figure this hand's ours and your life's the pot. We...."

Suddenly the saloon door swung open and Matt Bartleman re-entered. The three Bar B punchers froze in place, Cal's words fading in mid-air. Stoner crouched as if preparing to leap at his enemies, his hand tensed inches from his Colt, and his eyes turned the color of slate.

"Wait," Matt reacted to Stoner's move, slowly raising his arms to shoulder height. "Like I told you before, I'm not lookin' for trouble until Paw and Sam push me into it." He glanced disgustedly at the three Bar B punchers. "This wasn't my doing. I didn't set these three on you." Careful to make no aggressive moves, he stalked forward until he stood beside Stoner, then turned to face the three men. "You three better ride on back to the ranch," he ordered. "There'll be no shooting here today."

None of the three made a move.

Finally Cal spoke. "I figure you're the one better leave," he addressed Matt but his eyes never left Stoner. "After what he did yesterday at the Rockin' H and at the Loma spring your pa'll pay us a bonus to get rid of him. Besides, this is personal. No man's gonna do what he did to me and live."

"Paw sent you?"

"Naw," Cal smirked, lying easily since the orders had come from Barstow, "but you know as well as I do what he'd say about it."

Matt shrugged with irritation. He knew Cal was right. His father, Sam, Nate Barstow, and almost every rider at the Bar B would be happy to see Stoner dead. The gunfighter had made them all look like fools. But Matt didn't like the odds, three against one. And, in the short time they had talked, he had begun to like and respect Stoner. The man was no killer, nor was he hunting trouble.

"I know what Pa'd say about it," he agreed with Cal. "But I know what I'd think about it too, and I say no." He stared at Cal, his eyes cold and his face taut. "I also know what your problem is, Cal. I was standing outside the door there, listening. I figured you three were here to get Stoner. That's why I hung around." Bitterness crept into his voice. "You're right about one thing. My sayso doesn't go far at the Bar B. Paw and Sam run the ranch. If you ignored me and went ahead and killed Stoner, they'd probably pay you a bonus. But" he continued in a ringing tone, "if you killed me, they'd follow you to hell and back to make you pay. We Bartlemans stick together."

"We ain't gonna kill you," Dobbs cut in, "only him."

"I'm with him," Matt spoke with a calm confidence he didn't feel. He had never killed a man, and in the brief gunfight at the Rocking H the day before he hadn't even gotten his gun out of its holster. He didn't know how he would react if the shooting began. "You draw on him, you draw on me because I'll be drawing and shooting too."

Stoner remained silent, watching the three Bar B punchers as Matt talked. He noted their angry reaction to Matt's words. He noticed that after the first flash of anger Slicker's body relaxed and his hand moved away from his sidearm. That leaves two, Stoner thought.

"We don't want to kill you, Matt," Cal's words came out stubborn and clipped with anger. It was easily apparent that it was not friendship that forced him to speak. "But we're gonna kill that sneakin' bastard beside you. You get in the way, you'll get hurt and it won't be our fault."

"Not me," Slicker began sidling toward the door as he spoke. "I don't like the odds no more and I ain't gonna kill no Bartleman. They pay my wages," his eyes touched Stoner's face furtively and moved on. "Anyhow, I can wait."

"Damn you, Slicker," Cal shouted, fury and fear mingling with his words. "We made a deal with Nate."

"We still got a deal, but some other time," Slicker's answer floated over his shoulder as he edged through the door, his eyes never quite looking directly at Stoner but at the same time never losing sight of him.

"Your play," Stoner chuckled, looking first at Cal and then at Dobbs.

"I'll kill you you dirty son of...."

Cal exploded with blind rage. His hand grabbed for his Colt as the words spewed from his lips.

Before he could drag his pistol from of its holster, three things happened. Stoner's .45 slipped into his hand before Cal's fist had settled firmly around the handle of his weapon. Matt's pistol settled at hip level a moment after Stoner's. And Dobbs grabbed Cal with both arms, lifting the younger man off the floor and holding him there, helpless, his arms trapped at his sides. Cal struggled wildly, cussing and threatening Dobbs and all his ancestors for all time. For some seconds the struggle continued, but the younger man remained helpless, his feet hanging a few inches from the floor, his arms paralyzed. Finally he quit struggling.

"Let me down, Dobbs," he gritted.

"Okay, but we're leavin' peaceful-like unless you want to die alone. Besides, I agree with Slicker. I ain't gonna fight no Bartleman."

Cal tried to shrug. His eyes were locked on the pistol in Stoner's hand. He hadn't noticed Matt's draw.

"You should've killed me," he spoke with barely controlled fury, "because I'll get you if it's the last thing I do."

"I'll remember that the next time we meet."

"You do that, but there won't be no warnin'."

Cal's words shook with the fury in him. When Dobbs let him loose, he turned and, without another word, stomped from the saloon.

For a moment Dobbs stood silently facing Stoner.

"What he said goes for me too. So watch your back," he threatened expressionlessly before turning and following Cal.

"Sorry," Matt apologized when the door swung closed behind Dobbs, shoving his sidearm into its holster and turning to face Stoner as he spoke. "I should've sent those three back to the ranch earlier, before I left the room, but I didn't figure they'd follow orders, not from me anyway."

Stoner holstered his own pistol as he met Matt's embarrassed gaze. He grinned and shrugged his relief.

"I owe you one. Those three wanted to break me permanent-like. When you took a hand in the game, Slicker and Dobbs folded. Cal didn't have the cards to stay so he tried to steal the pot. It didn't work."

"Like Dobbs said," Matt cautioned, "watch your back. All three of those men'll shoot you in the back if they get a chance."

"Thanks," Stoner stuck out his hand and, without hesitation, Matt grasped it firmly. Stoner had already decided, the previous day, what kind of men Cal, Dobbs and Slicker were. The recent confrontation had simply reinforced his understanding. But he appreciated the gesture of friendship in Matt's warning.

"You still going over to see Pa and Sam?"

"Planning on it but I was hoping to grab a bite first."

"I'll tell you what," Matt offered. "I'll buy. That should give the good people of Chasco something to talk about, us eating together." At Stoner's quizzical expression, he explained, "Hell, the rumors are already spreading like a grass fire--about what you did here in the saloon, about the fiasco at the Rocking H, about the Bar B fracaso on the Loma. You've become something of a folk hero in the few hours you've been here and the conflict between the Bar B and Rocking H has already become a full-fledged range war in the imagination of the people. I heard this morning that you're the first of several gunfighters Mrs. Peters has sent for." He didn't mention that he had been present when the sheriff and delegation of concerned citizens visited his father and Sam.

Stoner shook his head with exaggerated dismay, "Yeah, after me come Bill Longley and Wes Hardin, and Clay Allison should arrive in a few weeks, but I don't know how the news got out. It was supposed to be a secret."

Both young men chuckled and, at Stoner's acceptance of Matt's offer, headed toward Chasco's single restaurant.

"I'm surprised Mrs. Peters hired you," Matt commented as they walked across the street, turning serious and showing a slight nervousness as he spoke. "I never figured her for hiring a rider with a gun rep."

Stoner studied Matt's face for a few moments, wondering what lay behind the question and pointed reference to his reputation with a gun. He decided to be as honest as Matt had been about his father and brother and about what the Peters family could expect from them.

"I was passing through Chasco, on my way west-- Prescott maybe, maybe toward Yuma and on to Los Angeles. Just riding with no particular destination." Stoner spoke with an apologetic grin. "I decided to stop for a drink and supplies. Chance put me in that saloon at the time your foreman decided to rough up Linda Peters." He shrugged. "I don't reckon you'd have let him paw her around either." At Matt's grunt of agreement, he continued. "Then she needed help getting Rob home. He was a little stoned."

Matt laughed, "Out of his mind and off his feet, I heard."

Stoner grinned and nodded agreement.

"She wanted help getting him out to the ranch. I agreed."

The two young men had stopped in front of the restaurant. Stoner glanced at Matt from the corners of his eyes as he spoke, a half-smile on his lips.

"Don't tell me you would refuse Linda Peters in distress."

Matt guffawed loudly, "I'm guilty like most every man in the valley. If she crooked her finger, I'd ride through hell."

"I reckon," Stoner agreed. "And out at the ranch I fell for Mrs. Peters. Two women like that? What the hell. I'm only human. If my mother was living, I'd want her to be like Mrs. Peters. If I had a sister, I'd want her to be like Linda Peters."

"Sister, hell!" Matt exploded with another burst of laughter. "Girl friend or wife, you mean. Don't give me that sister crap. Linda Peters is every man's dream."

The eyes of the two young men met in complicity. His half-grin still in place, Stoner agreed, "She sure makes my dreams worth having."

Laughing, the two entered the restaurant. Less than an hour later they emerged and walked toward the outskirts of town.

"That's her house, the woman I told you about, Dad's friend," Matt pointed to a small white house standing off by itself. "Her name's Nellie Thurston. She's a widow woman. Her husband died in a hunting accident a couple of years before Maw died." He paused as if embarrassed. "Dad helps her out a lot. He stays there when he's in town."

Stoner made no comment. He didn't see any need for one.

"I don't know how Paw's gonna take this," Matt shrugged nervously, "or Sam."

"You don't have to go with me."

"Yeah, I do," Matt stared at the house, his mouth set in a stubborn line. "If I'm along and they see we're friendly and all, they may decide to accept a truce."

"I hope," Stoner shook his head. "But from everything I've heard about them and what I've seen I wouldn't bet money on it."

"Why you gonna talk to them then? If you don't think there's any chance of them backing off?"

"Hope, like I said," Stoner's words were terse, but he softened them with a forced grin. "And the Peters women. For them I've gotta try."

At Matt's knock a pleasant female voice invited him in.

"I've got someone with me," Matt called through the open doorway.

"Come on in, Matt, and bring the gunfighter in too, but carefully," shouted a voice Stoner recognized as belonging to Joe Bartleman. "I've got a pistol so tell him not to make any quick moves."

"Put your gun away, Paw," Matt yelled as he led the way into the shadowy interior of the house, through the parlor, and into what Stoner took for Mrs. Thurston's bedroom. "He wants to talk. Besides, you can't shoot with your left hand. You'd wind up shootin' yourself or me or...hell," he added half-humorously as he and Stoner entered the room and he could see his father lying on the bed, with Nellie standing nearby, "maybe even Nellie."

"Ah-huh, well, maybe I should shoot you," Joe growled, "comin' in here with the man that shot me and your brother."

"I didn't know Sam had been shot."

"Don't be a smartass. Go on in the other bedroom and talk to your brother. Leave us alone."

Matt hesitated. Then, with a careless shrug, he left the room. As Joe Bartleman snapped at his son his eyes searched Stoner coldly.

"You've got nerve," when he finally spoke his voice was as cold as his eyes. "You come traipsin' in here packin' a weapon. Hell, I could shoot you and wouldn't no one say much."

Stoner studied the old man's face. Missing was the killing light he had seen out at the Rocking H, but it had been replaced by an uncompromising stubbornness glaring sullenly across the room. Joe Bartleman, Stoner figured, was a man who would kill for many reasons. In that way he didn't differ much from a lot of men. He was also a man with no compromise in his soul. He was ambitious. And he was a killer. One way or the other he would get what he wanted if he lived, even if it took a life-time and even if he had to kill anyone and everyone who stood in his way. He seemed out of place in the soft atmosphere of the bedroom, a softness created by lace doilies on the furniture, a bright Afghan on the bed, and water colors hanging from the walls. Stoner wondered if Nellie Thurston created the paintings herself and, if she did, what attracted her to Joe Bartleman.

"Maybe," Stoner answered Joe's threat, looking the older man in the eye, the makings of a smile on his lips. "Maybe you could shoot me. But the way you're holding that Colt, I'd say Matt's probably right. You'd hit anything but what you shot at, if you got the hammer back in time."

"Yeah," Joe rumbled, "I couldn't hit the floor once in three shots with my left hand. Which means I ain't very bright havin' a weapon in my hand at all. You could've killed me and called it self-defense."

"I don't reckon," Stoner chuckled drily. "Not without getting shot myself, anyhow. That isn't a prayer book Mrs. Thurston's holding," he nodded toward the woman's right arm. It hung in apparent relaxed innocence at her side, but barely visible behind the folds of her skirt was the black metal of some kind of small pistol. A derringer, Stoner figured. "And Matt, he made it plenty clear he's a Bartleman all the way. No, I came to talk peace, not commit suicide."

Joe hesitated for a few moments, looking Stoner over thoughtfully. Dobbs had reported earlier that morning about the events up on the Loma Linda. Joe had exploded at the failure of his men to take over the Loma Linda range, but his rage had soon burned to hot embers, becoming a controlled fury, as had his anger at his own failure at the Rocking H. He had begun to think clearly again, and to plan. He wanted the Rocking H. It had the best grazing land and the most stable water supply in the valley. With it, he could double the size of his herd. He would be the biggest rancher in the valley, one of the biggest in the territory. The thought of the prestige and power the Rocking H would bring him sent a faint smile glittering into the depths of his eyes and over his lips.

With an effort he forced his mind back to the moment. To take over the Rocking H, he once again reflected, he would have to get rid of the gunfighter standing near the door of the bedroom, unless he could find a way to do away with Mrs. Peters first, and maybe her son. He studied the man through narrowed eyes: a tall man in tattered jeans and cotton shirt, about the size of Sam and Matt, more slender, but heavier in the shoulders and arms, with bottomless blue eyes that seemed to balance between humor and death as if whatever happened could tip his emotions either way. His forehead was rectangular, his nose and mouth large, his cheekbones high and prominent, his chin square, the whole giving the impression of having been chiseled from stone, then sun-browned and weather-beaten until all excess flesh had ages since been stripped away. He wore a single Colt .45 on his right hip, low down with the holster tied around his leg.

Joe knew he faced a dangerous man, maybe the most dangerous man he had ever run into, but he was curious about what the gunfighter had to say. So he fought his anger in stony silence until he had himself under control.

"How's Sam?" Stoner broke the silence.

"The doctor gave him something for the pain. He's resting in the other bedroom," Mrs. Thurston answered the question, nodding her head toward the rear of the house and glancing at Stoner.

Stoner returned her nod.

"Peace?" Joe snorted derisively, glaring at Stoner, ignoring the question about Sam in his reaction to Stoner's earlier comment. "You shoot me and put Sam down with broken bones. You ambush Bar B hands and kill one of them, maybe two since Tate ain't showed up yet. You push our cattle off the water and grass up on the Loma. And you say you come in here to talk peace? I'll be damned."

"Tate headed north, for his health. Lew tried to rape Linda Peters; I caught him in the act," Stoner fought to repress a smile at Joe's verbal attack. I'll bet the man has two legal systems, he told himself wryly, a flexible one for himself and a rigid one for everybody else.

He hesitated in order to collect his thoughts. "As for you and Sam, you know damned well you were set to start shooting. I just beat you to it."

"That lush Rob Peters drew first. He...."

"I'll be damned," Stoner laughed mirthlessly. "Let's forget what happened at the Rockin' H. What do you want...really want...and don't tell me you want the Rockin' H."

"That is what I want," Joe glared at Stoner. "And I'll get it someday. The Bar B is the future of this valley. With the Rockin' H I can double my herd, put three times as much land in hay and grain as I've already got, hire twice the crew I already do, maybe more. As it is," he sneered, "Mrs. Peters and her brats'll lose the place in a few years anyway."

"Maybe," Stoner suppressed his irritation, returning Joe's glare. "But not without a fight."

"With what? Why?" Joe scoffed. "I wouldn't expect a wandering gunfighter to understand the vision I have."

"Vision or ambition?"

"What's the difference?" Joe shook his head scornfully. "I plan to unite this whole valley under one brand someday, the Bar B. I'll take care of the men that are with me. I'll crush anyone who gets in the way. The Rockin' H is the first step."

Joe's words startled Stoner into silence. The seconds ticked by on a large clock standing in the corner of the room. Most men, Stoner thought, would have hidden such ambitions or dressed them in more subtle words.

"What do the other ranchers say about that?" Stoner finally asked, aware of how hollow the question sounded.

Joe smiled coldly, "You're simpler than I thought. I'd be stupid to tell anybody what I planned to do, don't you think?"

"You told me."

Joe's eyes expressed his disdain and shrewdness. "You're a stranger here, a hired gun, a good one, but still a hired gun. Me and my boys could shoot you down or have you shot by somebody else, in a gunfight, from ambush, whatever, and nothing would ever come of it if nobody saw the backshooting. The sheriff would make a little noise, bury you, go through the motions of an investigation, and forget the whole matter in a week. Why? Because, like I said, you're a stranger here in the valley and I'm not. You're a nobody with a horse, a saddle, and guns. That's all. Me, I've been here since before this town was a town and I've had the Bar B almost that long. I'm a property owner. Compared to most people around the valley, I'm rich." Again Joe's eyes smiled their scorn. "But you're a fighter. A good one, I'll have to give you that. I don't want to fight you if I can get around it. You might get lucky and kill me or one of my sons. And besides, I could use a man like you. You're not only a fighter but you're smart," Joe stared thoughtfully at Stoner before continuing. "So I'm willing to let bygones be bygones and double your salary to come to work for the Bar B."

"If I don't take your offer?" Stoner asked.

"Leave the valley or you're a dead man."

"You don't give a man much choice."

Joe shrugged, "Enough."

"I was hoping we could reach some compromise. I was going to offer the Bar B use of the Loma Linda spring."

"For what I want the spring's worthless without the grass on the Rockin' H side of the fence. There ain't enough graze on my side for more'n a couple hundred head."

"I'd say that's plenty."

"Not for me it ain't."

"We could have maybe worked something out."

"We will. I will."

"Mrs. Peters won't give the spring up without a fight."

"How much of a fight is the question."

"No deal then?"

"I made you an offer."

"Yeah, I reckon," Stoner let his disgust show in the words. "An offer, and a threat if I don't accept it. I made you an offer too, use of the spring on the Loma. If you don't figure you can use it, that's your decision. But leave the Rockin' H and the Peterses alone."

"Or?" Joe grinned wolfishly.

"Or I'll come looking for you."

"If Mrs. Peters gives you leave," Joe laughed contemptuously.

Realizing that his attempted peace offering had failed, Stoner backed out of the room and left the house.

14

When Linda rode away from the corrals of the Rocking H, leaving Stoner and Tall Will staring after her, she reined her mount toward the desolate hills to the north. She wanted to avoid meeting other riders, any riders, including those from the Rocking H. She wanted to think and, she admitted to herself, she was afraid of riding where she might run into anyone from the Bar B. The incidents of the past two days had frightened her more than she wished to admit.

But anger predominated at the present time. She urged her horse to a dead run, soon entering the uneven ground that led into the higher mountains. When the house and corrals had disappeared beneath the broken horizon behind her, she coaxed her mount to a walk. A little later she found the faint trail she planned to follow.

As she rode, she cursed herself and she cursed Stoner, Stoner because of his presumption, herself because she had let her anger show again. Slowly, however, the gentle rocking motion of the animal under her and the rhythmic thudding of its hooves on the hard, sandy earth soothed her anger. She began to realize how childish her reaction had been. No matter how domineering his words had sounded to her ears, he had only been thinking of her welfare. He had probably not meant to order her around. Nor, from the look he had given her when she accused him of it, had he been trying to use the threat of danger to get her to go riding with him. He had simply been afraid for her.

"The man just rubs me the wrong way," she spoke aloud, patting her horse's neck when its ears turned toward her and it began to prance nervously. "Why?"

"Because of the physical attraction?" She formed the words to herself, embarrassed to say them out loud even with no one around to hear. More than once she had felt a pleasant warmth in her loins and a shortness of breath when some part of her body had come into contact with Stoner's or when they had been standing so close together that she could smell his maleness or sense the heat radiating from his body.

She was no innocent little teenager. She had been around aggressive males all her life. She had been around animals all of her life. She had been aware of the natural male/female relationship at least by the time she had learned to ride, if not before. And, being a good-looking girl and there not being enough girls to go around in the valley as she was growing up, she had had to fight off her share of over-zealous suitors even before she passed through puberty. And her situation had not been so very different back east. Men were men wherever they lived, she had decided; they thought that being men gave them certain rights.

So, she asked herself, why the hostility toward Stoner? There had to be something besides the fact that he turned her on physically. She had had similar sexual responses to other men, but she hadn't become so irritated whenever they suggested something was or was not in her best interest. Did she react so negatively to Stoner because his aggressiveness, in most cases, showed no signs of desire? She didn't think so. There had never been a scarcity of men wanting to take care of her, to tell her what to do and when to do it, sometimes sexually motivated, sometimes not. She had not necessarily found such demands offensive in the past, until the attempts at control became possessive. She had simply ignored them, told the source where to get off, or obeyed as her temper of the moment dictated.

So why did Stoner rub her the wrong way? As her horse walked higher and higher along the winding trail, she considered the events of the past two days, slowly, step by step, playing them over in her mind.

When she had completed her analysis, she again concluded that the problem lay in her, not in Stoner. He had only done what he considered necessary. He had saved her considerable embarrassment, maybe worse, in the Chasco saloon. At the Rocking H he had reacted to a perceived threat from the Bartlemans. He had saved her from being raped at the Loma Linda, possibly from being killed afterwards, and he had saved Rob and the other hands after she, Rob and Will had given him such a vicious beating.

So why, she asked herself again...why did she react so angrily when he tried to keep her from riding alone? Because he was a man who made his living with a gun? She didn't think so, although that was part of the reason. She had concluded that her mother was right. Stoner was a man who was good with a gun, but not a man whose gun was for hire. Because he had taken command of the Rocking H so easily? Earlier yes, she had been angry and suspicious when she had conspired with Rob to force him off the ranch. But no longer. She now agreed with her mother; Stoner had no interest in the Rocking H other than helping the owners.

So why? Why did Stoner irritate her so at times? She topped a rise from which the pond behind the ranch house was partially visible between two rocky peaks. She pulled her mount to a halt and sat staring at the tiny silver sheen of water. Twisted piles of boulders and scorched clumps of sagebrush and cactus dotted the barren slopes around her. Before her the land fell away for almost a quarter of a mile. The trail followed the slope downhill for half that distance, then curved and climbed again.

She sat her horse quietly for a long time, her eyes vaguely registering the desolate landscape surrounding her and the speck of water in the distance, images of Stoner floating through her consciousness. She tried to see him as she had seen him at first, a killer with a gun for hire. But the look in his eyes and the softness of his touch as he administered to her cuts and bruises at the Loma interfered. She again saw the look of surprise and delight on his face as he stared at her on the previous morning, on the porch, and the angry scorn with which he faced Nate Barstow and the other Bar B riders in the saloon.

Later, when she continued riding along the trail, she found herself singing happily.

She didn't notice the rider appear on a ridge several hundred yards in front and to her right. She didn't notice when some time later he trotted his horse out of a narrow canyon and rode into a stand of red cedar through which the trail wound. She didn't notice her horse's ears as they flickered forward, tracking the movements of the strange horse. When the trail skirted the lower edge of the trees, she didn't see the man sitting his horse half-hidden in the shadow of a bushy cedar.

"You've got a nice voice," he spoke when she had approached to within several feet of him.

She jerked, startled. For a moment she couldn't speak. Her heart beat wildly and her breath came in gasps.

"My God," she whispered hoarsely when she finally got her breathing under control. "You scared me. You shouldn't sneak up on a person like that."

"It wasn't difficult," Nate Barstow grinned at her suspiciously. "You'd think you were riding out to meet your best beau, the way you were singing and riding along as blind as you please. I could've driven a herd of steers up here, I think, and you wouldn't of known it till the first one rammed your horse."

"I guess," Linda answered tersely. The memory of Nate Barstow's hand on her blouse, dragging her across the saloon floor, assaulted her mind. She felt anger seeping into her gut, anger that didn't quite dispel the fright that had been part of her first reaction to his greeting. What was Barstow doing on this trail, she asked herself. Few people rode the mountains they were in. Fewer used the trail; it led nowhere but rather made a wide loop around the base of Puerco Mountain and returned to where it had started. It passed through some of the most desolate land in the area, a land filled mostly with rocks, brush, cactus, and an occasional stand of red cedar.

"You shouldn't ride alone out here," Barstow abruptly turned the conversation. "Outlaws sometimes hole up in the brakes back there," he pointed toward the base of Puerco Mountain. "I've seen plenty of bear and cougar up here too, and once or twice a bronco Apache. It ain't safe."

"This seems to be my day for masculine concern about my welfare," Linda's voice dripped with sarcasm. "I received the same lecture from Stoner before I left the ranch. I'll tell you the same thing I told him. Where I ride and whether I ride alone or not is my business. Not Stoner's, not yours, not anybody's but mine."

She started to rein her horse on down the trail. But while she had talked Barstow had eased his mount up next to hers. Before her horse could turn its head, he grabbed its bridle.

"Don't be so bad-tempered," he spoke harshly and then chuckled. "And don't be in such a hurry. I want to talk."

Nate was in a good mood. As he had many mornings, he had left the Bar B to look for Linda with little hope of actually finding her. But luck had ridden with him this time. He had just reined his horse into a wooded area from which he had a clear view of the Rocking H house and outbuildings, a wooded area he used often to spy on her and the Rocking H, when she spurred her mount toward the northeast. He watched her until he realized she was taking the old game trail that circled Puerco Mountain. Then, carefully keeping to the low ground and making a wide circle away from the ranch buildings, he had made his way across the small valley of the Rocking H and ridden to head her off.

Several years before, when Linda left the valley, he believed they had been close to an understanding. He thought she liked him and would eventually become his girl, maybe even his wife. But she had changed in the East, as he had been afraid she would. She no longer appeared satisfied with the simple, rough life of the valley people. She had quit attending the socials and dances and other gatherings. She didn't stroll the streets and wander through the stores of Chasco on Saturday afternoons, talking and laughing with the other valley people. She had quit attending church on Sunday mornings. She had stopped being the happy, pleasant girl who would dance a man off his feet or challenge him to a horse race.

And she had rejected his advances. More than once she had ridden out of her way to avoid meeting him out on the range. Three times, shortly after her return, he had ridden to the Rocking H to see her. Each time, after a brief chat, claiming she had to work on the ranch accounts, she had withdrawn to her room. She hadn't appeared again while he remained at the ranch. Later he had run into her several times in Chasco, but she had avoided being caught alone with him. During the first few months of her return to the valley, she had occasionally attended the dances in town. But even there she had avoided dancing or being alone with him whenever she could do so without making a scene. She also avoided dancing with the Bartlemans and the other Bar B hands. Then she quit attending the dances and began appearing in Chasco only in the company of her mother, her brother, or one of the Rocking H hands.

He decided that the rift between the two ranches had caused the rift between him and her. He considered quitting the Bar B and hiring on with the Rocking H. But he quickly rejected the thought. He knew the Bartlemans planned to take over the Rocking H and he didn't want to fight them unless the pot was sweet enough--say, Linda along with her half of the Rocking H. For that kind of a pot he would sit in on the game as more than a tool of others, maybe take care of the Bartlemans himself. Or hire it done. He knew where he could find men who would do away with anybody for a few dollars, no questions asked. A couple of them already rode for the Bar B. There were others who didn't work for the Bartlemans hanging around Chasco and the mountains south of it, waiting for an offer; like vultures, they sensed that before long men would die in the valley and they wanted their share of the blood money.

"Take your hands off my horse," Linda gritted.

"Come on," he forced himself to remain calm even though he could feel the red creeping up his neck. "I just wanta talk. You've been avoidin' me ever since you came back, like I had the plague or something. Hell, you didn't used to treat me like dirt. We were good friends before you left."

"Friends? What do you mean?"

"I mean we went riding together some. You went to dances with me. You let me kiss you. You said you liked me better than most of the other guys."

"I was a kid then," Linda explained as she continued trying to pull her horse from his grasp. "And I don't remember going out with you more than once or twice. Besides, people change when they grow up."

"I didn't," he insisted accusingly. "I mean, I didn't change. I'm the same man I was when you left."

"The other day, in the saloon, you didn't seem like the same man. You were an animal."

Nate let go of her horse's bridle and slumped in the saddle.

"I'm sorry about that," he groaned. "I had too much to drink. I wouldn't have done it if I hadn't. I sometimes get that way when I drink."

"You didn't used to," Linda commented softly, beginning to feel sorry for the man. She had liked him before she went east. Liked him, that was all, in spite of what he seemed to think. She had enjoyed his company, but there had been no love or anything physical between them as far as she was concerned, other than childish flirting and petting. When she returned, any interest she had had in him was gone. He was too aggressive, too intolerant of anything that stood in his way. He kept waylaying her in town, or at the Saturday night dances, or when she was out riding. He appeared at the ranch unannounced and uninvited. Her reaction had been to avoid him completely.

Nate shrugged off her comment. "A man sometimes drinks too much when his girl won't have anything to do with him. For you I'd quit drinking." He looked her over with a forced grin and continued, "I'd do about anything, I reckon."

"Yes," Linda said sarcastically, "like drag me across a barroom floor as if I were a sack of corn. And I'm not your girl."

"I said I was sorry," Nate glared at her. His voice had changed. So had his face. The pleading note had disappeared. Something cold and unbending had appeared in its place. Nervously Linda edged her horse away from him.

"We were friends," she said, studying his face for signs of violence. He had never been a kind and considerate man, she thought, and he had often been brutal with other men, even his friends, but before two days ago there had never been a reason for her to fear him. She found herself comparing him to Stoner, then angrily rejected the comparison. "That's all, just friends," she added. "We had some good times together."

"We can have some more good times," Nate spoke hopefully.

"No," she shook her head. "Not after the other day. I won't put up with that kind of treatment, not from anyone."

"I told you I was drunk," he interrupted indignantly. "It won't happen again."

"It better not. If you touch me again like that, I'll shoot you. I'll...," she stopped talking in mid-sentence, appalled at what she had said and at what she was about to say.

Nate burst out laughing. "That's more like it. That's the way I remember you before you went east, feisty as all hell and not taking crap from anybody. I'd just about decided you'd been ruined by all that two-faced, wishy-washy stuff they teach you in the schools. But maybe there's hope for you yet."

Linda smiled in spite of herself. She was well aware of Nate's scorn for teachers and for the East.

Her smile brought an answering smile to his face. They both visibly relaxed.

"I could ride with you for a while."

"I'd rather ride alone."

"You need someone to take care of you," Nate insisted stubbornly. "There's people in the valley that want you out of the way, and they don't care how."

Linda stared at him, startled. He could only be referring to the Bartlemans. She wondered if Stoner had been right, if the Bartlemans had come to the Rocking H to kill her and her family. With the thought came fear, and then a killing fury that purged her body of the weakness the fear had brought.

"The Bartlemans? They came to the ranch to kill us yesterday morning, didn't they?"

"I didn't say that," Nate's irritation pinched the corners of his eyes and turned his voice gruff. "I didn't even know they were headed for the Rocking H when they left. I found out later where they'd been, when a couple of the hands came back from Chasco."

"But you meant the Bartlemans when you said someone wanted us dead."

Nate decided he had talked too much. If the Bartlemans found out what he had told the girl, he would lose his job, maybe his life.

"I didn't say it was the Bartlemans," he tried to force a smile into his words but they rolled heavily from his tongue. "But that ain't the point. You can't go wandering around alone all the time. It ain't safe. There's lots of rough characters in the mountains all around the valley. You don't know what they might do if they caught you alone and unprotected up here. "Besides," he added lamely, seeing the anger building in her eyes, "you and your ma can't run the Rockin' H all by yourselves."

"You and Stoner must have been trained in the same school for would-be protectors of the fair sex," Linda commented sarcastically. "I can take care of myself, thank you. And my mother and I have Rob to help with the ranch, Rob and some very loyal punchers. We'll get by. Now," she added as she urged her horse on along the trail, "I'd like to finish my ride."

For an instant, frozen by her sudden move, Nate watched her ride away. Then anger at her rejection surged through him.

Violently he jabbed his spurs into his horse's flanks. With a frightened squeal and lunge the animal caught the girl's mare.

"Don't be so snooty," Nate growled, grabbing the reins from her hand. "You were a nice kid once, but you sure have grown up to be a shrew with a sharp tongue. I reckon you learned that from your teachers and eastern friends. Hell, don't I know it. Those damned hypocrites'd turn Wild Bill himself into a two-faced snob. They...."

"Let go," Linda gritted, swinging her fist in a looping roundhouse.

Her knuckles met Nate's nose at the precise moment when, still talking, he swung his face to glare at her. The impact sent tears rushing into his eyes and blood spurting from his nostrils. With an enraged yelp he grabbed the wounded member and at the same time swung his other fist, backhand. The fist missed Linda's ear and barely grazed the back of her head as her horse shied. If it had connected solidly, Linda thought fearfully, it would have cracked her skull or knocked her from her horse. Nate's fist was huge and had been launched with blind fury. But, at the same moment that Nate swung at her, she had kicked her boots into her horse's flanks and yanked on the reins, which Nate had dropped as he grabbed for his bloody nose. Her horse's first leap probably saved her from a broken skull or worse. On the third leap she had the mare under control. Swiftly she pulled it to a whirling stop. By the time she and the animal were facing Nate, she had her rifle out of its sheath and cocked.

Nate had not moved. He sat his horse stunned, one hand holding his dripping nose, the other chest-high and clenched around the reins. Linda relaxed until she noticed his eyes. He was staring at her as a grizzly might stare at its prey in the moments before it attacked. As she watched, her finger tensed on the trigger of her rifle, until she saw him also slowly relax, first his eyes, then his body. Deep inside her she felt a sigh of relief but she kept the rifle pointed at his chest and her finger firm on the trigger. She knew enough not to take chances with an angry animal. And Nate Barstow fit that category at the present time, she thought, even though his anger was held in temporary abeyance.

"What the hell did you hit me for?"

"You grabbed my reins."

"I just wanted to talk."

"I didn't know that and even if I did, you had no right to grab the reins."

In spite of his efforts Nate's voice reflected his rising irritation, "You know I wouldn't hurt you."

"Yes, you wouldn't," Linda laughed sarcastically.

"Damnit, watch your tongue," as he spoke Nate angrily kneed his mount forward. "I won't...."

"I'll shoot, Nate," Linda spoke loudly, insistently, hoping the words would stop him. "You come any closer and I'll shoot you."

Nate halted the forward motion of his horse.

"Why?" he asked in consternation. "I told you I won't hurt you."

"Why?" Linda asked in amazement, trying unsuccessfully to hide the angry disgust on her face and in her words. "I can't believe you. You waylay me on the trail and try to keep me from riding on my way. And then you ask me why I'll shoot you if you come any closer!"

Linda's fury burned itself out in her words. She noticed Nate's mortification, but she wondered if it wasn't superficial and temporary. She kept her rifle lined on his chest. She had seen more than one example of his sudden, brutal violence and heard of others. And help of any kind was a hard half hour's ride or more away. So she was not going to take any chances.

As she watched him closely, she asked herself what she had seen in him. The answer, she concluded, lay in her. Nate was the same man whose physical strength and aggressive behavior she had once found attractive. Somehow either her time back East or her passage through the teen years had changed her. Maybe both.

"You shouldn't treat me like I was nothing," Nate glared at her, feeling the anger expanding in his chest.

"If you don't like the way I treat you, stay away from me," Linda snapped. "I'm leaving. From now on just stay away from me."

As she spoke she reined her horse around Nate and back down the trail toward the Rocking H, careful to keep her rifle lined on the big man. Nate watched her silently, his eyes glittering furiously.

The section of the trail they were on meandered along the side of a slope. Above the trail the slope rose gently until it curved over the top of a rounded hill and seemed to merge with the horizon. Below the trail the slope dropped more steeply for fifty yards before it suddenly plunged two hundred feet straight down to the rocky bottom of a canyon. Except for the stand of trees which had hidden Nate on the upper side of the trail, nothing but low-lying sagebrush and cactus covered the slope.

When Linda began edging her horse around Nate, she reined it off the trail onto the lower slope, among several clumps of prickly pear. She kept her eyes and rifle trained on Nate, letting the mare pick its way through the cactus.

Nate watched her as a hawk watches a mouse make its way from one hole to another nearby, hoping the frightened creature will let its attention slip for a moment. Right then he wanted her, wanted her whether she wanted him or not. At first he had thought she was like other women he'd known, scared or playing hard to get. He had figured she just needed more time to get used to him, to him and what he could do for her, to what it would be like to have a man like him. He no longer felt certain of that. He still couldn't accept her rejection as final. But time and polite courtship didn't seem to offer an answer. He had tried that route. And failed.

What she needed was a man who wouldn't put up with her crap, his rage told him.

He watched her as she eased her mare off the trail and through the cactus. She tried to keep the animal facing him, which was a mistake, he knew. It couldn't see where the openings between the spines were as it sidled and backed along the slope. It was becoming more and more nervous with each movement. If it backed into a spine or set a hoof down on a bunch of them, it would probably panic. Without visible motion, he leaned forward in the saddle, muscles tense and ready to drive his horse toward Linda's mare. That he might send Linda and her horse tumbling downhill only added to the angry excitement that flooded his chest.

When the moment came, however, he reacted too slowly. The mare's right front leg connected with a clump of spines. The animal squealed and spun to the left, knocking Linda off balance and almost unseating her. Startled, she grabbed for the saddle horn with the hand that held the rifle. The weapon dropped under the mare's hooves and then tumbled down the slope until it came to rest against one of the prickly pears. As the mare darted to the left, its head moving toward him, Nate dug his spurs into the flanks of his horse, his body leaning forward and his hand extended to grab the bridle. It was at that moment that Linda's rifle dropped between the mare's rear legs. The animal bounded back to the right. The move startled Nate's horse; it swerved sharply. Nate lost his balance. His horse swerved again, frightened. Nate, realizing he was falling and afraid his horse might roll with him or he might catch his foot in the stirrup, threw himself from the saddle, landed on his arms and chest, and slid chin first downhill until he came to rest, breath completely gone, in a pile of sagebrush. His horse stopped a hundred yards up the trail and stood looking back at the scene, more curious than frightened after its flight.

Linda gained control of her mare before Nate could again breathe with some degree of freedom. She dismounted, recovered her rifle, unharmed, and remounted.

Impatiently she waited until Nate was again breathing comfortably, reining her horse back onto the trail and to what she considered a safe distance from the Bar B foreman.

When he stood up and glared belligerently at her, she spoke, "You can catch your own horse. I'm leaving now. But before I go, I have something to say," she paused for effect, although she didn't think Nate would heed what she said. "Stay away from me. You come near me when I'm out riding alone again and I'll shoot you. You understand?"

Nate glared at her. "You didn't watch out so good today," he sneered. "You just remember. You're mine. I'll kill anybody makes a play for you. And I'll catch you alone someday."

Fear mingling with her anger, Linda spurred toward home. She kept her horse at a trot until she came in sight of the ranch buildings. As she rode her fear dissolved little by little, leaving only the smoldering anger.

Two worries occupied her mind. The lesser was Nate Barstow. She could handle Nate, she believed. He still wanted her as his woman so he wouldn't do anything to jeopardize his chances of winning her, unless she did something to set his temper off.

The Bartlemans were a different matter. Nate's words had convinced her beyond any doubt that Stoner was right, that the previous morning the Bartlemans had visited the Rocking H to kill its owners. And they wouldn't stop with the one attempt, not Joe and Sam. She shivered and spurred her horse to a gallop the last half mile to the corrals.

15

Stoner swung to the north when he left town, then east, avoiding the trail that meandered through Bar B range and then over the pass into the small valley of the Rocking H. He wanted to avoid a confrontation with the three Bar B hands who had braced him in the saloon, in case they were planning to ambush him somewhere along the trail.

He headed for the desolate mountains that lay north of Rocking H headquarters, separating the ranch on that side from the main valley. As the afternoon was dropping rapidly toward evening, he turned into the faint trail Linda had ridden earlier in the day, unaware that it was the same trail. When he came to the spot where Barstow's escaped horse had stopped to graze, he pulled up to study the area, driven by the ingrained habit of many years. After a careful scrutiny of the broken, cactus-choked land between him and the horizon, he dismounted and studied the tracks at his leisure, keeping a wary eye out for any sign of movement nearby.

"Those hoof prints don't come from the stock in the Rocking H corrals, I don't think, but I could easily be mistaken," he mused to the dusty black watching him curiously. "I haven't been here long enough to be certain. But add them to the hombre's footprints and I don't reckon man or horse came from the Peters ranch. The hombre's tracks are too big even for Will."

He again scanned the surrounding area, slowly. Nothing seemed out of place, no buzzards, no four-legged scavengers.

"His horse must've thrown him for some reason," he commented as he unconsciously rubbed the black's ears. "Or the animal wandered off while he was sleeping last night, or taking a rest this morning. Maybe...."

The sudden realization that Linda had ridden into those mountains that very morning, possibly on the same trail he was following, sent his words crashing into silence. Quickly he mounted and urged his horse along the trail, backtracking man and horse. Worry dug its spiny fingers into his entrails.

When he reached the spot where Barstow had been waiting for Linda, he again carefully scanned the area before dismounting. Relief slowly eased its way into the tightness of his chest as he studied the signs of the meeting that had taken place.

"She got away if it was her, and it doesn't look like she rode all this way just to see him, Blacky," he spoke thoughtfully, trying to clarify his findings for himself. "It looks more like she didn't see him till he rode out of that clump of cedars there, unexpected like." He again began rubbing the black's ears, an unconscious habit he had when in the saddle and studying on a problem. "Must've been somebody she knew because she let him ride up close. Then something happened. Maybe he grabbed for her or the horse. Or maybe...hell, I don't know. Anyhow Linda's horse spooked and pranced off the trail. The other rider, he was dragged out of the saddle, lost his hold on the bridle or reins or whatever he had got hold of, and went tumbling down the slope. When he fell, probably, his horse took off hell for leather and stopped up there where the rider caught it. But what about Linda? She got off her horse down there by that prickly pear. Why? When she got back on, she took off toward home as fast as that other horse did the other way. And after the other rider caught his horse the bastard followed her, but at a walk as if he didn't care whether she got away or not." His hand stopped stroking the animal's ears and became motionless talons, rigid and curled.

"Unless she had too much of a head start or there were others waiting somewhere between here and the ranch, and he knew it."

He mounted and kneed the black to a trot, struggling successfully against his desire to spur the animal to a gallop in spite of the steep slopes along which the narrow trail began to wind and the uncertain footing caused by loose rocks and boulders on the trail itself. As he rode he kept telling himself that whatever had happened had taken place hours before. If something had happened he was too late to help. But the thought did little to ease his anguish.

Within a hundred yards, he found that Linda's horse had slowed to a trot, then a walk, while her pursuer had goaded his horse to a trot. After that, Linda's horse maintained its walk, increasing its pace to a trot when the trail became level and open. The pursuing animal continued its faster pace. As Stoner approached the ranch without signs of Linda being ambushed or caught, relief began easing its way into his chest and stomach. When he rode out of the hills and could look down on the buildings of the Rocking H, he pulled the black to a halt.

Overhead the sun had slipped behind a wispy cloud. Dark shadows of other clouds spotted the floor of the valley and the mountains in the background. A cool wave of air washed over Stoner as he sat looking at the peaceful scene below. He could see Linda and Rob standing near the porch talking animatedly. In one of the corrals Pate and Cactus were unsaddling two horses while another stood a few feet away awaiting its turn. One horse, a bay, was rolling in the dust in the far corner of the corral, while a fifth animal stood with head down drinking from the watering trough in the near corner.

"Well," Stoner spoke to the dusty black, "I see Rob and the hands're back. And Linda made it to safety okay. But for a bunch of people on the edge of a possible shooting war, they're not very alert. No one has seen me yet, I don't think." He sat quietly, studying the buildings and people and mountains beyond, letting the peace and solitude of the moment flow through him. As he watched, Linda and Rob entered the house, still talking. Pate and Cactus turned the last horse loose, hung its saddle on a peg in a lean-to beside the corral, and walked together to the bunkhouse. Stoner continued to sit his horse, motionless, wondering how, in such a short time, he had become so attached to the people and land of the Rocking H. Finally, with a gentle tug on the reins, he broke the silence, "Let's go see where that rider went, Blacky."

He returned to where Linda's unknown pursuer had veered from the trail. The man had ridden just below the top of the ridge that formed the wall of the valley, keeping out of sight of the Rocking H buildings.

Pulling his Winchester from its scabbard and holding the black to a walk, Stoner followed. About a quarter mile along the valley wall a dry arroyo split the ridge and dropped gradually onto the valley floor. The unknown rider's tracks turned into the arroyo. As he reined his horse into the watercourse Stoner noticed that another set of recent tracks, a few hours older than the ones he was following, came up the arroyo from the valley below. A brief search convinced him that they were made by the same animal he was presently following, that they had probably been made that very morning, and that, rather than turn toward the trail when they had exited the arroyo, they had set off parallel to it.

"If I was a betting man," Stoner commented softly, "I'd lay big odds he knew Linda was on that old trail and he was hightailing it to waylay her. Which he did," he added thoughtfully, "and which means he must've been watching the ranch from somewhere."

He followed the tracks to the valley floor. The arroyo turned into a dry waterfall about halfway down the ridge but a narrow, unused trail zigzagged to the bottom in a series of steep but scalable switchbacks. When he reached the bottom, Stoner found himself in a depression twenty yards or more at its widest and running the width of the valley. While in the depression, if he kept to the center and slumped in the saddle, a man on a horse could not be seen from the ranch, he decided.

After carefully scanning the slopes on the opposite side of the valley and seeing nothing he considered threatening,

Stoner urged his mount forward. He wondered at the carelessness of the strange rider. The man had made no attempt to hide his tracks. Was he so sure no one would follow him? Almost immediately Stoner answered his own question. Linda wouldn't tell anyone. She was a woman who took care of herself and skinned her own game, not a woman who figured she needed help or one who would let her problems cause trouble that might lead to a shooting. The rider, whoever he was, either knew Linda well enough to realize what her reaction would be or he didn't care if he was followed or not.

On the opposite slope the tracks veered to the right until they entered a stand of mingled pines and aspens. On the far edge of the trees the rider had dismounted and sat with his back against a huge Ponderosa pine. From the shadow of the tree he had a clear view of the Rocking H buildings and couldn't be seen from around them.

The thick layer of needles and leaves left less evidence of the rider's presence than had the open range but, after careful scrutiny of the area and of the upper slope leading away from the trees, Stoner decided the man had entered the stand of trees twice that day, once early in the day from up the slope and once late in the afternoon coming out of the valley. Each time he had sat against the pine and watched the activity around the buildings below. After the second visit he had ridden back up the slope.

"Toward the Bar B?" Stoner asked the black, which was standing nearby, reins trailing on the ground, as its master stood close to where the intruder had sat. "The foreman, the one they call Barstow? The feet are big enough." He considered his thoughts for a moment before continuing aloud. "If that's the case, I reckon his shenanigan in the saloon wasn't just a drunken trick he was ashamed of later, unless he tracked down Linda to say he was sorry. And that doesn't seem very likely, not the way the tracks read. Besides," he grinned at the memory, "the man didn't hit me as the apologizing type."

Stoner shrugged his shoulders and, mounting the dusty black, headed downhill toward the ranch house and corrals. Linda and Mrs. Peters were standing in the main corral, talking, beside the lean-to when he rode up. Mrs. Peters walked over and opened the corral gate for him.

"We were talking about you, Jacob," she said as she closed the gate and followed him to the horse trough. Without waiting for his answer she continued, "We were beginning to worry, what with you in town alone and the Bartlemans there too. We figured there was no telling how many Bar B riders were in town today."

"No problem," Stoner grinned at her as he stripped the bridle from the black and started to hang it on a fence post. "I...."

"I'll take that," Mrs. Peters smiled and reached for the bridle. "You get the saddle. I'm no longer strong enough to yank saddles around but a bridle I can handle."

Stoner looked at her and chuckled before handing over the bridle, then commented, "I reckon you can still saddle a bronc with the best of them, saddle and bridle him and put him through his paces before he knows what happened."

Mrs. Peters burst into spontaneous laughter at his quip. She knew he wasn't serious. She knew he was fond of her. She realized that, in the few hours they had known each other, she had become the mother he had lost early in life.

"So, what can you tell us?" Mrs. Peters interrupted his thoughts, making an effort to speak seriously. "Did you talk to the Bartlemans?"

Stoner finished unsaddling the black. As it drank at the trough, he rubbed it down with the saddle blanket, then carried blanket and saddle to the lean-to, followed by Mrs. Peters carrying the bridle. He would let the horse rest and roll in the dust awhile, and drink its fill, before feeding it.

"My mother asked you a question. Have the courtesy to answer her, please."

He had put the saddle, bridle and blanket in the leanto and backed out, still trying to remember what the Bartlemans had said and to formulate a report. Linda's angry words cut into his thoughts, cold and sharp.

"I was...," he started to retort in kind, but caught himself and stopped.

"Give him time, Linda honey," Mrs. Peters requested in a soft but insistent voice. "I expect he was thinking about what he wanted to say."

"He could just tell the truth."

"I know you had a bad day, honey, but don't take it out on Jacob."

Moments passed in tense silence. Stoner had caught the iron in Mrs. Peters' words and the angry resentment in Linda's.

"I'm sorry, Miss Peters," he forced the smile from his face and the humor from his voice, "but your mother was right. I was trying to remember what all happened and what was said. I meant no disrespect."

Linda made no return comment, but her stance, Stoner knew, clearly meant that she remained angry and wanted him to know it. He again suppressed a chuckle and began telling the two women what had happened in Chasco, including the meeting with Matt Bartleman in the saloon and the talk with Joe Bartleman, but not mentioning the three Bar B hands.

"Do you think the Bartlemans really will try again to kill us?"

All anger had disappeared from Linda's voice as she asked the question. Only serious concern remained.

"Yeah, if we don't do something about it."

"Like what?" Mrs. Peters asked.

"Like spread the word around that you think the Bartlemans planned to kill you when they came over here. Insist that they started the ruckus, which they did. Pate gave the doctor an earful when he and Cactus took the Bartlemans to town. Maybe the doc talked. Anyhow Matt said the townspeople knew about the fight and were upset about the danger to you two. A delegation went with the sheriff to warn the Bartlemans off." He looked at Linda but she refused to meet his eyes so he couldn't read her reaction to his words. "I think the bartender heard enough of what me and Matt were saying to guess at what Joe and Sam's intentions are. I don't know whether he gossips or not, but I haven't known many bartenders who don't." He paused briefly, collecting his thoughts. "What you should do is add your own bit to the gossip. When you talk to friends, tell them you really think the Bartlemans came here to start a fight and kill you two."

"You believe that'll help?" Linda asked, a note of surprise in her voice.

Stoner wondered if the surprise was because of what he had said or because he had said it. He shrugged uncertainly.

"I don't know. But you can't just sit and do nothing until those two come after you again. Public opinion is strong medicine. Tell everybody the Bartlemans tried to shoot you and you're afraid they'll try it again. Even if it doesn't stop them, it should make them more careful about how they go about their murders. Of course, you've still got to be careful," he glanced at Linda as he spoke but, again, she avoided his eyes. "You don't want them to catch you out on the range somewhere alone. Even on the trail into town there're lots of places a murder could be made to look like an accident."

"What would you do in our place?" Linda asked, surprising Stoner.

"Go after the Bartlemans. Matt's not in it, like I said before. Take Joe and Sam out of the picture and your troubles are over. You could live in peace with Matt in control of the Bar B."

"What about Nate Barstow?" Linda asked, her eyes full on Stoner's face.

Startled at the question, Stoner looked carefully at the girl. A picture of the large footprints back in the mountains to the north and on a slope overlooking the ranch buildings flashed through his mind.

"I never thought much about him, I guess," he answered lamely.

"Do you think he'd let Matt take over the Bar B, if Joe and Sam weren't around?"

Again Stoner glanced at Linda, to find her staring speculatively at him.

"Matt's tough, I figure," he shrugged. "He might be more than Barstow could handle. And he might not. I don't know." He remained silent for a while, thinking. Finally he shrugged. "I don't know Barstow well enough to say yes or no. I only saw him that one time and he was drunk. But Matt's no pushover. Besides, I could get rid of Barstow too."

"Where were you today after leaving Chasco?" Linda changed the subject, a slightly sarcastic smile playing over her lips. "Earlier, I saw you come out of the mountains to the north, on the trail I was riding today. But you didn't come on down to the ranch. You disappeared back into the mountains. And when you appeared again, you rode in from the south."

Her comments startled and pleased Stoner. She was observant. He had been certain that no one had seen him on the northern rim of the valley, but she had. He tried to picture the tracks at the spot where she had been waylaid that morning. He would probably never know everything that had happened, but the important thing was that she had escaped and set her assailant afoot. Maybe, he decided, she was even tougher than he had assumed.

Forcing his thoughts back to the present, he noticed that both women were waiting for an answer, Linda impatiently, Mrs. Peters curiously.

"Well," he said, grinning in spite of himself, "when I left Chasco I cut through the mountains between here and there to avoid Bar B land."

He related his experiences from the time he first found the tracks of the horse to his findings among the trees to the south.

"Once you saw I had escaped, what right did you have to trail me home and then go snooping around?"

Stoner felt his temper rise at Linda's words. He fought unsuccessfully against the increasing tension around his eyes and lips. For some moments he fought down the angry words that were boiling on his tongue.

"That was unfair, Linda," Mrs. Peters broke the strained silence. "Jacob was just...."

"I know, Mother," Linda interrupted, a contrite frown spreading over her face. "I'm sorry, Stoner," she continued without looking directly at the gunfighter. "I had no right to snap at you like that. You weren't the one that tried to ambush me. I don't know what...."

"Was it Barstow?" Stoner broke in to save her more confusion and embarrassment. He had suddenly realized that she was more upset and frightened by the incident than she wanted to show.

Linda nodded, not surprised that he had figured out who the intruder was and glad that he knew. Somehow, the simple fact that he knew gave her a sense of security she hadn't felt since Nate had spoken from the shadow of the trees.

For the first time since his clash with Nate Barstow and the Bar B riders in the Chasco saloon, she studied the man carefully. He was not an exceedingly handsome man. He stood tall, broad shouldered, granite faced, lean and lithe, built more for the speed and agility of the timber wolf than the brute power of the grizzly. Yet about him clung a rugged appeal frightening and attractive at the same time, a something hinting that primordial forces lurked just beneath the surface of his sun-browned, wind-weathered skin and snow-flecked eyes.

Not for the first time Linda wondered if her defensiveness, the guard she put up in Stoner's presence, rather than protection against him was a protective wall against herself, against powerful forces in her that at that very moment were surging uncontrollably somewhere in her vitals, answering the primitive forces in him.

"That, I reckon, will be the end of Mr. Barstow," Stoner spoke from a distance of three feet but his words tickled Linda's ears vaguely, as if they had come from a long distance.

"I don't think Nate would hurt Linda intentionally," Mrs. Peters entered the conversation, nervous fear in her voice. "But he has a hellish temper. And he doesn't abide anything standing in his way when he wants something. If she said no to something he wanted, at the wrong time...," she shrugged helplessly. "He's strong enough to kill a man with his fist."

Linda shook herself free of the spell her close scrutiny of Stoner had put her under.

"I can handle Nate, Mother. And I don't want you seeking him out for some sort of masculine duel over me," she directed her final words toward Stoner. "I've been solving my own problems since I was little. I can still do so without anyone's help, thank you."

Stoner made no comment. Mrs. Peters started to speak but held her peace. Linda wondered at her ambiguous reaction to her own words. There had been a time when having two men fighting over her was exciting.

But if two men like Stoner and Nate Barstow fought over her, one would be killed or crippled, she knew, and the image of one of them lying dead in the dust or on the floor of some dingy building sent a sick feeling worming its way into her stomach.

"I want your promise that you'll leave Nate Barstow alone."

Stoner sensed that her words held more plea than command.

"I reckon I can wait," he smiled at her.

"Wait?" she stared quizzically at him.

Stoner shrugged, "We'll clash sooner or later, I reckon, before this conflict with the Bar B is resolved, unless somebody else gets to him first."

"Isn't there something we can do to stop the Bartlemans, without fighting?"

"I don't know what. I didn't see any give in old Joe, and I don't reckon there's any in Sam, not according to Matt, at least."

"Maybe I could talk to them."

"Maybe, but I don't think...," Stoner caught himself and grinned. He had been about to tell Linda that she shouldn't go to town alone and that, especially, she shouldn't visit the Bartlemans without taking him or one of the hands along. The image of her probable reaction stopped him and put the grin on his face.

"Something funny about my talking to the Bartlemans?"

Stoner noted the flicker of anger in her eyes and the ice in her voice. He tried to erase the grin. But the attempt, her anger, his own inability to keep from irritating her--the whole situation sent waves of chuckles bubbling up from his chest like air bubbles loosed under water, out of control and irrepressible as they boiled to the surface.

"What did I say that's so funny?"

Linda's eyes flashed fire and she stepped toward Stoner, her fists clenched and her body tense.

Startled, Stoner took a quick step backward, then suddenly lost all control. Gales of nearly hysterical laughter rolled from his lungs and belly. Linda took another menacing step closer. He again retreated a step, but the laughter continued, making him weak and helpless. His laughter was contagious. Somewhere in the vacuum which was his mind at the moment he realized that Mrs. Peters was laughing too, a delighted trill of giggles which harmonized with the deeper notes of his. A few moments later Linda smiled tentatively, uncertainly.

"You remind me so much of my Jacob," Mrs. Peters declared gently after she got control of her laughter and caught her breath.

Her eyes sparkled but in the depths Stoner thought he could see a tiny pocket of sadness.

"I don't know why you keep saying he reminds you of Dad," Linda commented. "I don't see any resemblance."

"You surely remember how tickled he used to get when I got mad over some silly little thing? The madder I became the more he laughed. And the more he laughed, the madder I became."

Linda smiled slowly, tentatively, at the image her mother's words evoked. She glanced from Stoner to her mother. Her smile became a grin and then she too burst into laughter.

"I guess I did look silly, like a chicken attacking a wolf," she spoke to Stoner when she could catch her breath. "But you did too, grinning like a little boy caught stealing cookies and backing away with his hands behind him to protect himself from a whipping."

Stoner threw up his hands in mock supplication, "Truce?"

"Yes, I guess it's time we quit fighting each other," Linda imitated Stoner's imitation of seriousness, but the laughter sparkled in her eyes. "We might need all our energy to fight the Bar B."

She offered her hand. Stoner took it happily, knowing he was grinning from ear to ear but unable to control himself. The girl's hand, he realized, was larger than he had expected, but it felt warm and soft in his and sent currents of pleasure racing through his body. He found himself unable to let loose. The depth of her eyes, the light smile on her lips, the soft pressure of her hand--he was caught in a spell to which he gladly submitted.

Linda too found herself mesmerized by the contact of their flesh. She felt her knees go weak and her heart begin to pound. She realized that she was breathing heavily, as if she had just run a race. Silently she struggled against her feelings, angry and embarrassed. From the corner of her eye she noticed that her mother was smiling happily at the two of them, which increased her anger. With a final effort, she pulled her hand free.

"We have an agreement, then, Mr. Stoner--a truce between us. But I warn you," her voice became stronger as she spoke, the huskiness softening but not quite disappearing. "Don't interfere with me or my freedom. I'll ride where I want to and see anyone I want to, whenever I want to. Agreed?"

"Okay," feeling an almost irresistible urge to take her in his arms, Stoner reluctantly accepted her condition. As he acceded he made himself a silent promise. He would talk to the crew, each man separately. He would make sure that whenever Linda left ranch headquarters one of the hands shadowed her, a promise he found impossible to keep because Linda easily spotted the first two trailers, Will and Cactus, and sent them back to the ranch in humiliation.

"Thank you," Linda met his gaze.

"I didn't hire a killer," Mrs. Peters broke in after a long silence in which Linda and Stoner seemed lost in each other.

"What?" Stoner asked, stunned.

Linda stared at her mother, uncertain she had heard right.

Mrs. Peters met Stoner's glance with a smile on her lips, but her eyes remained serious, "You said the best way to stop a war with the Bar B was to kill Joe and Sam, maybe Nate Barstow. I won't have that. We're not killers, and I don't want you to be, Jacob, not as long as you work for the Rocking H. We'll protect the ranch and the people on it. If that means killing someone, so be it. But we won't go after the Bartlemans and kill them. That's murder."

"If you see a wolf or cougar after your livestock, you don't wait until it's made a kill before you shoot it," Stoner met the soft eyes searching deeply in his. "I figure the same's true of a human wolf. You go on the offensive as soon as you see it headed your way. If you don't...," he shrugged.

"I know," Mrs. Peters smiled sadly. "The best defense is a good offense. But human beings aren't animals. They have to take chances sometimes if they want to keep their humanity."

16

Later, when the two women had gone to the house, Stoner stood with one foot on the lower railing of the corral and watched the sunset paint the clouds pink and then, with slow, sure strokes, turn the pinks to violets and purples and finally, hurriedly, to ashy greys and blacks. Coyotes were hunting toward the mouth of the canyon, their sharp, yipping barks directing each other as they closed in on their prey. The wind picked up as the sun disappeared behind the western peaks. A chill began to strip the land bare of its blanket of remaining warmth.

Stoner felt the melancholy of the evening invade his soul. For a little while, with Linda's hand in his, the warm, soft fingers of love had caressed every corner of his being. For a moment, a brief, fleeting moment, she too had been touched by the same passion, he thought. He had seen it in her eyes and on her lips, and in a quick flare of heat in the hand that he held in his. But, like the sunset, her flash of passion had quickly turned cold. Her lips and mouth lost their glow. She withdrew her hand from his.

As the twilight turned to darkness and the cold began to spread through him, Stoner became aware that he was hungry, having arrived too late for the evening meal and having forgotten his hunger in his conversation with Linda and Mrs. Peters. He made his way to the cook house to see what he could con Chew Lin out of. Later he walked through the chilly, starry night to the lighted bunkhouse. Cactus sat on the edge of his bunk braiding a rope. Dodge lay snoring on his bunk. The other four hands were playing a desultory game of poker.

"You and Will here sure lead a tough life," Tack commented with a grin as Stoner shut the door quietly and walked over to the table. "We poor ignorant cowhands put blisters on our behinds ridin' from here to creation. We chase cow critters all day, what time we ain't diggin' postholes through pure rock and cuttin' ourselves up with barb wire. Then we ride back from creation, puttin' blisters on top of our blisters. And what are you and Will doin'?"

"There's the workers and the bosses," Will interrupted with a laugh. "Some men ain't no good for nothin' except workin' with their hands and butts, doin' what they're told. While some of us...."

"Whoops," Cactus shouted from his bunk, cackling noisily. "What you meant to say was while some we could name carry their brains in that there last body part, so they ain't good for much. They're always settin' around smotherin' the few ideas they do get, which in my many years of experience ain't worth a hoot anyway."

General laughter greeted his interruption.

"You old rooster," Will chuckled, "you're so dense and forgetful you wouldn't recognize a good idea if it bit you right between your eyes, on that buzzard beak of yours. And if you did recognize it, you'd forget it a minute later."

Again the laughter was general as they all glanced at Cactus's hooked nose and recalled instances of his forgetfulness.

"Play a few friendly hands, Jefe?" Sonora asked innocently when the hilarity died down. "I need some spendin' money and these other gringos're too tight to bet much. With new dinero in the game, I figure maybe we can get some excitement in it too. Sabes, some decent pots. Hell, there ain't been nothin' but a few pennies in the pot every game for the last hour."

"I'll be damned, you Mexican cardsharp," Tack shouted, his voice a mixture of humor and frustration. "You've won pretty near every hand we've played tonight. Nobody's got any money left to bet."

"Don't pay any attention to that bit about friendly hands Sonora mentioned, Boss," Pate spoke slowly. "He's the most unfriendly poker player I ever run into. He don't leave a man enough money to buy a beer for a lady friend, let alone two or three ladies, when he's down on his luck. A man'd die of loneliness if he played cards with Sonora more'n once a month."

"And at that he'd better know when to quit, like after he's only lost half his wages," Will cut in, laughing and clapping Sonora on the back. "But, what the hell, we figure it's all for a good cause. It goes back to Mexico to support the four wives and thirty-two kids our pard here left down there when he rode north, a half jump ahead of the federales."

"Four? Four?" Cactus clambered from his bunk and limped to the table. "Four?" he shouted again. "Look at the man. Look at how well fed he is." He tugged on Sonora's shoulder and the rider from south of the border stood up, playing along with the fun--grinning, flexing his muscles, sucking in his gut, strutting around the room with the arrogance of a torero after the kill. "Any man that eats that well now, at his age, and looks like that, must have really been something when he was young and full of sap. Four wives? Hell, give credit where credit's due. I'd say a dozen wives is an understatement. But to keep things on the reasonable side, let's say a dozen wives and another dozen women he never got around to marryin'. Now, just how many young ones does that come to?"

"Ninety-six for the wives," volunteered Tack, a forced expression of concentration on his face, "and another forty-eight for the other women."

"No, that's not right," Will roared. "Anybody knows it's a lot more excitin' with a woman that ain't your wife. "I'd say forty-eight with the wives and ninety-eight with the others."

"You're both full of bull shit," Pate laughed.

"Where'd you two get those stupid numbers?" Cactus tried to make himself heard above the uproar, but it was impossible. Everybody was shouting, nobody listening.

From a corner, Stoner grabbed a rickety chair that could have seen service in Valley Forge and dragged it to the table, between Will and Tack. Carelessly he searched through the pockets of his jeans, stacking on the table in front of him the few bills and coins he found, ignoring the noise around him as he counted his meager wealth. When he had finished his preparations, he looked around. The hubbub was beginning to subside. Cactus was limping toward his bunk, muttering loudly to himself about the youth and inexperience around him, and thus the profound ignorance in spite of the pervading conceit. Sonora had quit flexing his muscles and strutting around the room; he was standing near the table engaged in a friendly quarrel with Tack about who was the greater Romeo. Will was loudly expounding the joys of extramarital sex. Pate sat at the table, across from Stoner, with a half-vacant grin on his lips, fingering the coins in front of him, watching the antics of his comrades, and listening to the uproar. When he saw Stoner looking at him he shrugged and winked.

The two sat quietly, waiting, while the noise gradually died down. Eventually only Cactus's low muttering broke the silence.

"You peacocks ready to play poker?" Stoner drawled. "Me and Pate're waiting. I don't know why Pate's waiting so patiently but me, I need a stake. All those women raising my kids need to keep their energy up in case I decide to visit. And those poor little underfed children of mine, all two hundred eleven of them--you wouldn't begrudge them a few bites to eat, would you? No, I didn't figure you would. So sit down and contribute to the needy, you rich cowpokes."

"Hey, Sonora," Tack shouted as he plopped into his chair and scraped it up to the table, "do you really think this new capataz is old enough to have a female friend?"

"I don't know if he's old enough," Sonora leered. "But I think he needs some lessons from me before he again asks Miss Linda to go riding. I...."

"Lessons from you?" Will's voice rose above the laughter Sonora's words had elicited. "Lessons from you? He needs lessons all right. Any twelve-year-old cowboy could have told you that," Will's voice rose an octave as, bowing low to Stoner and grinning like a banshee at a wake, he created an exaggerated rendition of Stoner's morning failure. "Now Miss Linda, you hadn't oughta go ridin' alone. There're some real bad cowboys out there in the hills. And some lions and wolves and all kinds of coyotes and snakes hidin' behind the trees just awaitin' for some innocent little Red-Ridin'-Hood-type girl to come wanderin' by with her basket of goodies. You won't stand a chance, Miss Linda. Not without my brave protection, you won't. So let me ride at your stirrup and guard you and your precious little basket from the big, bad wolves. I'll be forever grateful and I promise to be a good little boy. Yes, Miss Linda, I promise. I'll keep my hands to myself. And no, Miss Linda, I'm not saying that just to get you alone. I'm not that kind of a man. I'm...."

As Tall Will bowed and scraped and accompanied his words with a comic imitation of Stoner's voice, inserting animal howls and growls and hisses at appropriate pauses, and occasional imitations of female indignation, the laughter again echoed off the walls of the room.

"You've made your point," Stoner laughingly interrupted the tall cowboy. "Now let's play poker, and I'll sure enjoy every penny I win from you."

"Win from me?" Will dropped into his chair. "That'll be the day. I was playin' poker before...."

Pate dropped the deck of cards in front of the tall puncher.

"Deal, Will; it's your turn," Tack grumbled. "You play poker like a horse with a burr under its saddle. But I'd elect you house dealer if we had one. You've given me three big pots tonight."

Will stopped talking and began shuffling the cards. Sonora explained the game to Stoner.

"This is just a penny-ante game, Jefe: three-cent limit, no ante, two raises, no wild cards, dealer's choice, cards tell the story. No arguments. No fights. We play for fun."

The evening flowed smoothly, one game drifting into another and mixing with it until time and action became a single current washing into the late hours of the night, the two distinguished only by occasional eddies of conversation, rough jokes, or an explosive, good-natured string of curses. Automatically Stoner studied the men at the table. He found himself relaxing more and more as the evening progressed. He realized how much he had missed the camaraderie of the bunkhouse before reaching the Rocking H. He had spent too many years of his life alone, he thought, wandering from job to job, place to place. With a warm feeling, he decided that he could safely turn his back on any man in the room and that he would trust them all in a fight, whether the odds for survival were in their favor or not. The Rocking H was lucky to have them, he figured. There wasn't a quitter or a turncoat in the bunch.

He smiled to himself, contentedly, as he studied their poker habits. Pate and Tall Will played like they did everything else. Will gambled with rough but good-natured pleasure, laughing boisterously when he won a good pot, swearing without rancor when he lost one, ignoring the odds against him if he decided to draw to an inside straight, and bluffing on nothing. Pate wagered deliberately, thoughtfully, but he too refused to back out of a pot once he had committed himself. Tack was a taciturn player, his normally jovial character withdrawn. He bet slowly, carefully, delaying the game as he thought each plodding step through and thus earning the irritation of his fellows. When danger lurked in the hidden hands around the table, he withdrew into his shell, either folding or silently calling the bets of others. Like Tack, Sonora showed a different side of his character in the game. Generally reserved and quiet, only occasionally joining the conversation and horseplay of the others, he was a noisy player and the one to be reckoned with in the game. The other hands all played according to a pattern. Not Sonora. He played with continuous commentary on the game, sometimes serious, sometimes humorous, as if paying no attention to what he himself was doing. But he played shrewdly, always

aware of which cards had fallen and which ones had not. His
pile of winnings slowly increased.

17

The next morning Rob and the hands scattered in two groups to begin working the rough country between the Bar B and the valley of the Rocking H. Stoner had suggested one larger group in case the Bar B attempted a quick retaliatory attack after their defeat at the Loma Linda. Rob rejected his recommendation.

"I don't think the Bar B will try anything until Joe and Sam are on their feet," he insisted. "Not after what we did to them at the spring."

Stoner remained at headquarters. He spent the early morning cleaning his pistols and rifle, patching an old pair of jeans, and repairing the hinges of the bunkhouse door. He had just finished the hinge and started off to inspect the barn and corrals when he caught a flash of movement near the house. Linda had stepped off the front porch and headed in his direction. She hailed him, asking him to wait up.

"Will you walk with me?" she asked. "I'd like to talk."

Stoner fell in beside her.

"I'd be delighted, ma'am," he tried to match her seriousness, but he found it impossible to keep the happy twinkle from his eyes and the half-smile from his lips.

"Don't make fun of me," Linda reacted with annoyance, mistaking his smile. "I couldn't sleep again last night. I lay awake most of the night thinking about how nasty I've been to you, after all you've done for me and my family." Nervously she pushed at the sleeves of her blouse. When Stoner started to speak she held up her hand to stop him and continued speaking hurriedly, as if afraid she might not say what she wanted to say if she didn't make haste. "I know I've apologized before. And I know, afterwards, I've gone right back to my ungrateful habits. I know you're trying to be helpful when you say I shouldn't ride alone. And I really am grateful, no matter how spiteful I sound. I want you to believe that."

She looked at Stoner beseechingly. He thought he had never seen anyone so appealing. He found it difficult to speak. His heart thudded painfully against his ribs, his breath came in gasps, his lips felt dry, his tongue felt swollen--as if he had been walking in the sun all day without water. Making a great effort he swallowed, once, twice.

"I wasn't making fun of you, Miss Peters," he finally forced out, his words almost a whisper. "I would never do that, never."

Linda stopped. He stopped and faced her. She studied his eyes and face for a long time before reacting.

"I know," she finally spoke, hoarsely. "I know. What I don't know is why I so often react negatively to what you say."

Stoner shrugged. "I affect a lot of people that way. I don't know why, but I do." An almost imperceptible frown crinkled the corners of his eyes. "Most of the time it's with strangers or people I don't know very well. I say something, not meaning anything by it, or I just look at someone, and the next thing I know I'm in a fight or being cussed out by somebody. It was no different when I was young, except worse maybe because I couldn't control my temper." He paused and forced a rueful smile. "I reckon that's one of the reasons I learned to use a gun. I had to defend myself from the trouble I was always getting into without knowing why."

Linda's rigid stance had softened as he talked. She again felt the powerful electrical force surge from his body into hers; her first reaction was one of resentment. But this time another feeling flowed in the current, something soft and tender and warm, something that made her want to reach out and touch the man standing so near, something that gave meaning and direction to the unbridled physical attraction. She wondered if she was falling in love with this nomadic gunfighter. The thought startled her. Finally she not only understood but also accepted, clearly, honestly, what had happened to her. The first time she saw Stoner, in the saloon, a powerful jolt had flashed through her loins and from there had exploded outward through every square inch of her body, leaving her weak and trembling. Since then the same thing had happened every time the man came near her. She found herself losing control over herself, and she became afraid, afraid of Stoner, afraid of the wild forces she was beginning to sense within herself and, most of all, afraid of what might happen if she once gave in to her desire. She was no prude, nor, she laughed to herself with a twinge of regret, was she a virgin. But her one brief affair, in the East, had been no more than a dalliance, an experiment brought on by curiosity and soon rejected because Peter, her lover, demanded more than she could give. He wanted to divorce his wife and marry her. She wanted neither to break up his marriage nor to marry him. When she accepted his advances she had not known of his wife. When she found out, it was too late to repair the damage done. So she shrugged fatalistically and continued the relationship, angry more at herself for believing Peter's lies without checking them out than at Peter. But when he proposed, she ended the affair. She didn't want to marry a man who had already cheated on one wife.

Linda started walking again, to gain control of her emotions. Stoner fell in beside her. They walked the rest of the way to the pond without speaking. There they stopped near the water, continuing the silence because neither one knew how to break it without returning to their previous conversation, which both wished to avoid.

Stoner pretended to study the pool of water. A barbed wire fence enclosed it, one section stretched across the span where the creek entered the pond, keeping larger game or stock from using it as a watering hole. The banks of the pond itself and of the stream for as far as he could see were of stones and boulders. From the clarity of the water it was evident that the bottom was also of solid rock. A small man-made canal ran from the water's edge to the house where, Stoner knew, it flowed into a large cistern behind the cook shed. It too was rock-bottomed and fenced and, at the point where the water left the pond, a large piece of metal sat in two slots; it could be positioned to start or stop the flow of the water. At the present time it was raised; the water gurgled softly as it moved along the channel.

Linda noticed the direction of Stoner's eyes and commented, "Father dug the channel. Actually he did more blasting than digging, because the whole channel goes through solid rock. I was twelve or thirteen. I'll never forget that year. Dad would make me and Rob go over there behind those boulders," she pointed. "Then he would set the charge and come running. In a few moments the earth would cough, varoom, and rock and dirt would fly into the air. Rob and I would jump and laugh with excitement and then help Dad clean out the rock fragments and scatter them around the area." She smiled sadly, "It was great fun, like every day was a special holiday."

"Your father must have been a good man," Stoner remarked, recalling what Mrs. Peters had said about her husband and the softness in her eyes when she talked about him.

Linda made no comment but her silence suggested that Stoner's words had touched deep emotions.

Stoner changed the subject, "A man could live and die happy in this valley."

"Yes," Linda murmured. She gazed around her, remembering her homesickness in the East. She had missed her family but, even more acutely, she had missed the endless days of sunshine and cool nights; the mountains with their dark green pine forests and the lower slopes of mingled juniper, sagebrush and cactus; the fields of wild flowers in the spring blanketing the valley and the mountainsides; the meandering stream flowing happily through the valley; and the pond where she and Rob had spent many pleasant hours swimming and playing. She had missed the riding, the ranch work, the campfires under the stars, and the dances and socials in Chasco.

"Yes," she cleared her throat. "This is what I missed in the East," she waved her hand in a sweeping motion. "There's nothing like it."

"Ah-huh," Stoner agreed.

Linda turned her gaze from the natural world to the man beside her. He was staring down the valley, his lips lifted in a contented smile, his eyes reflecting the soft, indirect sunlight escaping around the edges of a fluffy cloud. But he stood with his weight balanced lightly on the balls of his feet, his right hand resting near the handle of his pistol, his thumb hooked in his belt--ready, Linda thought, to spring into action at the least hint of danger. He's like some wild animal, always attuned to the slightest movement or threat.

"What do you want here, Mr. Stoner?" she asked curiously. "At first I thought you wanted to take over the ranch. Now I'm not so sure."

"I wish you'd call me Jacob, or Stoner, like you do sometimes" he met her gaze but avoided her question. "When you call me mister I feel like you're trying to put a fence between us."

"Maybe I am," she laughed nervously, then continued in a more serious vein. "But I would like us to be friends. Mother admires you a great deal. Rob seems to have accepted you. So I think it's time I do too."

"Call me Jacob, then."

"It's a deal," Linda stuck out her hand, "if you'll call me Linda."

Nodding agreement, Stoner took her hand in his and held it gently. Their eyes met. A hot blast of energy smashed into his gut. Again he found himself short of breath and unable to speak. And unable to let her hand go.

For a long time he stood there, her hand in his, looking into her eyes, her odor filling his lungs. Finally she smiled, pulled her hand from his, and broke contact with his eyes. When she spoke, her breathlessness equaled his own.

"You didn't answer my question, Jacob."

It took him several moments to recall the question. His mind was working with as much difficulty as were his lungs.

"I've answered the same question before, I think, but maybe not to your satisfaction. I reckon the main reason is that the Rockin' H gives me a place to call home for a while. Like I said, it's a place that makes a man want to put down roots. And you know how I feel about your mother. She's a good woman; she treats me like a human being, not like some wandering gunfighter. I couldn't ride off and leave her to face the Bartlemans alone."

"She has Rob and me, and the hands."

Stoner shrugged, "The hands are good men, all of them. They're one of the reasons I stayed on. They're loyal and, after a clash or two with Will," he smiled teasingly, "not all of his making, we get along great." He paused thoughtfully. "They're not gunfighters, but they'll all fight, no doubt about that. And Will and Pate are good with a sidearm, I expect. But the two of them aren't enough to stop the Bartlemans. I'm not sure all of us are. They've got a big crew and many of them were hired to fight."

"What about Rob?" Linda asked, momentarily irritated that Stoner had not mentioned her brother.

Stoner hesitated before answering. He didn't want to break the tentative rapport that had developed between the two of them, but at the same time he didn't want to lie. She had asked him a question; he owed her an honest answer.

"Rob'll maybe make a fighter someday, when he learns to listen and when he learns to control himself. A man's setting himself up to lose if he thinks he's better and smarter than he is. All the hands are pretty levelheaded, except maybe Will. They aren't easy to rile or lead into a trap. Will, he's got a temper, but he's seen his share of fights, I figure; it'd take a lot to fool him about a dangerous situation." He stopped talking, trying to collect his thoughts.

"You're talking about the fight up on the Loma," Linda interrupted. "Rob told me he ignored advice from the men.

He was upset and ashamed of himself. I don't think he'll be so stubborn in the future."

Stoner wasn't so sure about Rob. "I hope you're right," was his only comment.

Realizing that he was not going to say anything more, Linda shook off her irritation. Like Stoner, she didn't want to destroy the peace that had developed between them, no matter how temporary it might be.

"You're pretty good at avoiding questions you don't like," she smiled. At Stoner's startled look, she laughed out loud. "Someday when we know each other better I'll ask you about Rob again, and I'll expect an answer that doesn't sound like a preacher's evasions, a direct answer, and an honest one."

Stoner chuckled but he remained quiet because he sensed that she was not yet through talking.

Linda had turned to face him head on. He had no choice but to return her look.

"She's the most beautiful woman I've ever seen," he told himself. "She's proud and confident. She's happy with herself and with her world, and the only reason she gets mad at me is because she suspects I'm trying to destroy that world, or maybe change it in a way that would hurt the people and things she loves."

"You are a very interesting man, Jacob," Linda spoke clearly, precisely, looking him squarely in the eyes. "You are also a very capable man. You've shown more than once that you're skillful in a fight and that you know how to get other men to do what you want them to do. You've also proved that you're a considerate man. Cactus and Sonora both say you know a lot about ranch work, much more than you'll admit. You also sound like an educated man, although I believe the story you told Mother, that you've taught yourself. But what I don't understand is why, with all your abilities and everything, why you are a gunfighter."

Stoner found himself becoming lost in the vast depths of her eyes. With an effort he suppressed the hypnotic reveries that floated from her eyes into his and forced himself to think.

    "I didn't choose to be a gunfighter," he tried to organize his thoughts. "Like most boys, I reckon, I grew up with guns and had my dreams of being a soldier, a marshal, another Wild Bill Hickok, something heroic. Guns came easy for me, easier than for most. I just...," he shrugged. "A man has to defend himself sometimes. And things happen. I tried the outlaw trail, kind of wandered into it early as you probably know if your mom told you what I told her. That didn't work out because I didn't much get along with some of my companions in crime," he chuckled drily. "I tried the law, but it didn't work out either. I didn't like to kill a man or put him in jail for doing the dumb things I had done. And I didn't believe a man had a right to expect special treatment just because he knew the right people or had lots of money, or because his paw did. So I tried other things, bartending, scouting for the army, freighting, and cow punching. I found out I liked ranch work and it liked me so I stuck with it as much as I could, but there's always some bas...uh, pardon me, somebody recognizes me or doesn't like me and then it's stick around for the shooting to start or head for parts unknown."

    "You must have had a lonely life," Linda commented sympathetically.

    Her words startled Stoner. He'd never thought of his life as lonely exactly. Parts of it, yes. But then, he figured there was some loneliness in everyone's life. Besides, he had always been pulled in opposite directions, toward the solitary life and toward human companionship. One of the reasons he'd been attracted to cow punching was that he could have the best of all possible worlds--time alone in the mountains and desert, sharing his thoughts with only the wind and the howling coyotes on a dark night, and time with riding companions in the bunkhouse and around the campfire, time for jokes and laughter and stories of time lost.

    "There've been times when I'd call it lonely," he spoke slowly, thoughtfully, knowing words could not explain his feelings. "Lots of times. But those times haven't been any more or worse than what other people go through, I don't reckon, even people who live smack-dab in the middle of a town and are surrounded by family and friends. We want to be happy all the time. But that's only possible in a perfect place, some place like Heaven or the Garden of Eden or some other utopia we dream up. Life here on this earth isn't like that. It's mostly a grubby, lonely process, especially for us humans because we can think and dream. That's our character defect and that's our problem, I figure, and it's also what makes us unique and great at times. We can imagine perfect happiness and we're just arrogant enough to think that, with the right effort in the right place at the right time, we might get a little slice of it here on earth. So we do the damndest things. We go chasing all over God's creation. We lie, cheat, steal, hurt the people we love, march off to war, always with visions of better, happier times just over the horizon. We can't seem to accept that happiness is five parts contentment, four parts yearning, and only one part pleasure. And that it's inside us somewhere, not something just over the mountains, not something we can take from somebody else or win with a gun or sword."

Linda gazed thoughtfully at Stoner. What he had said touched her deeply, but she didn't know whether it was the cynic or the dreamer reflected in his words that most affected her, or the words themselves.

"Then why do you use a gun and why do you keep chasing all over God's creation, as you so well put it? What are you looking for?"

"What am I looking for?" Stoner mused as if to himself. "A place to call home. A ranch I can work at and build into a nice place for a family, a woman to work beside me the rest of my life, children who'll grow up around me and give me grandchildren someday."

Linda looked at him with increased interest before asking, "But why do you continue wearing a gun? If you didn't wear it, you wouldn't have to use it. You could stay wherever you wanted to. Nobody's going to shoot a man if he isn't armed."

"There are plenty of men," Stoner disagreed, "that would kill an unarmed person. All they need is a good enough reason."

Linda started to disagree. But images of the past few days' events flashed through her mind. Her vision of the world had been tarnished by those events, maybe changed completely. She realized that what she had said and been about to say now sounded naive to her. How it might sound to a man like Stoner, she couldn't guess.

"You're right," she found herself saying. "But let's not talk about such dreary things." She took his arm and pulled, smiling up at him. "Let's walk all the way around the pond and talk about you."

"Okay," Stoner returned her smile. "I'd like that, the walking together anyway. But we'll have to wade the creek and we'll have to talk about you some. What I've done wouldn't fill up all that time. And besides, I'm curious to know what the most beautiful woman I've ever had on my arm is like."

Linda's laughter trilled happily through the quiet air. As they walked she kept her grip on Stoner's arm, only letting go when they were taking off their boots and socks to wade the creek. She marveled at the mingled feelings his closeness caused in her, the sense of comfort and safety, of pleasure and happiness, and of something else indefinable that caused a yearning ache deep inside.

They sat for a long time with their feet dangling in the stream, side by side. They traded experiences from their pasts and hopes for the future. Finally, carrying their boots and socks, they waded the creek. Halfway across Linda stepped into a deep pool, slipped and, falling, grabbed Stoner, who also lost his balance. They both sat down in water that came up to their chests. Again Linda's laughter trilled through the quiet of the day. Stoner grinned.

"You're a real help," Linda laughed from where she sat near him, only her shoulders and head above the water.

"That's me," Stoner echoed her laughter. "The will was there but what can a man do with two left feet and no warning?"

He stood up, poured the water from his boots, and tossed the boots onto the bank. Then he reached for Linda's boots and repeated the process.

"Now what?" Linda asked suspiciously when Stoner turned from his chore and stared at her with an odd expression on his face.

"Now we see if a man with two left feet can do a better job of fording this creek, walking on sharp rocks, than a woman with two right feet can. Meaning, I'm going to carry you the rest of the way and pray that I don't make a jackass of myself by dumping both of us in the water again."

"That's not necessary," Linda said, a nervous catch in her voice.

"No," Stoner agreed, noting her nervousness and wondering if his voice reflected the butterflies flitting around in his stomach.

He reached for her. She stood easily, willingly, and put her arms around his neck. In a few moments, all too soon for Stoner, they reached the bank and he deposited her on a grassy spot. During the rest of their outing they were both more subdued. Linda was fighting her own battle with the powerful forces that contact with Stoner's arms and chest had unleashed in her. Stoner too had felt the wild mass of energy thunder in his chest. He struggled to subjugate it to his will. Elation battled with fear in his soul, elation that Linda seemed as moved by their contact as he was, fear that her pride would make her reject those feelings, and him with them, or that he was simply imagining her feelings.

18

The morning after Nate Barstow waylaid Linda he returned to the Rocking H. Mid-morning found him in the same stand of trees and brush from which he had spotted her riding off the day before. He was sitting with his back against a ponderosa pine watching the buildings below when she appeared and joined Stoner near the bunkhouse. A curse escaped his lips when the two set off toward the pond together. He started to rise when Linda took Stoner's arm but, with an angry mutter, forced himself to remain seated. He chuckled humorlessly when Linda slipped and fell, then swore furiously when Stoner picked her up and carried her from the water.

"You've just signed your death warrant," he spoke the warning aloud, feeling better for the threat even though Stoner could not hear it. "And you," he muttered to Linda's form in the distance, "I'll have you or no man will."

After the two young people he was watching had returned to the ranch buildings, Barstow mounted and headed back to the Bar B, seething all the way. When he rode into the ranch yard Cal was the only hand visible. Nate reacted angrily. The hands, he figured, were scattered around the ranch making a pretense of doing the work they were hired to do, except Cal, who was one of the laziest men Nate had ever run across.

"You guardin' the Bar B from a raid by the Rockin' H or the Apaches?" he asked sarcastically.

As he spoke he stepped from his mount and confronted the young puncher, expecting a sharp rejoinder, ready for it. The rage still boiled beneath the surface, rage at watching the only woman he wanted walking arm in arm with another man and smiling sweetly into his eyes as they talked. He wanted to smash something or someone, and Cal was available.

But Cal noticed the foreman's mood and bit off a sardonic reply. "No, boss," he spoke without looking at Nate, not wanting the man to see the angry glitter in his eyes. "Somebody had to stick around. There ain't nobody else here. Matt rode in this mornin' early, gave everybody their orders, and rode back to town. Joe and Sam are still in town, takin' it easy. The cook headed for town to pick up some supplies. A bunch of the boys rode in with him. The rest're scattered over the range doin' the chores Matt gave them. Wasn't nobody but me to watch over our headquarters."

Nate stared at the young gunman. He could sense the barely controlled anger in Cal's words, and he could sense the layer of fear and respect underlying the anger. Reminding himself that Cal too hated Stoner, he made himself relax, wondering how he could use that hatred.

"I figured you'd ride into Chasco again today, lookin' to finish what you started yesterday."

He forced sympathy into his voice, let derision curl his lips and glitter in his eyes.

"I planned to," Cal's words came out clipped and angry in spite of his attempt to hide his emotions. "I was gonna ride in with Slicker and Dobbs. But Matt seen what we was doin' and sent the other two to check the stock on our side of Black Bear Mesa. Told me to go along, but I said I was supposed to stay here in case you needed me." He smirked at the memory of his slight victory over Matt.

"What's Matt's beef about you ridin' to town?"

Cal shrugged, "You know Matt, old goody-goody Matt. He don't want nobody hurt. He told us to stay away from the Rockin' H gunfighter."

"Yeah, well," Nate spoke slowly, thinking, glaring at Cal, "what Matt wants and what we're gonna do are two different things. Joe and Sam want the man dead, like I told you." He paused to let his words sink in before continuing with a sneer in his voice, "The question is, are you up to it?"

Cal relaxed. His lips curled in a feral grin, "Just give me the word and you've got him."

"Like you did yesterday?" Nate chuckled sarcastically, then gave his orders. "Go get Slicker and Dobbs to help. From what they say, they hate Stoner as much as you do. Do what you have to to hurt the Rocking H and get rid of the gunfighter. Stay clear of Matt; he'll try to stop you if he finds out what you're plannin'. And I don't want Linda Peters hurt. Understand?" Nate glared at the younger man until he answered.

"Okay," Cal gave a surly grunt, then grinned suddenly, "but what about her brother and the old woman?

Nate still seethed from seeing Linda holding Stoner's arm and smiling up at the man. Angrily he considered what had happened between him and Linda the previous day and how she had avoided him ever since she returned from the East. His thoughts made his decision for him. He didn't owe Rob or Mrs. Peters anything and the Bartlemans wanted them dead. As for Linda, he no longer owed her either. In the past few days she had destroyed what little loyalty he had left. But he still wanted her in spite of the anger and hate struggling inside him with his desire.

"No skin off my nose if somethin' happens to them," he stared at Cal. "But I'm not givin' any orders about them. And whatever happens, no suspicious fingers better point to me. And nothin' better happen to the girl. Nothin'! Comprendes, amigo?

He glared at Cal until the younger man began to fidget and finally answered, "Yeah. We won't go near the girl. We'll catch the gunfighter out on the range somewhere, or in town. But if Rob or the old woman...," Cal shrugged, grinning cruelly.

For an instant he wondered if Barstow was afraid of the Rocking H gunhand, but quickly rejected the thought. He had seen Nate in action and knew the man feared nothing. Almost immediately he pictured Stoner and Matt both lying face down, dead, in some gully somewhere, himself standing nearby with a smoking gun, and he chortled to himself. Matt's interference in the saloon, in the trap he, Dobbs, and Slicker had set for Stoner, had enraged him. He had promised himself that one day he would exact revenge against Matt Bartleman. But his anger at Matt had been like a candle flame compared to the prairie fire of his murderous rage against Stoner. After the attempt in the saloon, he, Dobbs, and Slicker had waited outside Chasco for Stoner, hidden in ambush in the pass leading into the small valley of the Rocking H. After a couple of hours his two companions had tired of the wait and had ridden on to the Bar B. But he had remained, burning with bloodlust. Evening, twilight, and then full dark had found him still waiting. When he could no longer see to shoot he rode back to Chasco to search out and kill his prey. But Stoner had long since left. So Cal returned to the Bar B, rage burning in his gut, fed by the shame of having been beaten and, at his count, three times forced to take water from the man he had been hunting.

"Okay," Nate grunted. "I don't care about Stoner. You can leave his body for the coyotes. If somebody finds it, who cares. Nobody'll get upset about a gunfighter being killed. But any other bodies, you make sure they can't be found. And remember what I said about the girl. Anything happens to her and you're dead."

Nate stood watching as the young gunman walked to the corral, roped and saddled a horse, and rode away. He grunted with satisfaction when horse and rider disappeared down the far side of a slope. Until Joe and Sam were back on their feet, he figured, the game was his. He would make the rules. And he didn't want Linda harmed, not until he had had his chance at her.

At Black Bear Mesa Cal found Dobbs and Slicker loafing in camp, drinking coffee and playing two-handed blackjack for pebbles.

"If I was Nate, you two'd have your walking papers right about now," he shouted laughingly as he dismounted and tied his horse to the rope serving as hitching rail.

"Matt said we was to chouse all the Bar B cows off the mesa and drive them down to the valley."

He paused and grinned at Cal.

"Matt didn't know we was up here last week doin' the same thing," Dobbs put in. "So we sure as hell didn't tell him."

"I reckon Joe and Sam forgot to tell Matt," Cal laughed as he joined the two by the campfire.

"I reckon," Slicker agreed with a straight face. "Funny how Matt never knows what's goin' on around the ranch."

"Your deal," Dobbs tossed the cards toward Cal, then took some of his pebbles and some of Slicker's and dropped them in front of the newcomer.

"And you didn't figure it your moral duty to enlighten him none, did you?" Cal asked as he started to shuffle the cards.

"Nope," his two comrades commented drily.

"Well, I've got some new orders for you," Cal drawled the words, swelling with the importance of his mission.

He chuckled when the two of them looked up sharply.

When he finished explaining their mission he said, "Old Nate hisself give us these orders."

"Nate's declarin' open season on the Rockin' H, just like Joe and Sam want," Dobbs asserted thoughtfully, the card game forgotten. "But I'd bet anything those specific orders didn't come from the Bartlemans. They sure as hell wouldn't tell us to let the girl alone. Hell, they want all three of the Peterses dead, although they'd never admit it to no one but themselves."

"Yeah," Cal grinned. "They want the girl dead but Nate wants her in bed."

"Jesus, you're a lousy poet. Stick to chasin' cows," Slicker snorted. "And you ain't tellin' us anything new. Nate's been pantin' after the Peters girl like a hound dog in rut ever since she come back from the East. Hell," he laughed lecherously, "long before she growed up and left for the East."

"So, what do we do?" Dobbs changed the subject. "We sure as hell don't want Nate down on us. I don't ache to get my back broke." He paused as his eyes searched the faces of the other two. "But I don't want Joe and Sam gettin' a burr under their saddles neither. They're killers, worse'n Nate by a long ways, I think, both of them, and hell on wheels with a sixshooter."

"Nate didn't say when we was to return," Cal spoke slowly. "He just told us to kill that new gunfighter, do whatever damage we could to the Rockin' H, and not hurt the Peters girl. The Bartlemans, hell, they don't care if everybody on the Rockin' H dies, except Matt, and he don't count." He paused until his companions grunted assent, then continued. "I say we declare our own war in our own way. We take a few days, find a bunch of Rockin' H cows, rustle the critters, and sell them in Globe City. Anybody gets in our way, we kill them. Anybody comes after us, we kill them. We can do Nate's dirty work and make some spendin' money at the same time. Maybe we can make a stake and ride out if the Bartlemans don't like what we're doin'. Whatever happens," he added, glaring at his companions, "I want a shot at Stoner."

"What if no one comes along to try and stop us?" Slicker asked.

"We sell the cows and rustle some more."

"What about Stoner?" Dobbs asked doubtfully. "You say you want a shot at him, but so far he ain't been what I'd call easy to kill. What if he's the one that comes after the cattle?" He frowned as a chill swept over him at the mention of the gunfighter's name.

"If he gets in the way, he gets to be one we kill. If not, I'll hunt him up before I'm through," Cal bragged.

"If we don't kill Stoner what do we tell Nate when he asks why?" Dobbs asked thoughtfully.

"We tell him we couldn't catch the gunfighter alone away from the house, without the Peters girl. He won't like it, but he'll accept it if we get a Rockin' H puncher or two." Cal grinned maliciously. "Besides, if we don't get Stoner the first time, we'll just keep takin' a few head here, a few there. He'll come after them sometime and we'll get him when he does. In the meantime," he shrugged, "we'll get a stake. Nate won't say nothin' as long as he thinks we're after Stoner."

At the tentative nods of approval from his two companions Cal concluded, "Who knows? If this works, maybe we'll quit the Bar B and take up rustlin' for a livin'. We could make better money than the Bartlemans pay."

"The Rockin' H won't last that long," Slicker interposed, "not once Joe and Sam can ride again."

Dobbs grunted his agreement.

Cal shrugged again, "There's lots of other spreads in the valley with cows. And lots of ranches other places."

"Just as long as we don't touch no Bar B cattle," Slicker growled. "If there's one thing I don't wanta do, it's tangle with Joe and Sam."

"Yeah, and I reckon we'd better try them ranches in other places if the Bartlemans don't like what we're doin'. Fast," Dobbs grumbled.

When he was a young man in his twenties Thorn had made a good living stalking and killing men other men wanted dead for one reason or another, whether as a bounty hunter or a hired killer. Then a bronc had broken his right leg, which never healed correctly. He had found it difficult to move rapidly and stealthily through rough terrain on foot. So he turned from the lone-wolf life of the bushwhacker to riding with the pack, hiring his gun out to ranchers who paid extra for cowpunchers who could shoot and were willing to kill if ordered to. He didn't make as much money and he had to work harder, but he still made a decent living by his reckoning and he didn't live as dangerously. Usually his killing was done with others, seldom alone like this time.

While the three Bar B hands began rustling Rocking H cattle, Thorn began stalking Stoner, with a promise from Joe Bartleman through Barstow of five hundred dollars when his mission was successfully completed. He considered it a bonus that the target was Stoner. Killing the man who had ambushed and disarmed him so easily, and then forced him to repair the fence, would help heal his wounded sense of his own worth. He set up his ambush on a wooded slope about halfway up the valley of the Rocking H. Tying his horse to a sapling behind a jumble of boulders he settled down nearby, on a mat of pine needles he kicked together against one of the boulders. Before him the valley opened brown and green, the rocky stream of water meandering down its middle. He had an open shot to the valley floor two hundred feet below and rough terrain behind him through which to make his escape to the Bar B.

His chance came after a week and a half of waiting and watching the comings and goings of the Rocking H punchers. He reached his ambush site late in the day, too late to see where the work parties had ridden earlier in the morning. He had gone to Chasco the previous night and had returned late to the ranch, so drunk he couldn't remember the ride home. That morning he had awakened with a hangover like the inside of a hornet's nest. He moped around the cook shed drinking coffee until Nate threatened to break his gun arm.

He settled onto the mat of pine needles, his back against the rounded boulder at their head, his eyes on the valley below. And he fell asleep.

The next thing he knew he was lying on his side, curled in the fetal position, slobbering on the needles under his mouth. He jerked to a sitting position. The sun was sliding rapidly down its blue dome. Night would drop into place in a couple of hours.

Below him two riders were walking their mounts down the valley toward the buildings in the distance. The one on his side rode a dusty black horse.

"Stoner!" he muttered thickly and grabbed the Spencer propped against the boulder at his head.

He had an open shot, easy, he figured, although downhill. The riders were walking their horses abreast, talking, closer to the slopes on his side of the valley than to the stream.

"Don't seem worried about bushwhackers on these slopes," he muttered aloud.

He lay on his belly and scooted forward until the barrel of his Spencer rested on the tree trunk he had dragged into position for such an occasion. Carefully he sighted in on the rider on the dusty black and squeezed the trigger.

The two riders, Stoner and Tall Will, were discussing Rob Peters.

"He ain't gonna take your advice," Will growled in reaction to Stoner's explanation of how he had suggested Rob divide up the men. "Look what he done today. He sent out three work parties--Dodge and Pate together, you and me together, and Cactus, Sonora and Tate. He stayed at the house as home guard, just in case, like you said someone should." Will's tone turned sarcastic, "Then what? He shows up where we're workin' the foothills. Makin' his rounds to see how we're doin' and if we need help, he says. Bullshit," Will exploded, "he come out to make sure we wasn't goofin' off. See how fast he made tracks when he seen we had more work than we could handle in one day?"

Stoner chuckled at the memory of how quickly Rob left when Will showed him the brush and boulders that a recent flood and slide had deposited at the mouth of a long box canyon, effectively blocking it.

"We got maybe two, three hundred head up that canyon, and they got no way out to the stock tank between those round hilltops over there, except through here," Will pointed in the general direction of the pond. "There's some water in the canyon," he added, "but not enough without more rain than we generally get this time of year. Besides," he motioned to the steep slope above the blocked opening into the canyon, "another slide on top of this one, a bad slide, and we'll have a hell of a time gettin' it opened. Might take days." He stared into Rob's eyes and wondered if the man was listening. "We need to break it open every time there's a slide if we can." When Rob made no comment, he added lamely, "We could move the cows out and close the openin' so they can't get back in, but there's a lot of good grass in there."

Rob grunted, made no comment, and disappeared a few minutes later when Will and Stoner rolled up their sleeves and started moving boulders and tree limbs.

"It's his ranch, or will be someday," Stoner grunted, unwilling to get into a bitching session about Rob Peters. After the Loma incident he thought Rob had changed. But the man hadn't. Within days he had rejected most of Stoner's advice about sending out only large work parties, especially near the boundaries with the Bar B. Today he'd left the women unguarded, except for the cook. Stoner found himself hesitating about crossing Rob. He and Linda had reached a truce, a friendly truce. He was the happiest he had ever been, that he could recall. And Mrs. Peters! Her eyes gleamed when she looked at Rob. Stoner thought he would rather cut off an arm than ruin her happiness. I'll just have to work harder, cover more ground, and somehow make sure one of the hands is always at the ranch, he told himself.

"Yeah," Will agreed, "but it belongs to Mrs. Peters now, and when she's gone, half of it'll belong to Linda."

At that moment Thorn's finger was squeezing the trigger. Stoner pulled up, his head swinging toward the threat. Thorn's bullet broke through the air an inch in front of his chest and smacked into the cantle of Will's saddle.

Stoner didn't know why he had pulled up. An instinctive sense of danger, a flash of reflection off the rifle barrel, movement, something had caused him to yank the black up short and scan the hills. At the sound of the shot and the thwack of the bullet he drove his spurs into the black and reined him toward the tree-lined slopes downhill from the danger. He caught a flash of movement from behind as Will followed him. Then he threw himself down and forward, along the left flank of his mount, and swung the animal a little to the left, toward a rocky outcrop, the closest cover he could see.

The change of direction saved his life, again. He felt the tug of the bullet as it whipped through the back brim of his sombrero. In answer he grabbed his Winchester from its scabbard. Then he was in the jumble of brush and broken rock. He yanked the black to a sliding halt and dived for a narrow crack formed by a split in the rocky outcrop. Will tumbled in on top of him, knocking his breath from his lungs for a moment.

"Sorry, pard," Will apologized grimly, "but it ain't safe out there."

"Yeah," Stoner grimaced as he forced air into his tortured lungs. "But I think the shooter's after me, not you."

The fracture in the rock ran six feet in length, two wide, and maybe three deep. Underbrush rimmed its upper edges. Will had clambered over a few feet to give Stoner freedom of movement.

After a few moments of thought, Will agreed, "Yeah, thinking back on it, you probably felt the air from that first shot. The second one punched a hole in your hat," he picked the mentioned object from the ground, where it had fallen in Stoner's dive for cover. "Both shots came from the same rifle, I figure."

"Sounded like it," Stoner assented.

He pushed himself up and squatted beside Will. For several moments they remained silent as they studied their situation.

"We can't stay here, too cramped," Will broke the silence. "Before long we'll be so stove up we won't be able to move if he comes after us."

"Ah-huh," Stoner agreed, noting that Will was almost bent into three parts in order to keep his head below the edge of the fracture. "If there's only one."

"Only one rifle," Will reminded him.

"Yeah, and probably one bushwhacker," Stoner agreed.

"But could be others out there."

"Ah-huh."

"So, now what?"

"We go after the man that did the shooting," Stoner spoke slowly, studying the terrain around and above their shelter as he talked. "If there're other bushwhackers on the slope, they're probably fanned out. So we keep an eye out for any friends he might have."

"They could be together, waiting for us to come after them."

"Could be."

"I guess it don't make no difference," Will shrugged fatalistically. "We either go after him or find a way to run with our tails between our legs and maybe a bullet in our backsides."

"That's about the size of it," Stoner concurred, "unless we want to find another safe hole nearby." He paused, grimacing angrily, "Me, I don't like to be shot at. I say we flush the snake out of his hole."

"Lead the way," Will met Stoner's eyes. "I'm tired of Bar B snakes too."

"See that wash?" Stoner pointed uphill and to their left.

"Ah-huh."

"Looks like there's plenty of cover between here and there."

"Yeah," Tall Will showed his teeth in a grimace half grin, half snarl, "from the direction of the bushwhacker anyhow, if a man crawls."

"Head for the wash. I don't know where it runs or how far, but once you get into it, find a place where you can take off uphill without being spotted. Look for a way to flank the bushwhacker without him spotting you." Stoner met Will's questioning gaze. "I'll stay here for about ten minutes, then head up the slope, through the low ground that angles a little to the right of where the shots came from," he pointed to a seam where two hillsides seemed to merge as they descended from the heights above. "If we're lucky, one of us might get the first shot. If you catch a hint of another shooter," he added, his voice stressing the words, "get out; there could be more of them and even if there ain't, we don't want to flush two shooters. Head back down here. Fire a couple of quick shots to get my attention. I'll do the same." A fleeting smile crossed his lips. "We'll have to figure out something else, like maybe run with our tails between our legs."

With a quick "Luck," Will squirmed out of the split in the rock and snaked his way toward the wash, hoping the shallow depression deepened on its way up the hillside before it exposed anyone crawling up it to the fire of the man above. His hope failed him, but gave him a better solution. He had crawled no more than twenty feet up the wash when it ended against a vertical rock face eight feet high. At first he thought he was stymied, but a careful study of the ground to his left and right showed that the rock face ran at an angle uphill and to his left for twenty yards, then abruptly stopped. He quickly worked his way to the end of the outcrop and found the ground sloped around it, steeply but not impossibly so. Using handholds on brush and a small juniper he scaled the steep ground and soon found himself on a gentle, heavily wooded slope.

"I'm in luck," he mumbled out loud, breaking the eerie silence and calming the thud of his heart in his chest, adding cynically, "if Mother Nature don't get contrary and dig a ravine I can't get through between me and that damned bushwhacker."

As Will was ascending the slope, studying the terrain higher up and to his right, trying to figure out how high he needed to climb before he could turn and flank the rifleman, Stoner began his climb. In front of him a barren knob rose well above the surrounding shrubs and brush. On both sides of it lay jumbles of brush and boulders too thick to penetrate. On top of it he might be visible to the shooter. Stealthily, his rifle cradled in his arms, he snaked his way along the right edge of the mound, keeping as close to the shadows of the underbrush and small trees as possible. After what seemed an eternity he reached the tree-lined cover of the low ground he had chosen to follow. He stood and moved slowly upward, finding the going easier than it had looked from below. When he figured he was approaching the height from which the shots had come, he moved even slower, ghosting from tree to tree, outcrop to outcrop, carefully studying the terrain ahead of him before leaving one bit of cover for the next.

Thorn saw Stoner coming through the trees and thick brush, but he couldn't get a clear shot. Several times since missing his first two shots and watching helplessly as the two riders disappeared from his view he had decided to retreat and return another day. Pride and the wild desire to avenge himself on the Rocking H gunman kept him in place. Like most of the gunhands at the Bar B, he had heard of Stoner. He was aware of the legend that had grown up around the man and his ability with the Colt he always wore--his impossible speed and accuracy. Some said he had eyes in the back of his head, others that he had a sixth sense, others, more rational, that he never relaxed his vigilance, even while sleeping. Less known was his skill in the wilderness, but Thorn had heard that he was good, like an Indian born and raised in the mountains and forests. Mingled with his desire to avenge the insult to his pride at the Loma Linda surged another, deeper desire, to match his own native skills against those of the gunfighter.

So he waited. Like a spider at the center of its web he waited silently, ready to pounce, as Stoner ghosted through the pines and stands of aspen, catching only occasional, fleeting glimpses of the climbing prey.

What warned him this time Stoner could no more explain than he could what had warned him while he was peacefully riding the valley floor, talking to Will. He was darting from the cover of a rock outcrop to the thick trunk of a ponderosa when something, a movement of flesh or bush, a sound, something less tangible...something sent him diving into a tangle of brush and saplings as the shot cracked and the bullet nipped the cotton of his shirt, under his armpit, and whined off through the trees behind him.

"Damn," Thorn swore angrily to the world at large, "the son-of-a-bitch has the senses of a wolf."

A second later fear dissolved his anger. Nervously he studied the slope below for a glimpse of the second Rocking H hand, the tall puncher who had been with Stoner at the spring. Nothing moved on the slopes below his position. There was no sign of Stoner in the underbrush where he had disappeared. He could be circling to get behind me, Thorn thought, glancing to the right and left.

A cold chill shook his spine. No sign of Stoner. No sign of his companion.

The chill working at his spine and into his gut, hurrying him on, Thorn wormed his way through a slot made by the round boulder he had kept at his back and another, larger boulder that leaned against it. He should be moving more slowly, more carefully, he knew. But fear made him careless. Once through the slot he rose to his feet and, stooping low, scurried uphill to his horse, the icy fingers in his back tensing against the slam of a bullet. Quickly he ripped the reins free of the sapling they were tied to and mounted, raking the animal's flanks with his spurs as he settled into the saddle. At that moment he spotted the second Rocking H rider, in front of him, not more than ten paces up the slope, standing beside a huge pine, his rifle raised.

Tall Will had been angling along the slope fifty yards above Thorn when he heard the shot. The sound pinpointed the ambush site. Will hurried downhill, worried that the shot meant the end of Stoner. No sound followed it. No movement on the slopes below. Until he spotted the horse and, a moment later, a man darting toward it, rifle in hand.

Will stepped into the open, raising his weapon, settling it into his shoulder as the rifleman threw himself into the saddle and dug in his spurs. His eyes met those of the bushwhacker. He saw the flicker of fear and the frantic attempt to bring the rifle to bear as he squeezed the trigger. The bushwhacker slumped sideways, then slowly toppled from the back of the running animal, his head connecting with the trunk of a small ponderosa as he fell. He bounced several times and came to rest in a clump of boulders. The horse stopped forty feet further up the slope, standing undecided, looking back. Queasy at the stomach, Will studied the forest around him for movement or sound. Once he had decided that no other threat existed nearby, he checked to make sure the bushwhacker was dead, then walked uphill and returned leading the horse. He pushed the dead man's rifle into its scabbard and draped him over the saddle, tying him in place with short lengths of rope he found in the saddlebags. He was at his task when Stoner spoke from the shadow of the boulders that had served as Thorn's ambush.

"I was a second bushwhacker you'd be dead, Will."

"Jesus," Will started, grinning sheepishly. "I'm glad you ain't dead."

Stoner looked closely at him, noticed the upset under the grin, and changed the subject.

"Glad you came along. He had me pinned down. I didn't realize he'd sneaked off till I heard you shoot. Didn't know who'd been shot till I crawled through the boulders he was using. Sure happy it was him."

The two men looked at each other, the recent brush with death adding another level to their friendship.

Will and Pate took the corpse to the town marshal in Chasco.

After Will had explained the ambush and killing, he asked, "What now, Lije?"

"It's out of my jurisdiction, Will," Marshal Newel shrugged. "I could send for a territorial marshal but, hell, what could he do except check the wanted posters on the Bar B gunhands, and the one Mrs. Peters hired." He glared at Will, then Pate. "He could make a few arrests, maybe, if any of the wanted men stuck around long enough for him to find them, which I doubt would happen once word got out a marshal was on the way. He could warn the Bartlemans and the Peters family, for all the good that'd do. But you know as well as I do," he shook his head in irritation, "that there's no real proof the Bartlemans ordered the man to bushwhack you and that new gunfighter of yours."

"Stoner, that's his name," Will interrupted. "There's no doubt the bushwhacker was after Stoner."

"Okay," the town marshal shrugged again, irritation once more crinkling the lines of his forehead. "The bushwhacker worked for the Bar B, sure, but Joe and Sam'll deny they had anything to do with it. They'll say it was probably a personal thing like revenge for what happened up on the Loma Linda. Or they'll claim you shot him down in cold blood and now you're tryin' to make it look like self-defense."

"A marshal might scare the Bartlemans and make them pull in their horns."

"I doubt it. A marshal'll come in and ask questions. Not many people'll talk and the Bartlemans'll deny everything. It'll end up the word of the Rockin' H against the Bar B. That's the way of it. The Bar B's bigger and the Bartlemans're richer, so who'll the marshal believe?" He paused, smiling grimly. "The marshal'll leave and Joe and Sam'll start in again."

"What about the fight they started at the ranch house, with the Peters women present?" Pate asked icily. "And the ambush at the spring up on the Loma? You done anything about them?"

"I went to see the Bartlemans after you told me how the fight started at the ranch house, took a citizen's committee with me," the marshal returned Pate's cold glare as he spoke, his voice belligerent. "Joe and Sam claimed they rode to the Rockin' H on a peaceful mission, to make an offer for the ranch. They say this Stoner shot first. Matt, he refused to talk, but I figure he'll support his dad and brother if push comes to shove." He shrugged helplessly. "It's your word against theirs." He paused for a long time, considering what to say next. As an officer of the law he figured he should remain as neutral as he could in the upcoming battle between the two ranches, although his heart lay with the Peters family. "The citizen's committee warned them about hurting the Peters women, said the town wouldn't put up with women killing." Again he paused, thinking, not looking at either Pate or Will. "After Cactus brought that dead kid in I went to see them again. Asked them about the cut fence and ambush. They admitted to the cut fence and promised to deal from then on with Mrs. Peters for water rights at the spring. They said the ambush wasn't their idea, claimed it must have come from Barstow or over-eager hands. I talked to Barstow later and he denied giving orders for an ambush."

"Jesus," Will swore. "Those lyin' bastards."

"You want to say that to the Bartlemans, to their face? Or to Nate Barstow?"

Will glared at the marshal, then grinned sheepishly, "Not if I can get out of it. But I might have to someday."

"So, I reckon we're pretty much on our own," Pate interposed, "in spite of two ambushes and a shoot-out meant to kill Linda and Mrs. Peters."

The marshal shrugged, his eyes not meeting Pate's, "I'll talk to Joe again, warn him, but I already know what he'll say."

Will and Pate stalked from the office, angry scorn in the set of their shoulders.

Later, after the marshal left, Joe rolled out of bed and walked into the other bedroom.

"What the hell'd that yellow bastard want?" Sam growled.

Still recuperating from his broken bones, he had lost weight and his skin had turned pallid from lack of sun and wind. Dark rings circled his eyes, which seemed to have lost some of their strength also. His unkempt hair lay damp and oily on the greasy pillow.

"That damn Thorn didn't have what it takes. He ambushed the gunfighter when he wasn't alone. He missed and that tall, lanky drink of water they call Will got him."

"What now?" Sam cursed.

"It's gonna take a while before you and me get our strength back," Joe spoke sourly. "Then we'll figure out a way to get the gunfighter out of the way and go after the Peterses. Or go after them and forget about Stoner. Once they're gone, he'll drift."

"I thought you'd decided it was too dangerous to try for the women. Too many people in town might want our scalps."

"Yeah," Joe agreed grudgingly. "Maybe so, unless we can figure out an accident that won't point to us. Or some reason the citizens committee'd have to accept." He stared thoughtfully at the wall behind Sam's head. "I figure if the old woman was gone we could scare the cubs off."

"The old woman and Stoner maybe," Sam disagreed. "But hell, it'd be a lot simpler to get rid of the bunch of them. Then there'd be no one to stop us from takin' over the whole ranch."

"Yeah," Joe agreed tentatively and moved in another direction. "I don't figure we better send another killer after Stoner, not for a while anyhow. The marshal wasn't none too pleased about Thorn. He didn't believe me when I denied sending the back-shooter after Stoner."

"Not much he can do about it whether he believes us or not," Sam snarled.

"No," Joe agreed. "But he's a fighter, had his share of battles with Apaches and outlaws in his time. And he's got the ear of the citizen's committee, which is made up of some of the toughest men in Chasco. Don't underestimate him. Or them. We push too far too fast and we'll have to fight the town as well as the Rockin' H."

"I reckon we'll have to bide our time," Sam shrugged indifferently.

"Ah-huh," Joe agreed, adding thoughtfully, "unless Nate kills Stoner over the Peters girl, or kills both of them. Thorn said he heard Nate complainin' the other day about the two of them swimmin' together in the pond behind the Peters house. Said Nate was in a killin' mood."

"Maybe we should send him after the gunfighter," Sam suggested.

"No. Not yet," Joe disagreed. "Like I said, it's too soon. We'll take it easy until we're back on our feet. Then we'll figure out somethin'."

"Okay," Sam gave in, grinning, "but it'd solve a big problem if Nate killed the bastard over the girl. Next time I see him I'll put the spurs to him, tell him the latest rumors about Stoner and Linda Peters."

"Rumors?" Joe asked quizzically. "What rumors?"

"I'll come up with some," Sam laughed coldly.

Two days after the bushwhacking incident Stoner was riding up the edge of the valley. Pate had been left behind to repair a stall gate in the barn and stand guard. Rob had taken the rest of the crew to make a gather of cattle that had wandered down into the foothills and lowlands beyond where the creek entered the valley from the Loma Linda spring. They planned to brand the calves and push most of the older stock back into the upper canyons and slopes.

Rob had ignored Stoner, neither consulting him nor including him in the assignments.

The first time, Stoner thought as he rode, although not the first time my advice has been ignored, not by a long shot.

He had seen it coming, found it both amusing and irritating and knew that sometime soon he and Rob would clash, because Rob was slowly but surely returning to his true personality, arrogant and thoughtless, with a violent streak that exploded from nowhere. In the past week Stoner had been included in a work party only twice. The rest of the time he'd been left behind to guard headquarters. Today he had been ignored completely. Probably, he figured, because the evening before he had caught Rob beating his horse when it bumped him into the corral fence, causing him to tear his shirt and skin his arm. Rob's face, as he grabbed his bridle and lashed at the frightened animal, had been a mask of crazed savagery, his mouth split open in a snarl, his eyes unfocused. Stoner grabbed his arm on the third swing, angrily noting the blood oozing down the horse's muzzle.

Instantly Rob turned on his attacker, cursing, kicking, and swinging with his free arm. But Stoner let go of the bridle and grabbed him in a bear hug. Rob was no match for Stoner's strength. He continued to struggle for several minutes, then his body relaxed, although Stoner noted that the murderous rage roiling in the depths of his eyes never completely disappeared.

When Stoner released him, Rob dropped the bridle without a word, turned on his heel, and stalked toward the house. Stoner rubbed the horse down and put Rob's saddle and bridle in the tack shed. For Rob's sake he was glad none of the other hands or the Peters women had seen the interchange.

That morning Rob didn't look at Stoner as he told the crew what they would be doing, a recommendation that had come from Will the week before and which Rob had ridiculed at the time.

Stoner rode immersed in his thoughts, but not so deeply that he neglected the world around him. He caught the barely perceptible flash of movement on a slope to his right and reined his dusty black into the shadow of a boulder. Drawing his Winchester from its scabbard he sat quietly, patiently waiting, his senses attuned for threatening sound or motion. After a while a bridle chain rattled then stopped, abruptly, as if a horse had started to shake its head and been yanked up short.

"I'm comin' down," a deep voice sounded from behind a clump of junipers and manzanita.

"Come on," Stoner recognized the voice from his first day in Chasco. He jacked a shell into the chamber of his rifle. "But come peaceful."

Seconds later Nate Barstow rode into view and put his horse to the slope. He pulled up facing Stoner.

"You won't need that," he growled, nodding at the Winchester.

"You come to talk?"

"I come to kill you."

"Then I reckon I will need it," Stoner watched the big foreman but his ears and the periphery of his vision remained attuned to the shadows on the slopes above him.

"I didn't come shootin', did I? And I come alone," Barstow's voice remained an angry growl although he tried to force a neutral tone into it.

"Ah-huh," Stoner assented sardonically, letting his eyes roam the slopes.

"You think I need help to handle the likes of you?" Nate exploded furiously as he noticed the movement of Stoner's eyes, unable to control his emotions now that he faced the man he hated with deep, savage passion.

"Right this minute," Stoner's teeth showed in an insolent grin, "you need lots of help. I have a rifle aimed at your gut."

Fear flashed in Nate's eyes, then disappeared.

"Put the rifle away," he snarled, wondering if he had made a mistake in facing the gunfighter without a weapon in his hand, "and I'll beat you to a pulp."

Stoner studied the huge man, the insolent grin still in place, "I don't think that would be very bright. You probably outweigh me by a good thirty pounds, maybe forty."

"I didn't figure you for a coward," Nate gloated, sarcasm and suppressed anger underlying the taunting words. "But Sam said you wouldn't fight. Said you weren't much of a man without a gun in your hand. I reckon he was right."

"I reckon," Stoner's insolent grin spread to his eyes. "Would you like to try me with that Colt you've got? We dismount, stand facing each other, twenty feet or so apart, you start the shebang whenever you're ready. I won't draw till you do. Game?"

At first Stoner thought the big man would accept the challenge. A moment later, however, the flash of excitement in the foreman's eyes faded, leaving behind the murderous desire to rip and smash.

"No," Barstow's voice rumbled harsh and irritated. "I know some of the people you've killed, know how fast they were because I've seen them in action. It wouldn't be a fair fight."

"But a brawl no holds barred would be fair, even though I'm kind of puny beside your beef?"

"Scared?" Nate imitated Stoner's insolent grin, ignoring his question.

"You scared to face me with a Colt?"

"You know better'n that. I don't like the odds, that's all."

"Ah-huh," Stoner shrugged, "maybe that's the difference between us. I've been fighting the odds all my life."

Quickly he shoved the Winchester home in its scabbard and dismounted, moving backward into the open, "Hang your pistol belt on the saddle horn and get off your horse."

"You still got your sidearm," Nate growled suspiciously.

"Ah-huh, and I'm gonna use it if you don't do as I say. I'll get rid of my Colt when you're out here in the open where I can see you don't have a hideout gun."

With a sudden chuckle, half laughter, half snarl, the big foreman dismounted, unbuckled his cartridge belt, and draped it over his saddle. Unencumbered, he confronted Stoner. This was what he wanted, a chance to kill the gunfighter with his bare hands. He had rejected a shot from ambush. He had never yet bushwhacked a man and didn't plan on starting with the gunfighter. He had his pride and his code. When he killed, it was face to face, rifle, pistol, club, bare hands. He preferred his hands. There was something deeply satisfying for him in beating a man to death.

"I'm gonna break you in two," his eyes sparkled with the lust for violence.

"A man's gotta go sometime."

Keeping an eye on Nate, Stoner stepped to the black, hung his pistol belt over the saddle horn, and stepped back into the open to face his antagonist. Nate chose the moment he stopped to attack like a fighting bull maddened by the roar of the crowd. He thought he'd catch the smaller man with his balance on his heels, flat-footed, drive him into the dust. But Stoner stopped with his weight on the balls of his feet, lightly poised like a boxer or bullfighter, ready to dance in any direction. As the bigger man charged he feinted a left hook, noted the slight shift in Barstow's trajectory, and dodged to his left, dragging his foot behind him. Nate's leading ankle came up short against Stoner's leg, inches above the ankle. His following toe caught on the instep of Stoner's boot. His torso kept moving, a massive force with its equilibrium gone. He slammed into the earth on his chest and slid face first into a shallow wash, coming to a jarring stop against the far side.

With a curse, he scrambled to his knees and started to rise. He didn't make it. Stoner's fist caught him in the back of the neck. He lunged forward and up, roaring wildly. He barely made it to his feet when the toe of Stoner's boot caught him in the back of the right knee. His leg buckled. He threw himself backward, twisting as he moved, grasping frantically to get his hands on his elusive antagonist.

His right hand closed on air. His left hand closed on Stoner's ankle. He pistoned his feet into the earth, twisting his body and throwing it back and up at the same time while yanking on the captured ankle. Feeling his leg flying into the air, his head dropping to the earth, Stoner jammed his left boot toward where Nate's head should be. The spur caught Nate on the forehead, between the eyes, and ripped upward, taking flesh and a clump of hair with it. The Bar B foreman howled curses. He lost his grip on the ankle. Stoner twisted in the air as his motion flipped him head over heels. Like a cat he lit on both feet, bent forward, facing his raging foe.

His mind still blurry, blood dripping from ripped flesh starting at the top of his nose and ending deep in his hairline, Nate lunged. He wanted only one thing, blindly, instinctively, to get his hands on the smaller man and squeeze the life out of him.

Stoner, however, had had his share of rough and tumble fights. He knew that, if Nate did get his hands on him, solidly, he was a dead man. As Nate charged into him, head down, hands grasping, he clasped his arms under the man's massive neck and let himself be carried along by the momentum, throwing himself backward while at the same time jackknifing his torso and legs, his feet shoving solidly against Nate's belly. When he felt the earth at his back, using all the strength he could muster, still clasping Nate's neck with his locked arms, he heaved upward with his feet and torso. Nate flipped in the air, landing on his back. Stoner's momentum flipped him over onto his knees, straddling the bigger man.

Before the Bar B foreman could react, Stoner's fist struck out, knuckles extended, smacking solidly into his windpipe. Nate gagged. Stoner rolled free and lunged to his feet. Gasping and gagging, Nate was struggling to rise. As he reached his knees, Stoner's boot toe connected with the side of his head, above and in front of the ear. He folded, unconscious, his breath rasping harshly in his throat.

Stoner stood looking down a few moments, debating with himself about stomping his antagonist, breaking a few ribs, maybe killing him. He should, he knew. If he were lying there helpless, Barstow would stomp him to death without hesitation. Another consideration was Linda's safety, possibly her life. The man had been stalking her, doubtlessly still was. Barstow's death would free her. If he didn't kill Barstow and the Bar B foreman later hurt or killed Linda, he'd never forgive himself.

After a while he shook his head at his weakness and walked to his horse. When Barstow sat up a half hour later, moaning and holding his head, Stoner was sitting on a nearby mound of dirt and gravel, his pistol once again belted at his hip, his Winchester cradled in his arms. He stood up as Nate struggled to his feet.

"I should kill you," he spoke softly, as if thinking out loud.

Nate stood swaying, blood dripping off the tip of his nose, his hand holding his temple.

"You don't, I'll kill you."

"How?" Stoner let the insolence again creep into his voice. "Shoot me in the back?"

"I ain't no back shooter," Barstow growled sullenly without meeting Stoner's eyes. "Someday you'll walk through a door and I'll be waitin'."

Stoner studied the big man's face, again thinking that he was making a fatal mistake not shooting him down like a rabid animal.

"Anything's possible," he shrugged, "but if I catch you skulking around that stand of pines above the ranch house, the one you been using to stalk Linda, I'll shoot you like the skunk you are."

Surprise, anger, fear, shame--all mingled in the startled glance Nate threw Stoner. As he quickly swung his gaze to his horse and the trees beyond it, cunning mingled with the other emotions and soon predominated. Two birds with one stone, he gloated, remembering the first time he'd watched Stoner and Linda walking around the pond, and then recalling the recent times when they sometimes held hands, and worse for him, the afternoon the two swam together, laughing and splashing like two kids, while he watched jealously, furiously, from his ambush. Stoner was sweet on the girl. Nate wouldn't have to kill the bastard if he could get Linda. That would be revenge enough, more than enough. But, he told himself, I'll have to find a new ambush.

19

After the fight with the Bar B foreman, days passed at the Rocking H without incident, rolling into several weeks. Stoner found himself with no ranch work to do unless he forced his way onto one of the work parties. Most every day he checked the stand of pines where Barstow had lain up in ambush watching the ranch house, but he found no further evidence of the big man, and the self-appointed chore took little of his time. He ignored another stand of trees and brush twenty yards beyond the one Barstow had used, considering it too close to the other one, too obvious, for Barstow to choose it.

He often found himself in the role of headquarters guard because Rob assigned that chore only sporadically in spite of Stoner's sometimes angry advice.

Rob assumed command, consulting Stoner to satisfy his mother's wishes but ignoring any recommendations he received. Within a week or two of the ambush at the Loma he had again concluded that everything the gunfighter had done in Chasco and on the Rocking H had been done for the purpose of ingratiating himself into the family and eventually taking over the ranch.

"The bastard charmed Ma," he swore to himself one morning as he watched Stoner and Linda riding together up the valley. "Now he's after Linda. If I don't take care he'll be in the family legally, and next thing after that he'll be runnin' the ranch and I'll be workin' for him."

As the days passed peacefully, he became more and more convinced that the clash with the Bar B was over and that Stoner was exaggerating the danger for his own purposes. One morning he scattered the hands around the ranch in pairs, sending Dodge and Cactus into the brakes west of the spring at the Loma. He was going into Chasco with his mother, who was planning to visit friends and pick up supplies for the ranch. The previous evening, after dinner, Mrs. Peters had announced her plans for a day in town, with Stoner to accompany her. Rob and Linda had convinced her to accept Rob's company and leave Stoner to guard headquarters. Mrs. Peters had easily and happily agreed, rejecting Stoner's advice that she also take a couple of the hands along.

"Joe and Sam may still be in town. Other Bar B gunhands could be in town also," he explained. "Or on the trail. You could run into any of them, in Chasco or between here and there."

"I'll take a rifle," she touched Stoner's arm softly. "Rob will have his too. Besides," she continued with a disarming smile, "I don't think the Bartlemans will try to kill me again this soon. From what you and the hands say, they've been visited by Lije Newel and a committee of concerned citizens."

Stoner said he didn't think a citizen's committee would stop Joe and Sam for long, "They'll come up with something, like maybe an accident, or a bushwhacker who disappears afterward and can't be linked to the Bar B."

"Maybe," Mrs. Peters shrugged, "but not right away. I don't think they'll risk public opinion this soon after everything else that's happened."

Stoner was standing nearby, one foot on the lower rung of the corral fence, talking to Linda and Mrs. Peters when Rob gave his orders to the hands. Later, after the hands had ridden out, while Rob was hitching a horse to the buggy, he walked into the barn to inspect a wall that needed repaired. He walked out of the barn as Rob and Mrs. Peters were driving away in the wagon. Linda was still standing by the corral fence where he had left her talking to her mother.

"Come up to the house and I'll make you a cup of coffee," Linda offered, wondering if he heard the slight tremor in her voice.

She continued talking even as he accepted, hurriedly, nervously, trying to hide the pounding of her heart and the uneven rasp of her breathing. During the past weeks she had come to a clear realization, and a decision. Jacob Stoner was the man she wanted for a mate. She wanted him physically, immediately, whether that led to a long-term relationship or not. She wanted to feel his hands on her skin, touching her, caressing her body. She wanted to feel his hard body straining against hers.

Neither realization nor decision had been easy to come by, or to accept afterwards. Her pride and her aversion to killing and killers had been involved, as had her fear that Stoner was a tumbleweed, that one day he would tire of the sedentary life on the Rocking H and ride off, never to return. But, in his presence, she was happier, more comfortable than she had ever been with a man, felt more like a woman

Her desire had been difficult enough to admit into her consciousness, but accepting it as more than a transitory passion had been even more difficult. She had spent many sleepless hours trying to reject what first her body, then her emotions, kept telling her--that Stoner was the man she had always dreamed would one day appear in her life, no matter that he was not what she had dreamed he would be. Finally, one night in the early hours before dawn, she admitted to herself that he was the realistic manifestation of what she had dreamed her mate would be--a strong man with gentleness and love in his soul, a man capable of being a good husband and lover, and at the same time a man capable of standing tall in the face of nature's violence and man's cruelty. Such a man, she had admitted in the darkness of her room, would have to be a mixture of cruelty and kindness, like Stoner.

She had scorned Stoner from the first day of his arrival, scorned him and plotted violence against him, refusing to admit to herself the deep attraction she felt for him. Then, in the dark morning hours in her bedroom, she found herself wanting to submit to any demand he might make of her. She found herself shivering with suppressed desire and made the conscious decision to seduce him at the first opportunity, to make love to him with no strings attached, no matter the consequences, a decision that, every time she remembered it, made her burn furiously and shiver with mingled fear and anticipation.

Now the time had come. When her mother announced that she was going to Chasco with Stoner and asked her to go along, Linda made her plans. She refused her mother's offer and suggested to Rob that he take Stoner's place as escort. Rob was happy to go and they had easily convinced their mother to take him instead of Stoner. The final obstacle to her plans had disappeared when Rob sent all the men out to work the ranch, leaving her alone with Stoner, except for Chew Lin, of course, but Lin never entered the house, never came to the doors unless there was an emergency, and never discussed what he saw or suspected.

As Stoner accepted her offer of a cup of coffee and fell in beside her, she took his arm. Neither spoke as they walked slowly toward the house. They entered through the back door and into the kitchen. Stoner sat in the chair he had occupied on his first night at the ranch. A pot of coffee was always perking in the Peters household. Linda poured two cups, Stoner's black, hers with sugar. Neither spoke until she set the full cups on the table and took a seat opposite his.

"Rob scattered all the hands around the ranch," he broke the silence, worry in his voice. "Know where he sent them?"

"No," she answered tersely, not wanting ranch problems to interfere with her day. "But let's don't talk about the ranch. Let's talk about you." She darted a glance at him before again dropping her eyes to the table. After a long pause she continued, "You're a strange man, Jacob Stoner. One moment you're happy and cracking jokes, the next you seem so melancholy, as if ghosts from the past have appeared to torment you."

"They do, too often," Stoner smiled without humor. "I reckon I've always been moody. But you aren't Miss

Consistency, either," he grinned at her. "One time you're all charm and smiles. The next," he shrugged, "well, you've got to admit your claws can be pretty sharp."

They laughed together, easily, naturally, no longer uncomfortable in each other's presence.

"I guess I do change a lot," she spoke slowly, thoughtfully, having decided to confess the truth no matter how it sounded, in spite of the nervous trembling that had suddenly overcome her. "Mostly where you're concerned though, Jacob. To be honest, it's because I'm in love with you, I think. I've been fighting against my feelings for you ever since that first day in the saloon. That's why I was always changing, I suppose. One minute the Quaker side of me won, some might say the naive side, but in any case the side that considered killing a sin and thought that people who live by the gun are inherently evil. Even when I was a little girl," she smiled apologetically, for what she was saying, but found it impossible to meet his eyes, "the bible story that always haunted me most was the story of Cain and Abel. But I'm no longer a little girl expecting a perfect society. I'm beginning to wonder if Abel wasn't more than a little to blame for the falling out. I can no longer accept that Cain was guilty beyond redemption anyway."

She paused and shook her head in frustration, "I don't think I'm making myself clear, but what I mean is, I've begun to wonder if maybe we don't all have the potential to become killers, given the right circumstances."

She recalled her murderous anger at Nate Barstow on the day he ambushed her, and the fear that had kept her finger glued to the trigger of her rifle as she rode home from the ambush. There had been many moments on that ride when she yearned for only one thing, to put a bullet into Nate Barstow's brain for the fear he had caused her, for a fear that after that day, she knew for a certainty, would always be part of her reality.

She forced a smile and, reaching across the table, caressed Stoner's hand. He jerked as if touched by a hot branding iron.

"You're not just putting me on, are you, Linda?" he asked, his voice breaking slightly, a light shining in his eyes that Linda had never before seen in any man's.

"No," she answered in a whisper she knew came out as broken and husky as his.

As she spoke the word she felt her eyes mist over and for a moment the kitchen and Stoner dissolved into a liquid rainbow.

"That's all I've been thinking about for the last few days. I've lied to myself for so long and denied my feelings for you so much that...it's been tearing me apart."

She glanced down at her hands lying peacefully beside her coffee cup. Embarrassment turned her hot and sweaty. Inside, her chest trembled as if with a chill. But she forced herself to continue, "I don't know when I first realized how I felt. I do know when I first admitted my feelings to myself, consciously, that is, although I think my unconscious self had admitted them long before that and there was a battle going on inside me." She smiled sheepishly.

She paused and tried to steady her voice and gather her thoughts, which she sensed were coming unraveled. "I don't know, Jacob," she tried to smile but felt her lips form more of a grimace. "I just know I didn't want to love you. I wanted to love somebody with a steady personality and a steady, comfortable life ahead of him. At least, that's what I thought I wanted. But now," she grimaced again, "I think it was the East talking through me, that superficial veneer of an established and comfortable social order I acquired from a few years of schooling and living in the safe environment back there. It wasn't me, the real me, talking. I really want more than just a comfortable relationship."

She stopped talking. Their eyes met. They both felt the electrical charge in the air around them. Stoner started to reach for her.

"Don't, Jacob," her voice trembled again, husky, almost imperceptible. "Not yet. I want to talk. I need to," she forced a nervous laugh. "I guess I'm just afraid of the way I feel about you and I'm hoping words will make it easier...," again she forced a laugh. "To be honest, maybe I'm just delaying any final commitment, or maybe I just need to become used to my feelings before we...," she blushed furiously. "Say something, please," she blurted.

"Like what?" Stoner spoke uncertainly. "I've wanted you since the first moment I set eyes on you. It's been like a knife in my guts, whether you're near me or not. There in the saloon, when you asked me to help you with Rob, and the next day, and every day since, I've told myself that I should ride on, that there's no hope for me and, even if there was, that you'd be better off without me. I don't have anything to give you except uncertainty and danger."

"I'd rather have that from you than a long, sheltered life with someone I don't love," Linda reached across the table and touched his hand. This time she kept her hand on his.

"For that, even if there's nothing more, ever," Stoner spoke barely above a whisper, not daring to look at her for fear he would lose his train of thought, "I reckon I'll spend the rest of my life giving thanks. God knows, I'll never again look at a cholla jungle or a dust storm or a coyote catching a jackrabbit in the sage brush without seeing the beauty of it."

Linda's smile suddenly disappeared, although a soft glint of deviltry began to sparkle in her eyes. She asked, "Are you a religious man, Jacob?"

"Religious?" he blurted gruffly, startled by the question. He stared at her for several moments, indecisive, "What hat did you pull that question out of?"

She giggled at the shock on his face. "Just answer the question," she said. "You're the one who mentioned God as if you were his confidant."

He searched her face for some hint of where the question had come from and where it was leading. He didn't recall having mentioned God. For some time she met his gaze, then dropped her eyes.

"I know it's not a fair question no longer than we've known each other, and probably irrelevant too, but if we're going to be more than friends," again her eyes met his gaze openly, without wavering, although a splotch of red had appeared on each cheek, "I want to know all about you."

"Well," the word struggled out low and nervous. He swallowed and forced strength back into his voice. "Well, I think that's fair. And I'd sure like to be more than your friend."

"So?" Linda smiled shyly, again embarrassed by their mutual declaration but elated all the same.

"So, I reckon it depends on what you call religious." With an effort he regained control of his thoughts. "I haven't been inside a church since I was a kid, not more than a dozen times anyway. I've never liked all the threats of hellfire and damnation if you're a sinner, and the offer of brotherhood and love if you behave. I guess I just can't accept a God who says love me and do things my way or else," he concluded lamely, "especially when it's some narrow-minded preacher who's really doing the saying and claiming it's God. And when what he's saying is more custom than real feeling."

"You don't believe in preachers or churches, then?"

Stoner made a helpless gesture with his hands, "I can't say I do or I don't. I guess I never really thought much about it one way or the other." He frowned in concentration. "Churches? They serve a purpose, I reckon. They give people a chance to get together and socialize on a weekend, a day to relax a little and spend time with their neighbors. They give people hope for something better in some other life, if not in this one. They give people a reason for being good to each other, as good as they can be, being human and all. The real problem, though...people get the church and preacher all mixed up with God and truth, and they get their religious beliefs all mixed up with being good by their own standards. They forget the preacher's just another human like the rest of us and going to church isn't a substitute for accepting their neighbor no matter how odd he is. Worse, they forget they built the church so they could have a place to worship God. God didn't build it." He shrugged, still frowning in concentration. "As for preachers, somebody's got to run the churches, so I reckon it's best to have somebody run them who's done some studying on how," he chuckled, "although I think women could probably do a better job than the men seem to. They might cheer the sermons up a little at least. You know, have more singing happy songs and throw in some dancing and entertainment, and more ice-cream socials after church. And decorate the church a little better."

Linda found herself smiling while Stoner grinned at her.

"You don't really believe all that, do you?" she asked when he had finished.

Stoner took her hand in both of his, "I guess I believe that as much as I believe anything. I've always figured God would find most sermons boring and not worth much. The same with the people who run the churches." He paused, studying her face for signs of her reaction to what he had said, thinking. "All a person has to do is look around the world," he finally continued. "That's where you'll find God's words. In the beautiful bloom and the deadly spines of the cholla, in a steer that dies to keep a man alive, in a terrible summer storm and in the rainbow and the clean, blue sky afterwards, in the struggle to survive on the waterless desert or in a snow storm, both so beautiful in their own way, yet deadly too."

"You know," Linda moved her other hand to join the two that held her one captive, "you're a strange man, Jacob Stoner. I think I've said that before. If not, I've thought it often enough."

She took possession of one of his hands in hers and pulled it close to her while studying his face with soft, tender eyes.

"A gunfighter and a philosopher. What more?"

Stoner felt embarrassment warm his cheeks and forehead.

"I don't suppose you believe in the bible either?"

For a second Stoner wondered if she was being sarcastic, or if she was angry at what he had said. But, looking into her eyes, he found only a profound interest.

"Well?" Linda insisted softly but firmly when she thought he was going to ignore her question.

He shrugged helplessly, "I don't know what you want me to say, Linda."

She caressed the back of his hand with her thumbs. "What I want you to say is the truth, Jacob," she smiled at him. "I hope I'm not the shrew I sometimes appear." She felt her body turn warm and wondered if she was blushing again as she added, "If I'm going to be your woman and you my man, I want to know what makes you tick."

With his free hand he began softly tracing the outline of her cheek and lips. Nervously, a stranger to speaking so openly with a woman, he spoke in a low voice, "I can't say I'm real familiar with the good book. I've read some of it here and there, the Old Testament and the New, mostly the Old. I've heard it talked about plenty, of course. Every place a man goes, sooner or later it seems like there's someone who wants to quote the bible, or tell another man what God wants, or something. You know, a self-appointed preacher, a real preacher, somebody who's read some of the bible and memorized a few verses and reckons himself an expert on God's mind, some poor sap who's lost his own soul and thinks he can talk his way back to the straight and narrow. Most people won't talk religion, but there's always someone around that won't talk anything else. And I guess I'm a good listener when a man's got something he needs to get off his chest." Stoner paused and touched Linda's cheek before continuing, with a self-disparaging grin, "The way I get it, I figure the Old Testament tells us how the world really is. The New Testament is more like how we'd like for it to be."

Linda burst into delighted laughter. She stood up and pulled him up with her, moving forward until her body fit against the length of his, her face against his chest, her nostrils drinking in the mingled smell of horse, tobacco, lye soap, shave lotion, and man.

"If I have children I want them raised in the church," she murmured shyly.

"I don't reckon I'd fight that," he conceded, his voice a hoarse croak.

They stood silently as the moments passed, enjoying the pleasant, sensual comfort of each other's body.

After a while, the heat swelling in his loins, cupping her chin in the palm of his hand, Stoner lifted her willing lips to his. Their kiss was soft, reverent, hesitant. But soon the demands of passion drove their bodies together as if they could become one. His hands wandered of their own accord down her back, over her small, firm buttocks, moving between their straining bodies to her softly rounded belly.

"Not here," Linda gasped. "In my bedroom. Please."

Stoner lifted her in his arms and, following her breathless directions, stumbled toward the back of the house. Moments later he deposited her gently on her bed and stood looking down at her, savoring her warm beauty in the virginal atmosphere of the room. The walls and ceiling were of light oak. Watercolors of birds and flowers hung from the walls. A white rag rug covered the floor. Scattered around the room were small tables holding perfumes, cosmetics and other female items. Against the wall beside the bed, across from Stoner, stood a bookcase. On a tiny stand between the bookcase and the bed Stoner noticed a book entitled *Little Women*, a bookmark sticking from the middle of it. A white oil lamp stood guard on the other side of the bed, which was covered with a white quilt that hung to the floor on three sides. Sprawled on her back where Stoner had deposited her, Linda lay framed by the quilt, her dark hair spread in tempting disarray, her face flushed with mingled happiness and fear, her eyes swollen with desire and wonder, expectantly watching Stoner, her arms at her sides, her legs slightly spread, her light red blouse pulled tight over her heaving breasts, her skirt unable to hide the feminine roundness of her thighs.

Stoner felt a profound emotion flood through him, an emotion at the same time carnal and divine, an emotion more intense and pervasive than any he had ever felt, or imagined that he could feel. His hands trembling, breathing as if he had been running for hours, he began taking his clothes off, watching her as she watched him, mesmerized by lust and the purity of something he couldn't define.

When he stood naked before her, his desire evident in his swollen manhood and his heaving chest, Linda rose to stand facing him. She let her eyes drink in the broad shoulders and deep chest sloping into narrow flanks, the corded biceps and forearms, the muscular legs and flat stomach, his swollen manhood.

She felt her own juices increase their flow. Her legs quivered weakly. She began to strip, never taking her eyes from his body, fighting to control her breathing, wondering if he could hear the thump-thump-thump of her heart. She started with the buttons to her blouse, her hands moving slowly, hesitantly, teasingly, until she stood before Stoner as Eve must have appeared for the first time before Adam.

Stoner watched her, hypnotized by the sensuous, magical aura of the room and by her movements. He found himself unable to reach for her, as if the slightest stir would awaken him and destroy the moment forever.

Her breasts were large for such a slender woman, large, firm, proudly upturned, the nipples small and pert. Her belly rounded slightly, softly, invitingly. Her thighs dropped smoothly from her slender hips, silken, her legs long and athletic. The olive sheen of her body contrasted seductively with the dark patch of curly hair at the juncture of thighs and hips.

Suddenly the spell shattered, for both. Their bodies came together with the force of two powerful magnets. Their lips met. Linda's mouth opened invitingly, anxiously. As if with a will of its own Stoner's tongue penetrated the hot, sweet, moist depths, probing, searching, and frantically yearning toward the unreachable. Their bodies surged together, trying to become one.

With a single impetus they dropped to the bed. Moaning, pleading, demanding, Linda rose to meet Stoner as, thrusting wildly, uncontrollably, he entered her. The entry and the orgasm came as one explosive union.

Slowly they returned to the world and to each other. Pushing and pulling, Linda managed to roll Stoner over onto his back and stretch out on top of him, luxuriating in the feel of his hard body supporting the length of hers. Her cheek against his chest, with a smile of contentment that only she was aware of, she murmured, "Now I know what paradise must be like."

"Ah-huh," reluctantly Stoner forced his mind out of the pleasant fog in which it had been floating. "Now I know what making love to an angel is like."

Linda murmured something indistinguishable and snuggled closer. They floated back into the comfortable fog of lethargy. Later they made love again, slower, tenderly, exploring, teasing each other to the heights of sensual rapture. Afterwards, sated, Linda lying in the crook of Stoner's arm, her head on his shoulder and her fingers tracing delicate whorls on the skin of his lower chest, they talked about their love and their hopes for the future. Slowly their words became softer and softer until they drifted off to sleep. At mid-morning they awoke, made love once more, and again sank into a lethargic state half doze, half reverie, their limbs intertwined, Linda's face nestled in the hollow of Stoner's neck, her hair tickling his nose and lips, their thoughts and daydreams as intertwined as their bodies.

Shortly before mid-day, dressed, they wandered into the kitchen arm in arm. Linda began lunch and a fresh pot of coffee while Stoner headed for the washroom to fill the tub and lay a fire under it. Later, lunch over, refreshed with a hot bath, they were sitting on the porch, holding hands, quietly enjoying the shade and the play of light and dark on the mountains in the distance.

'Somebody coming," Stoner broke the silence.

Linda listened, straining. "I don't hear anything," she looked at him doubtfully, not relaxing her grip on his hand.

For a moment he said nothing more. Then, releasing his hand from hers and standing, he repeated his words, "Somebody coming. Fast. Riding around the pond."

A moment later Linda also heard the sound of the running horse. As Stoner stepped off the porch and turned toward the sound, she started to follow.

"Maybe you'd better stay here," he threw over his shoulder.

"You know better than that," she laughed without humor.

"Then get your rifle from the kitchen," was his only answer as he rounded the corner of the house.

She hurried into the house, grabbed her Remington and dashed out the back door. Stoner was standing near the bunkhouse, the corral between him and the approaching horse, his Winchester in his hands. As Linda ran to join him she saw the horseman top a low rise. At the same moment in which she recognized him and saw the blood on his chest, he reeled and toppled from the saddle, bouncing once on the rocky ground before coming to rest against a boulder twice his size. He made a move to rise but fell back and lay motionless where his body had lodged. Linda screamed, Stoner shouted, they both took off running, Stoner carefully scanning the horse's back trail and the surrounding foothills as he ran.

20

When they left the valley floor Cactus and Dodge entered a region of rocky gullies, landslides, and steep slopes covered with heavy brush. The two men pulled their mounts to a halt at the mouth of a rugged, steep canyon and stared disgustedly upward.

"I reckon we better get busy or we'll be here a month of Sundays," Cactus grumbled. "There's five main canyons comin' down the mountain, four besides this one, with side canyons everywhere, which makes it impossible to ride in anything resemblin' a straight line. But anyhow, we'll work the main canyons one at a time. We'll take the side canyons as we come to them through the main canyons. When we've gathered as many critters as we think we can handle, we'll move them down to the valley floor and scatter them. They'll stay there for a few days, I reckon, maybe a few weeks, the grass and water bein' better than they're used to. Maybe long enough for us to sort out the calves needin' brandin' and the young stuff we're gonna hold till we gather enough to make a drive," his grizzled face broke into a grin, baring a mouth half full of yellow teeth. "Leastways them's our orders, move the cows down to the valley floor. Tomorrow or the next day or the next the other hands're gonna start brandin' and sortin'." He paused, shaking his head and grimacing. "Rob's orders. He's good with ideas. I'll wait and see how well he follows through before I say what I really think."

"Ain't gonna be easy," Dodge frowned, staring up the canyon before them.

"The way I look at it," Cactus also stared up the forbidding canyon, "if we miss a few or some get away from us, don't worry about it. Hell, no need to lose sleep over a cow here and there. Nobody's gonna take them any place; they'll still be here next time."

"Where do we start this fandango?" Dodge chuckled, happy he had made the move to the Rocking H in spite of the tough chore ahead of them. The men on the crew were an easygoing bunch, unlike those at the Bar B, where there was always someone ready to throw a fist or a gun at the slightest provocation or, often enough, without provocation. In the past few weeks his gut had quit churning every time someone approached him. He even liked the hard work, he kept telling himself with surprise.

"On up this canyon," Cactus pointed to the broken, brush-infested opening in the escarpment ahead of them. "It might look like nothin' but a hole in the wall but it goes all the way to the top of the mesa, though sometimes it'll seem more like it's gonna tilt over on its back and fall off the mountain."

They set out, slowly, steadily. By early afternoon they had ridden over half way up the main canyon, in and out of a dozen side canyons, and they had gathered only nineteen head of cattle with three calves, which they had driven into a feeder canyon, where they planned to keep them until they had a large enough herd to make it worthwhile driving them down to the flats.

"We're movin' right along," Cactus commented as they sat their horses looking over the herd, "because there ain't no cows." Then he asked, "See much sign of riders on your side of the canyon?"

"Yeah," Dodge answered. "Old sign down at the bottom; the further uphill we get the newer it is. A lone horseman. I followed his tracks all the way up the canyon. He was doin' the same thing I was, only sooner, so he got all the good stock, I reckon. Most of these're his culls, I'd bet my saddle on it."

"That's what I figure," Cactus growled. "I followed a set of tracks too, on the left side of the canyon. One horseman gatherin' cows along the way, workin' the side canyons just like we was. I seen where they bunched the first gather in the middle of the canyon and drove it back up toward the top."

"Yeah." Dodge refused to meet Cactus's gaze. He had seen all the signs. A blind man couldn't have missed them, he didn't reckon. He wondered if Cactus figured like he did, that the Bar B was beginning a rustling war against the Rocking H. The thought shamed him because he had so recently ridden for the Bartleman outfit.

"They made two gathers in the lower half of the canyon. I saw where they gathered the second bunch."

"Ah-huh," Cactus started to interrupt, but Dodge continued talking.

"After the second gather the tracks're more recent."

"Some as recent as yesterday, I figure," Cactus spit at a clump of flowers on a nearby prickly pear.

Neither man realized that they were being watched.

Cal, Dobbs, and Slicker had established a lookout on the edge of Black Bear Mesa, in an outcrop of boulders that overlooked the valley floor. From their vantage point, with Dobbs's binoculars, they could watch the comings and goings all the way from the Rocking H ranch house most of the way up the valley. At first they kept watch diligently, hoping to catch Stoner riding out alone. Their anger for what had happened in Chasco remained seething hot for days. But it cooled, replaced first by boredom and then by greed. After days of watching in shifts and not seeing their target ride in their direction, they made other plans. While one of them spied on the Rocking H, the other two began gathering a herd of young stuff. When they had a bunch of thirty to forty, all three drove them south to Globe City.

Cal and Slicker agreed with Dobbs when he said, "I sure don't cotton to driving a bunch of ornery critters all that way. I didn't sign on with the Bar B to trail a herd. But what the hell, when they're our own critters," his words elicited a chuckle from his partners, "and there's all that money to be had at the other end, and all that rotten whiskey and them wild women to spend it on, well hell, work, here I come."

Cal let out a rebel yell and danced a jig.

"I'll be damned," Slicker grinned satirically. "We ain't busted our butts getting this bunch of cows gathered. Hell, we could've done it in a day and it's taken us almost a week. I don't reckon we're gonna push ourselves none getting' to Globe City. But while we're there," he leered, "I plan on workin' for two, a sponge and a jackrabbit."

Cal and Dobbs both greeted his sally with ribald comments and laughter. When they returned after selling the cattle and spending most of the money, they took up their rotation of spying and gathering cattle. They had completed the second drive and were almost ready for a third when Slicker, on duty with the binoculars, spotted Cactus and Dodge ride up the valley and turn into the brakes.

"Shit," he said when he reported back to camp, "there's two Rockin' H riders headin' up the same canyon we been workin'. "I'd bet my horse to a horny toad they're gonna drive that canyon for unbranded stock."

"They won't find much," Dobbs shrugged, less they start at the top.

"Nope," Cal grinned. "I don't reckon. But what they do round up, we're gonna take and add to our bunch," he gestured toward the head of the third main canyon from the escarpment, where the box canyon was that they used to hide the cattle they had gathered. "And we're gonna leave two dead Rockin' H riders behind. The next time Nate braces us up here I figure on telling him we've taken two scalps."

"He sure as hell didn't have no right to a split of the money we got for that second bunch of cows," Slicker growled. "We shoulda spent his share too, not kept it back like he ordered us to."

"Yeah," Cal agreed seriously, angrily, "but I sure as hell wasn't gonna ignore his orders, not with the mood he's been in since somebody cut him up. Sure like to know who done it." He paused, eyeing Slicker scornfully. "I didn't hear you tell him he couldn't have a share."

"Nobody's that dumb," Dobbs interrupted. "Nate's like a stud horse in heat. He'll kill anybody gets between him and that Peters filly. And worse, anyone that gets in kicking range of him until she gives in and takes the edge off his hunger. I sure as hell ain't gonna cross him about anything long as he's like he is."

"You and me both," Slicker added, irritated by Cal's comment. "As long as he's got a hard-on for everyone and everything, I ain't gonna brace him."

"As long as he's got a hard-on for the Peters girl, you mean," Cal leered.

"Same thing," Slicker shrugged. "He's been stompin' and growlin' around like a locoed bull ever since she come back from the East."

"Yeah, it's hard to understand," Dobbs spoke thoughtfully. "The way he talks about how all that education and culture's ruined her, you wouldn't figure she'd turn him on like she does."

"Hah, hah," Cal burst out gleefully. "It sure as hell ain't her education that gives him hot flashes."

Laughing and joshing about what attracted Nate to the Peters girl, the three mounted and reined their horses toward the canyon where the two Bar B riders were working. They rode at a walk, quietly, their glee submerged in thoughts of the clash to come. They had reached one of the narrowest sections of the canyon when they heard the sound of cattle in a side canyon. They reined in. Slicker and Cal waited with the horses while Dobbs scouted ahead.

"There's only two of them all right," he observed when he returned. "But they're skittish. They seen our tracks and they sure as hell know they should've found a lot more cows."

"What do you think?" Slicker asked.

"There's only the one way in and out of that side canyon," Dobbs answered thoughtfully. "The mouth's pretty big and the whole canyon's flat and wide, but not more'n a hundred yards long. There's a lot of cover at the opening, not much inside. If Cal goes in on the right, you on the left, and me down the middle, we'll catch them out in the open while we have the cover. Right now they're out in the middle, in plain sight and not more'n fifty yards from where we'll be. If we hurry we'll have them both dead in short order."

"When do we start shooting?" Cal asked, his eyes gleaming with murderous glee.

"From where I'll be I can see both of you move into position. When I start shooting, the game's open."

Minutes later Dobbs watched Slicker worm his way into a small clump of boulders near the left wall of the canyon. Cal had already disappeared into a tree-lined depression on the right. In the canyon itself, the two Rocking H riders sat their horses about seventy yards away, near the cattle they had gathered. Dobbs had recognized one of the riders as Dodge.

"Goddamn Judas," he muttered, aligning his sights on the ex-Bar B hand.

Two shots, to his right and left, echoed his. Dodge slumped, reflexively grabbed for the pommel, then slowly folded from the saddle, clearly dead before he hit the ground. With a startled yell Cactus spurred his horse toward the opening between Dobbs and Slicker. Dobbs carefully sighted on the fleeing rider's chest and squeezed the trigger. Cactus jerked and slumped along the neck of his horse, but he kept spurring frantically. Before Dobbs could get off a second shot the wounded rider had disappeared into a clump of tall brush near the canyon mouth.

Dobbs swore to himself. He had left his horse tied to a mulberry bush thirty paces behind him, in a shallow wash. He turned to run for the animal, thinking to chase after the wounded Rocking H rider. But he stopped before completing five steps.

"What for?" he asked himself.

He and his two partners had the cattle. If he chased the fleeing rider he might run into other Rocking H hands. The best thing to do, he concluded, was to gather the cattle that had scattered when they shot Dodge, as quickly as possible, separate out the culls, and drive the rest to the canyon where their herd was, then head the whole bunch south. He had lost his desire to kill the wounded rider or anyone else connected with the Rocking H, including Stoner.   Nate and the Bartlemans could kill their own snakes. Rustling Rocking H cattle had given him all the revenge he needed, and put money in his pocket besides. After a half dozen more drives, he figured, if he saved most of his share instead of spending it like he'd been doing, he could set himself up with a little place of his own somewhere like in Oregon or California.

He glanced toward his two companions. Cal was galloping in his direction, shouting and waving his rifle. Slicker was not in sight.

"What the hell you waitin' for?" Cal shouted as he spurred wildly past Dobbs. "That damned rider's gettin' away."

Dobbs watched the younger man disappear into the junipers. Then he turned and walked to his horse. Several minutes later he was sitting his saddle looking down at Dodge's dead body. A couple of blowflies had already found the blood on the dead man's chest. A line of ants was moving industriously between the pool of blood under the body and a mounded hole in the earth two feet away.

Dobbs shuddered, "Odd how things turn out, ain't it, old timer?" He spoke aloud, his voice made harsh by a feeling of guilt new to him. "You and me, we was bunkies not long ago. We got along okay, better'n me and these two bloodthirsty bastards I'm ridin' with now. I'm sorry I called you a Judas. Hell, I've had it with the Bar B too. I'll take what I can from this rustlin' of Rockin' H beef. Then I'm headin' west by north, away from Nate Barstow and the Bartlemans, before I wind up like you."

He dismounted and dragged the body into a steep-sided gully, where it quickly disappeared under rocks and sand. The burial gave him a sense of wellbeing again. He had just finished his chore when Cal and Slicker rode up.

"Catch him?" he asked without real interest.

"No, damn it," Cal hooked his leg over the pommel and began rolling a cigarette. "His tracks was easy enough to follow, him bein' in a hurry and all," he guffawed. "But me'n Slicker got to worryin' about ridin' into a ambush or a bunch of Rockin' H hands. So we gave up the chase and rode back."

Nobody said anything for a while. Slicker sat hunched over in the saddle, his eyes glued to his horse's ears. Cal continued to smoke his cigarette, a grin on his face as he recalled the shooting and the chase. Dobbs stared at his two companions for a few moments, then turned and looked at the cattle Dodge and his partner had gathered.

"We'd better get a move on," he said finally. "Could be they'll come after us soon as the wounded rider gets home." He waited for a comment but Cal and Slicker remained silent. "Looks to me like about a third of this herd's worth driving along; the rest are too old and tough, or too young to make it."

Dobbs soon had the chosen cattle moving up the main canyon. Slicker and Cal had ridden ahead for the cattle they had already gathered. The three planned to meet at the south end of the mesa, on Bar B land.

"I don't like runnin'," Cal had spoken with irritation when Dobbs had sent him and Slicker ahead. "We could set up an ambush right here."

"We could," Dobbs shrugged. "But we don't know how many riders they'll send after us. Besides, they'll be expectin' us here. They'll come in easy-like, ready for a fight." He paused and stared thoughtfully at his companions. "If we head out, there's lots of places on the trail south where we can set up an ambush, places a lot better than here. And lots of time to find out how many riders are comin' after us and figure the best place to cut them down."

Slicker agreed readily, Cal grudgingly.

21

Linda reached Cactus first, Stoner moving more slowly as he scanned the valley and every potential ambush spot within rifle range. Finally convinced that Cactus had not been followed by whoever had shot him, Stoner knelt beside Linda.

"There's a lot of blood," Linda spoke in a frightened whisper, "but I think he was only shot once, in the chest, high up."

After a brief inspection Stoner agreed. The bullet had gone in below the right shoulder and exited at the back of the armpit. He didn't think it had hit bone.

"He's lost a lot of blood," Linda continued more calmly. Then she added with a distressed shake of her head, "He's probably in shock, but I don't think he'll die. Do you?"

"I hope not," Stoner squeezed her shoulder gently, not knowing what else to do or say. Cactus was an old man, so who could tell for sure. With his hand still on Linda's shoulder he added, "We'd best get him to the house, doctor his wound, and get him to bed."

Between them they sat the old man back in the saddle. With Stoner holding him in place and Linda lugging the rifles and leading the horse, they soon reached the front porch. There, carefully, Stoner pulled Cactus from the saddle and carried him inside. The old puncher regained consciousness as Linda finished bandaging his wounds. Although weak from loss of blood, he told them what had happened and what he and Dodge had seen before the ambush, then insisted they help him to the bunkhouse and his own bunk.

"Damn it, Linda girl," he complained when she insisted that he move into her bedroom until he was well enough to get around on his own, "a man's a lot more comfortable in his own bed. I figure my wound'll heal faster there." He grinned weakly, and then fixed his eyes on Stoner. "And I can walk, too, boss. I need a little help, that's all. But I don't need nobody carryin' me like I was a baby."

"Okay, Cactus," Stoner returned the cantankerous grin.

They soon had the old man in his bunk.

"What now?" Linda asked as they stood side by side watching the old man's face swiftly relax as he dropped off to sleep.

"I've got to go see about Dodge, see if he's really dead like Cactus thinks. After that I'll see if I can track the killers," Stoner began loading his saddlebags from the wooden chest that sat at the foot of his bunk. "It sounds like they're rustling Rockin' H beef, so they probably made off with the herd Dodge and Cactus had gathered. If they did, they won't move fast, so I'll start there, where the shooting took place. If Dodge is alive, I'll bring him back here first. If not...." He shrugged. "When Will and Pate get back, send them after me."

"No!"

The word smashed into the silence of the room. Startled, Stoner froze, staring at the girl who, with one bound, now stood in front of him, her face less than a foot from his, her eyes flashing fire, her fists clenched. "I'm going along. They're Rocking H cattle. Cactus and Dodge worked for the Rocking H. Dodge lost his life working for the Rocking H. For me, my mother, my brother. The least I can do is help avenge his death and get back the cattle he was killed for."

Linda's words shocked her. They sounded so angry, so bloodthirsty. Vaguely she wondered about the changes that had taken place in her during the past few weeks. She almost giggled, nervously, at the thought of what her reaction would have been a few weeks previously.

Her words startled Stoner more than they did her. His first reaction was an emphatic no. But he looked at her face and realized that a refusal would do no good. She was going and that was that.

"If we catch them there'll be shooting. I don't want you hurt," he didn't expect his words to do any good, but he couldn't help trying.

"I don't want you hurt either," her jaw set stubbornly. "But you'll go anyway, won't you, even if the trail leads to the Bar B?"

"Somebody's got to take care of Cactus," he tried again.

"I'll tell Chew Lin to take care of him till Mother or Sonora gets home."

"Somebody should stay here to tell Pate and Will where to go. Cactus might still be unconscious," he spoke lamely, aware of how weak his argument sounded since Chew Lin would be there.

He started to tell her that she would get in the way, that worrying about her would hinder his actions, that she was not a fighter, that she was a woman. But he stopped himself in time, knowing full well that she would go in spite of anything he said or did and that such words, at the moment, might destroy the feelings she had for him. Besides, he told himself ruefully, she was a good shot and everybody had to begin somewhere. The thoughts didn't relieve his worries, though. He didn't know what he would do if she were killed, or if there was a good chance she might be.

"I'll tell Chew Lin where we're going, and I'll leave a note."

He shrugged helplessly, wondering how he had fallen for such an independent woman. The next moment he answered his own question--because she was all woman, just as had been the pioneer women who had moved westward beside their men, fighting when attacked, giving birth alone in the wilderness, cleaning, cooking, milking, helping with the clearing and planting and harvesting, doing whatever was necessary.

"We need to travel light, but I don't know how long we'll be gone or where they'll lead us, so bring a change of underwear and socks, and a couple of blankets," he shrugged helplessly before continuing, "and your rifle and plenty of ammunition."

He paused, thinking. "Leave a note on the table in the bunkhouse, another in the house, and fill a couple of canteens. I'll saddle up, tell Chew Lin, and have him put enough food together for a few days, in case the killers aren't Bar B riders and they run for it."

Twenty minutes later they were trotting up the valley. When they entered the canyon that Dodge and Cactus had been working, they split up, Stoner moving along one side, Linda along the other.

"According to Cactus there's plenty of cover most of the way to the side canyon, trees, boulders, breaks in the canyon floor," Stoner reminded Linda before they separated. "But cover works both ways. Any place that hides us can hide an ambusher." He paused and looked at her in silence for several moments, worried that he might be leading her into a trap but knowing that nothing he could say would keep her from going up the canyon. "I don't expect they're waiting for us but go slow in case," he admonished. "Anything moves, dive for cover."

When they reached the site of the ambush without incident, he breathed a deep sigh of relief even though he knew the real trouble would face them somewhere on the trail ahead, possibly some place where they were least expecting it.

They spent only enough time in the side canyon to verify that three men had ambushed Dodge and Cactus, that Dodge had been buried under dirt and rock, and that two of the ambushers had ridden up the main canyon together while the third had followed more slowly with some of the cattle. Before they left the mesa they understood the reason for the rustlers separating. On the far side the first two rustlers, driving another, larger herd, joined their companion.

"Three men and close to eighty head," Stoner mused as he and Linda sat their horses studying the tracks. "And not much more than two hours ahead of us."

"If we hurry we can catch them before dark," Linda spoke excitedly, spurring her horse into a lope.

"Maybe," Stoner found himself talking to the empty air as he urged his horse after hers, "but we won't be moving very fast through good ambush country. I don't plan on losing my new saddle partner if I can help it."

After leaving Black Bear Mesa, the country they rode through turned open. Brushy ravines, rocky slopes, and steep cliffs lay to either side of them, but they followed a trail that skirted the rough country and wended its way along rolling land. Stoner knew they were riding over Bar B range, so he kept his eyes peeled for any sight of riders. After several hours, they passed from the foothills of the Bar B range into pine-encrusted mountains where the trail wound through stony ravines and over springy beds of pine needles. Under the shade of the pines the day turned cooler, the sun dimming. Stoner called a halt to rest riders and horses. Refreshing himself and his mount in a small stream, he left the animal to graze on the banks of the water and took a seat on a nearby boulder.

Linda imitated his actions, but when he sat down to relax she protested.

"If we don't get a move on we won't catch them today."

"Maybe, but I figure we're only a half hour behind them. They don't appear to be in a hurry. Must not think they're being followed. They'll quit before we do, I reckon. They'll look for a place they can keep an easy watch without the cattle wandering off, a small box canyon or someplace backed up against a cliff face or...," he shrugged.

Linda nodded agreement and then smiled, "How do you know so much about what they will or won't do?"

He returned her smile, "Because I've been on both sides."

"Both sides?"

"Ah-huh," Stoner shrugged again.

"You never told me you were a rustler," Linda stared at him accusingly.

He returned her stare, a glimmer of a smile crinkling his eyes at the corners, "It's not something I'm proud of. So why would I tell my best girl? Besides, it was a long time ago."

They both laughed.

"I reckon it'll take me a lifetime to learn all about your past," she imitated his drawl.

"About the same amount of time it'll take me to learn about yours," he imitated her imitation.

Again they both laughed.

Once Linda had quenched her thirst in the stream she had remained standing near it, and near her mount, too nervous to sit. Now she walked over and sat down on Stoner's lap, leaning against him and putting her arms around his neck. For a long time neither moved nor spoke. Finally Stoner raised his head and glanced up at the patches of sky showing through the heavy canopy of pines.

"There's only a couple hours till dark. I figure the rustlers'll be bedding the cows down before long, maybe about now."

Leaning back, Linda studied him impatiently, then asked with mock sarcasm, "Does that mean we can go now? And what are we going to do when we catch them?"

Stoner had been asking himself the same question ever since they first began following the tracks of the rustlers. He kept searching his mind, desperately, for a way to keep Linda out of the action. He had deliberately kept their pace slower than necessary in hopes that some of the Rocking H riders would catch them, even though he knew his hopes were futile. He had thought of stopping for the night here by the stream, but he knew that Linda, if necessary, would ride on alone. Short of using force, he knew of no way to keep her from catching up to the rustlers.

"I reckon we'll catch them in an hour or so if we get a move on," Stoner answered Linda's questions, walking to his horse and beginning to tighten the cinch he had loosened when he turned the animal out to graze. "We can decide then what we'll do."

"Okay," she answered tersely, stubbornly, also preparing to mount. "But don't think we're going to do nothing. You've been dragging your feet ever since we left the ranch. And I know why," her eyes met Stoner's and her voice softened, "but you might as well get used to it here and now. I'm not a woman who'll stay home just because I'm supposed to, or because it's safe, or because you want me to. Not even after we're married."

Realizing what she had said, she blushed, but her eyes didn't waver. Stoner grinned teasingly although the fear continued its cold presence deep in his gut.

"Maybe that's why I can't wait to get married. I need some excitement in my life for a change."

Shaking her head in feigned disgust, Linda mounted. A few moments later they were once again following the wide trail.

22

The wagon ride to Chasco turned out badly. Mrs. Peters had looked forward to the time alone with Rob. She wanted to talk of his future and of the future of the Rocking H.

"I wish your father was here," she opened the conversation once they were through the pass and moving at a steady clip. "He'd be proud of the way you've taken over running the ranch."

Rob remained silent for so long that she began to think he was going to ignore her comment.

"I doubt it," he snorted when he did speak. "I've thought a lot about Dad lately." Again he paused until the silence became uncomfortable. "For years I thought he was the best thing ever sat a horse. Didn't figure he could make a mistake." He glanced at his mother out of the corner of his eyes, forcing a chuckle that sounded more like a grunt of pain. "Damn but was I ever a simpleminded kid! He kept me under his thumb, never let me do anything without his approval. He didn't figure I was good enough to run the ranch on my own, I guess."

"Your father gave you lots of responsibilities," Mrs. Peters struggled to keep the irritation from her voice. "When he thought you were ready for something, he let you do it. Your father loved you, but he just didn't think you were ready to take over the whole ranch."

"I know that, Ma," Rob cut in. "I loved him, too. But he wanted things done his way. That was why he didn't think I was ready. He wouldn't let me take over because I didn't always think like he did."

Mrs. Peters started to deny Rob's assertion. But she stopped herself. Rob was right to some extent. She had told Stoner the same thing. Jacob had never given his son complete responsibility for the ranch simply because he didn't trust the boy, and she had agreed with him.

"Well," she decided to drop Jacob from the discussion, "I'm proud of you, anyway."

Rob grinned like the little boy she remembered so well. She touched his arm, fighting the happy hurt in the pit of her stomach.

"You might not be in a few more days."

As he spoke he again glanced at her without turning his head. She made no comment, waiting for him to continue, a twinge of alarm pushing its finger against her spine.

"I figure to let Stoner go."

"Why? We need him."

"We need fighters, Ma, but we don't need Stoner."

He turned and looked at her, then looked away. He wondered if she would suspect what he really had in mind, to slowly get rid of the hands who were loyal to her and replace them with men loyal to him. Within a few months he expected to take over the ranch, become the real power if not the real owner.

Mrs. Peters recognized the stubborn streak in his voice and softened her own reaction, "I thought the two of you had an agreement."

Rob shrugged angrily, but remained silent. Mrs. Peters continued talking, defending the gunfighter even though she knew she was irritating Rob.

"Stoner's a good man to have around. You've seen what he can do. He's good in a fight and he's a good man. He wouldn't sell us out or desert us or anything like that. He's loyal."

"I don't see it that way anymore," Rob growled. "The more I think about it the more I think he was just lucky, lucky and shrewd enough to take advantage of his luck. Worse, he's probably got us in a war with the Bar B. There on the porch he could've got us all killed, drawing like he did on the Bartlemans and shooting them up. Now...well, when Joe and

Sam are one-hundred percent fit again, you can bet they'll come hunting for Rockin' H blood if Stoner's still around."

Rob's words irritated his mother. The only mistake Stoner had made, as far as she could see, was in not killing the Bartlemans when he had had the chance. But it was a mistake she could live with; she preferred it to the alternative. It showed that he was not a cold-blooded killer. He was not a man who could have continued shooting until all three Bartlemans were dead.

"The Bartlemans out for Rocking H blood won't be anything new," she spoke with an edge to her voice although she tried to force a softer tone. "What do you think they came to the ranch for in the first place? What about the ambush at Loma Linda?"

Rob misunderstood her reference to the Loma.

"All we had to do was wait till dark," he spoke with self-satisfied arrogance, forgetting that, when he had first gotten the full story of what Stoner had done to the Bar B at the spring, he had applauded the man and only faulted him for not killing several of the Bar B riders as an example. "We could've gotten away easy enough. There was no need to treat the Bar B punchers like Stoner did, making them drive their cattle back to Bar B land and fix the fence around the spring. We'll be lucky if there isn't some shooting over that too."

Mrs. Peters didn't know what to say. She had thought that Rob accepted the responsibility for his mistakes on the porch and on the Loma. Now she knew he had not. Somehow he had convinced himself that, without Stoner around to interfere, he could have resolved the two incidents with greater satisfaction for everyone concerned.

"So," Rob continued talking without looking at her, "I'm gettin' rid of Stoner. I'll send him packin' in a day or two."

She tried to think of a way to avoid a clash, but found none.

"No," she spoke softly, regretfully, after a long pause. "Like I said before, the Rocking H is mine. You're doing a good job running it so far. So you're free to hire and fire the hands if you think it's necessary, but not Stoner. He works for me and he stays."

"Goddamn it, Ma," Rob's voice rose to an angry shout. "The man's dangerous. I bet there's no way the Bar B'll make peace long as he works for us."

"They won't make peace if he isn't here, either, Rob honey. Joe Bartleman has wanted the Loma Linda spring for years. He's not about to stop till he gets it."

Anxiously, fighting her own temper, she watched the growing anger on her son's face but refused to be intimidated into a compromise with what she saw as the truth.

"Besides, now that your dad's gone Old Joe thinks he can take the whole Rocking H, and he'll make a try for it or my name's not Martha Peters."

"He stayed off our land when Dad was alive," Rob insisted stubbornly, "and by God he'll stay off it while I'm alive."

"You may be right," Mrs. Peters agreed verbally, to stroke her son's ego, although she had no confidence that, without Stoner's help, he could stop Joe and Sam Bartleman from doing whatever they wanted to. "But think of Jacob Stoner as added insurance."

"I'd like to think of him riding out of the valley."

Rob's words stopped the conversation. They rode through the growing dust and heat in silence, both buried in their own personal thoughts and worries. As they came in sight of the first cabins of Chasco Rob commented tersely, "I don't like the way Stoner hangs around Linda. That's gotta stop."

"That's a horse of two colors," Mrs. Peters reacted just as tersely, irritated by her son's jealous dislike of Stoner. "LInda hangs around him as much as he hangs around her, maybe more. Besides, she's a big girl now. She has a right to choose the men she wants to be around. And I don't think she could find a better man."

Nothing more was said until they rolled down the main street of town and up to the livery stable. Once the horses were cared for, mother and son separated. She headed for the general store, happy to be in town after so much time without leaving the ranch but worried about how Rob was sulking over their conversation. She planned to make her purchases and have them readied for loading on the wagon, then visit with friends. After extracting a promise from Rob that he would stay out of the saloons, she had agreed to meet him at the livery stable at four o'clock.

Rob moseyed around town talking with friends and acquaintances, picking up news. He learned that Joe and Sam had moved back to the Bar B the previous day. Nothing else. No rumors of an impending range war between the Bar B and the Rocking H, no rumors of retaliation although one of the old timers who frequented the benches in front of the bank commented with an owlish grin, "I reckon, I was that Stoner fellow, I'd make tracks so fast the dust wouldn't settle for a month. The Bartlemans didn't say nothin', but they ain't ones to forget a hurt."

After wandering the streets and businesses for a little over an hour, talking with anyone who had a moment to spare him, Rob found himself in front of the saloon. He hesitated, the memory of his promise to his mother and of his last visit to Chasco flashing through his mind, then he shrugged his shoulders angrily and headed for the door.

"I'll be damned," he muttered as he stepped into the smoky twilight of the saloon. "One little drink ain't gonna hurt nothin'."

Once inside he stopped to survey the room. The familiar odor of stale booze, tobacco smoke, unemptied spittoons, and unwashed bodies rolled over him. He took a deep breath and almost laughed. He felt like a man who had just come home after a long absence. In the center of the room a group of men were playing poker. He recognized Harry, the bartender; Johnny Zimmer, an old man who worked at odd jobs around Chasco and spent most of his free time playing poker; and Matt Bartleman. The other three he didn't know for sure, although he thought they owned one-horse spreads in the mountains northeast of town.

"Help yourself, Rob," the bartender called. "I can't leave this here game or Johnny'll steal all my money."

"He ain't got any to steal or I just might," Johnny's voice rose shrilly above the general chuckling at the table. "I never seen a worse poker player, less it's my horse."

The chuckles became laughter which soon returned to silence broken now and then by monosyllables as the players resumed their game. Rob grabbed a bottle from under the bar, pulled a glass from a stack nearby, and made his way to the poker table.

"You can have my spot when this game's over," the bartender said, taking the coin Rob handed him. "These card cheats've taken every cent I had, including the baby's milk money."

"Whooooeee!" one of the small cattlemen grunted. "The only baby you ever had, Harry, was that baby raccoon that got in the saloon...when was it?" He appealed for help from the other players, "Sometime last June maybe?"

"Ask Johnny," the bartender laughed good-naturedly. "My feelin's are he had a lot to do with turnin' that little monster loose in here. If I knew for sure I think I'd poison his whisky."

Johnny screwed up his wrinkled, bewhiskered face, feigning hurt innocence. "This's my home. We're brothers, Harry. I wouldn't do nothin' to my family or my home."

The other players roared at Johnny's words. The bartender stood well over six feet and was as skinny as a fence post. Johnny stood five six in his boots and weighed slightly over two hundred pounds. He was old enough to be Harry's father, if not his grandfather.

"We gonna jaw all day or play cards," growled one of the three ranchers, his eyes twinkling.

Rob stood behind Harry's chair, watching, as the game resumed. A twinge of guilt touched Rob for a moment as he poured himself a drink and downed it in one gulp. He had promised himself and his mother to avoid the saloon and drinking while in town. The next moment he shrugged his shoulders with irritation and took a gulp of the second drink. He wondered why he was planning to sit in on the game. Although he played poker from time to time, usually after he drank too much, he didn't enjoy it much, nor did he enjoy what he considered the inane, monosyllabic comments of the players as they slammed cards down on the table and raked in pots.

He glanced around the table. His eyes came to rest on Matt Bartleman and suddenly he knew why he would take Harry's place. He didn't like Matt. The feeling was mutual, he figured. That was why they had clashed so often over the years, from school-yard fights over an imagined slur to fights over girls at local dances and now to their struggle over land that the Rocking H owned.

Matt had been the first person he noticed when he walked into the room. Immediately an ugly desire to smash the familiar face had turned his gut sour. He studied the stack of chips in front of Bartleman and felt his anger rise at the size of it. Matt was winning. But that, he vowed, would soon change.

"Twenty dollars to sit in," Harry broke into his thoughts, rising, as the game ended with Johnny raking in the pot. "Five card stud, no wild cards, no ante, half dollar limit, three raises. From every pot the house takes a quarter."

Again Rob glanced at Matt and felt the anger wash over him.

"That's pretty steep, Harry," he grumbled.

Harry shrugged, "Nobody's drinkin' much today, not even Johnny. I gotta make money somehow. That or go hungry."

"Hell, Peters, don't be so damn tight," one of the three two-bit ranchers broke in. "I ain't complainin' and I don't figure I've got near the kind of money you've got."

Rob glared at the speaker, started to retort, but stopped himself. The man looked like he hadn't had a bath for weeks.

His clothes were no cleaner, nor were those of his companions. But Rob sensed something dangerous about the man, something explosive and brutal just beneath the surface. Nesters, he thought disgustedly. But he held his tongue, bought his chips, and prepared to play.

He filled a flush the first hand, three kings the second, winning both. Matt bet heavy in both pots. Success soothed Rob's earlier irritation. For the first half hour the stack of chips in front of him slowly grew. The three small ranchers lost steadily, although not a great deal. When they threw in their cards and quit, to be replaced by Harry and Aaron Whitman, owner of Whitman's General Store, Rob felt a sense of power. But he glanced at Matt Bartleman and he felt the bile again rise in his gut. It was Matt's money he had wanted, yet Matt's pile had stayed about even.

"I hear that new man you got out at the Rocking H is something with a six shooter. Faster than Reverend Lynch with the collection plate," Aaron Whitman commented as he stacked his chips and prepared to play.

Rob glanced up, frowning. The storekeeper was a short, stocky man with broad shoulders, short arms, a gut the size of a bushel basket, and a face that invariably wore a pleasant smile. Rob knew, however, that both the gut and the smile were deceiving. Aaron was a friendly man, a man who liked a joke and companionship, but one who could take care of himself when the need arose.

Aaron wasn't looking at Rob, though. His eyes and grin were focused on Matt, who returned the look and the grin.

"Fast enough I don't reckon I'll tackle him again."

"You or your paw," Aaron rumbled a laugh deep in his chest. "Or Sam."

"I wish I could say you're right about Pa and Sam, Aaron," as Matt spoke a frown replaced the smile on his face. "I think the gunfighter's okay, a good man to have around if people leave him alone. But Pa and Sam're too damn bull-headed for their own good sometimes."

"Or anybody else's," Aaron added as if adding amen to a sermon.

"We gonna play cards or are you two gonna talk all day," Rob growled, struggling to keep his anger in check.

He had to put up with a mother and sister, and a bunch of cowhands, who admired Stoner and sang his praises whenever his name came up. He wasn't going to put up with the same in town.

The game settled into the same routine as before, with one exception. Rob began to lose steadily, Matt to win. As he watched his stack dwindle and Matt's grow, Rob's temper rose to the boiling point. When his three nines lost an especially large pot to Matt's three jacks, he slammed his cards on the table and snarled, "You're damn lucky when you deal, Bartleman."

Matt glanced at him, "Come on, Peters. You know as well as I do I can't stack a deck, or deal off the bottom, or anything else. And I wouldn't if I could, not in a game with people I know."

"Hell, Rob," Harry cut in. "You could've folded. He had you beaten face up. You had two nines showin'; he had two jacks. You saw that easy enough. And the way he was bettin', it was clear as spring water he had the other jack from the deal, just like it was clear you had the other nine. That's why the rest of us folded early."

"Yeah," Johnny added, laughing, "far as I can recall, that's the first time today Matt's won on his own deal. He's a rotten dealer, worse to himself than to the rest of us. And he ain't no bluffer; anybody that's played cards with him much knows that."

Rob glared at Johnny, then at Matt. Matt returned the glare with a grin. Johnny told a joke, trying to ease the tension. Harry bought a round of drinks.

"Jesus, the world's comin' to an end," Aaron commented with a forced laugh. "That's the first time Harry ever passed out free drinks."

"I figure he wants to get us drunk and take our money," Johnny suggested with an affected simper.

"You keep actin' that way, he'll be after more'n your money," Matt leered at Johnny and chuckled.

"Won't do him no good," Johnny continued his charade. "I give that up a long time ago, before you was born. Little Bo Peep got it."

"You never had it to give up," Harry grunted as he finished passing out the drinks and took his seat again. "You was born experienced."

Johnny dealt amid hoots and boisterous comments on his morality. Silence settled in again, the clatter of chips, the click of glasses on the table. Rob continued losing, his temper rising with each pot, fueled by his dislike of Matt Bartleman.

When Matt's turn to deal came around again, as he shuffled the cards he said, "This is my last deal. I'll play till it's my turn again. Then I'm through."

"You can't quit while you're ahead," Rob growled.

Matt glanced at him without answering and began dealing the cards.

"Hell," Aaron answered for Matt, "that's when a man ought to quit. My problem is I'm always behind. I can't quit when I'm ahead."

"Yeah, well, he's not gonna quit. That's my money he's got."

Nobody said anything. Matt again glanced at Rob, noting the almost empty bottle on the table and the dullness in and around Rob's eyes.

I should have quit an hour ago, he told himself. Peters is mean drunk.

He dealt the cards and, when everyone else checked, opened the bet. He had a four down and a five up. He dealt the cards again and drew a seven. Johnny bet his king high. Matt raised. He didn't figure it was very smart of him to bet on drawing two cards to a straight, but luck had been with him and, for some reason, Rob's drunken comments had stirred the devil in his gut. He grinned.

"What you grinnin' for, less you got a five or seven down?" Johnny spoke, an answering chuckle rumbling in his voice. "And two fives or sevens don't beat the three kings I'm gonna have when you give me that next card."

"Hell, Johnny, I'm going after a straight," Matt drawled the words, accompanying them with a friendly chuckle. "I figure Lady Luck's got the hots for me today."

Everybody around the table echoed Matt's laughter, adding good-natured comments on his honesty or ignorance and about the vagaries of women and chance.

Except for Rob.

"It wouldn't surprise me if he drew two more cards to a straight," he sneered when the laughter and comments had died down, glaring around the table as he spoke.

Nobody answered or met his eyes. Rob felt his anger rising to the eruption point. He looked at the chips in front of Matt and at what he considered an insolent grin on Matt's lips. He filled his glass from the bottle near his right arm, knowing his hand was shaking and feeling the shame of it. He took a sip of the potent liquid. His anger ebbed a little, not much.

Matt dealt again. He received a six. Johnny drew another king, making him two kings and a ten showing. Rob drew an ace to go with another ace and a jack. Aaron and Harry had nothing showing. Johnny bet. With a leer, Rob raised. Harry dropped, muttering disgustedly. Matt raised. Johnny raised again. Rob started to raise Johnny's raise.

"Can't do that," Harry took the raise from the pot and returned it to Rob's dwindling pile. "The rules of the game was three raises."

Rob swore. "You're not in the game, Harry. You dropped. So keep out of it."

As he spoke he grabbed the chips Harry had returned to his stack and tossed them back into the pot.

"Don't make no difference," Harry spoke softly, his eyes glinting angrily. "The rules was set before the game started-- three raises. We all agreed. That's how we started and we don't change in the middle of the game less everyone's willin'."

"I say we up the limit, as many raises as a man wants."

"No, I don't think so," Matt cut in. "Harry's right. Rules are rules and we said three raises."

Rob glared at him, "You scared you'll lose a little of the money you've cheated us out of."

Matt returned the glare, struggling against his own rising anger. Finally he looked away and shrugged, promising himself he would never sit in a poker game with Rob Peters again.

"Ask the rest of the players, all of them," he clipped each word. "If they agree I'll go along, although you're being too damn high-handed about it."

Arrogantly Rob poled Aaron and Johnny, ignoring Harry, his irritation mounting as each rejected his proposal. He glared around the table before, with an angry flourish, grabbing his raise from the pot.

"Deal," he growled at Matt. "Let's see if you're good enough to give yourself the straight."

Matt started to answer, caught himself in time, and dealt another card to the three remaining players. Johnny drew a five, Rob another ace, and Matt a three. Johnny swore good-naturedly and threw his cards face down onto the pot.

"Three kings. That's a good hand generally. But not now, I don't reckon. I'd bet a dollar to a peso it's third best."

Rob stared at Matt's hand. Again he felt the blind anger flooding through him.

"Son of a bitch," he blurted. "You got the four or not?"

"It's your bet."

"I think you're bluffing."

Matt shrugged, "Bet and see."

Furious, Rob threw a dollar into the pot. He knew he should fold. Johnny was probably right that Matt had the straight and his own hand, three aces, was second best, just as Johnny's was third best. But humiliation gnawed at his gut, humiliation and a killing anger that he should be bested again by Matt Bartleman.

Matt called his bet and raised a dollar.

Rob counted the chips he had in front of him. Of the considerably more than forty dollars he had had at the height of his winning streak, only seven remained, thirteen less than he had bought into the game with. He threw a dollar in to match Matt's raise, then stacked the remainder beside the pot, cursing himself for a fool as he did so but unable to stop himself. Next he dug in his pocket and pulled out what remained of the money he had brought to town.

"Twenty-six dollars says I've got you beat."

Matt stared at him, wondering if he shouldn't refuse. There was a wild gleam in Rob's eyes and in the way his voice rose at the end. He teetered on the edge of a precipice. Anything could push him over.

Matt started to reject the challenge, but he realized that whether he accepted the side bet or not was irrelevant. Either way Rob would explode because he would lose, and that was the real problem, the losing, not the money.

Matt called the bet and turned his four over.

Rob stared at the card. "You cheating bastard," he gritted. "I don't believe that was all luck."

Matt struggled for control of his temper as he pocketed the money from the side bet and added the pot to his stack of chips.

"You know, Peters," he finally growled. "Someday you're gonna say something that'll get you killed."

"Not by you," Rob sneered.

As he spoke he shoved the table, furiously. Chips clattered, rolling and skipping in all directions. Glasses shattered and thudded across the wooden floor. The bottle that had been in front of Rob dropped unbroken, its remaining contents soaking the sawdust as it rolled toward the rear wall. Johnny and Aaron sat frozen in place, too startled to move.

"Goddamn it!" Harry shouted and reached for Rob. He moved too late.

Rob shoved the table and lunged at Matt. The table caught Harry in the thighs, knocking him into Aaron. The two went down, Harry on top, both momentarily stunned. The table missed Johnny, who stepped forward to help. When Rob dived for Matt his shoulder connected with the old man, catching him in the chest and catapulting him backwards, his feet in the air and his arms flailing wildly. He landed with a solid thud on his back and head, knocked unconscious.

Matt sidestepped smoothly as Rob lunged for him. His move evaded Rob and Rob's fist, thrown in a wild, roundhouse swing. The miss and his own momentum sent Rob to his hands and knees. For a split second he struggled to keep from toppling onto his face. Then, with a wild curse, he scrambled to his feet and faced Matt.

Neither man spoke. Matt stood balanced on the balls of his feet, waiting, an almost imperceptible smile crinkling the corners of his mouth, taunting Rob. His hands hung at his sides, but his fists were clenched, ready. His shoulders were hunched slightly forward.

Rob hesitated. Sanity returned, pushing the mad fog from his brain. He realized that he had hated Matt ever since he had known him and that the present fight was not about a poker game. It was about his hate and something else--his need to show his mother and Stoner and, more importantly, himself, that he was a man who could stomp his own snakes. With a roar he rushed Matt.

The fight ended almost as soon as it began. Matt stepped inside Rob's pummeling fists. A short jab crushed Rob's nose, sending blood splattering over both combatants. Another loosened a tooth. An uppercut connected with the point of his jaw. Rob floundered backward against the upturned table and wall. He clung there, one hand on the table, his shoulders against the wall, until his vision returned to normal.

Matt was standing ten feet away, grinning at him.

"Had enough, Peters?" he asked when Rob pushed himself forward and stood without support.

Rob didn't sense the dam of his anger burst wide open. He didn't hear the name he called Matt. He was only vaguely aware that his hand grabbed his pistol and yanked it upward.

He didn't hear Aaron and Harry shout for him to stop. He didn't hear the sound that sent Matt's bullet tearing through his ribs and exploding his heart. Nor did he hear the hurried shot that sent his bullet into the floor at Matt's feet.

"Jesus," Harry swore as Rob smashed back into the wall and slid to the floor, dead before he started falling.

"He was a wild man, blind, crazy wild," Aaron spoke barely above a whisper. "He wasn't that drunk, was he? If I'd known he was that drunk I wouldn't have played cards with him."

"My God," Harry swore again, too stunned to say more.

"Why'd he go for his gun?" Matt found his voice at last.

He felt weak and wondered if he would throw up. Carefully, moving slowly so as not to make his stomach queasier than it already was, he sat down on the only chair that, for some reason, had remained standing throughout the fight. He rested his elbows on his knees. His head dropped onto his hands.

"Somebody send for the doc," he mumbled through his hands, his dazed eyes staring unseeingly at the floor.

Harry was kneeling over Rob's body, "I reckon the doc'll need his buryin' tools, not the healin' ones. Rob's dead."

"Johnny ain't," Aaron's voice had not yet returned to normal. "He's got a knot the size of a turnip on his head and he says he thinks his arm's broken."

With a promise to hurry the doctor, Harry left the room.

Not ten seconds later the town marshal strode in, "I hear one, maybe two shots, and then I see Harry lopin' down the street like a coyote headed for the chuck wagon. So I come over to see for myself what was goin' on."

He walked over to Johnny, grunted, and continued on to Rob's corpse. He was a man of forty or so, thick of leg and trunk, with a bull neck topped by a head that looked too small to run the rest of him. He had been town marshal for almost ten years. Before that he had run a horse ranch on the west side of the valley, up against the foothills. One day he had gotten drunk in town, sold his ranch to a stranger, and the next day accepted the marshal's job. Most people figured the town had gotten a good bargain.

Aaron explained what had happened. Johnny and Matt seconded what he said.

"Harry'll say the same thing," Johnny spoke up as Harry entered with the doctor.

When Harry had told the same version of the fight the others had, the marshal shook his head, "Can't hold a man for protectin' himself, Matt," he said tiredly. "But who's gonna tell his maw? I saw the two of them ridin' in this mornin'. She's over at your house now, Aaron, visitin' with your wife and Sarah Gorton.

"I'll take care of the body," the doctor looked up from where he was kneeling over Johnny. "Johnny here's got a broken arm and a knot on his head, but he's plenty able to walk to my place so I can repair the damage. Harry can help me carry the body. You and Aaron tell Mrs. Peters that I'll have a casket ready in a couple hours. I reckon she'll want to bury him out at the ranch, near his paw. If she doesn't, let old Jimenez and his boys know so they can start digging a grave." He mopped the sweat from his brow. "Sorry, Lije," he glanced sheepishly at the marshal. "It's my military background, I guess. Giving orders comes natural."

"That ain't nothin' new, Doc. But what you said makes as much sense as you usually do." The marshal turned to Aaron. "Let's go, old man. You heard the boss."

23

Mrs. Peters, Matty Whitman, and Sarah Gorton were seated on the porch of the Whitman house, enjoying the shade and a slight breeze.

When Mrs. Peters saw Lije Newel turn in at the Whitman gate with Aaron, she figured he was coming to pay his respects. He had been a good friend of her husband. He was also a good friend of the Whitmans, so it seemed natural that he appear with Aaron. But when the two men stepped onto the porch and Lije doffed his Stetson, she noticed the tightness around his eyes. She glanced at Aaron. He refused to meet her eyes. Her heart skipped a beat as she glanced back at the marshal. He was rolling his hat with his hands, distress on his face and in his stance.

"Martha," he began hesitantly, then hurriedly summarized what he had come to say. "It's Rob. He and Matt Bartleman got into it in the saloon, over a poker game. Rob's dead. Shot."

"Oh, my God," Sarah Gorton exclaimed. "We heard the shots."

"They were so muffled, we thought they came from out of town some place," Matty qualified her friend's statement, deep sympathy in her voice, not so much for Rob, whom she had never liked, but for her friend, Martha Peters."

"No, they was in the saloon," the marshal reiterated, not knowing what else to say, still twirling his Stetson nervously, staring off into the distance rather than continue looking at the terrible grief spreading from Mrs. Peters' eyes to her mouth and chin.

"We were playing poker," Aaron broke in, feeling that Martha Peters should know the truth, "me, Harry, Johnny, Matt, and Rob. Rob was winning for a while. Then he started losing. Matt, he was winning right along and Rob didn't like it much. When he started losing. Rob, that is. When he started losing he made some nasty cracks at Matt, but Matt, he let them slide. Until the last hand. Rob called him a cheat once too often, I guess. Matt the same as told Rob he better shut up and Rob swung. He missed. But Matt didn't. He knocked Rob against the wall. Rob went for his gun."

Aaron noticed the look of mingled anger and grief on his wife's face and the growing anguish on Martha's. He stopped talking, realizing how deeply he was hurting Martha Peters.

"Rob missed. Matt didn't," he finished lamely.

Mrs. Peters felt she should say something, but her mind simply would not function rationally. Pictures of Rob at different stages of his life flashed before her closed eyes. She replayed their conversation on the way to town, what she could remember of it. She recalled her insistence on keeping Stoner in spite of Rob. She wondered if her decision had cost her her son. A lonely, empty ache began spreading in her chest where her heart would be. Tears seeped through her closed lids. She tried to stifle the wracking sobs, the struggle brief, violent, but lost before it began. Matty and Sarah helped her into the house. Aaron and the marshal stood by helplessly.

"Damn Rob," the marshal whispered angrily when the women had disappeared inside. "He never amounted to a tinker's damn. He wasn't worth one tear from Martha."

"Not when he started drinking," Aaron agreed. "I should've stopped his drinking when he started losing, or stopped the game."

"Hell, Aaron, Harry told me Rob started drinkin' before he got in the game. You weren't there yet so don't go blamin' yourself," Lije put his arm on his friend's shoulder. "Besides, you don't own the damn saloon so how was you gonna stop the game?"

Mrs. Peters sat quietly in the sunless room. At her request, her friends had left her alone, closing the door and curtains behind them. Her sobs continued unabated until her insides seemed as dry as the desert air in summer. Varied memories of her lost son floated in and out of her consciousness. For some time she let the memories flow of their own accord. But too many memories of the recent months since her husband's death began interfering with earlier, fonder images, distorting them, pushing them into the dark depths. She wondered how she had failed the boy. She asked herself if he would have become a better man if his father had lived. Finally she pulled herself together, washed her face in the basin of cold water Matty had left for her, and returned to the world of the living. All that was left of Rob, in her heart, was her love and her guilt. And her memories.

Aaron, Matty and Sarah were sitting in the living room talking in low voices. She returned their sympathetic smiles of greeting and sat down among them. Aaron explained the preparations that were being made at the doctor's.

"You'll stay the night," Matty took her hand. "We can make arrangement for the funeral tomorrow."

"No," she shook her head. "I'll take Rob home tonight. We'll bury him next to Jacob. Jacob would like that. I think Rob would too."

She refused their offer of an escort, insisting she would rather be alone with her son. She asked Aaron to get her wagon at the livery and load it with the supplies she had bought at his store, while she saw to Rob.

"I'll want to tell him goodbye one last time before we put him in the casket," she added, unsuccessfully fighting the quiver in her voice. "I'd also like to talk to Matt Bartleman."

"Why?" Aaron blurted, surprised.

Mrs. Peters ignored his question, "Could you find him and send him over to the doctor's, Aaron?"

"He wasn't to blame," Aaron searched her face for an answer to his question. Finding none, he shrugged and added, "I'll find him if he's still in town. But he might not want to see you, Martha. He was pretty upset."

"Please tell him, Aaron," Mrs. Peters returned his searching gaze without flinching, "and tell him I don't condemn him for what happened. I just want to talk."

"Maybe you should wait a few days, let yourself get used to the loss, before you talk to Matt. You might say something you'll regret."

"Aaron," Mrs. Peters failed to suppress her irritation, "I won't be able to accept Rob's loss in a few days or weeks. You know that. And I'm not planning to accuse Matt of anything. So please do as I ask, or I'll have to hunt him down myself."

She had spent a few minutes with Rob and returned to the doctor's waiting room when Matt showed up. She could tell from the drawn skin around his eyes and mouth, the slump of his shoulders, and the dull cast in his eyes that he was suffering from what he had done.

Oddly, she thought, at the moment she felt more sorrow for him and herself than she did for Rob, and sorrow for Linda, who had always doted on her brother.

She watched Matt approach, slowly, hat in hand. He started to speak but the words refused to come. She had never really disliked this Bartleman twin, in spite of her aversion to his father and brother, and in spite of how much he resembled them in looks and action. As a boy growing up in the valley, he had been as full of mischief and deviltry as the other boys, bouncing from one prank to another, from one fight to the next, with little if any sense of guilt. Yet, unlike with Sam and her own Rob, there had never been any sign of cruelty or heedless violence in him.

She touched him on the arm, "He was my son, Matt. I loved him. When I first heard what had happened, I wanted to strike out. I wanted to shoot you myself and...." She paused, trying to formulate her thoughts, fighting the ache that was again beginning to spread through her body. "But the anger soon passed. All that was left was the emptiness. I knew I would never talk to him again, never...," she stifled a sob.

"Don't, Mrs. Peters," Matt's voice broke, expressing his own anguish revived by hers.

For several moments they both struggled for control.

"I'd give anything if it hadn't happened," Matt broke the silence. "But it did and there's nothing we can do about it now."

"No. I.... Aaron told me what happened. You weren't to blame. You were just defending yourself."

"I know. But that doesn't make it any easier."

"Rob never liked to lose, not even as a boy. When he was drinking he was worse. A word, an action, or the slightest sign of opposition--anything could set him off. I've been afraid for a long time, afraid something like this would happen."

They talked on in the doctor's waiting room. The doctor came in, watched them for a moment, and discreetly left. No patients appeared to disturb them. They talked about Rob, telling stories of his childhood and youth that they remembered, making him seem better than he had been. When they separated, the wound that Rob had left in their souls had begun to heal. Later Mrs. Peters drove the wagon away from the doctor's home, the coffin in the back of the wagon.

24

At twilight Stoner and Linda came to a large park enclosed on three sides by the pine forest they had been riding through for some time and on the left by a steep, rocky cliff, at the foot of which lay a jumbled pile of huge boulders covered by brush. Automatically Stoner halted them at the edge of the trees. Carefully he studied the open area and the shadows surrounding it. Nothing stirred. Except for a squirrel chattering somewhere behind them and a jay scolding something off to their right, nothing disturbed the silence.

"See anything?" Linda asked in a hoarse whisper.

"No," Stoner answered, "But I smell wood smoke."

Neither spoke for a while.

"I smell it too," Linda said after several moments had passed.

At that moment a calf bawled, the sound muffled as if by distance.

"Over near the cliff face, in that pile of boulders at the edge of the clearing," Linda pointed. "That calf cried from somewhere in there, and I see the smoke."

Stoner also caught a glimpse of wisps of smoke rising above the boulders. In silent agreement, they dismounted and led their horses deeper into the trees, until they figured they were out of hearing range of the camp in the boulders.

"We'll tie the horses here, take our rifles and plenty of shells, head straight for the cliff, and follow it to their camp. The wind's in our direction so, if we're quiet and lucky, they won't know we're in the area until we get the drop on them."

As she listened to Stoner's words, a chill settled in Linda's stomach. She wondered how she would react if shooting started. After seeing Cactus she had been angry; she wanted to kill, or so she had told herself. Now she wasn't so sure. The thought of shooting into human flesh, or of being shot, unnerved her.

"Are you okay?" Stoner asked, giving her a questioning look.

"I'm all right."

"You can stay here with the horses if you want. I'd feel better if I thought you were safe."

Irritation smothered the chill in her gut.

"I know. But I'll never forgive myself if I don't go through with this."

"Okay, let's go," he touched her arm, cursing himself for not having made her stay at the ranch.

They soon reached the cliff and turned right. With difficulty they wended their way around fallen boulders, rocky outcrops, thick clumps of bushes, and twisted junipers and pines. Twilight had meandered well on its way to dark when they approached the clump of boulders from which the wisps of smoke rose. They realized that the cattle had been bedded down in an opening in the cliff face, hidden behind the boulders.

Once within hearing distance of the camp Stoner motioned Linda to a halt. They squatted behind a boulder the size of a chicken house.

"Jesus," Stoner recognized Cal's voice, "I can't wait to get these cows sold. I ain't gonna do nothin' but drink and eat for two days."

"After you take a ride on a whore or two," Dobbs chuckled. "I know you. You're young and hot-blooded. Me and Slicker'll see to the women after we shovel in some good grub and a barrel of rotgut. When you head for the grub and booze, we'll be headin' the other way."

"Yeah, well, I can't help it if you're old and wore out."

"Old maybe, not wore out. Just a mite more cautious and wiser, that's all."

Stoner recognized Slicker's voice. He took his hat off and glanced around the boulder. He could see Cal and Slicker. He could not see Dobbs but knew about where the man was. Silently he grunted his relief. He had worried that one of the three rustlers would be riding herd on the cattle, which would mean that he and Linda would have to split up.

"Cautious and wise," Dobbs repeated Slicker's words. "Me'n Slicker've learned enough to feed the fire if you want the heat to last a while."

"You learn the same caution when it comes to that stone-faced gunhand?" Cal's words dropped heavily into the silence that followed Dobbs's comment.

Dobbs answered softly, but irritation flowed with the words, "If Nate or the Bartlemans want him so bad they can go after him themselves. I've lost interest."

"Reckon he's followin' us?"

Dobbs shrugged, "The Rockin' H'll follow. We killed one of their men and shot up another."

"Maybe we better put out a guard tonight."

"Nah," Slicker interspersed. "Like I said, I saw the crew scatter this mornin' and the buggy head to town with a woman and man in it. Whoever's left at the house, it'll take time for them to round up some punchers to follow us. I figure we should start watchin' our back trail by noon tomorrow, earliest."

Dobbs agreed curtly.

All three outlaws dropped into silence. Stoner leaned over and put his mouth to Linda's ear.

"I figure they left their horses with the cattle. I'll circle that way, come up between them and the canyon mouth. When I yell, you throw down on them from here. Anyone comes this way, you shoot him. Comprendes?"

He squeezed her shoulder gently. She nodded but refused to meet his eyes. He wondered if he was doing the right thing in leaving her, but decided he had no choice. He needed to find a spot where he could get all three outlaws in his sights and, if a fight broke out, he wanted to draw as much of the fire as possible away from her.

With fear tightening his chest, he moved stealthily in the direction he had chosen.

Linda watched Stoner disappear silently among the boulders. A cold emptiness settled into her stomach when he merged with the shadows and brush. She peeked at the rustlers and drew back quickly, fearfully, although she knew they couldn't see her. The grey of twilight was settling closer and closer into the black of night and the two outlaws she could see were sitting staring into the fire. When they looked away from the blaze they probably couldn't even make out individual boulders more than a few yards from them.

She waited patiently, then impatiently. She wondered if Stoner had lost his way in the encroaching darkness. She peeped around the boulder again. Neither outlaw had moved. The one she couldn't see was talking, telling some kind of story, but she could only make out a few words here and there. She studied the two rustlers in sight. One was a boy, no older than Rob, the other a middle-aged man, probably as old as her father had been when he died.

They don't look like killers, she told herself dubiously.

She shuddered at the thought of killing one of them. At that very moment she heard Stoner's voice, seeming to come from beyond the fire.

At first Stoner had moved swiftly through the deepening shadows, but as he neared the mouth of the opening in the cliff face the brush thickened. His pace slowed to a ghostly crawl. His heart hammered in his chest, telling him he had left Linda behind, alone and a target for the rifles of the rustlers when the action began. And begin it would, he had no doubts. Cal was too volatile to give up without a fight. Dobbs and Slicker, more careful, wiser, as Dobbs had bragged, would fight also, simply because they would fear a lynching at the hands of the Rocking H. Stoner knew the smartest move would be to shoot the three killers as they sat by the fire, giving them no more chance than they had given Dodge and Cactus. At the same time he knew he'd give them an opportunity to surrender.

Not for himself, he grimaced, but for Linda, because she would never forgive him if he shot the three men in cold blood.

The irony, he thought, is that the safest way, for her, is to just shoot them. Yet it's because of her that I can't. And if anything happens to her....

He didn't finish his thoughts. He had just moved into position less than ten feet from the nearest outlaw, Dobbs, who was squatting on a flat stone with his face to the fire, his side to Stoner. To Dobbs's left, across the fire from Stoner, sat Slicker, hunched forward on a rounded boulder, his feet not quite touching the ground. Near Slicker, his back to Stoner, stood Cal, balancing his weight first on one foot, then the other, as if full of a nervous energy that kept him ceaselessly in motion.

As the three images impressed themselves on Stoner's mind, he made his decision. He rested the Winchester on the boulder behind which he lay, drew his Colt, rose with a leap, and bounded into the circle of firelight.

"Don't move!"

His voice shattered a moment of silence by the fireside. He crouched menacingly, his pistol aligned on Cal's chest.

With a curse Cal whirled and crouched as his hand dipped toward his holster. His fingers barely caressed the handle of his sixgun before Stoner's first bullet smashed into his middle just under the "vee" of the ribcage. The flattened piece of lead came to rest against his backbone. He fell backward, to a sitting position, bent almost double, unable to catch his breath, then slowly rolled onto his side, paralyzed and dying.

Stoner saw none of this. His finger had no sooner squeezed the trigger on his first shot that he was swinging the barrel of his Colt toward Dobbs. He had decided, before stepping into the firelight, that Cal was the primary danger. He was on his feet and he would start the action. But Dobbs was next. Stoner had him figured as more dangerous than Slicker, faster, quicker to react, unafraid. Besides, Linda couldn't see Dobbs but she could see Slicker. Stoner was counting on her to take Slicker out of the action.

Dobbs had made a fatal mistake. He hesitated at the sound of Stoner's voice, trying to penetrate the encroaching darkness for signs of other attackers. When, from the corner of his eye, he glimpsed Cal's hand flashing downward, beginning the gun battle, he was still squatting. He frantically struggled to stand, his legs reacting stiffly, trying to draw as he rose. He realized he was too slow. The barrel of his pistol had barely cleared leather when the chunks of lead slammed into his body, one in the throat, low down, the other through the heart. He died on his feet.

Where's Slicker? The question echoed through Stoner's mind, leaving him cold. He sorted through the impressions of his mind and realized that the outlaw had disappeared into the shadows, in Linda's direction, when the firing began. He gathered air to shout a warning. Not fast enough. Two shots split the night, one from Linda's rifle, the other from a pistol. Stoner's warning shout became an animal cry of fear. Heedlessly he leaped the fire and ran through the night toward where he had left Linda.

Linda had been watching Cal and Slicker when Stoner shouted his warning. His words froze her in place, on her stomach, hidden by the boulder around which she was peering, her rifle pointed toward the campfire, butt against her shoulder. Shocked motionless, she watched Cal crouch and reach for his sidearm. She heard the shot and saw Cal drop to a sitting position, as if something had yanked his legs out from under him and he had tried to catch himself by throwing his upper body forward. She watched, horrified, as he slowly rolled onto his side. She heard the two shots that instantly followed the first one, two shots that almost sounded like one. She watched as Slicker dived from his perch and stumbled rapidly in her direction. For a moment the significance escaped her. He was no more than a man moving away from danger. She scrambled up to face him. Then a sharp fear sliced through her chest. Her senses cleared.

Slicker was not more than ten feet from her, running bent over, trying to merge with the shadows on the ground. In the gloom she saw his hand dip toward the holster at his hip. She tried to shout, to tell him to stop, to tell him she didn't want to kill him. But nothing came out of her mouth. Her lungs heaved with the effort. Slicker's hand was coming level. She felt herself pull the trigger. From a distance she heard her shot. And Slicker's shot.

Slicker continued running, slowly toppling forward until his face, then his chest and legs, hit the ground. His feet kicked at the rocks and dirt at her feet for several seconds, as if he were still fleeing Stoner's gun, and finally ceased their spasmodic movement. He lay still. Linda couldn't take her eyes from the body. Bile rose into her throat but she fought it down. Stoner's shout penetrated the cold fog that had twined itself around her mind. She heard herself answer; the next thing she knew she was in his arms. She didn't see him stop to check Slicker before he moved to her.

"Jesus," he whispered in her hair. "I was scared you'd been shot."

"He's dead?"

"Yeah. You got him square in the chest."

"I shot him."

Stoner held her at arm's length and tried to see her eyes, but it was too dark. Her voice had held no emotion, yet he had sensed a quiver somewhere deep inside it, a quiver of approaching nerves.

"I killed him."

"It was you or him, honey. You had to shoot. I only wish you hadn't waited so long. He could have shot you too."

He pulled her against him and stroked her hair. She began to shake uncontrollably.

"I killed him!" she shrilled as if she were alone and he hadn't spoken.

Her trembling became worse, violent. She tried to push free of his embrace, but her hand slipped from his chest. She began to babble hysterically. Without hesitation, he pushed her to arm's length, held her there with one hand, and slapped her face sharply. The crack of his palm on her cheek brought sudden silence. The trembling stopped. Her body recoiled from his.

"You...bastard," she gritted, swearing and attacking him at the same time.

Hard pressed to defend himself in the darkening night, not wanting to hurt her, he stepped backward to avoid her swinging fists. The heel of his boot caught on a half-buried rock at the same time that her right fist connected with his nose. He sat down with a thud, in a scattering of sharp rocks.

"Damnit, Linda," he shouted, his own anger flaring before he realized that she was no longer attacking him.

"Oh, my God. I'm sorry. Are you hurt?"

Linda stooped beside him, her hands fluttering over his shoulders and face.

He could feel the warm trickle of blood running from his nose, over his lips, onto his chin. Avoiding her hands, he explored his nose with his fingers. It wasn't broken. He figured the blood would stop soon. Taking his bandanna from his hip pocket, he held it to his nose and stood up, pulling Linda with him and telling her that she had bloodied his nose, nothing more.

"Remind me not to sock you again," he chuckled, holding her close for a moment. "You're quicker'n a starved sidewinder."

"I'm sorry I got mad; I realize I was becoming hysterical."

"I'm sorry I hit you," he squeezed her against him. "But I thought you were gonna have a nervous fit. I didn't know how else to stop it."

A few minutes later they returned to the campfire. A quick exploration found bacon, beans, and flour among the supplies of the rustlers. There was a small spring in the mouth of the opening where the cattle were being held. Linda set to preparing a meal while Stoner dragged the bodies back against the cliff, under a low overhang which he walled up with boulders and as much sand as he could break off of the sandstone cliff face directly above the bodies. Later he went for his and Linda's horses.

After they finished eating and cleaning up they sat by the fire talking. Linda had been too upset to eat much. She was too distraught to sleep, afraid the man she had killed would haunt her dreams. He had already begun haunting the edge of her senses.

Stoner tried to comfort her, but he did little good. The horrible visions remained. Finally, toward morning, she slept fitfully, to dream over and over of shooting the running outlaw, moaning and frantically jerking half-awake after each reenactment. Stoner hovered all night on the verge of wakefulness, because of Linda's suffering and because a pack of coyotes spent the night in the area, attracted by the blood. Until the first grey of dawn the pack lingered nearby, afraid to approach too closely, too hungry to wander off, filling the darkness with their yips and howls of frustration.

In the grey of first dawn Stoner fed the coals with fresh wood, then wandered off to empty his bladder, wash up, and fill the coffee pot with water from the spring. He returned to find Linda frying bacon. While she visited the bushes and spring, Stoner searched for the biscuits and dried corn Chew Lin had sent with them. When Linda walked back into camp, he had finished cooking the bacon and had softened the biscuits in the hot grease. By the time they had eaten, the coffee was boiling.

"God, that smells good," Linda spoke for the first time as Stoner poured her a cup of the steaming liquid.

"How do you feel?" Stoner watched her closely as he waited for her answer.

They had made a hard ride the day before. They had a tough drive ahead of them with only two people. Much of the time they would be driving the cattle over Bar B range, which could mean a fight if they were spotted. They both had to be alert, in top form, even if it meant resting a day before they started back.

"I can make it," Linda's lips set stubbornly. "I didn't sleep much, but I don't think you did either." She put her hand on his. "Every time I woke up I could feel your eyes on me."

"I was worried."

"Worried I might have a relapse?" she teased.

Feeling a slight tinge of embarrassment, he shook it off and answered gruffly, "Maybe, but more worried that you were hurting. Besides," he grinned suddenly, boyishly, his face lighting up through the dark spikes of beard, "the music those coyotes were playing was a little off key. Kept me awake."

Before they left the area they piled the dead men's gear near the opening into the cliff wall and turned the Bar B horses loose. They didn't expect anyone to find the gear but they had no way to carry it without the rustlers' horses, and they didn't want the burden of extra mounts. They would have enough to do driving the cattle.

Once the herd had been set in motion, Linda took the point. The cattle followed passively, still tired from the hard drive of the previous day. Stoner rode the flanks for a while, alternating as the ground rose and fell on each side of them, then fell in at the drag when they entered an area of rolling terrain, his bandanna over his nose as protection from the dust and stench.

They met Tall Will and Pate well after mid-morning.

"We set out soon as Cactus told us what happened," Will spoke for the two, his eyes studying Linda. "But we didn't ride in to the ranch till late. By the time we got to the canyon where the shootin' took place, it was too dark to trail you. So we camped there and set out again this mornin'," he paused and stared at Stoner, then gestured at the cattle. "There was three riders pushin' those cows. There wasn't no sense you leadin' Linda into trouble like that."

Before Stoner could more than shrug his guilt, Linda reined her horse forward. Anger and tiredness made her voice harsh, "Where I ride is none of your business, Will." She glared at the tall rider. "You've been around the ranch long enough to know I do what I want to. And don't go blaming Jacob. He had no choice. After all, Dodge and Cactus worked for me and my family, and the cattle belong to us. I was going after the herd whether he rode with me or not."

"He should have waited for us," Will insisted stubbornly, a sharp pain of worry and jealousy punching at his gut. "You could've gotten hurt."

"So could've Jacob," Linda's voice softened, aware of Will's feelings for her, but she refused to concede to his point that she was a woman and so should leave the fighting to men. "And so could've you and Pate if we had waited."

She reined her horse away and, with a wave of her arm, indicated that the conversation was over. They soon had the cattle moving again. They crossed the Bar B without incident and abandoned the cattle on Rocking H land, at the edge of the valley below Black Bear Mesa. The stifling heat of late afternoon had settled over the land when they turned their mounts toward the ranch house.

25

As they rode into the yard Sonora stepped from the shadows of the barn to greet them, rifle cradled in his arm.

"Expectin' trouble?" Stoner nodded toward the weapon.

"Just takin' no chances. We heard you comin' and wasn't sure who it was," Sonora answered.

Tack came ambling up from the area of the front porch, also carrying a rifle. "Your maw wants to see you, Linda," he spoke with an edge of sorrow floating in his words. "You, too, boss," he nodded to Stoner. "I'll take your horses."

Mrs. Peters sat in a corner of the living room, her shoulders slumped, her face creased with sorrow. She stood and hugged Linda silently for several minutes, then gestured for her and Stoner to take a seat. She paced nervously for a moment before again sitting down. Tears trembled in her voice as she spoke.

"We buried Rob this morning. If I'd known you would be back today we would have waited. But we thought...," her voice broke. She struggled to regain control of herself before continuing, "I...we didn't know when you would return. Or if...," again she stopped, choked.

Stunned, Linda stared at her mother. A cold emptiness spread through her chest and into her throat. Buried Rob? She tried to concentrate but found her mind in a whirl of emotions.

"You buried Rob? Why?"

She blurted the words, realizing she sounded irrational but hoping she had not heard her mother correctly.

Slowly, haltingly, in bits and pieces, between angry interruptions from Linda and soothing probes from Stoner, Mrs. Peters told the story of Rob's fight and death as she had heard it. When she finished no one spoke.

Stoner watched Linda closely. He had sensed the tension mount in her as the story unfolded. Toward the end she had lowered her eyes to her fists, clenched in her lap. She hadn't raised them even after her mother's voice faltered and stopped. Stoner could see the blood seeping from the palms of her hands where her fingernails dug into the flesh.

"Matt Bartleman will die for killing my brother," Linda broke the silence, her voice the harsh, aching growl of an animal that has just found its young killed in their lair.

While she had listened to her mother relate Rob's final hours, she had listened to other voices from her childhood. She had recalled the hours she and Rob had spent swimming in the pond, the hours on horseback exploring the valley and foothills, the fights, the times they had stood as brother and sister against the world. Through her memories and the soft, hurt voice of her mother floated the love and the loss.

"I want you to kill Matt Bartleman," she turned to Stoner. "If you don't, I will." She shuddered at the fleeting image of the rustler she had shot so recently. "Or I'll find someone else to do it."

"It wasn't Matt's fault, Linda," Mrs. Peters spoke with a sad acceptance of the fatality of Rob's death. "He's a nice boy, Matt is, not like Joe and Sam. You know how Rob could be. He had a nasty tongue sometimes, especially when he was drinking. Like I said, he insulted Matt and then attacked him. And he drew first. Matt was only protecting himself." She paused as a sob took her breath for a moment. "I just wish I'd made him stay with me. He'd be alive now."

"You can't blame yourself," Stoner broke in, shouldering some of the blame to help ease the older woman's pain. "If I'd gone to town with you like you asked, the fight wouldn't have happened."

"No," Mrs. Peters gave him a grateful look, "but he might have been with Cactus instead of Dodge, or he might have gone after the rustlers and...."

"This is getting us nowhere," Linda interrupted angrily. "Are you going to kill Matt Bartleman for me?" She glared at Stoner, daring him to refuse her.

"No, he isn't," Mrs. Peters answered before Stoner could come up with a way to reject Linda's demand without angering her further. "He works for me and I won't let him."

"He may work for you," Linda forged blindly, heedlessly ahead, "but he's my man." She hesitated, momentarily startled by her declaration, but shrugging her shoulders in stubborn acknowledgement of what she had admitted to her mother, she continued. "Or at least he was."

She glared at Stoner, imperiously holding up her hand for silence when her mother started to speak.

"Matt's no killer, honey," Stoner watched Linda's eyes turn even colder as he spoke, but he forged on, knowing he had no alternative but to reject her demand. He couldn't hunt Matt Bartleman down and kill him simply because he had defended himself. "I'll ride to town to find out what happened, but I figure it'll be just like your ma said."

"I don't care how anyone thinks it happened," Linda's words were clipped, her eyes impersonal, cold. "The Bartlemans attacked us here on our porch. They ambushed Rob and the hands up in the hills. They killed Dodge and wounded Cactus and stole our cattle. Now they killed Rob. And Mother tries to tell me it was self-defense? I don't believe it. It was a setup. And even if it wasn't, Rob was my brother. I loved him. I want the man who killed him dead." She stared at Stoner, waiting for him to say something. When he remained silent, she continued, "If you won't help me kill his murderer, I'll do it myself."

"Linda," Mrs. Peters spoke sharply, "you're asking Jacob to kill an innocent man."

Linda ignored her mother. Stoner met her eyes. He flinched at the anger and determination he saw there, and at the hurt, which he knew came not only from Rob's death but also from his refusal to help her avenge that death. He thought of the changes that had taken place in her since his arrival in the valley. He knew she had reached a crucial point in her life, a fork in the trail that he had passed many years before--to follow the path of hatred and vengeance or the path of self-control.

He tried to reason with her again, hopefully, "You don't want to kill an innocent man, Linda, not knowingly."

"Innocent?" she laughed hollowly. "How can you say he's innocent? He killed Rob!" She glared at Stoner. "After all that's happened you think it wasn't planned? And even if it wasn't, what difference does it make? He killed my brother." Her voice broke. For the first time since becoming aware of Rob's death she began to cry, a few isolated gasps at first, then a torrent of wracking sobs. "I'll kill him for that."

Sobbing uncontrollably, she ran from the room. Stoner sat motionless, his eyes focused toward the back of the house where Linda had disappeared. He started to rise and follow her but Mrs. Peters stopped him with a shake of her head.

"I think she's best off alone. She's a stubborn girl, and emotional," she forced a sad smile. "She doesn't like either one of us much right now. She thinks we're betraying her and Rob. But she'll get over it." She paused. "I'll go talk to her in a little while, after she's had her cry. You'd better stay out of her way till tomorrow."

After Stoner left the room Mrs. Peters sat alone with her anguish, her mind wandering erratically over the past few days and the more distant past of Rob's childhood. Evening shadows gave way to darker shadows. She slept fitfully in the chair, unaware when she was awake and when asleep, her mind skipping uncontrollably through the past in both states as if they were inseparable. Eventually the lamp ran out of oil. The room plunged into darkness. She slept less fitfully, her dreams focused on Rob's childhood, her promise to talk to Linda forgotten. Sometime toward morning she awoke and went to bed, where again her sleep became tortured and as changing as the sands.

Linda didn't fall asleep until long after she heard her mother stumble through the dark house to her bedroom. For hours her conscious self, like her mother's, flitted uncontrollably through her memories of Rob and their years of growing through childhood together. Her memories, however, were interspersed with visions of violent retribution against Matt Bartleman. When she finally did sleep nightmares of Rob rotting in his grave haunted her unconscious mind, giving her little rest until after sunlight had penetrated her bedroom.

She awoke late, tired, her stomach in knots, her mind no longer focused on Rob's death but on vengeance against his killer. She washed and dressed carelessly and picked absentmindedly at her breakfast. She avoided her mother's attempts at conversation. After breakfast she returned to her room, took her Spencer and the Cooper .31 that Rob had given her on her return from the East, loaded both weapons, put extra cartridges and the pistol in the pockets of her jacket, and sneaked out the back way to the corral.

Within minutes she was riding toward Chasco. She planned to find Matt Bartleman and kill him. Alone. Rob had been her brother. Avenging his death was her responsibility. After Stoner's refusal to help her, during the night while she lay awake dreaming of revenge, she had considered asking Will or Pate to help her. Either one would do almost anything she asked. But to accept either man's help for a killing would tie her to him in a way she didn't want to be tied to any man except Jacob Stoner. She shook her head and grimaced at the irony. The man she loved had refused to help her. Two men she didn't love would help her, but she refused to ask them for fear they would expect more in return than she was willing to give.

With an effort she forced her thoughts to the task at hand. But she found it impossible to concentrate for long. Her mind insisted on meandering uncontrollably between memories of Rob, stark visions of Matt Bartleman dying a violent death, and the bloody image of the rustler she had killed. Soon all three became intermingled in her mind. She lost track of time and the terrain around her. Before she realized it she had ridden into the pass leading from the little

valley of the Rocking H into the main valley, and into the
ambush set by Nate Barstow.

26

Nate Barstow had left the Bar B before dawn. He had been at his new lookout above the Rocking H in time to watch four of the hands ride down the valley and turn into the hills far east of his position. Later he watched Stoner follow in the direction the crew had taken. His first thought was to follow the gunfighter and shoot him from ambush. He rejected that thought for a more satisfying revenge against the man, kidnapping Linda. He considered riding in and taking her by force, but he mistakenly figured the cook and two men remained; he had learned about Matt killing Rob Peters the night before. And Mrs. Peters was there. He didn't want Linda killed in gun battle. And he didn't want a posse on his trail when he left with her.

He didn't know that Dodge lay in his grave, that Cactus lay wounded in his bunk, and that only Mrs. Peters and the cook stood between him and his prey. So he waited. His patience was rewarded when he spotted Linda leaving the ranch at a shuffling trot. Swearing happily he mounted and cut across country. His objective was an area of the pass where the trail wound through huge boulders before switch-backing to its highest point and then dropping into the larger valley. Once he had Linda, he decided as he rode, he would take her north, maybe all the way to Montana. If things worked out, he would marry her. If not, there were lots of places on the way north where a body would never be found.

The ambush turned out easier than he had expected. He found a spot within a few feet of the trail, a narrow space between two boulders surrounded by juniper and pinyon pine. Sitting in the saddle he was invisible from the trail. Yet, once Linda passed him, he could spur his horse and be at her side before she realized what was happening. She had nowhere to escape. To her left a cliff face rose straight up. To her right the jumble of boulders he was using for cover effectively kept her from fleeing in that direction. In front of her the trail rose in sharp switchbacks for a hundred yards; anything faster than a walk would send her over a drop-off that began at ten feet high just beyond the boulders and slowly increased to almost two hundred feet at the top of the switchbacks.

Nate gloated as he waited, letting his mind roam through images of Linda stripped naked and helpless at his feet to making love to her while she returned his caresses and their mutual passion mounted on waves of pleasure.

He became so mesmerized by his reveries that he almost missed her approach. Only the sudden movement of his horse's ears penetrated the warm fog that had enveloped him. Instinctively he leaned forward and put his hand on the animal's muzzle to keep it from snorting its greeting.

A moment later Linda passed his position, her mount at a trot. Luck was with him. At the same moment that he dug in the spurs and his horse lunged forward, Linda was pulling her horse to a walk, getting ready to make the first turn into the switchbacks. Before she realized what was happening his horse forced hers into the cliff face and his hand grasped her horse's bridle, taking control.

Linda reacted instantaneously. She grabbed for her rifle while at the same time raking her spur along the flank of the horse pressing against hers, catching it in the juncture of the rear leg and the belly. With a shrill cry the animal swung its hind quarters away from the pain. Linda dropped into the open space between the two animals and rolled back down the trail, desperately trying to scramble clear of the stomping hooves as her horse tried to push clear of the cliff face and Nate tried to force his mount to hold, not yet realizing that she was gone.

She hit the ground on her shoulder, losing the Spencer at the impact. The rifle slid over the edge of the trail into the underbrush a few feet below. She started to clamber after it. But at that moment Nate won control of both animals and dropped to his feet, the two sets of reins in his left hand. With a deft movement of his other hand he drew his sidearm and fired. Pebbles and sand exploded inches in front of her hands. She froze, her startled gaze locked on Nate's face.

Cocking his pistol again he leered at her, "I didn't mean to come that close, but what the hell, I'm not Wes Hardin. The next bullet, though, I'll put in one of those pretty legs, if I don't miss and hit something vital."

"What do you want?" Linda pushed herself to her feet.

"Don't play dumb," Nate jeered.

Linda felt a chill slam into her gut. With an effort of will she kept her legs from collapsing.

"You touch me and I'll kill you."

As she spoke she realized how empty the threat sounded. The lust in Nate's eyes and the set of his mouth said clearly that nothing short of the death she had threatened would stop him from doing what he wanted to with her.

"You used to want me to touch you. Hell, we might have gotten married if you hadn't gone east to that damn school."

Linda studied Nate's face. The mockery had disappeared from his voice. The lust had gone from his eyes and lips, to be replaced by a wistful sadness.

"I was a child," Linda angrily cursed herself for blushing. "Besides we were never that close and I never wanted you to touch me that way."

"Don't lie to me," Nate snarled. "What about that last summer before you went east? We had some hot times, especially that June night in the Carter wagon at the dance in Chasco." His voice turned soft, melancholy, his eyes gentle, as he spoke. "There was a freak storm. It was colder than a lone doggie in a Montana snowstorm, but we were plenty warm and snug under all those blankets. Hell, you sure didn't stop me from doing about everything I wanted to." When Linda refused to meet his eyes he continued, "Except what they call the consummating act." He made an angry snort meant for a forced laugh. "And I reckon we'd have done that if that damn brother of yours hadn't found us."

Linda remembered the incident all right, but not with the nostalgia that Nate was evincing, nor with the same interpretation. He had been a young man new to the valley by a couple of years, with a reputation as a tough customer, at least ten years older than she was. She was not yet seventeen, fascinated by his age, his size, his strength, the aura of danger that clung to him, the way other men, older men as well as younger, deferred to him. More than once she had felt herself swept along by his aggressive, reckless passion. But she had always pulled up short, turned cold at the last moment by the threat of a commitment that she might not be able to get out of later. At such times she clearly saw Nate for what he was, a self-centered man who took what he wanted, when he wanted it, regardless of the feelings of others.

Besides, as she recalled it, she had gone out with him less than a half dozen times, and he had been only one of several men she had been seeing at the time. She had been fascinated by him, nothing more, nothing truly serious anyhow.

"Maybe," she reacted to his final comment, "but I doubt it. I would have backed out that time just like I did before." She felt herself blushing again and angrily shook her head, "We only went as far as we did because I couldn't stop you. You were too strong and didn't care what I did or didn't want to do."

"Naw, not that time," Nate ignored her final comment, eyeing her speculatively, a self-satisfied smirk on his lips. "I was ready for you. I'd had my fill of your teasing, so I made a deal with Carter." He chuckled mirthlessly. "Why do you think him and his old lady never showed up at the wagon after the dance ended? They bedded down with the Simpsons. We had the wagon to ourselves for the night. Would have had, but along comes your brother and bang, the fun's over. I never did learn who told him we were out there or there would've been one less windy cowboy around."

When Linda remained silent, Nate ordered her to mount up.

"What about my rifle?"

"Leave it. If you're good I'll buy you another one. If not, you won't need one."

The words, the leering smirk, the cold appraisal his eyes made of her body caused a sick chill to settle in Linda's stomach. As she mounted and gathered the reins, her right hand dipped into the pocket of her coat to make sure the pistol still lay hidden there.

She debated drawing the weapon and shooting Nate. He sat his horse less than fifteen feet from her. She couldn't miss from that distance. She rejected the idea even as her hand convulsively tightened on the pistol grip and her finger caressed the trigger. The ambush had made her horse skittish. It was still trembling. Any quick movement on her part might set it off, not to mention a gunshot so close to its ears. If she missed the first shot or only wounded Nate....

And then there was Nate with his .45 in his hand, pointed in her general direction. She loosed an involuntary groan of disgust. It might be suicide to draw on him when he had the drop on her. Angrily she cursed herself for a fool and began to force her fears aside. The sick chill in her gut slowly dissolved, to be replaced by an iron resolve. She would kill him the first chance she got.

Nate motioned her to take the lead. Wordlessly she obeyed, unwilling to give him the satisfaction of asking where they were headed.

"You're as stubborn as you always were," Nate chuckled as she rode past him. "I always figured a horse and a woman should be broke quick and hard, but in your case I'm gonna enjoy doing it slow and easy. There's a lot of miles between here and Montana. By the time we get there, if we do, I'll have you wearing a saddle and bridle and prancing to the gait I call. And liking every second of it."

Linda made no comment, but the cold, empty feeling returned to her gut. Montana sounded like the end of the world, with hundreds of miles of hell in between.

Matt Bartleman had watched the final moments of Linda's capture from the top of the cliff above the trail. He had left Chasco soon after Mrs. Peters, but he had spent little time at Bar B headquarters, preferring the solitude of the hills to the pleasure Sam took in joshing him about the killing of Rob Peters. Within hours of reaching home he had packed food and gear on a pack horse and ridden into one of the roughest sections of the Bar B, the corner above the pass between the valley of the Rocking H and the main valley. The previous day he had spent the daylight hours riding the steepest slopes he could find and hunting anything whose tracks he came across. He had killed one coyote and three jackrabbits. He had put two bullets within inches of a big cougar, but the animal escaped down a ravine too steep and overgrown for Matt's horses to descend. So far this morning he had seen nothing to shoot at.

"You're a great hunter," he had scoffed at himself moments before he spotted Nate Barstow.

He was sitting on a boulder from which he could see the pass below and at the same time look out over both valleys. Nate had ridden out of the foothills and cut straight for the pass, pushing his horse. His curiosity aroused, Matt studied Nate's back trail, wondering if the Bar B foreman was being chased. But he saw no evidence of pursuit. As he watched, Nate rode into the pass where he hid in the crevice between the boulders. A chill tickled Matt's spine as he realized that Nate was setting an ambush for somebody. He studied the big man's back trail again, then let his eyes roam over the trail that entered the pass from both directions. He couldn't see much of the trail in the valley of the Rocking H; it wound through too many arroyos, piles of boulders, stands of trees, rolling hills. He had almost given up when he spotted Linda ride out of an arroyo and enter the pass.

Relief washed through him momentarily as he thought that Nate and Linda Peters had a meeting set up in the pass. Everybody on the Bar B knew Nate had the hots for the girl. Matt had heard plenty of crude remarks about the two, but he had never known if Linda felt anything for Nate. Now.... The chill returned as he studied the fissure that hid the Bar B foreman. A man didn't hide like that from someone he was meeting, unless the other person didn't know she was being met. He drew his pistol, thinking of firing a warning shot, but hesitated, deciding that Nate was playing a harmless trick. The big man had a rough sense of humor.

Then it was too late; he was too far away to help. In consternation he watched the attack. He watched until the two had ridden through the pass and turned across Bar B land. For some time after they disappeared he studied on the direction Nate had been riding.

"Southeast," he mused. "Ain't nothing in that direction but Bar B and worthless land beyond. Unless he's swinging that way to miss the area around the ranch house, where most of the hands'll be working, or to throw off any pursuit." He tried to recall any semblance of shelter in the general direction Nate might ride after avoiding Bar B headquarters. "Could be heading for that old nester's shack in Mule Deer Canyon," he told himself finally. He shrugged and shook his head, pity for Nate's captive overwhelming him for a moment. "After that, there's lots of places to hide east, south or north."

Hurriedly he descended the slope to where he had hobbled his horses, cursing himself for having left his rifle hidden with the saddle and supplies, near the hobbled animals.

"But what the hell," he mumbled aloud, angrily, trying to excuse himself in his own mind. "I reckon I wouldn't have shot Nate even if I'd had the rifle. Too long a shot, downhill, the girl in the way, and, shit, up till she went off her horse I figured he was just pulling his normal roughhouse stuff."

He tried to force fear for the girl from his mind as he turned the pack horse free, took his rifle from the cache, leaving the supplies to pick up some other time, and saddled his mount. He would need a cool head if he planned to catch Nate and free the girl before anything happened to her. If he did save her, unharmed, it might make up for killing her brother. The thought lifted his spirits. For the first time since he had killed Rob Peters, he sensed the possibility of redeeming himself.

However, as he headed his horse out of the broken hills, the worry returned. By the time he worked his way down to more level ground and found the trail of his quarry, he would have lost two or three hours. He shuddered involuntarily. A lot can happen to a person in two or three hours.

Nate and Linda made slow progress across the Bar B. Afraid that he and his captive might be seen by some of the ranch hands, he kept to the wooded, rough ground, avoiding the trails, angling southeast from the pass in order to give the ranch house a wide berth. When he had almost reached the far border of Bar B land he swung to the northeast. He arrived at his destination a couple of hours before nightfall.

Linda's spirits fell when she saw the ramshackle hut with the rear section of the roof collapsed. The building reflected her own feelings. On the first part of the ride she had kept her hopes up by plotting ways to escape. Once while traversing a steep slope she and Nate had entered a recent slide area. Nate's horse had sunk in loose gravel and spooked. Seeing her chance, LInda sank her spurs in her horse's flanks. But Nate had rolled from his floundering mount and grabbed her horse's bridle before it had taken its first jump. The horse tried to run as she frantically raked its flanks. The effort was futile. With a mighty heave Nate yanked the animal's head around his chest, throwing it as if he were bulldogging a steer.

At the last moment, as the squealing horse crashed onto its side, Linda threw herself from the saddle. She felt her ankle catch between the saddle and ground, then wrench free as she rolled and skidded downhill. When she came to a halt she was dazed and sore from one end to the other. Her elbows were scraped raw, as was the side of her face. Her ankle had twisted when it caught on the saddle. A number of bruises covered her body. The knees of her jeans were ripped and her blouse was torn in several places. Despondently she tried to brush the sand from her clothes and hair.

"There's a spring where we're headed. You can wash up there."

She glanced up to see Nate sitting his horse a few feet away, leering and holding the reins of her mare.

Her anger boiled over. She grabbed for the pistol in her pocket. It caught on the fabric, then ripped free as she furiously yanked on it. Blindly, instinctively, she brought it level, searching for her target.

She found it, too late.

As her hand dropped Nate spurred his horse, simultaneously loosening his grip on her mare's reins. The large horse smashed into her just as her pistol aligned on its rider. She catapulted downhill, landing on her back and sliding through sand and stone until she came to rest against a ledge. The pistol landed a half dozen yards downhill.

"You think I didn't know you had that toy pistol? Hell, I felt it back in the pass." He grinned widely. "You try that again and I'll give you a hiding you'll never forget," his grin disappeared as he spoke. "If you'd hurt your horse I'd give you a hiding now. And make you walk till we found another one."

Frightened, trying to ignore the pain in her body, Linda refused to look at him.

"You know better than to treat a horse like that, Linda."

"I'm not the one that threw it."

"No," Nate conceded reluctantly as he retrieved the pistol, his irritation clear in his tone, "but you sure as hell're the one that caused it. Just remember what I said about bein' good. You're with me till I say you're not. You try to escape again and you'll wish to hell you hadn't." Having given his warning, Nate relented. "You can clean those cuts when we get where we're goin'. Won't be long now."

It wasn't. In less than two hours they were sitting their mounts quietly, eyeing the abandoned nester's shack.

"Some more of the roof's fallen in since I was here last, but I reckon it'll do for the night," Nate broke the silence. "Come on," he added as he dismounted. "I'll clean the place up some and shore up the roof a little. You clean yourself up at the spring," he motioned toward a stand of cottonwoods on the slope behind the cabin, "and fix those scratches." He handed her a pint bottle of whisky, half full. "After that, make a fire and cook us up a meal. What food we got is in here." He handed her his saddlebags, adding apologetically, "There ain't no stove and the chimney for the fireplace has caved in, so I reckon you'll have to cook on a campfire, but there's plenty of firewood from the caved-in roof. You won't have to go looking for it."

Later, when they had finished the meal, Linda scraped the dishes with sand and washed them off with water she heated in a pan Nate had found in the cabin. Nate watched her closely, his desire growing with each movement she made.

"You could say this's our weddin' night," he announced when she had finished her chores, studying her face for any sign that she shared his growing passion and nervousness.

He had committed himself, he thought. He had made his vow to himself about what he would do if he ever got her alone. He didn't plan on backing out. Yet in his own way, he realized, he loved the woman standing near him in the firelight. He wanted her for his own. He wanted her softness and her surrender in the night hours, and her dedication to his other needs during the day. In her eyes, in her face, in the way she stood before him he looked for traces of her feelings for him. He found nothing but fear and a smoldering anger. His own anger rose in answer to hers.

"I'm goin' to wash up at the spring," he leered. "Get ready to deflower the virgin which, I'd give odds, ain't as pure as the fallin' snow. Not after all that time back east."

Linda returned his stare but made no comment.

Nate burst into forced laughter, the noise raucous and suggestive of suppressed violence.

"I'll have you tonight, so you might as well enjoy it."

When Linda still remained silent, he continued with a sardonic grin on his lips, "If you're thinkin' I'll change my mind or someone'll come along and rescue you, you might's well quit thinkin'. There ain't no one within miles of this shack. And me, well, I sure won't change my mind. I been thinkin' about something like this for a long time. At first I figured to do it all legal-like, but after you gave me the brush-off I began plannin' it the other way."

"You won't get away with it," Linda fought the despair rising in her. "Jacob Stoner will track you down and kill you. If he doesn't kill you, I will. You can't watch me all the time."

"Stoner," Nate pronounced the word with jealous anger, fingering the scabby line on his forehead. "You sure do go through the men. Before he rode in, story had it you were sweet on that tall cowpoke called Will. But you sure have been playin' up to that gunfighter since he hired on, playin' around in the crick and pond with him."

"Do you believe everything you hear?"

"I believe my own eyes."

"You've been spying on me," Linda accused him angrily as she realized the implications of what he was saying. She recalled Stoner's warnings and how she had ignored them.

"Spyin'?" Nate queried with an angry grin. "Keepin' an eye on my property till I could claim it, I'd say."

Linda forced a wounded note into her voice, "Is that what I am to you, Nate? Property? Baggage?"

"You know better than that, Linda."

Nate studied her thoughtfully, wondering why the change of tone. "I said I'd marry you if you'll have me. I want you for my own. I don't like it when you let other men hang around you like hound dogs after a bitch in heat."

"You have a way with words," the sarcasm escaped her before she could stop it.

Nate shrugged, glaring at her through eyes turned icy, "I may not be as honey-tongued as those educated fellows you've been used to, but I don't reckon Stoner has anything on me when it comes to brains or fightin'."

Afraid of the look in Nate's eyes, Linda changed the subject, "Why would you marry a woman who doesn't love you?"

Jeering laughter burst from Nate's lips. "Love!" he snorted scornfully. "I don't figure you know what it is."

"You figure wrong," Linda didn't try to hide her irritation although she felt her knees shaking. "A man has to be sick if he thinks he can force a woman and she'll learn to love him for it."

"You and your goddamned education," Nate clipped his words furiously. "You used to like it when I didn't take no for an answer."

"I was a child then, Nate. I didn't know what I wanted and I didn't know what a real relationship between a man and a woman was supposed to be like," Linda glared at him in disgust, her fear forgotten. "I admit I was a flirt at times. But so were most of the girls. And the boys." She paused to catch her breath from the rush of angry words. "I admit I sometimes liked it when you were aggressive. But that was different. I was a child, like I said, and I thought I liked you. Besides, when I said stop and meant it, you stopped. This is different. You said you're going to force yourself on me tonight and that I'll learn to like it. At the same time you say you want me to marry you. I think that's sick."

Nate shook his head stubbornly, fighting the rage that was rising in his chest.

"Women don't like weak men. They like a man that'll take the bit in his teeth."

"That depends on what you're talking about, Nate," Linda's anger at Nate's attitude burst forth again in spite of her attempts to reason with the man. "You force me and I'll hate you forever. Don't ever turn your back on me because I'll kill you if I get the chance."

Nate studied her through half-closed eyelids. She was a beautiful woman, a woman whose dark eyes promised the extremes of tender affection and wild passion, a fit mate for a man among men. The way she looked straight at a man, challenging his manhood; her slender, graceful carriage; the delightful sway of her hips and the proud, thrusting breasts sent shivers of pleasure coursing through a man, enslaving his mind to a desire he couldn't control. She was a woman a man would kill for, or die for, Nate thought. Watching her in the fading daylight, across the fire, he was overcome by an unquenchable thirst. At the same time, bitter doubts about his project began to seep into his consciousness. Behind Linda's soft sensuality, behind the promise of hidden fires ready to burst into flames lay an iron resolve that he had glimpsed only recently. A chill tingled his spine, as if someone had just entered the date of his death in the eternal logbook.

He shook himself disgustedly, trying to throw off the sense of doom. He had what he had wanted for a long time, alone and at his mercy. No one knew he had kidnapped her. At the Rocking H they would figure she was still in town. No one would begin worrying about her for a few more hours, maybe not until the next day. When they did decide something had happened to her it would be too late.

In fact, he exulted to himself, it was already too late. It was too dark to follow his trail. Even the next day, he figured, what few tracks he had left would be nearly impossible to follow because he had covered them well, circling, riding the rocky ridges and pine-covered slopes as much as possible, avoiding the trails. He had accomplished his goal. No one could stop him. So why the worry?

With a curse for himself and his gloom, he bounded to his feet.

"Like I said, I'm gonna clean up, get ready for my bride. However, just in case the bride might take a notion to wander, I'd better take her along."

He grabbed Linda by the wrist and, lifting her to her feet as if she were a child, pulled her around the cabin toward the spring.

Terrified and angry, Linda dug in her heels. But resisting him was like resisting an avalanche. Reluctantly, afraid she would lose her footing and be dragged over the rocky ground, she quit struggling and kept up with him. She tried to think ahead, to plan, but her mind was a turmoil.

On the bank of the small pool formed by the spring Nate stopped and grinned at Linda, "Let's go swimming."

"No thanks," she shivered. "It's getting cold."

"Yeah," Nate glanced at the darkening sky, "but the water'll make you feel good. Take the aches and pains away. When we get out we can cuddle by the fire to warm up. There's some blankets in the cabin we can use. I left them the last time I was here."

Linda remained silent, afraid to say anything. Nate felt his mood change. His gloom faded. The pleasant heat in his groin returned. Accompanying it was a joy he hadn't felt for years. Suddenly he burst out laughing, an animal rumble in the gathering darkness. Effortlessly he lifted Linda in his arms and tossed her into the middle of the dark, cold water, his laughter increasing at her shrill scream. With a sweep of his hand he unbuckled his belt and deposited it, Colt and all, in the grass at his feet before he followed her. His dive carried him into her as she was scrambling toward the far shore.

"Gotcha," he shouted happily, grabbing her around the waist and diving again.

When they came to the surface Linda was coughing and gagging.

"Damn you, Nate Barstow," she sputtered as soon as she could breathe again. "You almost drowned me."

She struggled to free herself, but she might as well have been struggling against the embrace of a grizzly. Nate held her with one arm around her chest, her arms pinioned in his clasp.

"I reckon there's no doubt I'll be damned," his laughter rumbled once more. "So I might as well enjoy getting there."

He turned her like a toy and pulled her against his chest. She had begun to shiver in the chest-deep water. Her shaking body inflamed his desire. With his free hand he pulled her face to his and hungrily kissed her cold lips, unaware that her shivering had turned to fierce struggles to free herself from his arms, oblivious that her lips did not respond to his bruising kisses, not realizing that she had managed to free one arm.

When her fingernails raked at his eyes, he cursed mildly and grabbed her wrists. His passion driving him blindly, he dragged her to the bank of the pond. There he forced her down on the grass, on her back, ignoring her struggles. Sitting astraddle her to hold her in place with his weight, imprisoning her wrists above her head with one hand, with the other he unbuttoned her wet blouse.

"You might as well quit struggling and enjoy it too."

He threw his head back and laughed, a wild roar of conquest in the gathering darkness. Exhilarated by the sound, excited by her struggles and by her warm softness under him, he rolled onto his side and reached for her belt buckle, one hand still holding her hands immobile, one leg holding her body in place.

27

Earlier that morning Joe and Sam Bartleman had watched Nate ride out of the Bar B. Angry curses from the bunkhouse as the foreman stumbled around getting dressed and later the nervous whinnying from the corral as he caught and saddled his horse brought them out of their bunks in the main house, onto the sagging porch. They sat in rickety wooden chairs, boots and jackets thrown on over their long johns to protect them from the cold, night air, watching the big man emerge from the shadows of the corral and disappear into the surrounding gloom of approaching dawn.

"That bastard's crazy," Sam grumbled. "Ain't no woman worth the time he spends tryin' to waylay the Peters girl. Not when there's plenty of women ready and willin'."

Joe gave a grunt meant for a chuckle, "Me and you know that. But Nate's got the sickness. He don't want a short ride or two. He wants to own the filly."

"I gotta admit she's all woman," Sam returned the grunt. "She'd give a man one hell of a ride. But she's just one more woman." He paused with a snorted sneer before he continued, "I didn't get a chance to tell you last night, what with that drunken poker game goin' on in the bunkhouse, but I followed Nate's tracks again yesterday, after he rode in-- backtracked him. He was in a new hideout in the hills above the Rockin' H. I wonder if that cut on his forehead come from getting' caught by one of the Rockin' H rannies in his other hideout. I asked him how he got it and he growled like a she-bear just out of hibernation," Sam chuckled at the memory.

Joe made no comment.

"Anyhow," he continued when he saw that Joe didn't seem much interested in Barstow's spying on the Peters girl or in how he got the scratch up the center of his forehead, "There ain't no mistakin' the tracks that hammerhead of his makes. The right hind leg pulls in a mite. And there sure as hell ain't nobody else I know of wears boots as big as Nate's."

"Spit it out. Don't beat around the bush all day."

"His hideout's less'n two hundred yards from the house. I could sneak in there, shoot the old woman and girl, and leave somethin' to make it look like Nate done it."

"Leave what?"

"That little pocketknife? The one with his name on it? He used to sit around parin' his nails with it all the time."

When Joe nodded, Sam continued, "It irritated the crap out of me so I swiped the damn thing. Hell, you remember him pissin' and moanin' for days about that goddamn knife and how his first true love gave it to him."

Both men laughed uproariously at the picture of Nate's anger over the missing knife, at how he had searched every man on the crew and gone through their personal belongings, not once but several times over the days after the knife disappeared.

Joe chuckled. "We didn't get a damn thing done around here for two weeks. He had every man-jack on the crew lookin' for that damned knife. They musta searched every cranny on the ranch."

"In groups of three," Sam grinned at the memory, "so the guilty man couldn't pull no shenanigans."

"What do you think?" he asked after a few moments.

Joe considered Sam's proposal in silence. He wanted the Rocking H, with its sheltered valley and permanent water. He didn't care what happened to the owners as long as he got the land. But whatever happened to them, he, Sam and Matt had to appear innocent. Or the Peters women had to disappear without witnesses who would talk.

The earlier, botched attempt to shoot the Peters family in a gun battle and call it accidental had been stupid, he figured. If it had succeeded it might have put his neck and those of his sons in a noose. In the days following the fight at the Peters house, as he lay recuperating in her house, Nellie had reported more than one conversation she'd heard around town threatening lynch-law if anything happened to the Peters women.

Joe explained his thoughts to Sam. "Now," he concluded, "Matt's killed the Peters boy. The women though...."

"Christ, Joe," Sam interrupted, "you ain't getting' soft on me, are you?"

"Don't bet your life on it," Joe growled. "I just don't plan on losin' a son or puttin' my own neck in a hangman's noose."

"Like I said," Sam reiterated. "I can shoot the women, leave the knife, and wipe out all evidence that I've been in Nate's ambush spot. Anybody searches up there'll see nothin' but sign of Nate' big feet, his hammerhead, and the knife."

"Yeah, I reckon," Joe mused. "But if you only get a shot at one of them, make sure it's the old lady. The girl'll more'n likely sell out under pressure, now her brother's gone. Not Martha Peters."

Sam stared at Joe in the gathering light of day, "What about the gunfighter? And the other hands?"

"Don't get too ambitious, too sudden," Joe grunted coldly. "That's a good way to get yourself killed or in prison." He paused. "Besides, they don't own the place so they ain't no threat if the women're dead." He stared at Sam in silence. "Let's take it one step at a time, where it counts. Kill the girl and the old woman both if you can get by with it easy. If you can only get one of them, make sure it's the old lady. Then we wait a while, see what happens before we make another move."

"What the hell," Sam grunted after a long silence. "I might as well get started today. Nate don't stay over there more'n a couple hours. I reckon he's tryin' to catch the girl alone, at the ranch or out ridin'. Soon as he sees what they're doin' for the day, he heads back here, then rides over there in the afternoon again."

"Don't let him catch you on his trail."

"I can take care of Nate," Sam shrugged. "But what I was sayin' is, I'll wait a couple hours and then ride on over there. If I get lucky I can maybe get rid of both the Peters women today. From the little I've seen they don't ride out much, just hang around the house and corrals."

Later that morning Sam left his horse in a grassy ravine almost a hundred yards from Nate's new ambuscade. His first destination was a brushy knoll near the Bar B foreman's hideout, then on into the hideout after he was sure Nate wasn't there. From the knoll he could see the approaches to the house and the new hideout, just as he could to the old hideout. More than a dozen times over the past months he'd followed Nate from the Bar B and spent a few hours on the knoll, watching the house and waiting to see what Nate would do.

After a quarter hour of careful scrutiny he had not yet spied Nate but he spotted movement in the shadows of the ranch house. A moment later the Peters girl walked into the sunlight and made her way to the barn. She wore jeans and a green blouse; her dark hair drifted over her shoulders. Within a short time she appeared again, this time on horseback, riding toward the pass leading to Chasco.

Sam almost missed Nate, but from the corner of his eye he caught the flash of movement and a few minutes later, watching carefully, could see Nate in the distance riding hell for leather toward the pass.

"Go get her, Nate," he chuckled lewdly. "Me, I'll take the old woman."

His chuckle became a broad grin as his words tickled his funny bone, bringing to mind a picture of himself and the old woman in a passionate embrace. The image turned his chuckle into cruel laughter. It wouldn't be the first time he had killed another human from ambush. Nor would it be the first time he had killed a woman.

The first had been a whore in Globe City. He was seventeen. He had been drunk when he bought her favors, too drunk to perform. She laughed at him and kicked him out of her shack, but she kept the money he had given her. Later she had ridiculed him in the saloon where he had propositioned her, in front of his friends. He did nothing at the time, afraid he would be suspected if he did. Two months later he returned, sneaked into town at night, waited near her shack until she was alone, broke in, and cut her throat. He had never told anyone, not even Joe, that he'd killed her. Nor had he told anyone about two of the others, a miner he'd ambushed and killed for his sack of gold dust, a cowboy he'd shot in the back for the hell of it, beside a lonely campfire they had shared one night after meeting on the trail to Prescott. He had buried the bodies of both men and, as far as he knew, neither had been found.

Sam continued watching the Rocking H ranch house. Sometime later Mrs. Peters appeared and walked to the bunkhouse, disappearing inside. Within minutes she came out of the bunkhouse and returned to the house. Except for the horses in the corral, Sam saw no other sign of life.

Deciding that he would shoot her when she appeared again, Sam made his way to the Bar B foreman's hideout, trying to leave no trace of his presence. Once inside the stand of trees and bushes, he settled down to wait. For a half hour nothing moved in the ranch yard below. Then Mrs. Peters again separated from the shadows of the house and walked toward the bunkhouse. She stopped a few yards short of the low building and stood staring in his direction.

A cruel smirk curled Sam's lips and glinted in the murky depths of his eyes. He estimated the distance to the woman at maybe a hundred and eighty yards. It was a clear shot, slightly downhill, no wind, nothing between him and his target. He lifted his Sharps.

"Hold still, old woman," he grunted as he took aim, froze, and squeezed the trigger.

The rifle cracked. Mrs. Peters folded, turning as she dropped face first into the dirt, her left side to Sam. Quickly but carefully he shot her two more times, tossed Nate's knife into the dirt, and headed for his horse, sticking to rocky ground or terrain covered by pine needles whenever possible. He laughed exultantly as he mounted and rode for the Bar B, sure that he had left no trace of his presence.

Mrs. Peters had been carrying a small pail of stew to Cactus when she spotted the rider leave the foothills far up the valley and turn in the direction of the house. She stopped to watch, wondering if the horseman was Stoner returning. She knew he had been upset by his spat with Linda the previous evening. She also knew he felt guilty about the deaths of Dodge and Rob. She had her own load of guilt and easily recognized the same symptoms in him. Twice in the night she had seen him up, smoking cigarettes at the corral, easily recognizable in the moonlight. At first light she had found him in the chow hall, drinking coffee he himself had brewed before Chew Lin had stirred. She had tried to talk to him, to share her own sense of guilt and worry, but he had been uncommunicative, not brusque, simply brief in his answers to her questions. Later, after sending the men for Dodge's body, he had been like a caged tiger, constantly moving between the corrals and the bunkhouse.

Finally she had cornered him at the corrals and told him to find something to do somewhere else. He had given her a rueful grin, promised to send Will or Pate back as soon as he caught up with the hands, and quickly saddled. Now, she thought, she wished she hadn't sent him off. Linda's secretive departure had her worried. She was afraid the girl had set out to find and kill Matt Bartleman. If Stoner had been around when she left, he could have ridden with her or, if she had refused his company, followed her, maybe prevented a disaster.

Soon after spotting the rider along the edge of the valley, Mrs. Peters recognized the huge frame of Tall Will. Relieved and apprehensive at the same time, she decided to send him after Linda. His temper made him untrustworthy, explosive, especially where Linda was concerned, but he would give his life to protect her.

At that moment the world dropped out from under her. She felt a heavy blow and then nothing. She didn't feel the next two bullets. Nor did she see a dark cloud momentarily hide the sun.

Will heard the shots--one, a pause, two more in quick succession. He had not seen Mrs. Peters standing near the bunkhouse, but he knew the shots came from the spur of hills south of the house. His first reaction was that Linda or Chew Lin was hunting. He immediately rejected that thought; the spur of sandy ground covered with anemic trees and brush was barren of game worth hunting. Seldom did anyone from the ranch enter the area, except to pass through it into the mountains beyond. As for target practice, Linda always shot down by the pond and Chew Lin only fired a weapon on his rare hunting expeditions.

An icy wave of fear slammed into his gut as another thought hit him. The spur of hills was a good place for a bushwhacker to shoot at anyone moving between the house and corrals.

He kneed his bay into a lope. Minutes later he saw Chew Lin dash across the yard and kneel near the bunkhouse, beside a man already kneeling there, over what appeared to be something on the ground. The man, he figured, was Cactus. The other form? Was it a woman? Fear again washed over him like a flash flood. He spurred his horse to a wild gallop. When he rode into the yard and threw himself from the saddle, Cactus was standing, staring in the direction from which the shots had come, a look of stony sadness etched on his face.

Will dropped to his knees beside the still form. It was Mrs. Peters, not Linda. One bullet had cut a groove an inch deep along the top of her head from left to right. Another had smashed into her chest from the side, immediately below the left breast. A third had entered her body through the top of her other breast. She was dead. She had died instantly, he figured; any one of the shots could have killed her.

Several emotions seeped into his belly as he looked down at the woman he had come to respect so much, almost to love like his own mother--relief that it wasn't Linda, guilt at his feeling of relief, anguish at the loss, and rage at the sneaking coward who had killed such a good woman.

Chew Lin, who had hurried toward the house just as Will galloped into the yard, soon returned with a blanket. They wrapped Mrs. Peters in it and carried her to the living room, where they deposited her in her favorite rocker.

"I'll dig the grave," Will's voice cracked.

"No," Chew Lin spoke angrily. "You go after the killer."

Will stared at the Chinese cook, startled at the angry insistence. He had never heard Chew Lin give an order not having to do with food supplies and eating.

"I dig the grave. Cactus can't. I can. You go after the killer."

"Okay," Will was glad to agree. His rage was eating away at his other emotions over Mrs. Peters' death, dominating them and deadening his feelings to anything but his need for vengeance. Grabbing the reins of the bay he started toward the corral to throw his saddle on a fresh mount.

As he turned on his heel, he stopped. Something was missing. Linda!

"Where's Linda?"

"She headed for town shortly after Stoner left, Mrs. Peters said," Cactus shrugged helplessly. "Sneaked off before anyone knew what she was plannin'. Mrs. Peters was upset. She was gonna send Stoner after her when he got back."

A pang of jealousy punctured Will's chest, but he forced it away. He still loved Linda, he realized, in spite of his efforts. For some time he had been aware of the developing relationship between her and Stoner. His first reaction had been anger. He considered calling Stoner out, forcing him to fight with fists or guns, but soon rejected both possibilities.

"One way you'd be a dead man, the other you'd spend a few weeks on your back," he had warned himself aloud more than once, laughing ironically at himself as he spoke. Then seriously, "Besides, he saved your life."

He continued to hesitate, however. Linda in town? Alone? He turned back to Cactus and Chew Lin.

"The others ain't far behind me. Tell Stoner Linda's in town alone."

With their okay echoing in his ear Will again headed for the corral. Within minutes he was riding into the spur of hills south of the house, riding a grey horse with plenty of stamina.

Cactus and Chew Lin had pointed out a general area from which they thought the shots had come. Will rode a quick circle around the area, hoping to pick up tracks coming or going. He had almost completed half the circle when he found Nate Barstow's tracks galloping from the grove of trees.

He set off in pursuit, figuring he was following the tracks of the fleeing bushwhacker. When he reached the pass and came to the spot where Nate had ambushed Linda he stopped to study the ground, puzzled. After several minutes, he had given up and decided to continue his pursuit when he spotted the Spencer on the slope, almost hidden by the underbrush.

His heart did a flip when he recognized the rifle. He had often watched Linda fire it. A metal plate with her initials on it was attached to the left side of the stock. He held the rifle in his hands and stared at it, more confused than before he had found it. The timing was wrong. Linda had ridden out right after Stoner, according to Cactus and Chew Lin. Mrs. Peters had been shot after Stoner reached the canyon where Dodge had been buried and he, Will, had returned down the canyon to within sight of the house. Unless Linda made a detour or something....

He shook himself, unconvinced by that line of reasoning. If Linda had detoured very far she would have taken some other way to Chasco. He wondered if he was following the killer or someone else who had ridden from the ambush site before the shooting.

In the next moment he shook off his indecision and kneed his horse in the direction the horse with the leg that turned in had taken. The killer or not, he appeared to have kidnapped Linda. And his were the only tracks Will had found in the area where the shots had come from. When he came to the place where the tracks of Matt's horse merged with those he was following, he decided that there must have been two bushwhackers holed up in the hills near the house. One had taken off after Linda when she rode toward town while the other had remained behind and shot Mrs. Peters.

He grimaced and swore under his breath, urging his horse to a canter. As he rode he studied the three sets of prints. Linda's captor seemed in no hurry. He appeared more intent on not being seen and on losing any potential pursuers-- riding the low ground, keeping to hard, rocky terrain whenever possible, winding through ravines and heavy stands of brush and trees, reversing his direction from time to time. Following him and his captive would have been slow, tedious work but for the third rider, who made no attempt to cover his tracks.

Will kept his mount at a rapid trot, only occasionally stopping to make sure the third rider was still following the tracks of Linda and her captor.

"They've got us by two to three hours," he leaned forward to rub the grey's neck as he spoke. "With luck, we'll cut their lead in half by nightfall, maybe more. But we better keep a sharp eye out. We can't be too far behind the bushwhacker that shot Mrs. Peters."

28

Linda struggled frantically, in vain. With one hand Nate held her wrists in a crushing grip, grinding the wrist bones together and bruising the flesh. The weight of his thigh and knee over her thighs imprisoned the lower half of her body. No matter how much she struggled, she could not free her hips or kick anything but the ground. Luckily the ground was soft from water seepage and the thick grass or her heels would already be bruised.

Suddenly Nate grunted a curse. His free hand had been working to unbuckle her belt, a wide, three-pronged leather affair. All three prongs worked as a unit. To try to fasten or unfasten them individually was impossible, which Nate had been trying to do. Each time he had one out of its hole and reached for the next one, the first one slipped back in.

In spite of her helpless situation Linda almost giggled at his frustration. A second later, however, she was once more struggling and cursing her tormentor.

Intent on his task, deciding he needed both hands to unfasten her belt, Nate clasped each of her wrists in one of his beefy paws and yanked her arms down to her sides. Swiftly, driven wild by his passion, no longer trying to be gentle, he reversed his position and knelt on her chest. The weight of his buttocks rested between her chin and breasts. His knees and shins pressed her arms into the ground. She was effectively immobilized from the waist up. Once again he reached for her belt buckle. She swung a leg at him, then another, trying to hit his head with a knee. He laughed, boisterous and happy, as his forearms and elbows warded off her thrashing legs, catching her just above the knees.

A moment later he grunted his success. The buckle came free. With a lusty chortle, feeling the tight, pleasurable throbbing at the crotch of his own pants, he began stripping Linda's jeans from her body. He ignored her threats and pleas and violent thrashing. Now that success seemed so near, he no longer felt driven. He worked on one leg, pulling and tugging until it was free. Then he reached for the other one.

"What's going on down there?"

Nate froze. His eyes darted toward the sound. He recognized the voice. It belonged to Matt Bartleman. But it had come from the shadows up the slope toward the cabin. He couldn't see its owner. Worse, he couldn't tell if Matt had a weapon in his hand or exactly how far away he stood.

"What the hell you doing here, Matt?" he asked, frantically searching the shadows for sight of the man.

"I was hunting up above the pass this morning, Nate. I saw you take the girl. I've been following you all day."

"Yeah, well, you can keep on hunting," Nate felt anger and fear mingle in his gut.

He tried to recall where he had dropped his pistol and gun belt. He didn't figure Matt would shoot an unarmed man. The kid didn't have it in him to kill in cold blood. But he wasn't a pushover, either. He had proved that when he killed Rob Peters. He was tough and he was as straight as a rifle barrel. He would take Linda back to the Rocking H if he could get her away from Nate. And he would take Nate to the marshal in Chasco. Unless Nate could figure a way out of the trap he was in.

"I've found what I was hunting for, Nate. Just come up out of there. Careful. You're in the moonlight. I can see you and the girl plain as day almost."

He paused to shift his stance. Nate caught the movement and a moment later could make out Matt's dark silhouette.

"Stand up, Nate. Take your hands off the girl and stand up. I've got you covered so don't try anything dumb. You know I'm good with a pistol. From this distance I can't miss."

"Okay," the Bar B foreman grunted as he stood up. "I'm coming peaceful."

For now, he thought, as a killing fury smothered him. He stood and walked slowly up the slope. He had almost reached the halfway point when Matt stepped from the shadows of an oak and advanced toward him. Nate stopped walking and braced himself for a lunge.

Come on, he growled to himself. Keep coming. Just a few more steps.

He estimated the distance between them at fifteen feet and Matt was still closing in, moving too swiftly over the shadowy, uneven ground. He studied the approaching figure, trying to see the face and eyes, but he could only make out the shape of the head surrounded by a splotch of dark hair and darker clothing. With concentrated effort he spotted the dull glint of a pistol, held waist high.

When Matt had closed the distance to ten feet Nate braced himself. Two more steps, a voice gloated in his depths, two more steps and you've got him.

Suddenly Matt stepped in a hole camouflaged by leaves and the black shadows along the ground. Off balance, unable to stop, he lunged forward, flailing wildly with both arms to keep from falling. As his right hand flew skyward he pulled the trigger, already cocked and ready to fire. The shot echoed deafeningly beside his ear, disorienting him further. Desperately he fought to regain his balance. But it was too late. His first lunge brought him within arm's reach of the Bar B foreman. The wild shot had gone off less than a foot from Nate's face, blinding him temporarily. But he was already reaching for his victim, and for the pistol. One hairy paw closed on the barrel and ripped the Colt from Matt's grasp, the other crashed into Matt's face, knocking him to the ground, stunned.

The Colt in his grip, confident that his fist had put Matt out of action for a few seconds, Nate stepped backward, once, twice, fighting to clear the bright lights from his eyes. When he could once again penetrate the darkness, he glared at Matt, who was trying to sit up.

"Might as well stay down," he grunted what he meant for a chuckle. "You'll be there permanent soon as I pull this trigger."

"Shoot and be damned," Matt growled, trying to staunch the flow of blood from his nose with his hands. "Anybody dumb enough to do what I did deserves what he gets."

Nate felt anger rise in him, killing anger, at the youth's cool reply. He had never liked Matt. The boy was too easygoing, too quick to serve as peacemaker, too willing to see the other person's point of view. He would have killed Matt long before if not for Sam and Joe. They paid his wages, good money for little work, and they were too dangerous to cross.

"You don't think I'll kill you, do you Matt?"

Matt ignored the jeer. Nate's anger flared out of control. He cocked the pistol and pulled the trigger in one fluid motion. Matt grunted explosively and toppled onto his side. Nate fired again. Matt made no sound.

From behind Nate came a wild scream. He turned, a lewd grin forming on his lips.

When he had risen and walked up the slope, freeing her of his weight, Linda had frantically pulled up her pants and begun searching for Nate's pistol, all the while wondering at the irony of a fate that had sent Rob's murderer to save her. Sobbing and cursing with outrage, she crawled through the grass, searching blindly with her hands. She had almost given up when Matt's shot cracked the silence of the night.

A moment later she heard the thud of Nate's fist against flesh and the sound of Matt's falling body. Deciding the two men were fighting but unable to see them in the dark shadows of the slope, she increased the frenzy of her search. Then she heard their voices and she realized that Nate had Matt's pistol. She shivered, frantic, and her hand touched leather.

She drew the heavy pistol and scurried up the slope, cocking the weapon as she moved. She had covered most of the distance to the two men when Nate's voice rose tauntingly, followed closely by the two shots.

Nate's voice and bulk had identified him for her, thus making Matt the long, dark shadow on the ground in front of Nate. At Nate's first shot and Matt's grunt she stopped, shocked that any man could kill so cold-bloodedly. At the second shot she found her voice. She screamed with rage. She aimed at Nate's bulk and pulled the trigger. Somewhere inside her it registered that Nate had turned just as she fired. She thought she saw him stagger. But he took a step in her direction, silently, menacingly. Swiftly she cocked the pistol and fired again. And a third time. Twice, subconsciously, she noted flame spurt from the weapon in Nate's hand. She noted the flame and heard the crack of the shot. But the impressions seemed so distant, so muffled, that it was almost like somebody else had sensed the sound and the flame.

After her third shot Nate seemed to hesitate. Automatically she cocked her weapon to fire again. As her thumbs pulled the hammer into place, Nate took a half step, swayed, mumbled something unintelligible, and tumbled face first to the ground. For several seconds incomprehensible sounds tumbled feverishly from his throat, as if he was trying to tell her something. Slowly the noises died. His feet kicked at the dirt. Then nothing.

Linda remained where she stood, frozen, the silence washing the conflicting emotions from her soul. After what seemed to her a long time the night resumed its normal life. In the distance a pack of coyotes returned to the hunt, yipping on the trail of some frightened animal. A tree limb cracked and fell with a thud. An owl hooted nearby, its eerie noise soft and haunting. Something small moved along the ground behind her.

Finally she approached Nate's body. She nudged him with a toe. He didn't move. She dropped to her knees and felt for a heartbeat. Her hand came away covered with warm blood, which she tried unsuccessfully to wipe off on the dirt and leaves at her feet.

Convinced that Nate was dead, she moved on to Matt. She could find no pulse, but he was breathing, shallowly, raspingly. It was too dark to see so she explored his body with her fingers. High on his right chest, under the collar bone, she found a hole that was bleeding very little; she could not find an exit hole in his back. Along his right hip she traced a furrow that glanced off his hipbone and cut a deep groove through his upper thigh before, apparently, spending itself in the earth somewhere. The latter wound was bleeding profusely but was not life-threatening. The hole in the chest scared her. She prayed that the bullet had not punctured the lung.

The final words of her prayer reverberated through her mind like cold water sloshing in a glass.

"A prayer for Matt Bartleman?" she asked herself disgustedly, "for Rob's killer? I left the ranch to find and kill him. Now I'm praying for his life."

The killing anger flashed hot and wild again, consuming her emotions and leaving them like dry ashes in her chest. What her mother had said about the manner of Rob's death came back to her, as did Stoner's refusal to hunt down and kill Matt for her. She tried to think of Rob and all the fun times they had had growing up, but all she could think of was how self-centered he could be at times, and how cruel. For the first time since hearing of his death she admitted to herself that her mother was probably right; he could have forced the fight. It was like him, especially when he was drunk.

She stared at the unconscious man stretched out before her, helpless and maybe dying. He had risked his life to save her. He deserved her help even if he had killed Rob. But how? His wounds needed immediate attention. He needed to be kept warm in the increasing chill of the night air. He weighed too much for her to carry him up the slope to the cabin, and dragging him might aggravate his chest wound and kill him. Yet all the gear and the fire were up there.

She rose and hurried uphill, determined to bring the necessary supplies to Matt and to rebuild the fire beside him. If she could get him through the night alive, in the morning she could figure out how to get him to town and the doctor.

She had covered slightly over half the distance to the cabin when a shadow stepped from a tree to her left. A cold fear plummeted from her throat to her chest. She had dropped Nate's .45 when she knelt to examine Matt's wounds.

"That you, Linda?"

The voice rose barely above a whisper, touching her with its familiar drawl as she spun on her toes, ready to flee. The panic that had taken control of her body began to subside. Her heart rate dropped off instantly. With an effort she brought her breathing under control.

"Oh, my God," she croaked. "Is that you, Will?"

"Yeah, it's me," Will continued speaking softly, worried about what threatened from the darkness down the slope.

He had been close enough to see the glow of the campfire when the first shots had sounded. Not knowing what to expect, he had tied his horse to a shrub and continued on foot, cautiously. The second group of shots had sent him running through the darkness, blundering into trees and brush and, once, plunging head over heels into a ravine, until he forced himself to again move with vigilance.

Creeping along when Linda might be dead or dying had been the most difficult thing he had ever done in his life, he thought. Every step brought a new image of her suffering. Every step was a torture, worse than had been each minute of the day as he followed the woman he loved and her captor, not knowing what might be happening at any given moment.

"What's goin' on down there?"

"Nothing," she forced her voice to its normal tone. "Nate Barstow's dead." She hesitated and then plunged on. "I shot him. Matt Bartleman's shot bad. He needs help."

"You killed Nate and shot Matt too?"

Will's shock rang in his voice. He had listened to Stoner's account of the clash with the three rustlers, but his mind refused to accept Linda's part in it. For some reason he couldn't accept the image of her killing someone. It destroyed the picture he carried in his soul.

"No, Nate shot Matt. Matt was trying to help me and, well, he made a mistake and Nate shot him. I shot Nate. I'll explain later. Come on, Matt needs our help."

She took his arm and led him back down the slope. As they walked she briefly related what had happened at the spring, omitting only the details of the attempted rape. She ended with an explanation of what she planned, followed by a request for Will to help her.

Without comment, led by Linda, Will stepped down the slope to make sure Nate was dead, then turned to Matt. Linda was right, he decided as he inspected the wounds with his hands. Matt needed attention right away. He was still losing blood. If they didn't get him warm soon he might go into shock; his body was already shaking.

Will remained silent for a long time, kneeling over the wounded man. A killing rage flared in his chest. One object of his rage was dead, beyond reprisal. The other, the one he considered Mrs. Peters' killer, was wounded and unconscious, possibly dying. He fought a silent battle with nothing to vent his anger on. He started to tell Linda that her mother had died, that Matt had killed her. He started to tell her to leave Matt where he was, to die as a killer should die, alone and untended. But he caught himself. He glanced at the night sky. Heavy clouds were advancing at an alarming rate. They covered the western half of the heavens in empty darkness. The eastern half, though, sparkled like black velvet studded with diamonds.

Slowly his anger dissipated. He couldn't tell Linda about her mother's death, maybe in the morning, but not that night. The girl had suffered too much in the past few hours, more than she had told him, he was certain. As for Matt Bartleman, he shrugged helplessly. If it were up to him he might let Matt die, save the trouble of a trial and a public hanging. But he couldn't tell Linda that without telling her about her mother.

"You go on up to the fire and get things ready," he ordered curtly, hiding his sense of his own impotence. "Make a place for Matt somewhere in the cabin. I'll carry him up the slope."

"You think that's wise?"

"Maybe, maybe not. But there's a storm movin' in. It'll dump rain on us before mornin'. It's best we keep him warm and dry as possible."

Accepting his logic, Linda hurried up the slope. Embers glowed in the ashes of the campfire. She started laying firewood on the embers. Will staggered up with Matt as the embers began to flame.

"Put him there," Linda pointed to a blanket she had spread by the fire. "Then fill the canteens at the spring, please."

As she spoke she emptied what water remained in her and Nate's canteens into the pan she had used to heat water after supper. She set the pan in the edge of the fire to heat and turned to Matt. His face had taken on a grey pallor. His breathing was harsh, ragged, but stronger than it had seemed earlier. Carefully she removed his shirt, unbuckled his belt, and slipped his pants down to expose the jagged groove starting at his hipbone. The bleeding had stopped, so she wrapped him in the blanket and turned away, waiting for the water to heat before she cleaned his wounds.

By the light of the campfire and the flickering rays of a limb she had turned into a torch, she searched the cabin for a dry spot. She chose a place near the front wall, where space existed for the three of them to stretch out under what was left of the roof. Hurriedly she moved the remaining blanket into the area and began building a fire nearby, on the earthen floor. With the fire the three of them could remain warm even if the temperature plummeted during the coming storm.

She was bathing Matt's wounds when Will returned with the canteens.

"There's a pile of rocks and boulders near where Nate's body is," he spoke softly as he watched her work over Matt. "I'm gonna drag him over there and cover him so the coyotes don't get to him. The Bartlemans can send somebody out for the body if they want." When she made no comment he continued, "After I've done that, I'll go get my horse. I've got a blanket behind the saddle. It's gonna cool off a lot when it rains, but with my blanket, the blankets you've got here and the saddle blankets, and that fire in the cabin, we should be plenty warm." He paused before adding, "We'll move Matt when I get back. It ain't gonna rain before that."

At her nod of approval he turned and disappeared into the night. By the time Linda had finished cleaning and bandaging Matt's wounds, Will had returned and tied the horses off in a grassy area near the cabin. Together they moved Matt under the roof and bedded down on each side of him. Between Matt's moaning and the storm that dumped buckets of rain on them before sunrise, they slept fitfully, rising long before first light.

"Could've been worse," Will grumbled good-naturedly as he sat in front of the cabin watching the grey light creep over the land, munching some of the dried beef and biscuits Chew Lin had sent with him. "The wind blew rain all over us, but we could've been cold as well as wet."

"And hungry too," Linda agreed as she handed him a cup of coffee, also compliments of Chew Lin. "How did you find me?" she asked after a few moments of silence.

"Matt was trackin' you. I followed him, although I didn't know who it was. Wasn't hard. He...."

"Why were you following Matt?" Linda interrupted, curious.

Reticent, but realizing he had no right to keep her mother's death from her any longer, Will told her everything.

"Nate Barstow wasn't the killer, not if Mom was killed when you say," Linda fought to control her voice. "When I left the ranch I rode straight to the pass. He waylaid me there."

"I didn't never figure Matt for a coldblooded killer," Will spoke thoughtfully, not looking at Linda.

Without a word Linda rose and walked away from the cabin, her eyes blinded by tears. Sometime later she sat down on a large flat boulder on a promontory overlooking miles of undulating black forests sloping downward in an uneven flow to the golden-brown desert far beyond. Overhead no cloud marred the clean blue dome or impeded the first rays of the sun. Several feet away, on the edge of the boulder top, a lizard appeared and watched her suspiciously, its orange throat pulsating. A wolf spider moved through the leaves nearby. Two crows began quarreling in a tree to her right.

Linda neither saw nor heard the world around her. Slowly the tears dried, to be replaced by a smoldering rage. First Rob. Now her mother. Both killed by the very man who had been shot trying to save her from rape, maybe death. But why had he tried to save her? She asked herself that question over and over. Had he and Nate planned her abduction and her mother's death together, one to carry out the kidnapping, the other the murder? If so, why had Matt challenged Nate the way he had? To save her for himself? To force her to sign over the Rocking H to him?

"It doesn't make a damn bit of difference," she spoke aloud without realizing it. "He'll hang if I have to pull the rope myself."

With her vow echoing in her mind, she trudged heavily back to the cabin. Will had broken camp and was sitting on his heels in front of the cabin, talking to Matt, who lay on a travois Will had made, awake but with his eyes closed. The horses were saddled and packed and grazing on a patch of grass nearby, except for Matt's, which was hitched to the travois.

"Matt says he didn't kill your maw," Will spoke after studying Linda's face for several moments. "He says he was in the rocks above the pass when Barstow took you."

"A lying murderer's alibi," Linda snarled.

"No, I don't reckon," Will insisted. "He told me what happened when Nate ambushed you. He told everything just like you did last night, all the same facts, includin' you droppin' your rifle when you rolled off your horse and scrambled back down the trail. And includin' Nate's warning shot when you was crawlin' over the side of the trail after the rifle."

Linda glared at Will, then at Matt, whose eyes struggled open, then closed before they could focus on hers, as if they were simply too heavy to control. Again Matt's challenge to Nate Barstow echoed in her mind. She replayed as much of the conversation as she could remember. Matt's words, his scorn, Nate's surprise at Matt finding him, his anger at the interference, and now Matt's knowledge of what had happened in the pass--everything suggested that Matt could not have killed her mother.

But he could have returned to the Rocking H from the pass, she told herself. After all, he hadn't reached the cabin much before Will, although admittedly Will had made better time because Matt hadn't tried to hide his tracks like Nate had. Moreover, it would have taken a great deal of luck and excellent timing to reach the ranch and find his victim waiting in the open, and afterwards make the fast, brutal ride to the cabin, a ride that would have left his horse lathered and dead on its legs. She tried to remember what Matt's horse had looked like when Will led it up to the cabin the night before. Her memory suggested that, of the two horses, Matt's had been in better shape.

She shook her head angrily. Matt had killed Rob. Whether or not he had fired the shot that killed her mother, he was implicated. There were only two other people in the valley who would have wanted her mother dead--Matt's brother and father. Whichever one of the three had pulled the trigger had done it because the other two also wanted it done. She glared at Matt. Unconsciously her hand touched the pistol she had confiscated from Nate and carried stuck in the front of her pants. She thought of drawing it and killing the wounded man. She thought of leaving him there by the cabin, to die alone and untended. Finally she turned away disgustedly, realizing that she could not kill a wounded man, especially one who had been instrumental in saving her from a sickening attack, probably eventual death. Muttering furiously under her breath, she mounted and reined her horse into the trail that led away from the cabin, toward the Rocking H.

A few moments later she returned and, without a word, took the reins of Nate's horse from Will, before again urging her mount into the trail. Will followed, leading Matt's horse.

29

Having not only dug up Dodge's corpse but also spent several hours checking on the cattle in some of the side canyons in the area, Stoner and the Rocking H crew rode into the ranch yard an hour or so after dark. Chew Lin had just finished digging Mrs. Peters' grave. Briefly he explained what had happened, including Linda's earlier departure for town, then relinquished shovel and pick so that Dodge's body could also be returned to the earth.

"You go fix something to eat," Stoner ordered the cook as he took the lantern and implements. "We'll dig another grave and then eat before we bury Dodge and Mrs. Peters."

"We goin' after the killer, Jefe?" Sonora asked, taking the pick and beginning to break ground for Dodge's grave.

"First thing in the morning. No sense going tonight. Couldn't see anything anyhow. But in the morning me and Pate'll take out after the bushwhacker," Stoner replied, unable to hide the worry in his voice. "You and Tack're going after Linda. I don't like her riding around alone. I figure she's the next target." After a moment of silence he added, as if trying to convince himself, "I reckon she's staying in town overnight, with friends."

"Yeah, I reckon," Tack agreed as he took the shovel from Stoner's hands. "And you're right as rain about her bein' the next target."

After supper Cactus recited the Lord's Prayer over Dodge's grave. The old outlaw had been buried in the tarpaulin they had rolled his body in to bring it back to the ranch. Mrs. Peters was lying in the house, in a rough coffin made by Cactus. They had decided to delay her burial until Tack and Sonora returned with Linda.

The next morning, as they saddled and packed their saddlebags, Pate broached the subject that had been worrying them all.

"Will should've been back by now."

Nobody responded but they all stopped working for a moment and stared up toward where the shots that killed Mrs. Peters had come from.

When they had mounted, Tack said, "Wish me and Sonora was goin' with you, boss. We want a shot at the killer for what he done to the boss lady. And if he got Will too...."

Stoner and Pate reined away, Stoner with his mind on Linda and the worry that she had not returned from her trip to town.

When they approached the general area from which the shots had come the two riders split up, Stoner angling right, Pate left. There were several places where a rifleman could have set up an ambush. Stoner and Pate planned to circle the whole area, then meet on the far side. They wanted to find all tracks leading in and out of the area. They didn't want to make any mistakes--overlook something, follow the wrong set of prints, or destroy a clue.

Stoner's fear for Linda became sharper and sharper the further he rode. He kept remembering Nate Barstow and his hideout in the clump of pines, even though he'd found no further evidence of the Bar B foreman's presence in the area since their fight. Soon he came across the two sets of tracks leading toward the pass. He dismounted and studied them. One of the horsemen had been following the other. The lead set had been made by Nate Barstow's horse, the same horse he had been riding when he ambushed Linda.   The second set was made by Will's dun.

"If Barstow was the killer and Will was following him," he mused aloud, scratching his horse's neck, "it was long after Linda headed for town."

But the words did little to ease his fear. His examination complete, his gut still cold and empty, unable to rid himself of worry about the direction and timing of the tracks, he mounted and continued circling. Fifteen minutes later he met Pate.

Stoner explained what he had found.

"Fits," Pate doffed his flat-crowned sombrero and, with the sleeve of his shirt, wiped the sweat from his forehead and eyes. He told his story, ending with, "Looks like the first hombre hung out in that clump of pines a lot recently, watchin' the house." Pate shook his head angrily. "The second hombre followed him in yesterday, on foot, tryin' to hide his tracks. He left his horse up there," Pate motioned uphill. "I figure he moved in when the first hombre took off toward the pass. It was the second bastard that shot Mrs. Peters. I found where he took the shots, I figure. And I found this."

He extended his open hand. A knife lay in his palm.

"It's pretty clear who owns the knife." He showed Stoner the engraved side. He stared in the direction of the Bar B, his eyes cold, his lips a rigid line. "I reckon I can follow the bushwhacker back to where he came from though. He's not as good at hidin' his tracks as he thinks he is."

"You don't believe Barstow was the killer?"

"I reckon the first hombre was Barstow if you're right and his horse is the one has the leg that turns in." Pate paused thoughtfully before continuing. "Anyway, his boot prints say he was a big man. The second hombre wasn't so heavy. Couldn't weigh much more'n I do. And I didn't see any sign he'd snuck in there before, though I seen his sign on that knob up there," he pointed his thumb over his shoulder, "like he'd been there before. He...," Pate shrugged. "I reckon he's one of the Bartlemans or somebody they hired. If it was a Bartleman, it was Sam; I'd bet a year's wages against a warm beer. Joe's too old to go sneakin' around bushwhackin' people. Besides, he's too heavy for the tracks. And Matt? I don't figure he'd shoot a woman."

"How long did the killer wait in there?" Stoner gestured toward the stand of trees.

"Hour. More. Less. I don't know," Pate answered thoughtfully, his eyes as bleak as Stoner's.

Stoner told him about the day he had followed Linda through the hills, about Nate Barstow waylaying Linda and about the traces of Barstow in the stand of trees farther along the slope.

"Wish I'd knowed that," Pate growled, making a pass at his forehead with his shirt sleeve. "Barstow wouldn't have been around yesterday."

Stoner accepted the criticism without comment. Pate was right. He should have put an end to Barstow.

"I reckon Will might get first whack now," Stoner stared off toward the pass as he spoke.

"Yeah," Pate agreed dubiously. "I hope so, but Will's no good at trailin'. No patience." He scratched his head before continuing. "Sonora now, he's somethin' else. And Tack ain't no slouch. If Barstow took Linda, they'll find him."

"Can they handle him?"

"Don't know," Pate settled his hat on his bald head. "I don't know how good Barstow really is, just what I've heard. But there's three of them after him, and every one of them'd kill him to save the girl."

Pate continued with a grimace that was meant to be a grin, "Hell, boss, we both know Barstow didn't head for the pass like the devil chasin' a sinner just to kill the girl, if he was after her, which we can't be sure of. If he caught her she's still alive, more'n likely." He paused, searching for words to say what he wanted to say. "Maybe used a little, but none the worse for wear. Tack and Sonora, they'll find her if Will don't. And they'll bring her home."

Or die trying, he wanted to add, but didn't. Stoner's suffering and indecision were plainly written on his face.

"If you need to go after her too, I'll understand. Hell, she was my woman, nothin' could keep me from followin' and killin' the bastard that took her, or findin' out she was safe. Besides, I can track this other murderin' coyote to his lair and make sure he don't kill anyone else. I ain't above playin' the bushwhackin' game with bushwhackers."

Stoner shook off his vacillation with an effort of will.

"You don't figure he's taken her back to the Bar B?"

"Nope. From what you say, I reckon he don't want her dead. Not right away. So he'll take her out of the valley, maybe up in the mountains somewhere away from people. The Bartlemans want her dead. He won't take her to the Bar B." Pate stared at Stoner for a few seconds of silence, letting his words sink in. "The problem is, though, we don't know for sure he took off after Linda. And we don't know if he caught her or not."

"I do," Stoner answered flatly. "Hell, I won't be worth a damn to anyone until I find out what happened to her. Probably not then if...."

"Yeah, I reckon," Pate made another failed attempt at a grin. "Any orders before we separate?"

"We both know where the killer's tracks will lead. Keep watch on the Bartlemans. If they ride out follow them, but leave me some kind of sign near the ranch. I'll meet you at the Bar B tomorrow, before sunset, unless...," he shrugged. "If I'm not there by sunrise the day after tomorrow, head back to the Rockin' H and wait for me. Keep any of the hands there that show up. It's time we stopped the Bartlemans, permanently."

"Okay," impulsively Pate stuck out his hand. The jealousy he had once felt for the Rocking H foreman, over Linda, had lost its sharp, angry ache some time ago. The envy remained, but all other feelings had given way to respect and admiration. "I'll camp in the hills south of the Bar B ranch house."

Stoner took the proffered hand, gripped it for a second as he met Pate's eyes with a promise to see him soon, and then reined his dusty black away.

He felt a twinge of guilt at abandoning the hunt for Mrs. Peters' killer. After Linda, he promised the interior ghost of the older woman, after she's safe, I'll hunt the coward who shot you. But you know how much I love your daughter. And she might be alive.

His mind shifted gears. He began to blame himself for Mrs. Peters' death and for anything that might have happened to Linda. He had always been a man who believed the best defense consisted of a good offense. Yet he had waited, biding his time because Mrs. Peters wanted it that way, gaining a false sense of security from his early successes and from the love and trust of the Peters women.

With an effort he forced his mind away from his morbid thoughts, still fighting the painful lump in his throat caused by memory of Mrs. Peters and his worry about Linda.

While Cactus watched Stoner and Pate ride away he unconsciously flexed his right shoulder, moving his arm in a circle. It was still plenty stiff and sore, and it wouldn't take much to start the bleeding again, but most of the pain was below the shoulder; it hindered his use of the arm but didn't restrict it. When the two riders disappeared into the rolling hillside, he turned and walked purposefully toward the bunkhouse. Fifteen minutes later, armed and supplied with a day's rations and water, he kneed his horse into the trail toward Chasco.

Linda would probably have returned from town the previous day unless something had happened to her. The thought of her in danger or lying dead somewhere had eaten at his gut the entire night. He would have ridden out with Tack and Sonora if Stoner hadn't ordered him to stay put.

But now, he told himself as he rode anxiously toward town, with Stoner gone, there was no one to keep him at the ranch. If Stoner fired him later for disobeying orders...well, it wouldn't make any difference if Linda was dead. He wouldn't want to stay on without her or Mrs. Peters around anyway.

30

Joe and Sam were sitting on the rickety porch of the Bar B drinking rotgut whiskey and talking when the rider appeared.

"You say the old lady's dead?" Joe asked again. "And Barstow took off after the girl?"

"Yeah," Sam chuckled. "To both questions. Again. Jesus, how many times you gonna ask?"

Joe ignored him. "And Barstow ain't returned, so I reckon he caught the girl."

Sam shrugged, taking a long pull at his beer, "I reckon. But, hell, you know Nate. He could be in town, drunk and raisin' Billy-be-damned because he didn't catch her."

"We'll know soon enough," frowning, his lips forming a thin, cruel line, Joe pointed toward the approaching rider.

The two men remained silent until the squat, swarthy rider pulled up near them.

"Find him?" Sam asked, irritated when the rider, without saying a word, cocked one leg over the saddlehorn and began rolling a cigarette.

Little Oak, the swarthy rider, half Cheyenne, half French, was the best tracker on the Bar B crew. A few hours after Sam's return from the Rocking H the previous day, when Nate hadn't returned, Joe sent him out to find the Bar B foreman.

"Sam saw him ridin' away from the Rockin' H this morning, headin' toward the pass that leads to Chasco," Joe had explained. "I want to know where he is, but I don't want him to know anyone's spyin' on him."

"Did you find him?" Sam repeated sharply as Little Oak silently stuck his cigarette in his mouth and lit it.

"Nope," Little Oak spoke flatly, slowly, between puffs, smoke dribbling from mouth and nose. "I made a mistake. From what Joe said, I figured he was headin' for Chasco. I rode there first and had to backtrack. By the time I got to the pass it was too dark to do any trackin', so I bedded down there. This mornin' I found tracks that said Nate waylaid a woman and rode off with her. The Peters girl, I figured. Hell, Nate's been slobberin' around after her for years." Little Oak leered. "I followed Nate and the woman, and two other riders trackin' them. Two riders separate. One of them riders was Matt. I know that horse of his."

Little Oak paused to take the last drag from his cigarette before flipping it into the dirt.

"Goddamn it, Oak," Sam growled. "Finish the story."

Enjoying Sam's impatience, Little Oak spit into the dirt, wiped his mouth with his sleeve, grinned briefly, and continued, "I come across them over the other side of Black Rocks, followin' the trail south of here that runs into the main trail we take to Chasco." He paused and shrugged. "I figure they're headed for town. There's three of them--the Peters girl, that Rockin' H puncher they call Tall Will, and Matt. They're pullin' Matt on a travois. Reckon he's wounded or sick or somethin'."

"What about Nate?" Sam asked belligerently. "You were sent to find Nate."

Little Oak stared at his horse's ears. He suppressed the grin before it reached his eyes and mouth, realizing it wouldn't do to gall Sam too much. The man was dangerous and unpredictable.

"They was leadin' Nate's horse," he looked at Joe as he spoke. "They ain't no mistakin' that big plow horse he rides."

"I'll be damned," Sam exploded. "You sure it was Nate's horse you saw?"

Joe interrupted, "You say there was just the two of them and they was leadin' Nate's horse?"

"Yep."

"And Matt on a travois? How did he look?"

Little Oak shrugged, "Couldn't tell much. I hid in the Rocks till they rode out of sight, then I hightailed it back here. But Matt never moved that I could see."

"They wouldn't have Nate's horse if he was still alive," Sam put in.

"Or bad wounded," Little Oak corrected him slyly.

"Go take care of your horse," Joe ordered Little Oak, wanting to be alone with Sam so they could decide what to do.

"If he was wounded they'd have him on a travois, like Matt," Joe mused as if to himself. "No, Nate's dead. That tall puncher must've killed him and wounded Matt, saved the girl."

"Or Matt and the puncher tackled Nate together," Sam cursed. "I wouldn't put it past Matt to help save the Peters girl. He thinks he's a goddamn knight in shining armor. He...."

"It don't make no difference now," Joe interrupted, his disappointment in Matt clear in his voice and expression. "But this could be the chance we been waitin' for." When Sam suddenly grinned as if sensing the direction of his thoughts, he continued, "I was hoping Nate had done away with the girl, one way or the other. If he hadn't, I was plannin' on waitin' until things died down before we went after her." He chuckled at the macabre humor of his words before adding, "A period of mourning, you could call it. But now maybe we got the best chance we'll ever have, with the girl out there and nobody to protect her but that tall bastard I been meanin' to kill for a long time now anyhow. We kill her and that tall puncher. Hide their bodies and spread the rumor Nate killed the cowhand and made off with her." His lips split in a feral jeer. "If we get caught, hell, we say we figured the two of them killed Nate and was plannin' on killin' Matt. We was just tryin' to save Matt and the girl got caught in the crossfire. We can't lose."

"What about the men we take with us?"

"They'll be in on the killin'. They say anything, they'll put a noose around their own necks."

"What about Matt?"

"He's a Bartleman. He might not have the guts to kill a woman but he'll keep his mouth shut if I tell him to."

"What about the sheriff and that citizen's committee that visited us?" Sam asked, already having gladly accepted Joe's decision, but wanting the problems out in the open.

"Won't be nothin' they can prove," Joe mused thoughtfully, not liking the idea of antagonizing some of the most powerful and influential people of the area, but determined to take advantage of the luck that had come his way. With the girl dead, he figured, he could take over the Rocking H. No one would stand in his way. "It'll be over quick. Some'll be suspicious as all hell, but in a few years they'll forgive and forget, treat us like nothin' happened, especially since we'll be the biggest ranchers in the valley."

"What about Stoner?"

"Like I said before, ain't much he can do if the owners of the Rockin' H are all dead. If he hangs around we can hunt him down and kill him easy enough. Won't nobody brace us for killin' a gunfighter."

Sam agreed, only too happy to swing into action which promised violence.

He headed for the bunkhouse and corrals to round up what men were available. Within minutes a cavalcade of horsemen left the Bar B, headed by Joe and Sam.

From a hill behind the ranch house Pate watched them ride out before he hurried back to his horse and angled through the pines to their trail. He left his neckerchief tied on a shrub near the point where he joined the trail.

31

Hampered by the travois, Linda and Will made poor time. Matt never complained although they could tell he suffered. He had developed a fever in the night. The fever seemed to ease somewhat as the morning progressed, in spite of the burning sun and the jolting motion of the travois. However it never quite dissipated completely, leaving Matt weak but conscious of the continuous jolting pain of motion.

They met Tack and Sonora around mid-morning.

"You two look comfortable," Will greeted them as he and Linda topped a rise and saw the two punchers sitting their horses at the side of the trail. "All you need's some shade and a rocking chair."

Happy grins splitting the stubble of their cheeks, the two riders answered Will's greeting with jibes of their own. Quickly Will told them his and Linda's story.

"So we're taking Matt to Chasco," he ended.

"After that we swing by the Rockin' H to pick up Stoner and Pate," Linda interrupted tersely, making up her mind about the problem that had been plaguing her since she learned of her mother's death: What to do about her killer, or killers? "Then we head for the Bar B. It's time the Bartlemans pay for what they've done."

Will started to argue but one look at Linda's face stopped him short. Her eyes were cold and unbending, her mouth a thin line of steel. With a startled glance at each other, Tack and Sonora turned to the task of getting the procession into motion again. Soon they were riding, with Linda leading, Tack following with the travois, Sonora next with the dead man's horse, and Will bringing up the rear. They were traversing rolling grassland dotted with clumps of sage, boulders, isolated junipers, and an occasional knoll like the one Tack and Sonora had awaited the others on. Above them the sky remained a sheet of blue flame, fed by the sole object in the void, the blazing sun.

They had been riding for a quarter of an hour when Sonora grunted sharply and pulled his horse to a halt.

"What the hell, Sonora, you...," Will started to comment as he pulled in his mount to keep it off the heels of the led horse, biting the words off short as Sonora dropped from the saddle and bounded off into the desert, soon disappearing in the brush.

"I reckon he's heard somethin'," Tack stated in a low voice. "Gone off away from our noise to listen better."

"Or seen somethin'," Will added, studying their surroundings suspiciously. "We couldn't be more'n a mile or two from Bar B headquarters. He could've spotted one of their riders."

"Could be," Tack answered softly, his head cocked to listen.

Minutes passed. Their horses became restless. Matt groaned, having fallen into a fitful sleep as soon as the horses stopped moving. Linda had just decided to start the group riding again when she spotted Sonora trotting toward them from near the top of a ridge almost a hundred yards to the front, weaving through the sage and other brush, disappearing for long moments, then reappearing briefly before disappearing again. He soon joined them.

"Bar B riders on the other side of the ridge, headin' this way," he explained quickly as he mounted. "Twelve. They're coming fast so I didn't take time to make sure, pero...I think I saw Sam and Joe a la cabeza."

"How much time do we have?" Linda asked, struggling to keep her voice from breaking with the fear pounding in her chest.

"Dos, tres minutos, maybe a little more."

"About enough time to reach those boulders," Will pointed to their left as he spoke, to where a few boulders lay clustered at the foot of a cliff. "They catch us out in the open we ain't got a chance. We reach those rocks, we can maybe hold them off. For a while anyway."

"What about Matt?" Tack asked.

"We can take him with us," Will spoke uncertainly. "Try to make a trade, his life for ours."

"You wouldn't do that, and Sam and Joe wouldn't trade anyway," Linda answered, once again in control of herself. "But they'll see that he gets to the doctor if we leave him here. That'll get rid of one man, maybe two. Improve the odds some. Give us a better chance of surviving until Stoner and Pate find us, if they do."

"Here they come," Sonora warned in a low voice, pointing.

Two riders appeared on the crest of the ridge. One of them turned and shouted, then both charged down the slope. An instant later a compact group of horsemen boiled over the hill after the two scouts. Out of time, out of options, Linda and the Rocking H punchers spurred their horses toward the boulders Will had pointed out. Seconds later, bullets buzzing the air like angry yellow jackets, thudding into the ground, ricocheting from rocks, they dropped off their racing mounts and dragged the frightened animals into cover.

There were fewer boulders than Will and Linda had thought, but they were strategically placed. The cluster they formed had not resulted from a slide, as seemed evident from a distance, but had rather resulted from the cliff face splitting at ground level. A chunk the size of a large cabin had fallen outward. Over time it had become part of the ground itself, creating a mound several feet higher than the surrounding area, except at the base of the cliff, where a small bowl, almost a cave, had been formed, a depression deep enough for a man to stand in without being able to see over the floor of the mound itself. The rocks and boulders strewn around the mound ranged from pebble size to the size of a large black bear curled up for hibernation.

While the others began returning the fire of their pursuers, Sonora hastily gathered the reins of their horses and dragged the frightened animals into the depression, where he hitched them to a scrub juniper before taking up his position at the perimeter of the mound.

The firing had stopped. The Bar B riders had retreated out of rifle range, except for two. Those two were leading Matt's horse and travois and Nate's horse toward the huddle of their fellow riders, casting nervous glances behind them.

"I could pull the picket pin on both those sidewinders before they get out of range," Tack grunted as he plopped down to the left of Linda.

"Let them go. They're trying to help Matt."

"Yeah," Tack growled in return, "help him to safety so he won't get hurt when they come after us. There'd be two less to deal with later if I took them out now."

"No," Linda insisted.

"Think they'd let me live if I rode out there with a white flag?"

Linda didn't answer. Tack was right, she knew. The Bartlemans wouldn't honor a truce of any kind. Nor would they give any quarter in the battle that had already started.

But she couldn't bring herself to kill men who weren't shooting at her. Nor could Tack. Otherwise he would have shot the two riders without a comment.

"Anybody hurt?" she asked.

"No" came two grunts.

"But one of them was," Sonora spoke softly from beyond Tack. "Tack dropped him before he got out of range. I seen him fall as I was comin' back from tyin' off the caballos. He's layin' out there a hundred yards or so, straight between us and where we left Matt. Muerto, I bet. That's his caballo headin' for home," Sonora pointed to a bay trotting toward the ridge over which the Bar B riders had just come.

"There's another one gonna be a mite sickly for a few days," Will spoke up from several yards to the right of Linda. "That must be him they're sendin' off with Matt." They all watched as one of the riders led the horse and travois in the direction of Chasco. "From the looks of him settin' that saddle, they maybe should send someone else to take care of him."

No one spoke for several minutes as they watched the lone rider and two horses. The travois showed only occasionally through the sage and cactus.

"What'll they do now?" Linda asked, already knowing the answer but feeling the need to talk. For the first time since they had turned to race toward the boulders she felt herself begin to shake. An icy fear had begun to spread in her chest.

"Don't know," Will spoke for all of them. "We got a good position here. We're back in under the cliff face so it won't do them no good to work their way up to the top. They can't see us from up there."

"I bet they'll work their way in close, try to pick us off," Sonora added softly.

"Won't do them much good if we don't get careless. Unless they get lucky. We got good cover and we can see down through the brush for a good ways."

"Menos along the foot of the cliff."

Will and Linda studied the terrain on both sides of their shelter. Sonora was right. The winding cliff face itself, uneven ground caused by water runoff, boulders that had broken free and rolled only a few inches or a few feet before coming to rest, as well as shrubs and stunted trees, gave sufficient cover for their attackers to creep to within yards of them.

"Not much room for more than a couple men on each side, though," Will commented.

"Si," Sonora agreed. "But I bet they can put three or four riflemen a lo largo de la escarpa and keep us pinned down while the rest try to move in."

"I guess we ain't in as good a position as I thought," Will added worriedly, "Ridin' in, I saw a couple of washes plenty deep enough for good cover. And not more'n a hundred yards from us, at the nearest." He pointed to two lines of brush heavier and greener than the rest. "They keep us pinned down from those gullies and get riflemen close in on the sides, some of us maybe ain't gonna make it."

His comment brought silence for a long time; each person studying the surrounding terrain, trying to come up with an escape route but failing. They were surrounded and outnumbered. Any attempt to escape would put them at the mercy of their attackers.

"If we can hold out till dark...," Linda broke the silence, her words trailing off as her eyes found the sun overhead. Darkness was a long, long way off.

Suddenly, from their left, near the cliff, came a crashing of brush and shouts. In the distance the Bar B horses started milling, their riders shouting and pointing. Three of the riders dropped from their mounts and began firing in the direction of the noise.

"Don't shoot," Linda shouted as Will raised his rifle. "It must be a friend."

She pointed at the Bar B riders.

"I wasn't plannin' on shootin'," Will growled. "Just getting' ready in case."

Seconds later Cactus burst out of the brush twenty yards from their sanctuary. Hobbling, favoring his right side, bent over at the waist as if to duck under the hail of bullets, he propelled himself through the intervening undergrowth and into their midst, losing his balance at the last minute to dive head first into a pile of sagebrush.

"Jesus, you old bastard," Will shouted as he roughly dragged Cactus to the cover of a boulder. "I never figured I'd be happy to see your grizzled mug. What the hell you doin' here anyway. You're supposed to...."

Will suddenly stopped talking. Cactus' face was deathly white. His teeth were gritted with pain, his eyes glazed.

"Aw, Cactus, I'm sorry," Will dropped to his knees beside the old-timer. "I forgot you was wounded."

Quickly he inspected the old man's shoulder. The bandage held. The wound was not bleeding. As he sat back in relief, though, he noticed that the front of Cactus' shirt and Levi's was soaked with blood. Apprehensively, tenderly, he unbuttoned the shirt. A bullet had entered from the side, below the ribs, and had torn its way out the other side.

"Christ," Will groaned, the words ripped from his depths as he stared helplessly at the dying man.

"Let me see what I can do," Linda spoke from Will's shoulder. "You go back and help keep watch. Send Sonora to help."

"He must've been wounded back a ways," Will spoke without moving. "He's lost a lot of blood. It's in his boots and his pants're soaked and his shirt...."

"Go keep watch," Linda gave him a gentle push. "I'll take care of Cactus."

As Will crawled back to his position on the line, Linda explored Cactus' wound with her fingers. The bullet had left little more than a pucker where it had entered, a fist-sized hole where it exited between two ribs. Linda hurried to the horses. Hastily searching the saddlebags, she found several shirts and clean socks. Scurrying back, she found Sonora bent over the wounded man. They used the shirts and socks as compresses to stop the flow of blood but only succeeded in slowing it. Finally Sonora caught her eyes, shook his head sadly, shrugged, and crawled back to his position next to Tack.

"Ain't no use in that," Cactus spoke so softly she almost missed what he was saying. "Sonora knows. I'm on my way to another life."

She took his hand, "Oh, Cactus...." She stopped, unable to continue because of the sobs rising uncontrollably in her chest.

As she knelt beside him, watching his struggle with the pain, watching him fight for air and fade before her eyes, a fierce hatred swelled in her chest. She cursed herself for not having turned Stoner loose on the Bartlemans, before Rob's death, before her mother's death, before.... Somehow, she promised herself, she and the others would get free of the trap they were in. After that, she would declare open season on the Bartelmans. She would see them dead, no matter what the cost.

Cactus drew a ragged breath and let it out slowly. His body relaxed. His legs twitched several times. His kidneys and bowels voided the detritus of his mortal life. His eyes focused on eternity.

"Oh, Cactus," Linda repeated, as if somehow the words might bring him back or, at the very least, help ease his journey into the beyond. For a while she continued holding his hand, recalling pleasant times during her childhood, times when Cactus had taken her riding or brought her a present from town.

"I'll take him now, Linda."

She looked up to find Will kneeling beside her.

"There's a little ledge back there that forms a kind of cave, near where the horses are. I can put him in there and cover the opening with rocks. We can come back after him later, like we did Dodge."

She pulled back and watched as Will half carried, half dragged Cactus toward the rear of their temporary shelter. After Will disappeared she continued kneeling for some time, motionless, her mind a blank. Then, with an effort, she rose to a crouch and again took a position on the line. When she scooted into the opening between the two boulders where she had left her rifle, she scanned the area before her. The only sign of life was a hawk floating the thermals high and to her right. Carefully she studied the area where the Bar B riders had been grouped, then the expanse of terrain to the right and left. Nothing.

"What's going on? Have they left?"

"Naw," Sonora answered. "Two of them rode off to the left. Dos más a la derecha--two more to the right. I figure they'll come in along the cliff wall. The others? Pues, mira esos arbolitos, those little trees, on the other side of the trail. Just past where we was settin' our horses when the Bar B riders reached the ridge. They took their caballos in there. One of those two main washes runs through those trees."

"They ain't there now though," Tack broke in, his voice low. "Four of them are in the washes all right, but a lot closer. The others? They could be anywhere. In the washes with the others. Takin' care of the horses. Holed up in some spot we ain't seen yet."

Linda noticed weakness in his voice. "Are you hurt, Tack?" she asked, her concern causing her voice to rise shrilly.

"Nothin' to worry about. They got me in the leg when we was ridin' in. I lost some blood but Sonora bandaged me up. I'll be okay long as I don't have to walk much." He hesitated, then forced a chuckle. "So if you're plannin' on makin' a break on foot you'll have to do it without me."

Linda considered his words, but quickly rejected them. Trying to break out of the trap on foot would be a major mistake, she decided. They couldn't do it without being spotted, just as Cactus had been spotted and killed. They would be caught in the open, on foot, outnumbered, trying to protect a wounded man. Their best bet, she decided, was to wait until dark and ride out. Some of them might escape in the confusion. If they could hold out until dark.

32

From almost a half mile away, sitting their horses in the shade of a Ponderosa pine high up on the slopes of Barrel Peak, Stoner and Pate had watched as the Bar B riders spurred their mounts over the ridge, glancing worriedly at each other as the firing commenced.

At the pass Stoner had picked up the trail made by Linda and Nate Barstow. He had followed their hoof prints at a rapid clip, trying to work out the identity of the riders who had made the other tracks as he rode. He was fairly certain of Will, and of Tack and Sonora. But the other tracks puzzled him. Eventually he gave up trying to figure out who had made them, satisfied with the knowledge that one set was following Linda and her captor and being followed by Will, while the other two sets were fresher, one very recent.

He had spotted the Bar B riders long before they entered the trail. Recognizing Joe and Sam Bartleman in the lead and figuring his life wouldn't be worth the price of a cowhide if they caught him in the open, he reined his horse into the shadow of the Ponderosa pine. He was still sitting his horse silently, watching the riders disappear around a sloping bend in the trail, when Pate rode warily out of an arroyo and into the trail less than three horse lengths away.

"Getting a mite careless, Pate," he spoke softly, chuckling as Pate whirled in the saddle, his pistol half clear of the holster.

"Yeah, I reckon," Pate grinned his relief. "Trailin' a killer makes a man blind to other things. And nervous. You might be a little more careful about how you speak to a fellow."

"Find out anything?" Stoner changed the subject.

"Yeah, Sam Bartleman's ridin' the killer's horse."

Neither man spoke for a while after Pate's words. A fiery blast of anger shook Stoner, then turned to ice in his gut. He stared in the direction the riders had taken, an unspoken promise of vengeance stirring in the darkest caves of his soul.

Quickly, to occupy his mind and break free of the anger holding him in its spell, he told Pate what he had found in the pass and since, on the trail.

"So," he completed his information, "Will, Tack and Sonora are out there somewhere. Maybe Linda. And the Bar B's between us and them."

At that moment the Bar B riders broke into the open a half mile away. A few seconds later the two advance riders spurred over the ridge in front of them, followed by the main body of riders. Soon after they all disappeared the shooting began. Certain that the target of the chase was the Rocking H, possibly Tack and Sonora, Stoner sat the saddle helplessly, listening. Concentrating with all his effort on the sound of firing, he followed the brief attack and flight toward the cliff face. He fought the urge to gallop blindly to join the battle. His gut turned cold when the firing ceased. He had counted four or five rifles answering the fire of the Bar B, the thought.

"We better get a move on or the war'll be over before we get there," Pate's words cracked in the silence. His eyes glittered with suppressed violence. His mouth twisted in a snarl of rage.

"What's that?" Stoner pointed to the right of where the Bar B gunhands had disappeared.

A horse and rider walked into view, seeming to appear from a fissure in the bottom of the ridge.

"Hell," Pate spoke in a hoarse whisper. "That's Cactus. I'd know that spotted grey of his anywhere."

As they watched, Cactus spurred his horse up the ridge, angling toward where it met the cliff. He soon disappeared over the top. Less than a minute later the firing started again. When it stopped Stoner and Pate looked at each other without a word. Neither wanted to say out loud why he thought the firing had ceased.

As one, both men reined toward the spot where Cactus had disappeared. Sporadic firing from beyond the ridge gave them hope.

Near the top of the ridge they dismounted, tied their horses in a stand of aspens, and ghosted upward until they could see the entire battlefield without being seen from below.

They watched silently. They couldn't determine who remained alive among the besieged, but they counted four rifles answering Bar B fire. Stoner prayed that Linda was among those alive.

"Looks like they're gonna attack from both sides and the front," Pate broke into Stoner's thoughts.

"Yeah," Stoner agreed, forcing his mind to the battle at hand. "The riflemen out front will keep the defenders pinned down while those attacking from the sides close in to within twenty or thirty yards. Once they do it's goodnight, Molly. Whoever's in those rocks won't be able to do anything but keep their heads down and pray the bullets don't find them. That'll be when the fight shifts focus. Those coming in from the sides will keep the defenders pinned down while the ones out front close in."

After a few moments of silence he continued, "Think you can take care of the two headed this way, then make your way in, if I can keep those men out front busy?"

"Yep," Pate replied tersely.

"Don't take any chances. Make sure you get both of them."

"You got it, boss," Pate spoke with a deadly grimace on his lips.

Stoner offered his hand. Pate returned his grip.

"Bring them out if you can," Stoner spoke, his eyes probing Pate's.

"If I can," Pate answered, a deadly gleam in his eyes. "If I can't," he shrugged, "one more rifle'll help. The Bartlemans won't take us cheap."

"I'll do what I can from behind them," Stoner promised.

With a final "good luck" he made his way back to the horses, mounted the black and, kneeing the animal down to the foot of the ridge, made his way to a point beyond the trail where he could easily scale the slope. He prayed that the far side was as simple to descend. When he reached the top of the ridge he spotted a wash below him. It appeared to intersect the trail and continue on toward the cliff face. He studied the open area in front of the defenders, until he spotted the two groups of attackers, one in the wash that began below him, he figured, the other in another wash further on. Beyond the attackers, for a few moments, he caught a glimpse of two Bar B killers moving along the cliff face. Fear for the defenders turned his blood cold. He forced himself to ignore them and turned back to the two gullies.

"Good cover for bushwhackers," he muttered, "and for bushwhackers of bushwhackers."

Seconds later he had hitched the black to a scrub oak at the foot of the ridge, in the wash, and was moving rapidly, silently toward the intermittent sound of battle. His mind on the battle, trying to pinpoint the exact positions of the besiegers, he didn't hear the Bar B horses. They were picketed in a wide bend of the wash, near the outside corner, where a small pool of water had turned the surrounding area green. Stoner passed through a line of saplings and into their midst before he realized they were there.

After Stoner left, Pate eased along the ridge toward the cliff until he came to a place where a slide had left a shallow fissure, the rim and bottom covered with sagebrush. Lying on his stomach, he wormed his way into the crack, facing the way he had come. From his position he had a commanding view of the entire slope of the ridge for fifty yards. The two Bar B bushwhackers, he figured, would approach along this side of the ridge, under the rim, so as not to be seen by the defenders in the rocks on the other side. He settled in.

He didn't have long to wait. Within minutes he heard the crunch of approaching steps.

"They're about as cautious as a bull in heat," he grunted softly in satisfaction, "but I don't reckon they're expectin' any trouble. They figure they got this whole section of the territory to theirselves."

Soon a shapeless sombrero grey with dirt and age appeared bobbing toward him, then another of similar vintage. The two men approached in single file. A tall, thin gunman wearing soiled Levi's and a flannel shirt of indeterminate color strode in the lead, his sixgun tied low on his right hip, a rifle swinging from his left hand. A shorter, heavier man skulked in his wake, armed only with a rifle which he carried in the crook of his arm.

"You don't have to like it," the tall man was saying. "Orders is orders. No prisoners. If you don't have the stomach for killin' you shouldn't oughta hired on for gunfighter's wages."

"Hell, I don't mind the killin', Slim," the shorter man grumbled. "You oughta know that. What pisses me off is killin' the girl right off. What a waste. Like I told Sam, I'd take her off in the mountains somewhere and enjoy myself for a few months. Then get rid of her. Wouldn't nobody know...."

Pate's first bullet slammed into the shorter man's belly like a sledgehammer, coming to rest against his spine. Frantically gasping for air that he couldn't get, he took two awkward steps to the side, then slowly toppled onto his face. Two hours later, in a pain-racked delirium, his body shut down forever.

The taller man was fast. But not fast enough. His first shot nipped the outside of Pate's left thigh. He was diving sideways, desperately levering another bullet into the firing chamber, when Pate's second bullet smashed into his chest and exploded his heart, killing him instantly. He landed on his side, his dying reflexes triggering a bullet into the distance as he collided with the earth, slid onto his face, kicked as if trying to turn over, and lay still.

Rifle at the ready, Pate approached the two gunmen. Once he was certain they were no longer a threat, ignoring the shorter gunman's pleading eyes and frightened, breathless grunts, he glanced in the direction Stoner had taken. The major problem, as he saw it, was out front, in the men Stoner had gone after. For a second he thought of following Stoner, to help him, then shook his head to clear his thoughts and headed along the cliff face. His job was to help his friends defend the rocks against the immediate danger, the two gunmen approaching from their right.

When Stoner burst unexpectedly through the first line of saplings and found himself among the picketed horses, the Bar B guard was standing on a ledge, in the shade of a scrub oak, staring toward the position of the Rocking H punchers. He was a slovenly man, big, in his early thirties, going to fat around the middle. Dust lay thick on his unkempt beard and hair, hiding the grease underneath. His rifle lay near him, propped against the side of the wash. He whirled as one of the horses snorted at Stoner's sudden appearance, almost tripping over his own feet. Fear froze him in place for a split second when he spotted Stoner. His eyes flickered toward his rifle, beyond his reach. His shoulders slumped as if he were going to give up without a fight. Then his hand streaked for the .44 strapped on his thigh.

Stoner had been holding his Winchester at hip level as he cat-footed through the wash, the barrel pointed forward, his left hand holding the rifle steady, his right hand at the trigger guard. He spotted the sentry and whirled toward him, firing from the hip as his body squared up to the target, levering another shell into the firing chamber almost before the first had exited the barrel. Once, twice--both shots ripping through the Bar B gunhand's shirt, killing him instantly.

His senses on a hair trigger, while his victim was still falling, Stoner slid behind the milling horses, his eyes scanning the area for another man, another weapon. Neither seeing nor hearing anything that might constitute a threat, he slipped through the rest of the trees and trotted along the wash, keeping low, trying to estimate the distance to the Bar B gunmen ahead. Slowly the gully deepened until the sides stood a foot or two higher than his head. When he figured he was no more than forty or so yards from the gun shots before him he slowed to a walk. Soon he came to another bend. As he started to step into the curve he spotted a rifleman ahead, lying on a slope near the lip of the ravine. He froze, and slowly withdrew until he could study the area before him without being seen. The gunman he had seen kept up a slow, steady fire.

"Helping keep the Rocking H pinned down while his friends sneak in along the cliff face," Stoner growled to himself.

Carefully he studied the area before him. He could see only the one rifleman, but from somewhere to the left of the Bar B gunman sounded the sporadic fire of another weapon, a Spencer rim fire, he thought, but he couldn't be sure.

"Damn," he swore softly. "Where the hell is that other bushwhacker?"

He wanted both men dead, quietly, without advertising his presence. There had been ten horses in the wash. He didn't know if all of the Bar B horses had been stashed there. He didn't know if some of the gunmen had been killed in the clash with the Rocking H riders. So he had to figure on ten men, at least. Four were attacking along the cliff face. He had killed one. There were the two in front of him. That left three more unaccounted for.

Another image gnawed at his vitals as he studied the gully before him, sometimes in the form of fear, sometimes as hope, always driving him forward: Linda alive, trapped in the boulders.

He cat-footed into the bend, wanting to reach a point from which he could get a shot at both bushwhackers. The man on the ledge continued his sporadic firing, his back to Stoner, unaware of death approaching. Stoner continued creeping forward, to within forty, thirty, twenty yards of the rifleman. Still he couldn't see the other man.

He took another step. At that moment the rifleman on the ledge turned his head toward his unseen companion. He started to speak, spotted Stoner from the corner of his eye, let out a yelp, and tried to roll onto his feet while frantically swinging his rifle in Stoner's direction. Stoner fired, and fired again. His first shot chipped a rib, ricocheting into the soft dirt beyond. His second bullet tore through the man's throat, tearing through the neck vertebrae, sending a spray of blood shimmering into the sunlight as the gunman dropped from the ledge, dead before his body hit the ground.

As he fired the second time, not waiting to see the result, Stoner bounded forward. In two leaps he came face to face with the second bushwhacker, rushing headlong in his direction. Not ten feet separated them when, almost simultaneously, each man caught sight of the other. Both rifle barrels flashed upward, spouting flame in a desperate bid to beat its assailant.

Stoner felt a sickening blow above his right ear. He felt himself walking backward, toppling. Then, vaguely, somewhere in the recesses of his subconscious self, he felt the earth smash him from shoulder to thigh.

After that, nothing.

33

Pate made his way along the foot of the cliff, walking, trotting when the brush and rocks grew high enough to hide him from the Bar B riflemen and the earth extended itself level enough. Most of the time he crawled or snaked through low brush, over rocky, broken ground. He passed Cactus' dead grey. Eventually he came to the open section where, unknown to him, Cactus had met the bullet that killed him. He stopped to study the desolate stretch before him. As he considered it and the riflemen who had already spotted him moving toward the besieged Rocking H hands and had begun firing at him when he showed himself, an involuntary shiver convulsed in his gut. There was little chance he could cross those barren thirty yards unscathed.

The memory of Cactus' dash over the ridge toward the cliff flashed through his mind and another cold shiver touched his spine. He remembered the firing after Cactus passed from his sight. And he had just seen Cactus' dead horse. With little more than a cursory glance, he had counted seven bullets in the animal.

Again he studied the terrain between him and the Bar B riflemen. The two in the far wash didn't have an unobstructed firing angle. The uneven ground and several scrubby trees between their position and the ground he had to cross were in his favor. But the two in the near wash had a straight, clear shot, a shot of not more than a hundred yards. He again turned his eyes to the terrain in front of him. Running boldly across that stretch, he would be like a turkey in a turkey shoot. Carefully, foot by foot, he studied the open ground. There seemed to be a slight depression at the very foot of the cliff, probably caused by water runoff.

He considered staying where he was. He had a good defensive position in a depression. He had a commanding view of the valley far beyond the riflemen in the washes. He could easily hold off a half dozen men approaching from the direction he himself had.

He discarded the thought almost as soon as it entered his mind. His comrades needed help. Four of them were still firing. He could make that out easily enough. But he didn't know if any were wounded, or how badly, or if they knew about the two Bar B gunmen sneaking up on them from the right.

With a decisive grunt, he crawled from his depression toward the foot of the cliff. He had covered no more than four or five yards when he heard two quick shots from the near wash, a pause, then two more shots that almost sounded like one. He stopped, puzzled. The two riflemen had been firing alternately, slowly and inconsistently. The first two shots he had just heard, he felt, had come from one rifle and not one of those he had been listening to since he started making his way along the foot of the cliff. The second set of shots had come from two different weapons, one the same one that had fired the first two shots.

Stoner, he thought.

Instinctively he scrambled to his feet and dashed for the cover of brush, rocks and broken ground thirty feet before him. Bullets began splatting around him. Seconds later he dropped safely behind a mound of broken rock and earth.

After he had caught his breath, he continued toward his destination, no longer worried about the Bar B sharpshooters in the nearest wash. The firing had stopped from that direction. But he continued moving cautiously, keeping some kind of cover in front of him. He didn't want to be shot by his friends in the rocks ahead.

"There ain't no more firing from that wash to the left," Will spoke in a whisper.

"What happened, do you think?" Linda asked, her voice barely audible.

The two had moved to the left perimeter of the boulders, Linda near the foot of the cliff, Will near the front, from where he could watch the wash as well as the approach along the cliff. Sonora and Tack had taken up positions along the right perimeter. They were already returning the fire of the two Bar B men who had attacked from that direction.

All four hunkered low, dreading the ricocheting bullets and the shreds of splintered rock the bullets splattered in their path. Will already had a deep scratch on his left cheek, from his ear to the side of his chin. The back of his shirt was ripped across the shoulders blades. Blood seeped through the rip, staining his shirt in a widening circle. Linda had dug an inch-long sliver of rock from her bicep. The bleeding had stopped.

"I don't know," Will shrugged. "They could've pulled back, I reckon. But I doubt it. The Bartlemans ain't about to give up now they got our tail caught under a rock." He paused. "I don't figure they run out of ammunition either. It's strange though. We heard those shots out there by where the ridge and cliff meet. Then nothing. Now those four quick ones out in the wash. Like somebody's dying out there, several somebodies maybe."

"You think Jacob has found us?" Linda's voice rang with a glimmer of hope.

"All that's left is Stoner and Pate."

Will fought the rising tide of hope that matched Linda's. Hope could lead to carelessness, he thought, and carelessness could get somebody killed as long as Bar B killers remained on the loose.

Minutes later he heard the brush of cloth against stone. He moved his rifle barrel to cover the spot where he thought the noise had come from. Out of the corner of his eye he noted that Linda, too, had heard the movement and was focusing on the same spot, a jumble of sagebrush and rocks thirty yards away, good cover for snipers.

Linda heard the voice first. A heavy weight, cold and lifeless, had settled into the pit of her stomach at the first sound of movement. Within seconds, however, it had been replaced by burning anger. When she noticed motion in the brush and heard the scraping sound again, it took all her self-control not to shoot. But she forced herself to wait, concentrating on a patch of dull blue that she glimpsed between two small rocks covered with low sage. If that little patch of color moved again, she promised herself, she would shoot into it.

"Hey, Rockin' H."

Linda and Will froze.

"Hey. It's Pate. Anybody in there?"

"Jesus, Pate," Recognizing the voice, Will grinned from ear to ear. "I never thought I'd be happy to see your ugly face."

"Oh, God, Pate," Linda exclaimed happily, patting him on the shoulder as he crawled into the rocks between her and Will. "Is Jacob with you?"

"He's out there," Pate waved his hand away from the cliff. "I'd bet anything that was him stopped the firin' from the wash on the left." He paused to study their shelter.

"How many still shootin' besides you two?"

"Tack and Sonora," Will answered, "but Tack's shot in the leg. He can't walk."

"What happened to the two Bar B men who were sneaking along this side of the cliff?" Linda asked.

Pate explained briefly how the two gunmen had died.

"That means we don't have to protect ourselves from that direction." Linda analyzed the situation. "We don't have to worry about those two men in the wash to the left, it seems," she pointed. "Jacob should be headed for the other wash by now. We'll leave them to him and concentrate on the two at the foot of the cliff. There're five of us and only two of them. We should be able to drive them away."

"It ain't a good idea to depend on Stoner completely," Pate advised in a low voice. "Too many things could happen."

Will and Linda both nodded approval of Pate's advice.

All three were thinking the same thing. If Stoner could get to the two riflemen in the wash, even if only to divide their attention, the besieged could maybe effect an escape along the cliff face to the left. If not, if they could keep the shooters at bay for the rest of the day, they might escape with the horses as soon as night covered them in darkness.

They discussed the two possibilities. No one expressed what they were all thinking, that Stoner might have been killed or badly wounded during the recent spate of shooting or that he might not survive his next attack. Linda knew that her first responsibility was to the Rocking H defenders, to help them escape the siege with their lives, but she almost cried aloud at the thought of leaving Stoner behind, maybe wounded or dead.

34

Stoner heard the firing as if it came from the bowels of the earth. He struggled to open his eyes, to lift his arms. Each movement sent waves of pain and nausea flooding through his body.

A moment of panic hit him as he remembered the second rifleman, but he forced himself to relax. Slowly the nausea receded. The pain eased a little.

He wondered how long he had been out. He could feel the barrel of his rifle under his hip.

He listened, unmoving. Except for the sporadic firing he could hear nothing.

Carefully he opened one eye, then the other. He found himself looking into the face of the first rifleman. He recognized the young man called Wib and sadness dropped a thick, black blanket over his soul. He tried to look away but couldn't. Wib's eyes were staring straight at him, unseeing, his face twisted in a grimace of surprise and pain. Stoner shuddered.

For a long time he remained motionless. He lay on his stomach, his head twisted to the side. He could see little except the dead man and the slope he had been firing from.

Where was the second rifleman? Dead? Alive? Standing behind him?

Only one way to find out, he told himself.

Quick as a cat, with an effort that sent the pain again shrieking through his skull, he scrambled to his knees, trying to twist around and draw the .45 at the same time.

The second rifleman lay on his side not five feet away.

"Jesus," Stoner breathed aloud with relief.

Carefully he studied his surroundings. He couldn't tell how long he'd been unconscious. He sat down near the side of the wash, to ease his headache and the queasiness in his stomach and to listen to the battle. With his fingers he touched the source of his pain, a deep groove running along the side of his head. Just touching it set the pain to shrieking again, so he decided to ignore it.

He sat quietly until the queasiness ebbed. Then he moved to a position from which he could study the battle. After several minutes of watching and listening he decided that there were two men in the other wash, two men up against the cliff, to the left of the Rocking H, and five Rocking H shooters. Pate must have made it, he thought, feeling a sense of relief. But that left one Bar B rider not accounted for unless his first count was off. And he was beginning to have a bad feeling about that. He hadn't come across Joe or Sam yet.

"I reckon it's up to me to clear those two bushwhackers out of the other wash," he muttered as a panoramic view of the battleground flashed before his eyes. "We'll have to worry about any back-shooters not accounted for when the time comes, if I don't run into them between here and their friends."

He debated going directly to the other wash, on foot. It was the shortest distance, the quickest way. But it would be over open ground, terrain visible to the two groups of riflemen near the cliff because of the slope of the land, although invisible from the position of the men in the other wash. He opted for the long, safe way around. He couldn't fail the besieged Rocking H. Moving slowly at first so as not to aggravate his headache, he started back up the wash. For a while the nausea returned, but it soon disappeared, leaving him feeling whole except for the dull throb of his wound. He found his horse where he had left it, mounted, crossed the ridge, and followed it to a point opposite where he thought the second wash began. Leaving the black in a stand of pinyon pines, he re-crossed the ridge. Soon he was ghosting along the gully bottom.

He came across the two bushwhackers where the wash opened onto the valley floor. Both men were lying on their stomachs in a jumble of boulders, firing sporadically at the rocks hiding the Rocking H crew and talking between shots. Although Stoner didn't have a decent view of either man, he recognized Joe Bartleman from the rumble of his voice.

He studied the terrain he had to cross and the two men he planned to kill. He considered shooting from where he squatted, but immediately rejected the idea. He didn't have a clear shot at either man. If he missed, or only wounded one of the men, he might wind up in a standoff, and that wouldn't do. Both men had to die. As for the terrain between him and them, during its last fifty yards of existence the wash became as straight as the flight of a crow. It slowly petered out until it turned into little more than a natural furrow in the ground, the only cover along what was left of its banks being an occasional shrub or a boulder uncovered during flash floods. On the other hand, Joe and his gunman were facing toward the cliff, concentrating on the position of the men they wanted to kill. Even with the scarcity of cover, Stoner decided, he had a good chance of closing in on them without being seen.

His decision made, he began snaking forward while using what cover he could.

He had reached the pale shadow of a burro bush fifteen feet from his objective when Joe's companion spoke, "Damnit Joe, I tell you I hear something."

"Your imagination, I reckon," Joe chuckled, the sound raspy in the silent heat.

Joe and his hired gun stopped firing, looking around and listening intently. Stoner forced himself to remain motionless, trying to merge with the burning ground.

Finally, after minutes of intense concentration, Joe spoke again, "Like I said. It's your imagination."

"Yeah, I reckon," the other man agreed reluctantly.

The two men returned to their shooting. Stoner eased his .45 from its holster. Leaving his Winchester in the dirt beside him, he rose to a crouch, his eyes glued to the two men before him.

Joe fired and started to say something when his gunhand, with a curse, exploded to his feet, whirling to face

Stoner as he rose. At the same moment Joe also spotted Stoner from the corner of his eye. Frantically he flipped onto his back, swinging his rifle as he rolled. Both men fired too soon. Joe's shot flew toward a small, fluffy cloud overhead. His gunhand's bullet buzzed past Stoner's ear like an angry hornet. Stoner's first shot hit Joe at the bridge of his nose, tore through his brain, and ripped out the back of his skull, splattering blood, bits of meat, and splinters of bone over earth and rocks. His second shot smacked into the unknown gunman's chest like a sledgehammer. The man dropped as if smashed by a boulder from above, dead before he started to fall.

Stoner had thumbed another round into the cylinder, ready to fire again if necessary, when something tugged at his sleeve. He dove into the boulders that had sheltered his two assailants. Not quickly enough. A second bullet dug a shallow furrow across his shoulder a split second before he hit the ground.

Pate, Will and Linda had joined Sonora and Tack. The latter two kept the two bushwhackers along the cliff face pinned down while Pate and Will answered the fire from the wash. Linda had stationed herself between the men, in a spot from which she could fire at both enemy positions.

"This tradin' bullets is about as much good as tryin' to milk a bull," Will commented during a lull in the firing.

"I don't see no other way," Pate answered. "Not till nightfall anyhow. We can't attack those two yahoos," he pointed toward the jumble of bushes and boulders at the foot of the cliff. "Too much open ground between us and them. The same goes for them two in the gully out there." He paused, scratching his head thoughtfully. "We could retreat along the foot of the cliff. But like we've said more than once, it's too dangerous to take the horses and too dangerous to be caught on foot somewhere between here and the Rocking H. While we was trying to lead the horses over the rough ground between here and the ridge, we'd be targets for those two bushwhackers in the gully. They wouldn't have a clear shot at us but, hell, they'd pick the horses off like picking off a covey of quail on a sand dune. Worse, those other two'd be yapping at our heels all the way to the ridge. Which brings us to the same place we got to the last time we had this talk--wait till nightfall."

When Pate stopped talking, Linda and Will considered his words thoughtfully. Linda felt an overpowering sense of discouragement. They had had the same discussion several times during the past few minutes and always came to the same conclusion: There was little they could do except defend their position until dark. What added greater depth to her depression was her fear for Stoner. For a long time they had seen no sign that he still lived, not since the shots in the first wash.

She again glanced at the gully which still hid two Bar B bushwhackers, then scanned the area between it and the wash on the left, as she caught herself doing unconsciously every few minutes.

At that exact moment she saw a figure stand up just beyond the position of the Bar B riflemen. A split second later another man rose into view, nearer, his back to her. She recognized the first figure. It was Jacob. A violent happiness clogged her throat, forcing tears into her eyes. Jacob was alive.

Suddenly the shots sounded. Her heart leaped, then pounded violently at her ribcage. With terrible relief she saw the second figure fall from sight. Then the first dropped, suddenly. Almost immediately, horror-struck, she realized that the last few shots had sounded from nearby.

"Stop it!" she screamed.

Will, closer than Pate, glanced at her in consternation.

"That was Jacob," she told him, her mind awhirl. "You shot Jacob."

"Oh, Jesus," Will exclaimed, looking uncertainly at Pate. Slowly, apprehensively, he replayed his shots at the man in the gully. Two men had stood up almost simultaneously, one with his back half turned to the Rocking H position, one almost facing it. Will forced the images to return to his mind. He concentrated on the nearer one, then the farther one. "I don't think I hit Stoner," he stated firmly, relieved at his conclusion. "Stoner was the one farther away, almost facing us. I only shot once. I was shooting at the other one, the closer one. I saw him drop just as I shot. I think Stoner dropped right after that."

"Yeah," Pate's anguished words rose to little more than a whisper. "That other one was Stoner all right. I didn't recognize him before he fell, but as soon as Linda yelled I knew it was him. I fired at him twice. Lord, I hope I didn't hit him."

"Hey," Sonora's shout interrupted them. "These two bushwhackers are retreating. Qué pasó out there in the gully?"

Will glanced at the wash. Nothing moved. The firing had stopped. Slowly he exposed himself. When no one fired at him he stood up. Stoner must have killed those two back-shooters, he thought. If he did he's probably like us, huddled down in the gully waitin' to see if there're any others skulkin' around somewhere.

A flash of movement caught his eye. Turning, he saw Sonora dart from his position and dash along the open area that separated the Rocking H position from the last two Bar B riders. He heard Tack shout for Sonora to let the two men go. But Sonora ignored him and dove into the underbrush beyond the clearing, his bloodlust up, angry that he had had to cower among the boulders for hours without a clear shot at the enemy. Will gave a wild shout and took off after Sonora.

Seconds later he bounded into the underbrush where Sonora had disappeared. He paused to get his bearings before moving forward, silently. He could hear nothing but the sound of the wind rumbling through the distant pines. Twice he thought he heard movement in front of him. Once he heard the crunch of a boot on rock. Anxious to charge ahead, he forced himself to move silently, slowly. He figured he had travelled five, six slow, excruciating minutes when his patience was rewarded.

Voices rose ahead and to the right, up against the cliff. A few more steps and three figures emerged from the underbrush and scattered boulders.

Sonora stood with his rifle ready in both hands but pointed heavenward. Not twenty feet away slouched the two Bar B hands he had been trailing. They stood several feet apart, facing Sonora, their rifles clasped in their left hands, their right hands hovering near their sidearms. The man nearest Sonora stood in a crouch. About my age, Will thought, short devil, skinny, ugly as a starved coyote with mange, probably gets his kicks out of scaring kids and old women. The other one, though, the one closest to me, he looks okay--fortyish, I suppose, clean, kind of sad looking eyes like those of a beagle hound, going to fat in places, looks like he'd fit in a family portrait.

"Looks like a standoff to me," the older of the pair grunted, edging backward toward a stand of high brush.

Will moved to his left, hoping to find a spot from which he could get a clearer shot at the pair. They hadn't spotted him yet.

"We have the edge though, Mex," the younger Bar B hand added through his handlebar mustache. "You might get one of us, but the other one'll get you sure."

"Tal vez," Sonora shrugged, his eyes gleaming angrily at how easily he had been caught out in the open, with the barrel of his rifle pointing at the clouds. "Pero quién sabe? Maybe I can get you both. That would be very good, muy bueno. I don't think scum like you should ride in the sun."

"You son of a bitch," handlebar mustache shouted, his clawed hand darting for the pistol hanging low on his thigh.

Realizing that the fight was beginning, Will threw his rifle to his shoulder, at the same time roaring to distract the Bar B gunhand nearest him, who, at his friend's curse, had fired his rifle from the hip and was already pumping another shell into the chamber. The ruse worked. The man swung toward Will, the fear of death shining from his eyes, his hands working wildly to bring his rifle to bear on the new threat. Will's first shot sledged him in the stomach, doubling him over. The second bullet hit him in the top of the head, smashed through skull and brains and ricocheted from a boulder beyond.

Swiftly pumping another shell into the chamber, Will swung to face the younger Bar B gunhand. As his eyes focused on the target, he froze. The man was standing straddle-legged, his arms at his sides, his pistol dangling from his right hand, a glare of consternation on his face. He glanced at Will, his mouth moved as if trying to say something, then he slowly toppled onto his face.

Will shivered and turned toward Sonora.

"Ah, Sonora," he whispered involuntarily, momentarily paralyzed.

Sonora lay on his back, his eyes staring sightlessly at the fleecy clouds overhead, his right hand on his chest. From between his fingers bright red blood oozed. Another wound, in his throat, flowed more freely.

Shaking himself from his paralysis, sadness and anger alternately taking control of his emotions, Will strode to the older man for whom he had developed a sense of family and friendship over the time they had ridden together. "Sonora," he groaned as he knelt beside the silent form, not realizing he was speaking aloud, "you were a man who would give everything you had to your friends if you thought they needed it. I wish to hell I'd started shooting as soon as I spotted those murderin' scum. You might be alive right now if I had." With an effort he pulled himself to his feet and turned away, making a promise as he did so, "I'll be back to bury you proper, Sonora. Soon as this fight with the Bar B is over, if it ain't already."

35

Stoner never quite lost consciousness, but for a long time he couldn't force his body to respond to his commands. He lay in a fog of paralysis, trying to reconstruct what had happened. Finally he worked it out to his satisfaction. He had killed Joe Bartleman, but the other rifleman had been killed by a bullet from somewhere else. Simultaneously as he saw the gunman drop, he had instinctively dived for cover, only to feel the blow on his back and another blow to his head. The first blow had knocked the breath from his lungs, the second had sent the shrieking pain coursing through his head again.

As he lay there, his arms and legs refusing to answer his commands, he thought he heard shooting. When feeling and control returned to his limbs after what seemed like an eternity of silent struggle, he explored his head. Another, smaller wound had appeared near the groove of the bullet wound. Forcing himself to ignore the throbbing pain, he opened his eyes and raised his head. He found himself staring at a rock twice the size of his fist. Bits of blood and hair clung to its rounded top. His blood and hair. Carefully he explored his back as far as he could reach. Nothing seemed to be broken but the bullet had dug a deep groove until it ricocheted off a rib. Holding his head to minimize the violent throbbing, he sat up and looked around. As he had thought, Joe and his hired gunhand were both dead. From where he lay, he could see clearly that the gunhand had been killed by a bullet in the back of the neck.

"Your friends or mine?" he asked the corpse musingly as he reloaded his Colt and holstered it. "Whoever it was it turned out lucky for me, unlucky for you."

Painfully he forced himself to his knees and crawled to Joe's body, which he grabbed by the boots and unceremoniously pulled from between the boulders the man had been using as cover. Avoiding the puddle of blood-soaked sand as well as he could, he crawled between the boulders and peered at the Rocking H position. A thrill coursed through his chest when he spotted Linda and Pate standing in plain view. Linda was alive and they must have cleaned out the remaining two Bar B gunmen. He relaxed, letting his head fall onto his arms to relieve the continued throbbing pain of his head wound. After a few moments he pushed himself to a sitting position, and then stood. Tenderly he explored the furrow on his head with his fingers. It seemed to have stopped bleeding. He touched the gouge on his back. It was still bleeding, but was not as sore as the head wound.

He stood up straighter as several questions began stirring under the blanket of fog that seemed to have settled over his thought processes: He was certain there had been another Bar B rider, so where was he? Had there been three men creeping in on the right of the Rocking H position? He didn't think so. Most important of all, where was Sam Bartleman? Had he died somewhere along the foot of the cliff? Or was he the missing rider? If so, had he gone to the ranch for reinforcements or was he hiding out somewhere?

Once again Stoner glanced toward the Rocking H position, anxiously. Linda and Pate were galloping toward the wash.

"Drop the rifle, raise your hands away from that hog-leg, and turn around. Slow."

"Damn," Stoner swore as he dropped the weapon and turned. There were five of them grinning at him, Sam Bartleman and four men, all gunfighters and killers from the looks of them. All carried rifles. Three wore two guns slung low around their waists. All had the hard-bitten look of men who had seen violent death and had often faced it themselves. One was a tall, angular galoot with long, greasy black hair and a pock-marked face. His right ear was missing. He watched Stoner with the amusement of a man who enjoys watching others die. Stoner pegged him as the most dangerous of

Sam's four gunmen. Another, short, thin, not much beyond his mid-teens, grinned vacantly at Stoner as if watching an animal ready for butchering. The last two had round bodies and faces covered with unkempt beards, both black but one with flecks of grey in it. Above each beard, black eyes glared around a bulbous nose. One looked twenty years younger than the other. Father and son, Stoner decided.

Anger struggled with fear for control of his emotions, anger at himself for not watching his back more carefully, fear for Linda and the others, who were riding into a trap. Almost immediately, however, he forced the fear and the anger aside. A cold, murderous rage replaced them. Like a cougar getting set to spring on its prey, he tensed, his senses alert, waiting for his chance. He would die here and now, he decided, but he would take Sam Bartleman and as many of the other four as he could with him.

"You weren't easy, but it was only because we was too goddamn dumb to know what we was hearin'." Sam cursed, then grimaced and added, "We left some men back along the trail, in case you or other Rockin' H rannies came along. Somehow you missed them."

Glaring wolfishly at Stoner, he continued, "We watched you top the ridge and followed you in. Weren't more'n fifteen minutes behind you, but we lost you when you ducked in that other wash where you killed Wib and the other two. We heard your shots, I reckon, but we thought they was from our men, shootin' at the boulders over there," he shrugged toward the cliff face. "I was afraid you was after Joe so we come on over here and had to double back, but missed you somehow. Then we lost some time worrying about bein' ambushed, so you got to Joe anyhow." His glance veered to Joe's body. When he returned his gaze to Stoner a cruel hatred glittered in his eyes. "Your friends are on the way. Hear them?" He sneered and spit. "I was gonna wait and shoot you in the back when your friends rode in, then kill them. But after I seen you killed Joe, I figured you deserve a better fate." He attempted a grin; he looked like a rattlesnake opening its mouth to strike. "We're gonna tie you up, let you watch while we have some fun with your friends, then I'm gonna shoot every damn one of your fingers off. You ain't gonna die, not today. I want you to remember this day for a long time, and what you was like before you met me." Sam tried to grin again, with no more success than the first time. "Bates," he spoke to the father and son, "you and Cole go get his sidearm and tie him up. Hurry. Hear them horses comin?"

Sam glanced at Bates. As his eyes moved, his pistol swung slightly off center.

At that instant Stoner's hand streaked toward his sidearm, all emotion replaced by a desire to kill. His first and second shots, the second an echo of the first, smashed through Sam's ribcage two inches apart and burst through the heart. Sam died instantly, but not before he realized his mistake. As Stoner's hand dipped and rose Sam desperately swung his pistol back in line and triggered a wild shot. The bullet hit Stoner in the left forearm, breaking the bone halfway between wrist and elbow.

Stoner barely noticed the break. His third and fourth shots were meant for the tall, angular gunman. But his target had stepped behind the youngest member of the quartet when Stoner went for his Colt. The skinny youth took both bullets through the right eye. He flopped backward into his companion, dead but saving Stoner in his dying.

The tall gunman had already triggered one shot at Stoner when the dead youth collided with him, sending him stumbling backward, dancing and waving frantically to keep from falling. Off balance, desperate, he fired wildly, his bullet ricocheting from a nearby boulder. His first shot had torn through the collar of Stoner's shirt, burning flesh at the juncture of neck and shoulder on its way through but otherwise doing no damage. He never got off a third shot. Stoner shot him twice, once through the throat as he was trying to push the dead youth away and again, through the heart, as he was falling.

Coldly deliberate, but with an angry curse of frustration and fear that he would never again see Linda, Stoner dropped the Colt and dove for his rifle.

He never reached the weapon. Bates and his son Cole had ducked behind a boulder when Stoner fired his first shot. Now, from the safety of their refuge they opened fire. A bullet from Cole's rifle caught Stoner high in the chest just as he started his dive, driving him to the ground. Another, from Bates' .44 broke his collarbone. Seeing their victim motionless on the ground, Bates stood up and took deliberate aim.

"I don't reckon we'll collect any money for this killing," he grunted, "Joe and Sam both being dead. But I'm sure as hell gonna enjoy killing the bastard that spoiled the easy money."

36

Sonora and Will had no sooner disappeared than Linda turned toward the horses.

"I'm going out there," she stated in a voice that brooked no opposition. "Stoner may need help."

"We should maybe wait for Sonora and Will to get back," Tack frowned at her.

"That might be too late," Linda impatiently threw over her shoulder. "Jacob was hit; I'm sure of it. I saw him fall. He needs help."

The sick fear had grown inside her in the past few minutes, telling her that she was already too late. Angrily she tried to shake off her ominous feelings but found it impossible.

"I'll ride along," Pate spoke guiltily as he too hurried toward the horses, worried that he might have actually hit Stoner.

As she and Pate led their mounts from the jumble of boulders, Linda spoke quickly, nervously, "Wait for Sonora and Will, Tack. If everything's okay out there I'll wave. If I don't wave...."

"If she don't wave, you're on your own," Pate growled as he mounted. "We won't be no help."

With those hasty words he spurred to catch Linda, who was galloping wildly toward the wash, driven by her fear that Stoner had died in the fusillade of shots from the Rocking H.

They had covered more than half the distance to the wash when the firing started. With a savage scream of fear, Linda spurred her mount unmercifully, driving it to a dead run over rocks and cactus and broken ground. Pate fought to keep his horse close behind her.

Linda and Pate galloped into the wash just as Bates reached his feet and Cole was pushing himself up to join in administering the coup de grace. Intent on murder, neither man had heard the sound of running horses replace the shooting for the past few seconds. Nor had they remembered Sam's reference to the near approach of Stoner's friends. The sudden appearance of the two horses and riders startled them, freezing them for the precious moment it took for Pate to drop from his horse, rifle ready and firing. His first shot glanced off Bates' hipbone and lodged under the ribcage. His second sledged into the man's midriff. Bates dropped to a sitting position, an expression of pained anguish slowly turning to fear when he realized he couldn't breathe. Pate's third shot splattered the top of his head onto the rocks beyond. Bates' body slowly, grotesquely toppled onto its back, kicked at Pate several time, and accepted its fate.

Linda had not hesitated when she spotted the two Bar B gunmen. With an instinct born of anger and desperation she drove the spurs to her mount, yanking him directly toward the two men. Her action sent Bates darting to his right, giving Pate the extra fraction of time he needed to get off the first shot. Cole reacted slower. He still had one knee on the ground when Linda drove toward him. He dove to his right but Linda's mount was trained to the rope. It swerved smoothly, bringing Linda alongside the dodging youth. Without a second thought, her anger at white heat from a brief glimpse of Stoner's body as she bounded into the gully, Linda swung her rifle and fired it one-handed, the barrel almost touching Cole's face as it discharged its deadly piece of lead.

Cole dropped, motionless.

Linda reined her horse in and kneed it toward Stoner, ignoring the carnage around her. Swiftly she dropped from the saddle and knelt beside the broken body of the man she loved.

"Oh, God, Pate," she whispered, "he's shot everywhere."

Pate, who had come to stand nearby, dropped to his knees beside her.

Together they inspected the unconscious Stoner's wounds, then rolled him onto his back. Linda took his hand and held it in hers, tears glistening in her eyes.

"Yeah," Pate agreed sorrowfully. "He's shot up bad."

A few seconds later he added, "He's got a broken collarbone, looks like." He pointed to the chest wound, "That bullet's still in there. We'll have to get him to town, let the doc cut it out."

"Will he live?" Linda asked, needing reassurance rather than information.

Pate shrugged, "The chest wound ain't life-threatening, I don't reckon. The bullet's high. I don't think it nicked a lung. The other wounds, they'll be sore for a while, especially that collarbone, but they ain't gonna kill nobody. Yeah, he'll live if he don't bleed to death or get blood poisonin'. He's strong. He'll make it," he stated uncertainly.

"I feel like I'm already in hell," Stoner mumbled, trying unsuccessfully to chuckle. The pressure of Linda's warm hand holding his had pulled him from his unconscious state.

"If you are, I'll come and get you," Linda laughed through her tears. "And when I get you, I'll never let you go again."

"If that's a proposal, I accept," Stoner again tried to smile, his words a hoarse whisper. "Paradise sounds better than where I've been any old day."

Linda bent to kiss his lips.

"I reckon I'd better find the Bar B horses and get all the bodies loaded," Pate stood up, a mingled sense of loss for himself and happiness for Stoner restricting his breathing. "We can let the town marshal bury them."

He looked up at the immense distance of land and sky. He would be moving on soon. So would Will, he figured. But Stoner would be staying. He had found what they were all searching for.